Fragments

Shattered and Shattering

By

Gary Battle

Fruition Literary

Preface

Many of us know what its like to feel broken, sadly that is life in our fallen world. But all of us come to this world lacking something and it is our destiny to find it and live gloriously as God has intended. In many ways, the Fragments series is a long breakup letter and ode to the stupidity of my 20's. It began in December of 2007 as a simple story about a girl forced to start a new life. By 2012 God had flushed out character after character, leaving me to figure out how it all came together and why it matters. Sadly, I was too deep in a bottle to take on the work and thus the delay.

Simply put, "Fragments" is the story of five sets of siblings who unknowingly become the pawns of a mysterious young woman, in the destruction of a trans-national company. The life and plot of the woman known as Jade, provides the backdrop to the web of half-truths, untold encounters, and the different forms of othering brought forth by the five families.

Much like when the time came to name the work itself, the hardest part of understanding the characters was finding the right name for each one. Over the course of the almost ten-years it took to finish Fragments, several of the characters underwent two to three name changes, which is why so many have aliases. The novel itself drifted through six titles before "Fragments Shattered and Shattering" was chosen.

Contents

These six things doth the lord hate: yea, seven are an abomination unto him: a proud look, a lying tongue, and hands that shed innocent blood, an heart that deviseth wicked imaginations, feet that be swift in running to mischief, a false witness that speaketh lies, and he that soweth discord among brethren.

-Proverbs 6:16-19 KJV

The desire for freedom is preceded by oppression; a yearning for God's law is born of destitution of human license and corruption; glamour of riches is in thrall to poverty, hunger, and debt.

-Toni Morrison,
Playing in the Dark

Acknowledgments

As cliché and unpopular as it may have become, first I'd like to thank God, who allowed me to travel the world with his mercy and grace covering me—even the few too many times I left both collecting dust. Without the countless chances I was given to see, interact with and become the "fragmented" there would be no book, no story, and no me.

I would like to thank my parents, Gary Battle, Sr and Terrie Artis. My father, for tirelessly slaving away as a truck driver and trying to push me to constantly do better. To my mother, who was caring and patient, one of my first teachers, my ally, and friend. The three of us have been through a lot together and separately but God has been faithful. To you both I promise to keep striving for a better me. To my sister, Christah, thanks for encouraging me to just plug away no matter how high the word count climbed. To my little-est sister, Brittany, thanks for reading it to give me the Romance/YA lover's perspective.

I would like to thank Ashely 'Campbellina' Campbell for suffering through the rough-rough draft that I for some reason thought was a polished story with a few plot holes. Your ideas, suggestions, and attention to a lot of the details really helped breathe new life into this piece. They also helped me better understand why I chose to present each character in their particular light.

I would like thank my friend Tran Tang for letting me quietly study her family and the Tang ideal of family and cultural values. To my friend Yewande Mohammed Adaba for telling to take my time and make it happen.

I would to thank Brittani Pleasant at B. Pleasant Law Firm in San Antonio, Texas. Thank you, Brittani, for taking time out of your packed schedule to make sure my courtroom scenes were believable and accurate.

I would also like to thank Ms. Joy Lewis of Emmanuel Writing Services and Mr. James Bryant Jr. for saving me countless IQ points by highlighting my various grammar issues, word misappropriations, redundancies, and clearing metaphors, so that I felt comfortable moving forward with the piece.

Finally, I would like to thank many of my various friends, associates, mistakes and mishaps who compositely sparked the beginnings of a number of the characters, story lines, and precarious situations found throughout the work.

The Families

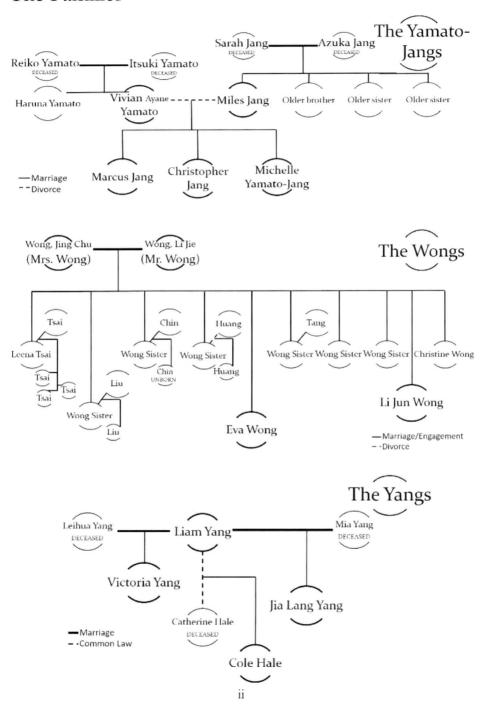

The Yamato-Jangs

Sarah Jang DECEASED ——— Azuka Jang DECEASED

Reiko Yamato DECEASED ——— Itsuki Yamato DECEASED

Haruna Yamato · Vivian Ayane Yamato - - - - - - Miles Jang · Older brother · Older sister · Older sister

——Marriage
- -Divorce

Marcus Jang · Christopher Jang · Michelle Yamato-Jang

The Wongs

Wong, Jing Chu (Mrs. Wong) ——— Wong, Li Jie (Mr. Wong)

Tsai · Chin · Huang · Tang

Leena Tsai · Wong Sister · Wong Sister · Wong Sister · Wong Sister · Wong Sister · Christine Wong

Tsai · Chin UNBORN · Huang

Tsai · Liu · Li Jun Wong

Wong Sister · Eva Wong

Liu

——Marriage/Engagement
- -Divorce

The Yangs

Leihua Yang DECEASED ——— Liam Yang ——— Mia Yang DECEASED

Victoria Yang · Jia Lang Yang

Catherine Hale DECEASED

——Marriage
- -Common Law

Cole Hale

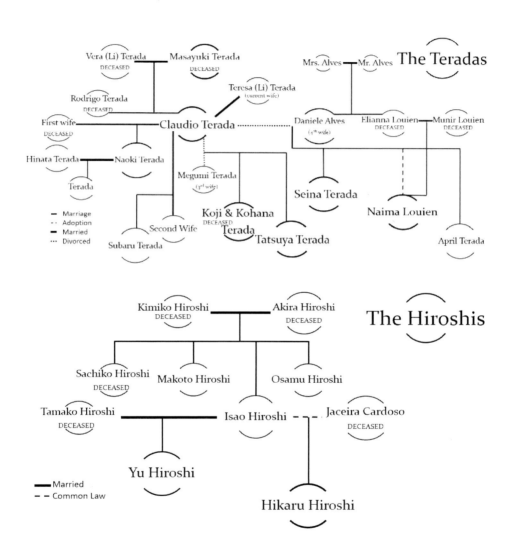

1. The Director

Yokohama, Japan, March (9 Months Ago)

A tapestry of blues painted both sky and sea, as icy winds blew in from the Tokyo Bay, and up the Katabira River. The winds cut into Jade as she made her way from Yokohama Station to Blue Mountain coffee bar, *to meet him.* Jade brushed aside side-swept bangs, zipping along the K1 Yokohane Line underpass, the streets nearly emptied by the frigid winds. She paused only to rewrap her scarf and adjust the large bag on her shoulder, hardening herself to the cold.

When Jade packed in Taipei, jeans, a pair of calf-high boots, and her thickest winter coat seemed reasonable. But as she stumbled into Blue Mountain reeling from the cold, she realized she was wrong. Jade went to the restroom, sifting through her bag deciding to don the demure charcoal grey skirt and blazer typical of an "office lady," paired with the plainest block heels she could find.

"I'll need to buy a real coat if this goes like I planned it," she mumbled noting her reddened nose and ghostly white complexion in the mirror. Her skin was creamy like honey and milk tea, with a rosy undertone paired with sweet almond-shaped eyes. This version of Jade was a bit of a stretch compared to the wind-shocked visage she glimpsed in the mirror.

A year ago, Jade underwent a *few* minor surgeries so that she could pass through this region not as the youngest heiress of an international plastics company, but as someone barely visible. The result was a Eurasian look, a slender nose, wide yet 'Asian' eyes, and full lips. This led her to take the new name—Jade Wang.

"He'll be back today for sure," Ah Fan, Jade's co-conspirator, informed her the moment she had the new passport in hand. "He just

1

finished some training. Now is your chance."

Without reservation, Jade booked a last-minute flight, Taipei to Tokyo, in hopes of meeting Second Lieutenant Robert Harris, the man she was following. Presently, Jade Wang sat in the Blue Mountain Coffee Bar in Yokohama during the slow thaw of a Japanese spring. She glanced over a newspaper, rubbing the last of an acidic lotion on the palms of her hands, further erasing any lingering prints. Jade blew on her hands to cool the slight burn as she had since she left Switzerland with Ah Fan. The coffee bar was quiet, all but empty on a cold day like today, during the lull between breakfast and lunch. Jade was on her third espresso when a headline grabbed her attention.

アメリカの化粧品外科医がパートナーを殺害し、日本に姿を消す
American cosmetic surgeon kills partner and disappears in Japan

"Miles Jang." She murmured, stumbling over the Katakana—that strange pointed alphabet used in Japan for both emphasis and things foreign. A chill crept up Jade's back as she continued to read the story. Miles Jang, a California-based cosmetic surgeon is alleged to have killed his business partner and fellow surgeon in his hospital room.

Memories of Jade's mother were triggered. The ever-present smell of lemongrass and lavender were all that was left for her to reminisce about. Even when faced with photos, they didn't match the face Jade remembered. She knew she wasn't special—growing up without her mother, with a distant father but, that was the reason she was here.

Jade shifted from that notion back to the paper. It was then She heard the doors open and close with the incoming of the lunch crowd. Within what seemed like seconds, the bar jolted to life as customers issued orders, and waiters doled out menus.

"Irashaimase!" The workers chanted as more people entered the coffee bar. Suddenly Jade looked up from the paper and spotted him—her mark—her kill. Robert Harris, dark haired and green eyed, he came to sit with his back to the clouded glass dividers facing her.

"Goyukuridozo." The waitress placed a drink on Robert's table. Jade sipped her coffee and continued to read—or pretended to. In thirty minutes or so, he would stand, beginning the chain reaction—the splitting of atoms, binding his life to hers. She, throwing coffee, would jump up—dressing the target and the floor. Then she would slam into him, with a firm and convincing bump. There it would unfold, the first life chosen, and compelled to this sorrowful sonata. But for now, she simply watched—waiting.

"Gomensai!" She shouted, her entanglement already spun, her coffee on him. Target hit, hole in one. "Sorry," Jade said bowing and a waitress rushed over to clean the coffee on the floor. Jade grabbed napkins and Robert knelt to help.

"Are you okay?" A thick, American accent coated his lips. Jade stopped cleaning, and looked into inviting lush green eyes. It was the hum of the coffee shop all around that pulled her back from virtually drowning in those eyes.

"I'll pay for your jeans to be cleaned. Were they expensive?" She asked, her face wrinkled in dismay, eyes narrowed with worry as she bit down on her lip.

"No, not really." He shook his head, laughing.

"Jade Wang." She smiled, tucking hair behind an ear, scribbling on a napkin. "Here's my number. I'll pay for it, I swear."

"I'm Robert, Robert Harris. It's-it's okay, you don't have to do that." His teeth gleamed into an uncontrolled grin. He was clearly interested in her.

Jade has watched this man for months from a distance, and now she has him cornered. Three years she's planned this, beginning with the compromised printer in Hong Kong. She has looked into nearly every detail, and weighed almost every option. Ah Fan, the Indonesian hacker, was a guiding hand, a wise and helpful informant. He was an invaluable resource, barring their brief relationship. But Robert was the first and last piece, the point coming full circle. Jade thought to learn more about the man, but wanted the courtship not to seem rehearsed. She knew the basic things, first the Army—four years, then the Air Force for the commission and of course his work in engineering.

Jade grined, glancing down at a text message from Robert as she strolled down Shibuya's neon-stained sidewalks. She melted into the mass of bodies push-pulling as the sun set. *He's the one*, she thought. She-cat and he-mouse, and she laughed aloud. Then, without notice, a wave-like rush overtook her thoughts—the proverbial pebble skipping the pond. *Naima would be perfect for this*, Jade scoffed amending the thought: *this is a one-woman job, no loose ends, no loose cannons,* she shook her head. *Now I need the decoy*, she noted. Whom she found in Michelle, some seven weeks ahead.

Lovely Distractions
Tokyo, (7 months ago) June - December, 31st

Jade knew the instant she saw Michelle, this was the kind of woman she was looking for. Her first sighting of the girl came through Mrs. Wong— Auntie Jing, as Jade's sister called her. Jade sat, in June's growing humidity on the patio of Gar Eden, waiting for her food and playing games on her phone. She heard shouting then saw Li Jun run past her table, and down the street.

She knew Wong Li Jun, of the *moderately*-wealthy Tokyo Wongs, was one of ten or twelve Wong children and the only son. Such a sighting could only mean the eventual appearance of his mother, Mrs. Gloria Wong— Auntie Jing. Jade would have simply disappeared for fear of running into Mrs. Wong, despite not actually knowing anyone in Japan. But Jade glanced up and saw a woman blow past her in a blur of long blonde balayage colored hair— Enter, Michelle, the decoy.

"Come on Michelle, come on!" Li Jun called back to her, pausing briefly to look back. Michelle looked like an Olympic sprinter as she caught and promptly passed Li Jun with Mrs. Wong gaining speed behind them. She was beautiful, *a commercial come to life,* Jade thought—Though her hair was a bit much. But beyond that, Michelle was mesmerizing, and Jade was mesmerized. Much darker than Jade, Michelle had creamy-dark caramel skin, defined cheeks and thick perfectly arched eyebrows. So, Jade barely flinched as Mrs. Wong went by in a rippling of air, her chemically curled hair flapping in the gust.

Jade only knew of the Tokyo Wong's because of her sister, who shared a Chinese name, and a room with Li Jun's older sister, during their time at Sorbonne. Jade also recalled her sister had a short-lived fling with Li Jun in New York, but by then she had done her research and decided to make Michelle her decoy.

Inside of a week, Jade amassed extensive knowledge of the Wong's, and she had an idea of the relationship between Li Jun and more importantly, Michelle. Yet, strangely enough, there was no record with Japanese immigration or in any Japanese system of a Michelle that matched the woman Jade saw from the patio. So, Jade turned to social media, the enemy of all those in hiding.

She started with Li Jun's Instagram, where she saw a handful of photos with Michelle, but no tag. In one of several photos, they appeared to be somewhere in China or Hong Kong in a boat. The first three images of her were from a shoot of some kind in Asakusa. Here things turned in Jade's favor. Jade shifted to the website for the modeling agency run by Li Jun's sister and she was rewarded with a last name—Yamato.

Intrigued, Jade dug deeper and found a Michelle Sarah Yamato-Jang of Newport Beach, California. She was a recent graduate of the University of Southern California, but Jade found no record of her in Japan. Her research stopped here, and this was her first grave mistake. Jade looked for an opening with the knowledge she obtained. *A woman in Japan illegally could easily disappear once all was said and done.*

Jade decided the best play was to corner Michelle in a store she frequented. So, she went to Sacai Aoyama four days in a row before Michelle returned. The balayage hair was replaced by a silky jet-black waterfall that carelessly draped her face in long feathered bangs. She had that guitar-shaped body Brazilians the world over are known for, despite being an American. Jade stood at the rear of the store tipping around over-active kawaii fashionistas as Michelle floated from one rack to another.

It was clear to Jade that Michelle was the result of at least two kinds of people coming together, with almond eyes and caramel skin rich in vermillion undertones. Yet the thing that pulled at Jade was the way Michelle moved. Most beautiful women know they are appealing, and often put on airs because of, or despite their looks. Michelle moved as if she were invisible. She didn't care how others saw her. She didn't care who she *should* be. Michelle had no battle to wage with Du bois's double consciousness. She won. She had removed the white gaze to simply exist in her own skin as she desired. She was dangerously free, or so Jade thought then. This was her state of being and each moment Jade watched, Michelle was candid, enthralling, and sensual.

Michelle stared at each item she touched, looking past them in search of something, shifting from dresses to shoes to purses and belts. With less than five haphazardly picked outfits, she strolled to the fitting room. Jade followed, casually picking up a dress from a rack. She put it on then waited for Michelle to emerge. When Michelle walked past her, Jade stepped out from behind the curtain, looking back in the mirror of the stall.

"Excuse me," Jade called.

Even before Michelle spoke in that sultry alto, with those bright eyes, and long eyelashes, Jade knew this was her decoy.

"Can I get your honest opinion about this dress?"

"Yeah." Michelle nodded, brushing the long-feathered bangs back from her face.

"How does it look on me?" Jade gestured to the red baby doll-style dress she had thrown on. She was going for funny, but Michelle chose to be endearing instead.

"It's definitely your color but the cut isn't too good for you," Michelle smiled, with only a hint of sarcasm, and turned to her own stack of clothes, then plucked a white and navy-blue sun dress from the pile. "Try this. It'll look really good on you. It's too small for me. You know, the cake region." She gestured to her hips, thighs and buttocks with a smile.

Jade laughed, taking the dress, "Thank you, I'd gladly pay for a bit more cake." She said looking over her shoulder toward her own body. Post check-out, Jade invited Michelle for a drink, and in the months that followed they became fast friends.

The Wong's, by comparison, were an epic saga. Wong Li Jie and Wong Jing Chu, Li Jun's parents, both went to school in San Francisco only a few short years before Tiananmen Square. After marrying, Mr. and Mrs. Wong attempted to become American citizens for fear of returning to China or Vietnam. Their citizenship was denied. After Mr. Wong obtained his medical degree, they flew to Japan to start a new life.

Mr. Wong became a heart surgeon and Mrs. Wong went on to open five restaurants in quick succession. Overtime, they managed to send eight of their ten children to study abroad. Li Jun came to work for his older sister as she laid the groundwork for what would become a modeling agency, building each other's careers in the process. It was only after seeing Li Jun's pattern of dating the talent, that the Michelle Yamato angle became crystal clear.

It all seemed dream-like now, that Jade has been in Tokyo these past nine months, building a fake life and all the trappings that came with it. It still annoys her that by no will of her own, she has again entered the circles of the rich and famous. Jade sat on the set of Michelle's commercial shoot, on New Year's Eve, wondering how she and Michelle became 'friends's at all. Yes, Jade liked Michelle, but she was still just a means to an end. She lingered on that thought, trying to push away the fact she was no closer to acquiring the access codes than she was the day when she first met Robert. Jade also had no clear understanding of how she would leverage her target's vulnerabilities. Yet, here she was. I've just been spending hundreds of thousands for shiggles, she thought annoyed by her shortcomings, and tallying the expenses: the two fake passports, hiring other hackers to help cover her tracks, and renting an apartment—all to enhance the Jade Wang facade.

Jade shifted her attention to the sound stage when filming began. She was still amazed at how the decoy simply came to life in the blink of an eye. The stage was on a raised platform set up like a bedroom. A Roman inspired bed sat on the left side of the room, covered in a chocolate and gold duvet, and framed on all sides by sheer chocolate curtains. The curtains swayed in the breeze created by the fans outside the frame. Michelle sat to the right of the bed at a vanity table styled in ornate gold trim. Light from the sound stages's artificial moon spilled in from the balcony on the far-right side of the room.

An ad such as this was ideal for a woman like Michelle working in Japanese fashion. She was too exotic for regular roles in film or tv, never mind her limited Japanese. She, like many girls with her background, straddled that chasm between 'brown' and 'yellow,' dangerous and intriguing; ambitious and scary. Her skin was like desert sand at dusk. Her eyes even before the make-up artist's brush pierced hearts like passion lights a flame. Michelle spoke the Asusu anya—the language of the eyes— one whose words would not be tamed. Often her demeanor alone disrupted the atmosphere of respect and civility when navigating amongst Japan's powerful and elite magnates. She sat in black lingerie under a purple kimono, embroidered with white cranes, with the garment loosely wrapped around her. The camera crept closer from behind.

"God has given you one face and you make yourself another," her voice rang across the soundstage. She inched to the mirror, a hand beneath her chin. "Yet, they fit seamlessly together as if ammunition in a gun." She stared into her eyes drifting to eyebrows and full lips, applying blood red lipstick. "Only with effortless match, from KMR, can two faces be one." A breeze floated in from the balcony, moving the curtains lining the bed.

Michelle stood and the moonlight danced on the glistening kimono, the cranes swaying with every step as camera one followed her. She slowly walked toward the balcony and into the light of the soundstage's moon where camera two waited to capture her spark.

"Find your effortless match today," her voice echoed across the set.

"Cut," Li Jun yelled, leaping to his feet. "Beautiful. Let's call it." He shouted. A smile enveloped his amber colored face, his jet-black pony tail swaying down his back. His almond eyes narrowed with joy and his lips pulled back to show white-almost-straight teeth. He was dressed in that careless way artsy types do, khaki pants and white sneakers with a green button-down shirt unbuttoned nearly to his sternum.

On the soundstage, Michelle let out a deep sigh, closing the kimono and throwing her hair over one shoulder. She moved toward the dressing room and Li Jun intercepted—cutting off her retreat. Behind Li Jun, Jade stood quietly tittering at Michelle's foiled attempt.

"I hope you still intend to keep modeling. Even after this leave thing is over." Li Jun said trying to ease the tensions he knew were still present.

"Of course I do," Michelle stared at him blankly, tucking hair from her face. "At least for a little while anyway," she shrugged, trying to keep the kimono closed, with feigned politeness. "Well," she said, punctuating her escape, when Li Jun placed a hand on her arm. Jade's eyes widened at that.

Michelle stopped.

Slowly her eyes trailed up Li Jun's arm.

"Yes?" She asked curtly. The raised brows pulled Li Jun's attention away from the sarcastic smile as the crew began the task of packing the equipment.

"Look, I was out of bounds with you and that guy from the D and G shoot. I—" He started, but couldn't finish.

"You were," Michelle stared at him with one brow raised, to insure he felt the weight of her disapproval.

"I'm sorry," Li Jun countered, pausing to comb stray hairs from his face back into his ponytail.

"As you should be," she said flatly, "I don't belong to you. And you haven't given me reason to want to," her brow furrowed in an 'are you done' expression.

"Let me give you one," he paused, biting his lip. "We could go out tonight, then go to the party and bring in the New Year right," he smirked, searching for signs of a smile returning to her face.

At the back of the room, Jade made her way over to the buffet; picking up snacks for what she knows will be another episode in the life and times of Li Jun and Michelle.

Michelle sighed loudly. "Our relationship is strictly professional now. I'll see you later," she said, walking away, hair and kimono swaying. Michelle bowed to the production crew as she passed. Then without preamble she thought of how she had called from that shoot, just before Christmas. It was midnight, in Japan, and Victoria answered Li Jun's cell phone with that over exaggerated British accent. *Hoe bag*, Michelle thought glancing back at Li Jun.

Jade came closer, pulling Michelle from her thoughts. "So, this is your job?" Jade smiled, glancing at Li Jun over Michelle's shoulder. "It's not as hard as you make it out to be."

"You're not the one dealing with the bullshit." Michelle scoffed, rolling her eyes as they strolled off the set en route to the dressing room.

"But weren't you the one who chose to ride that bull, by the horns and into town?" Jade replied.

"You're right but I chose to leave him alone too. He's the one not getting it." Michelle brushed her hair back from her eyes.

"No worries, I will be a more than adequate third wheel this evening." Jade chuckled. This would become her second grave mistake.

"Good." Michelle leered, opening the door to the dressing room. "I'll owe you one and if you wear that Gucci dress I gave you, I might be able to pay you back with a man," Michelle winked stepping inside.

"Michelle I'm sure you're aware I am not that kind of girl." Jade followed, then and closed the door.

Shades of Her
Tokyo, In transit, December, 31st

Wait downstairs

That was the text Li Jun got while on the subway, to Michelle's apartment. He rode, the Chiyoda to the Hibiya line toward Naka-Meguro, alongside the muffled clack of the moving cars. He started the conversation, **be there in twenty.**

Amongst the eerie quiet that often makes up commuting in Tokyo, Michelle came back with, **Wait downstairs**

The dreary fluorescent lights sucked all liveliness from the red chairs lining the tightly packed subway car. But as Li Jun sat staring at his phone, irritation suddenly swelled in his chest. His face went blank, a layer of blood pulsed across his otherwise golden amber skin. He decided then and there to walk to Michelle's apartment to cool his ego, and attempt to quell the anger disguised as irritation.

He surfaced from his thoughts near Meguro station not knowing how he ended up so far-off course. It was the press of bodies zipping here and there all around that forced Li Jun to seek solace along the quiet avenues that melded into Michelle's neighborhood. The cold seeped through his coat and gloves. Li Jun had lived in Tokyo all his life, but the cities damp winters bested him year after year. He wasn't dressed for wandering about the city, certainly not with the threat of snow.

Li Jun walked to her apartment hat in hand, wishing to broker peace, forgiveness or whatever: for his temper, and his assumptions. He strolled down a street emptied by the cold. The quiet neighborhood was more like the hub of some small town, rather than a segment of a buzzing metropolis.

Li Jun knew it was wrong to outright accuse Michelle of cheating on him with no proof. What stung was that she simply scoffed before reading him his rights.

"Yet Tori answered your phone at midnight, man who claims to love me." Michelle said, gathering her things. "Jun you should also know we have to be together for me to cheat." That was the last thing she said to him before moving her clothes to her apartment.

By the time Li Jun reached Michelle's building, the air was thick with a wet cold that prickled the skin, before seeping into the body. He stood outside of the building, his long hair pulled into a ponytail and his skin like redden clay still soft to the touch. It was his expression that was hardened by the cold.

Li Jun questioned whether or not to go inside. *Was what awaited him worth it? Was the experience worth the maintenance? Was what— they— had— enough? You love this girl, right,* he walked into the lobby, shaking off the cold. Li Jun glanced at his phone, eight fifty-three. "Come on Michelle we're gonna be late." He mumbled, thinking of their first meeting and how quickly time flies. When they met, he was on his way to work, the rainy season just over and the heat was settling in. She had been walking to the subway— beautiful, he thought, in a sexier variation than the usual aesthetic.

Michelle was walking in Asakusa, ripped tank top and baggy ripped cargo pants. Captivating is the word he used when they spoke. She laughed and shrugged him off, but she let him take a few photos.

Now, he stood waiting with his back to the elevator taking in the decor. The lobby was designed to attract the nouveau riche to the moderately-well-off middle class. The over-styled furniture was uniquely shaped in various shades of cream paired with accent pillows in feasting reds, wine, and rust colors. The tables were covered in dark wood with oversized vases of orchids placed at eye level with the observer. Floor lamps dotted the low-lit space appearing to have been crafted from paper and wood during the Edo period, as if to remind the tenants and their guests they are still in Asia. Li Jun observed all of this for the first time, while waiting downstairs—feeling like a delivery boy. He was dressed in a black tux, black shirt, with the top two buttons undone, formal—with a twist of casual chic. He let out an exasperated sigh, slowly thawing, but ready to go.

"Come on, woman." Li Jun grumbled just before he heard the chime of the elevator and turned to the doors opening behind him.

Separation
Meguro-ku, Tokyo, December, 31st

"Hey!" Li Jun said, a smile appearing on his face, but failing to reach his eyes. Then shock took root, as his eyes met Jade's.

"Michelle, it's perfectly alright," Jade objected sweetly as they stepped from the elevator.

"I'm telling you, the other dress was amazing," Michelle said. "It was the one for tonight. You'll only pull pedophiles looking like a fourteen-year-old," Michelle added as she and Li Jun made eye contact. Michelle moved past him, to check her make-up in the mirror closest to the front door. Feeling this odd sense of tension, Jade avoided the crossfire by texting Robert, who was away working in Misawa. Still playing at demure, Jade wore a plain black dress underneath the ill-fitting black and white pea coat. Her face was framed by side-swept bangs that flopped, oddly over her eye on occasion, messily, not sexy—never sexy.

Jade needed to be cute, maybe even beautiful, but forgettable in the end. Long hair, but not too long, cut along the shoulder blades: black, straight and limp, for the effect. Furthermore, Jade befriended this Michelle, from Newport Beach, to drive the point home, to ensure she and by extension her sleight of hand would be overlooked.

Michelle's presence would allow Robert's engineering prowess to work on Jade's behalf. That was the plan, six— nine months ago—though Jade has made little progress other than an elaborate cover life. And now there is the boy-girl drama between a cheating model and cheating photographer to deal with. Or something along those lines, she thought rolling her eyes as she sent the text.

Michelle avoided Li Jun's eyes. Fur in hand; she was breathtaking in a backless halter-strap white dress. The sight lit a fire in Li Jun's blood as he leaned against one of the sofas. Michelle looked him over, stopping to tuck her freshly flat ironed hair. She pulled mascara from her clutch and placed it on the table in front of her, touching up her eyes and lipstick as Li Jun continued to watch her.

"Jun, you look sharp." Jade said, her eyes lit with laughter.

"Hey Jade," he diverted from Michelle. "You look nice too."

"Thank you," Jade nodded, as a stale silence covered the lobby, seeming to wilt even the flowers. "Okay. Let's go." Jade said, clapping her hands and slipping out in an attempt to give space to the issues at hand. She walked to the sidewalk as Michelle strolled toward the door behind her, when Li Jun grabbed Michelle's arm, again.

"I thought it was just you and me." Li Jun said flatly, still pouring on the charm with a slight smirk.

"Those days are over. Why can't we be adults about this? We work together that's it." She pulled away, almost dismissing him.

"What do you mean why? And you're the one ignoring me. I still care about you." He wanted to say love— 'I still love you,' *but it was unleashing these fettered emotions that brought us here,* he thought.

"Not as much as you think." She shook her head, pulling a golden blonde strand from his long jet-black ponytail. Michelle held the hair for him to see, but dropped it as he reached for it and an explanation. "My stylist—" He began, but Michelle walked out the door to catch up with Jade.

"Oh-could you possibly keep my keys for me? I don't have any pockets in this dress. And I imagine we'll be checking our coats," Jade asked Michelle, refreshing the sweetness in her voice. She and Michelle walked along the street, with Li Jun following. The swooosh of slow-moving cars and the click of Michelle's heels the only other texture to the quiet stroll.

"Sure."

"He cares for you Michelle and you're absolutely gorgeous. Why wouldn't he throw a fit if he thought you were cheating?"

Michelle cut her eyes at Jade as another car swooshed past them. "There's nothing to be said. I'm not a thing and I don't do possession," she shrugged, buttoning her coat, while glancing at Li Jun.

"You certainly love making Eva hate you. First you date him against her will, and then you drop him. Are you sure you'll still have a job after this?" Jade asked, sounding much wiser than her twenty-one years would suggest.

"We were never dating. Let's just enjoy ourselves tonight, okay?" Michelle said, her eyes locked on Jade.

A soft breeze lifted Michelle's perfume conveying the scent to Li Jun. The crisp smell of exotic fruits, a hint of rose floating in a sea of lavender with the dangerous incorporation of vanilla. The mix was seductive. He inhaled deeply, knowing the smell of fruit and roses would quickly fade. The lavender would evaporate giving way to the more overpowering fragrances. But the vanilla, *it* would linger, as it had since July, on his sofa, in his bed, and on every pillow in his apartment, fortified by each of Michelle's visits. Li Jun's mind began to drift, like a coil unwinding,

He suddenly remembered an afternoon floating along the Yangtze with Michelle. But Li Jun stopped this memory, trying to hit delete in his mind, still unable to forget her taunting words: I— don't— love— you.

His whole life Wong Li Jun had walked the line of Chinese zainichi, a foreign resident. He was always too Japanese for his Chinese peers abroad, and yet too Chinese for the Japanese people at home. He thought by being with Michelle, the constant guesswork at her true intent would be minimized by her American upbringing. He knew by pouring his feelings out to her he would never be branded as rude or brash as often happens in Japan. Instead, he was a liar, insincere, or hollow. Now after "reeling it in" at her request, his motives have become opaque. Li Jun gushed and ogled over Michelle but he knew, she didn't feel his love—perhaps she never had.

Li Jun stopped walking, the fragrance drawing him back to reality as the vanilla mixed with the smell of bread from a nearby bakery. They stopped at a crowded corner in Shibuya, the flash of ads on the screens overhead momentarily staining the crowd's skin, hair, and coats in vivid colors. Li Jun looked at Jade and Michelle, and sighed. He took in the glow of the neon lights, on billboards and signs. Looking closer at the vista he scoffed, as an image stared at him from one of the billboards. It was Michelle. He had taken that photo, launching her career and transforming her into an unstoppable force in the industry.

 She was draped in a white-nearly see-through dress, offset by a thicket of black waves down her back—skin glowing. The expression was neither daring nor bold, but mysterious as the glance drifted away from Li Jun's lens. The image of her floated above the streets, full of color and life as Tokyo buzzed with the New Year's dawn. The cross-light changed, Jade and Michelle stepped onto the street. Only a foot or so away, it was an ocean. It was distance further then he knew possible.

2. Terada Fifteen-o-Seven

Shinjuku, Tokyo, December, 31st

One of the crown jewels of Claudio Terada— unofficially one of the richest men in Asia—stood in Shinjuku. Fifty-eight stories of shopping, restaurants, offices, and even a hotel, Terada Fifteen-O-Seven was known for its glass-walled ballroom and panoramic views of the city. It was an icon of the Tokyo skyline, a building so impressive it bore the family name.

The Teradas built their wealth during the nineteen forties, beginning with Masayuki Terada, Claudio's father, and Terada shipping. In the upswing of the fifties Masayuki Terada took up real estate, snatching up properties on both sides of the Pacific in and around Sao Paulo, Kanagawa and Chiba.

By the time Brazilian-born Claudio came to power, in the early seventies, he simply managed the company. Yet it was Claudio's acquisition of Tokyo Broadcasting System Holdings and its twenty-eight affiliate news networks in the early eighties that made people in Japan take notice. By the time he weaseled his way into telecommunication through large shares of SoftBank, Docomo, and AU, Mr. Terada was a legendary shark. In 2015, he bought and renamed Shinjuku Park Tower, then renovated much of the space. The famed ballroom and the prestige that came along with it are why Eva Wong has hosted her New Year's Eve Party here year after year.

Many Japanese celebrities often declined the invite, sending their regrets, due to deeply ingrained Shogatsu rituals. Shogatsu marks a time of refreshing in Japan. Similar to Thanksgiving and Christmas rolled into one. It is noted by traveling to one's hometown, spending time with family and visiting temples before the rush of the new year kicks into high gear. But as many things do in Tokyo, the agency and its parties have gained momentum, becoming a powerhouse agency in the far east.

Tokyo lay at their feet, the backdrop on all sides, as Li Jun and Michelle entered the famed ballroom together, with Jade following behind. On the left side of the room there was the larger of two bars, with another placed directly across from it. Off in the far-right corner, there was a stage and live band playing soft music to the still trickling in crowds. At the center of this was a marble sunken dance floor surrounded by a sea of patterned burgundy carpet, bathed in the light of dim chandeliers. The space would feel romantic, with the city stretched out on the horizon, twinkling toward a new year. Yet it was Michelle's sighting of Li Jun's sister—her agent, Eva Wong that put the last nail in that coffin.

Eva strolled toward Li Jun, Michelle and Jade as if walking on clouds. She wore a black lacy gown, trailing her every step.

"Let's get a couple of drinks and network," Michelle said to Jade, trying to slip away as Eva came to meet them. Unlike her younger brother, Eva was fair with dark brown hair cut to her collar bone but pulled up for the occasion. She was thin and beautiful by every standard in this country. Her beauty was inexplicably compounded by the French accent that clung to her words. Yet, Eva's concern first and foremost was always her business, thus, making her a nag. The band shifted into 'Fly Me to the Moon' by the time Eva was upon them.

"Hi, Michelle-Jun, I'm glad you finally made it."

Eva placed a hand on Li Jun's shoulder, plastering on her 'work smile,' as Michelle called it. The only smile she knew of.

"Good Evening," Michelle grinned back, tucking hair behind an ear as Li Jun stood sandwiched between them, and Jade attempted to go unnoticed.

"Oh, Michelle I have a shampoo commercial for you once you come back from your, *vacation*. So, don't do anything too drastic to your hair. I'd hate to add extensions on to the bill." Eva ran her fingers through Michelle's hair, scowled, then released the hair.

Michelle simply stared at her.

It was nearly impossible to miss the tension as the two women spoke to each other, burning between indifference and distaste. That was the reason Michelle changed the tide. "Eva, this is my friend, Jade," Michelle said carelessly throwing the spotlight elsewhere. Jun chuckled, remembering that he taught her that trick, as he downed a glass of champagne.

"Jade, nice to meet you, I'm Eva Wong. You wouldn't happen to know Victoria Yang, would you?" Eva paused, looking Jade over head to toe.

"The fashion model, no." Jade beamed, her heart rate slowly climbing, with the realization that Eva might remember her, from before the surgery on the one occasion they'd met.

"You remind me of her in a way, have you ever thought about modeling?" Eva asked, her hands clasped, poised and modelesque herself as she shamelessly tied the introduction back to work. Michelle giggled to herself, turning her head away, while Li Jun shook his head.

"I'm absolutely too shy for that." Jade smiled.

"That's too bad. Well, are you new to Tokyo?" Eva asked. Li Jun sighed, knowing where the conversation was headed.

"Yes, I've been here for about six months or so,"

"So, about the same time as Michelle," Eva was determined to play the ever-gracious host. The usual questions ensued: What brought you to the city? What's your occupation? Have you been to, and so on and so forth, until the hand was played.

After the conversation had run its course, Eva turned her attention back to Li Jun. She whispered something to her brother over a shoulder while Li Jun grabbed a drink, using the other hand to palm Michelle's butt. Michelle rebuffed him. She elbowed Li Jun and tucked her hair behind an ear, then turned to Jade to start a conversation.

"Just get over there," Eva shoved Li Jun away before turning her sights to Michelle.

"Michelle, you should go with Jun and chat up some of our clients."

Eva's smile was tainted with a twist of sarcasm, or was that just her face, Michelle could never really tell.

"By the way Michelle, stick to vodka sodas. You're looking heff-te. We're having a tape session next time you come in." Eva narrowed her eyes, the dangling gold earrings chiming with each syllable.

"Got it." Michelle nodded, and turned to Jade.

"I'll catch up with you later,"

"Alright." Jade nodded back, just before Michelle left with Li Jun

"Again, it was good meeting you, Jade. Have a nice evening," Eva beamed.

"It was very nice to make your acquaintance," Jade said, before Eva walked away.

Her cover, still safely intact, Jade's focus moved to finding alcohol and avoiding Eva at all costs. The last time she had a drink must have been, four months ago. With money getting tight and playing the goodie-two-shoes to Michelle's 'bad-and-boujee' persona, there was little to no me time for Jade. She missed her days of drinking in the boarding school dorms with Naima. Just as she dismissed Naima from her thoughts, Jade locked eyes with a man at the bar. She approached moving through the crowd like a lioness through the brush—with ice in her veins. She smiled at the bartender and he quickly finished with his customer and came to her.

For now   double gin   tonic   extra   lime   please
"Toriaezu, daburu jin tonikku ekusutora raimu, onegaishimasu."Her

Instead   gin s o d a   extra   s o d a
Japanese was flawless. "Kawarini, jin soda ekusutora soda." She longed for the taste of a gin and tonic, but she could not risk dismantling all her work so she amended the order.

"I'm fairly certain you're not old enough to drink." The man at the bar said to Jade with a Posh British accent.

"There's only one way to find out," she echoed back in the same accent, brows raised and lips curling upward.

"I'm Jon,"

"Stephanie," Jade said moving the bangs back from her eyes—sizing him up.

水 く さ い
MizuKusai
Shinjuku, Tokyo, December, 31st

At the entryway to the ballroom, veteran model, Victoria Yang arrived solo. At the top of the stairs she paused, holding a hand up to stop the security guard from opening the door. Victoria tucked a few stray hairs from her face, patting the loose ringlets that hung to the middle of her torso. As thin as a rail and armed with ivory skin and blue-black hair, Victoria Yang has remained one of the world's top models for the last decade.

Victoria graced more than seventy magazine covers over the course of her amazing modeling career. Turning back to the stairs, she posed for the press who were stationed like hungry dogs just outside the ballroom. After a few different angles, Victoria turned back to the door. Nodding to the security guard, she entered the ballroom. As the gold lacquer doors closed behind her, she whipped any trailing portions of the gold dress away from the door for dramatic effect. No press until midnight that was Eva's golden rule.

Some star-struck Korean pop sensation, whose name Victoria couldn't remember, turned to her with martini in hand.

"Victoria you look amazing."

A conversation followed with Victoria half listening as the live band played Banana Lemon's 'Joyride.' She nodded, picked up a glass of champagne, smiled politely.

"I saw Jun come in with some girl. You know— beautiful, exotic. Last time we chatted you and Jun were engaged. Why would you two call it off?" The singer asked, allowing the implications to float between them.

Victoria stared at the girl's oversized diamond necklace and ring clashing with her Christmas-elf-green gown.

Who dresses these people?

"I noticed," Victoria said, in her prim Singaporean British accent, with an attitude at odds with her true feelings. "It seems he can't keep his hands to himself. At this point I think he's slept with every woman at the agency, other than Eva." Even as the words left her mouth, Victoria knew she still loved Li Jun—the depth of this 'love' to be examined at some later date. Victoria cut her eyes across the room, appraising Wong Li Jun with the exotic beauty, looking past the Korean singer, to the couple, while pretending to listen.

Victoria could almost feel the tension between them. Michelle's body was rigid. She smiled with clients not even looking at Li Jun. Knowing Jun, Michelle caught him with his tongue down another woman's throat or with panties too small to be hers. Seeing Li Jun and Michelle like this, made Victoria feel good about Li Jun ending their relationship, yet ridiculous for still being attracted him.

She felt like an idiot for letting Li Jun quietly break their engagement—for Michelle no less, to date her, to be with her. Victoria felt like a complete buffoon for giving her body to a man who didn't want to marry her—left her—and had no problem bedding her while his new boo, Michelle, was away. This realization paired with her observations of them tonight rankled her even further.

Victoria twisted her earring, quietly cursing that friendly drink with Li Jun, last Christmas while Michelle was in Hawaii. The drink somehow spilled over into a night of bliss. She was still secretly pleased she answered Li Jun's phone while he was in the shower, and even more pleased she gave Michelle a piece of her mind.

"Tsap tsing gia." Tori mumbled, as the singer changed topics, to something about L.A. fashion. On the other side of the room, Eva spotted her friend and slipped away from chatting to aid Victoria.

"Beka, Merry Chris—Um, Happy New Year" Eva smiled, her arms

spread to embrace the girl. Victoria covered her mouth, trying to hide her smile as Eva and Beka stepped back from one another. "I thought you were working on a new album,"

"No, we start in March." Beka shook her head.

"Oh, after your nose and jaw surgery, right? I forgot." Eva nodded to herself, Beka was taken aback.

"It's nothing to be ashamed of, darling." Victoria chimed in, before handing her champagne glass to a waiter.

"Well, I have a girl at the agency that writes amazing songs and she's performing tonight. I think you'll like a few of her upbeat tunes, and if you're still around you two might be singing a duet this summer." Eva smiled at the icy phrase, adding a note of dismissal at the end—signaling that the singer be on her way.

"That sounds amazing. Well I have to go." The pop singer bowed out. "Eva this is a great party, one of your best!"

"That means a lot coming from you." Eva and Victoria smiled as the girl walked away. "I hate that girl, she's so…fake." Eva rolled her eyes.

"I know. Her manager really needs to reel her in. The girl's only eighteen." Victoria added, shaking her head. They laughed watching a cornered viper—turned lost sheep; wander off to mingle as more celebrities began to pour in.

"You know those Korean singers have short shelf lives." Eva sneered as Victoria burst into laughter. "There'll be a new one just like her next week. Better voice, better legs and she'll be tossed out on the heap, unless she's giving it up." Eva smirked, with raised brows.

"I've missed you," Victoria laughed, stressing British 'o.' "Let's get some drinks. We need to catch up."

They sat at the bar laughing, filling the time with stories of the months since last they saw one another.

"And where is Yu?" Victoria asked, realizing the missing piece.

"He wanted to come but had to work."

"Work, on New Year's Eve?" Victoria stopped to sip her Cosmo, very sex-in-the-city-esque. "Doing what, might I ask?"

"I don't know." Eva paused. "Some shoot in Kenya."

"Okay." Victoria quietly stared, allowing the band's version of Taylor Swift's 'Style' to fill the space between them. "So, Jun came with some exotic girl." Victoria waved to someone in the distance.

"Michelle. They're by the other bar with clients." Eva pointed with her eyes. "When you become my VP, this May—" Eva began.

"It won't interfere with business." Victoria cut her off.

"Good. I'm setting everything up now, my little workhorse," Eva smiled. "—Oh, by the way, I just met a girl that reminded me of your sister. It's been years since I've seen her. How is she?"

"Well, she's going through that rebellious heiress stage."

"She'll grow out of it, hopefully." Eva beamed as Victoria waved to the designer, Kili Mono.

Victoria's smile faded. "Well, I have to go play nice with all the usual people." She said hoping to close the subject. "Give me a call tomorrow. So that we can really catch up."

"I will." Eva nodded and Victoria walked away.

As the evening dragged on, Victoria became irritated by the watered-down drinks—the eavesdropped conversations—and the subtle stabs of shade. Victoria returned to the conversation at hand.

"The plan is to shoot in the Spanish Village so it'll look like different love stories, playing out in different areas of Spain and the track is awesome." Alex, another musician friend, said to her.

"If you'd like I could donate to the shoot." Famed shoe designer, Kili Mono chimed in, with her husky Spanish accent.

"That would be awesome." Alex nodded, following Victoria's less than discreet glances to Michelle and her group of junior models, gathered near the windows to their right. The spectacle: star actor of that new action thriller coming on strong. "Do you know her?" Alex asked, shifting the conversation.

"Not really." Victoria countered.

"It looks like she needs help." He walked over, extending a hand as Victoria and Kili followed alongside. "Nice to meet you, Michelle," Victoria heard Alex say, coming within ear shot.

"Victoria, how have you been?" Michelle asked. They hadn't seen each other since autumn, before that awful exchange at Christmas.

"Wonderful." Victoria replied. "This is Kili Mono," she extended a hand to the designer as Michelle and the other junior models looked at her in awe.

"Hello." Kili waved with a smile.

Feeling Victoria's intensity, the other models shifted conversations to each other and split off, almost instinctively, leaving Michelle and the actor to the titans. This allowed another conversation to spring up followed by Victoria and Michelle's long dreaded question: "How do you know each other?"

"It's a long story." Michelle laughed.

"It can't hurt to tell," Victoria edged her on.

"Well, I was in Paris at a New Year's party with my family—" Michelle started, recapturing Kili's attention.

Michelle didn't mention Victoria and Adrien Depaul leaving the bathroom, or his lingering hungry stare at the then seventeen-year-old Michelle. Nor did she discuss the earring she left on the table, inviting him to follow her. Michelle also left out the time frame she dated him, age nineteen, alongside the discovery of his wife and daughters.

"You know she'd be great for the lead in our music video." A man cut in with an offensively strong Aussie accent, referring to the same job just accepted by Victoria. The Aussie winked at Michelle. She stared at him unfazed, that was when the glass from his hand slipped to the floor and shattered. Everyone jerked back, as rich Hennessey-stained carpet, satin shoes, and white shirts alike. Alex led the drunken Aussie off, toward the back exits. The small crowd dispersed to clean themselves up, leaving Michelle and Kili.

"I loved that Dolce and Gabbana ad you did." Kili smiled, "Why don't we set up a meeting? I've been looking for a new face to work with." She handed Michelle her card.

"I'd love to," Michelle was astonished.

Victoria, who happened to overhear, was enraged. This went completely unnoticed as Kili strolled back to the bar. Michelle looked at the card then glanced at the band playing a familiar song she couldn't place,

'Work' – Rihanna, it occurred to her.

"What a mess." The hot shot actor said, coming back to chat with Michelle. He pointed to the drunken Aussie then shifted his sights to the window, staring out at lights as far as the eye could see.

"I'm fine. That bitch was a fucking tease." Michelle and the actor, heard the Aussie say, over Drake's portion of the song. Michelle looked at the actor, who scoffed, then sipped his Rum and Coke. Victoria, grabbed a security guard to help Alex.

"Hontoni yopparatte, sono gaijintachi." The actor laughed, as Victoria moved to open the door, allowing a security guard to escort the Aussie and Alex out. Another guard appeared a moment later, carrying the Korean singer, Beka, in a flash of green satin.

"Well I'm going to find my friend," Michelle said, before walking away.

"Why do you speak so much English? Nihongo sabete."

"Watashimo gaijin desuyo, Kenchi." Michelle grinned. "Shranagatta?" She laughed before walking away.

'She's Asian,' the typical onlooker would say of the California-born beauty. Yet, despite 'the look,' Michelle's grandmother came from Eritrea and her grandfather from Nigeria, both professors in those days. Michelle's mother was the problem, at least when it came to living in any White or Asian community. She and Ms. Yamato were almost twins, one carved from ivory the other sculpted from sand. Though Michelle inherited the eyes, nose and cheekbones from the Eritrean side of things, her mother's imprint was always there.

"*Gaijin*, I hate that word." Michelle muttered, trying to avoid the masses surrounding the bars. *Gaijin, foreigner, literally outside person,* Michelle thought.

It's not a slur, one might say. And it is not people being lynched, hung, spat on, all because of skin, because of perceived belonging, or the lack thereof. That is what her grandparents faced – her father's parents, in the sixties in DC when it was still very clearly 'the south.'

Japan's form of othering is not unique. This foreignness exists everywhere. In parts of Tokyo and much of Japan, foreignness comes with not-so-sly sideways glances and stares, dismissal at hello, whispers just outside ear-range, and being treated like a foolish child. Or pure fascination. These are the fines of being in this country, not as the standard, the norm—as the exception rather than the rule. It is white fragility but dyed macha in all its tepid subtlety with 'color-blind' discrimination, keeping all the structures intact yet changing the vista –from canvas to khaki. All of this is paired with the refusal to know. Refusal to see—hear—or smell the elephant trapped in the majority's cage.

This kind of insularity causes closed-mindedness to things not focused on the central group. There's also an expectation, going far beyond intercultural tolerance. The anticipation is simply this: being invited, one should (must) do things the Japanese way. Ultimately, the goal is assimilation into society, to take on the Japanese perspective, though not completely: eighty-twenty—seventy-thirty maybe—depending on where you are in Japan. But this should be done in a generation or less.

Many times, the warmth from this place and these people, although present, is barely felt. It's something like heating a stadium with a campfire. Until someone warms up to you, rarely is it the other way around or mutual, God forbid, without protocol. 'The chanto way of making friends.' Mizukusai-distant, distance all the kimarimonku, and formalities. There are too many unnecessary words, not enough necessary ones—and even fewer actions. Yet there is a kindness in many of these cool, distant vessels.

Michelle wandered through the crowd of drunken celebrities among the swirling chaos of rich people and an open bar. Michelle walked towards a free seat at the bar, sat, and ordered a drink. A man appeared at her side.

"I've heard a lot about you, Miss Yamato." He smiled.

"Really?" She turned, thinking business might be the topic.

"May I get you a drink?" He asked.

"No need." She pointed as the bartender placed a toasted almond in front of her—ordered to spite Eva.

"Excuse me," A second man appeared, on her left in a glistening black tuxedo. He spoke in a rich savory tenor that caught Michelle off guard.

He was young. Michelle thought he was Korean, from the look of him. The oblong face and gelled side-part-cut found in every Korean drama, and the flat inky brows that tapered down at an angle. His eyes, warm and welcoming were placed neatly on the sides of a slender nose just wide enough to be 'ethnic'. High cheek bones adding a touch of definition to his face. His jaw and upper lips shaded in a thin layer of stubble that crept to surround a mouth of pink lips.

"Eva sent me over to discuss something with you. Do you have a moment?" The second man asked.

Michelle picked up her drink, and paused, to assess the mouth more closely. The top lip was slender, much like the nose, yet the bottom lip was full, thick, and *damp*. He beamed and she felt the desire to back away from him, not knowing why. He was Asian she knew but not fully, with a slight accent she couldn't place. His skin was dark for this country, with a color liken to a croissant.

"We were just—" the first gentlemen retorted, but couldn't finish.

"I realize that." The second man smoothly cut him off. "I was sent by Eva Wong to personally discuss a few details with Miss Yamato's upcoming campaign, if you don't mind." He smiled and the first gentlemen relented, before walking away.

Michelle stayed, intrigued by the ruse of this Asianesque man.

"I'm Seina." He said. "Do you mind if we sit somewhere away from the noise?" He glanced at the bar.

"No. I don't." She gave him a half smirk.

Michelle sat at a small table near a window, across from Seina. It was a quiet corner of the room that felt as though the rest of the world had simply fallen away. Melodies from the band were the only faint reminders they weren't alone.

"So, is Seina really your name?" Michelle asked, breaking the brief quiet.

"Would you believe me if I said yes," he raised an eyebrow.

"No." She laughed, crossing her legs. She stared at him; unsure of what he was after, liking his slick expression, and cunning eyes. "Why did you step in? Eva obviously didn't send you." There was something magnetic that kept her attentive.

"I wanted to talk to you alone." Seina beamed, "I saw you across the bar and came over. Time was just on my side." He said, and familiarity closed in.

Just as quickly as Michelle was intrigued by him, her stomach turned. An inside logic clicked, and it all became too much. The armor was adorned, and unexpectedly the woman was replaced by the general. She shifted her attention to the window. Another Drake and Rihanna tune playing. The glow of the Tokyo skyline illuminated the space between and around them. *It was 'Take Care,'* the song Michelle realized as Rihanna's hook, shattered their quiet. "Smooth." She nodded.

"I like to think of it as a charming characteristic. Are you involved with anyone Michelle?" He leaned in, an arm on the table, the other hand clasped around his glass.

"Aren't you forward?" She placed her chin on her hand, leaning on the arm of the chair.

"You haven't answered the question." Finishing his drink, Seina stared at her as an array of colored lights glided across Michelle's face.

"We're already on shaky ground. I don't know your name."

"Tonight, I don't have a name." He grinned as Michelle sipped the last of the toasted almond.

"Well," she said surreptitiously, "tonight, I'm married." Michelle smirked back, uncrossing her legs and standing.

"Your husband should be more attentive to you." He said turning in her direction.

"Good night, and thanks again, Seina." She said walking back to the larger bar.

Complications from Roppongi
Shinjuku, Tokyo, December, 31st – (2 hours before midnight)

Jade stepped from a bathroom stall, zipping her dress. She turned to Jon, the Brit from the bar as he zipped and buttoned his pants.

"I'll see you later?" He asked, smiling.

"I'm not done with you yet." Jade ran her fingers through her hair, still using the British English, as a man walked out from the next stall embarrassed. He quickly rinsed his hands and left, leaving Jade and Jon to a symphony of laughter. Jon moved closer to kiss her and she pushed him back, "Bye." She said, as she walked out the bathroom.

Jade wove through the crowd as her purpose for still being here began to take shape again. As Jade moved away from the bathroom, she faintly heard a voice over the music.

"Lia…Lia, is that you?" Seina grabbed her attention.

Jade turned to face the voice.

"I thought that was you. Aren't you a little young for plastic surgery?"

"What are you doing here? I thought you were living in Italy." At least that's what her Intel and Ah Fan's research concluded. Jade gave Seina a cold stare. "It's my dad's building and I'm working for Terada Industries." He smiled, with a shrug. "What are you doing here?"

"I'm with a friend." Her words were sharp and cold.

"Small world." He was taken off guard by her tone and lack of explanation. "Would your friend happen to be her?" He pointed to

Michelle sitting at the bar. "I saw you with her earlier."

"She's off limits," Jade said shifting to walk away.

"Is she seeing anyone?" Seina stopped her.

"She's the mistress to some rich chef named Marcus. He bought her an apartment and she just ended it with Jun." *Or so Jade thought at the time.*

"Jun who?"

"Li Jun Wong—Jun, Eva's brother." She said in a sing-song way trying not to roll her eyes.

"Oh-okay, thanks Lia," he nodded, walking away.

"It's Jade." She grabbed him by the forearm, jerking him back to her.

"As in Kung-Fu-grip-Jade." Seina laughed looking at the arm, before slipping Jade's grasp and walking away.

Jade shook her head and walked to the bar–freshly spotted by Michelle. Their eyes met again as Jade slipped past the throng of celebrities, socialites and the obscenely wealthy posted protectively around the alcohol. Jade cut past a couple of older gentlemen discussing discreet jewelers and the Christmas gifts each got their mistress.

"Thank you, its Vivienne Westwood." One woman said in Japanese to another gesturing to her gown as Jade noticed the huge Harry Winston diamond on her left hand. I thought this was Tokyo not New York. She rolled her eyes at this showboating, when she finally reached Michelle at the bar.

"Was he trying to chat you up?" Michelle tittered as Jade sat down beside her. "You looked like you were about to punch him."

"I guess dehydrated-men aren't just a western phenomenon." Jade smiled. "He was asking about you." She said to Michelle batting her eyes.

Michelle's eyebrow rose and fell. "Let's bring this new year in right," she said shifting topics, beaming and throwing an arm around Jade.

"Okay, what's a good drink to get me started?" Jade asked scanning the crowd. "You know I don't dri—" she began as she spotted him— Chris— in the sea of faces. She was breathless. The shock was like rocks in the pit of her stomach. He was the third person tonight she knew. The feeling was compounded at the fact that she even remembered him, especially at this angle—In this lighting.

Jade met him in a club in May. She was at a low point since coming to Japan. She was in Shinjuku, no Roppongi— she liked the 'danger' or thought nothing of it. Jade was high, the first time since Amsterdam with Naima. Smoking at a VIP table with a cool-good-looking Nigerian dude, who thought he might get lucky.

Oh, how they laughed, oh how they kissed.

Chris appeared from nowhere, the color of wet sand, incisive almond eyes, and thick wavy hair slicked back from his face. He hit her leg knocking the joint to the floor.

"Asshole" she roared over the lights and music. Chris turned to her, brows lowered, eyes dismissing—no sign of remorse. She stood, Olu, her Nigerian, stepping into the mix. Chris swung, knocking Olu into a wall. Olu swung back before crashing to the floor with his mouth bleeding. Chris looked from the man to Jade. "Meet me outside, asshole." She said propping Olu up in his booth with security on the way. Jade would never admit it, but she was intrigued and turned on by Chris' blatant disregard.

"I'm Chris," he said to her later outside the club, hand extended, and face bruising; then— she woke up— in his bed— in his arms.

This, her third grave mistake, was in direct connection to her first. She found Chris sexy, even though he was western, Californian, and cocky— three things she absolutely hated, but she wanted him. Jade saw herself as being the complete opposite in every category, still she was drawn to him.

"A long island," Jade heard Michelle say to the bartender, as she continued to watch Chris.

Here he stood, cocky, sexy, cool with a *slut* on his arm. Had Jade not slept with him, again, just two weeks ago, seeing him here wouldn't have fazed her, but the encounter was intensely satisfying. The woman on Chris' arm, looked like one of those car magazine girls, the form-fitting dress amplifying the hourglass figure— somehow Jade knew she came from money.

Michelle moved closer, attempting to see what had caught Jade so off guard. Next to Michelle, Jade's face was a soft thing, sweet like pink cotton candy wound in a sweep of excitement. Her features were womanly but not quite, she, still a budding lily at twenty-one. Jade's eyes were almond-esque, her skin like rose tinted porcelain. The black hair made her look European but not quite.

"What are you looking at?" Michelle asked, as the bartender handed her the Long Island.

"I thought I saw someone I knew." Jade turned away as her eyes met Chris' across the room to the sound of Taichi Mukai's 'Touch'— *how ironic,* she thought.

"Give this a try." Michelle said handing Jade her drink, and scanning the crowd. "What is he doing here?" Michelle wondered aloud as Jade took a sip from her glass.

"That's good." Jade croaked in relief, eyeing the glass as Michelle watched Chris' date kiss him and walk away.

"Hey Jade, my brother is here. Come on. I'll introduce you."

Brother, Jade thought. *Brother?*

Ho lang kan

"The girl has a fucking brother," Jade mumbled. The Singaporean English surfaced as she was slowly losing her cool. Reluctantly, Jade followed Michelle and she saw the brother in question.

"Chris, what are you doing here?" Michelle asked with Jade in tow.

"I'm just hanging out. You?" He smiled, drinking champagne as his eyes drifted to Jade. He stood in a bespoke black tuxedo, Italian by the cut. Jade traced every inch of him. At six-four, with a muscular build, Chris oozed confidence, but most importantly sex— much like Michelle. But if Michelle was fire, this man was lava. His woodsy cologne wafted in Jade's direction, as her eyes settled on his.

"I'm working," Michelle stared at him, Chris' half smile enhancing his dimples.

"You're always doing something you do anyway, *for work.*" He said in a husky baritone. His squared off jaw tightening at his attempts not to laugh.

"Real funny, why are you here?" Michelle crossed her arms.

"Marcus and Devina decided not to come, last minute. So, I'm here, with a friend."

"And where is this friend?" Michelle asked as Jade looked away from him, trying to cover her disappointment at the use of the word friend.

"The bathroom, Barbara Walters," Chris nodded to Jade. "Who's your friend?" He smiled as Jade decided to play the stranger.

"This is Jade. Jade this is my brother Chris. Chris Jang if you ever need to hire a hit man." Michelle glanced at Jade, all too seriously.

"For what," He laughed. "I won't do anything you don't ask me to do. It's nice to meet you, Jade." He licked his lips, hand extended, smiling as their eyes met again, his lingering.

"It's nice to meet you too." She simpered, not shaking the hand. "Why the different surnames?" Jade found herself asking trying to avoid Chris' eyes.

"That's a long story but our 'parental units' were on the outs when I was born is the simplest answer," Michelle said leaving a keen opening for her and Chris to pass banter. Looking for similar features Jade need not look very far. It was apparent in an instant, the two nearly twins, with a different look to them somehow. *He really is her brother*, she thought.

"Shut up." Michelle hit Chris again.

Chris laughed in a deep rumble, all the while, watching Jade. When his date approached, Chris introduced her, changing little about his demeanor.

"Nice to meet you both," Alyson, Chris' date said before, placing an arm around his waist and a hand on his chest.

Michelle was right, I should have worn that dress. Jade sighed.

"So, Alyson where are you from?" Michelle asked.

"Busan." She glowed, smiling and flinging hair off her shoulder.

"I thought you were Korean. You're gorgeous. Chris always finds such beautiful women."

"Thank you." Alyson laughed. "Well, he's not too bad. I could maybe see why."

"How did you two meet?" Michelle asked. Jade was half listening.

"Well—" Alyson began. Chris whispered something into her ear, she laughed and hit him. "I met Chris a few months ago, when he and your mother came to sample a few bottles for the restaurant."

"Korean, huh? She's been cut up a few times too. Like that's all natural." Jade mumbled, giving Alyson the one over.

"So does your family own a winery?" Jade cut in.

"Yes, that's right." Alyson smiled, teeth gleaming.

"Well, I think you two should go now." Chris leered. "It's past your bedtime, Michelle." He wrapped an arm around Alyson's waist.

"Bye Christopher." Michelle sneered as Eva appeared.

"Excuse me," Eva said slipping in, like lightning— in Wong fashion. "Michelle, do you know where Jun is?"

"No." She surveyed the room as Chris and Alyson slipped away—off to some corner. "The last time I saw him, we were talking to the tall man from Malaysia."

"Alright, well don't forget you're on in 30, then right after is the countdown." Eva nodded, walking away, another of her increasingly-less-subtle reminders to avoid the press. Michelle sighed and turned to Jade.

"I have to get ready. At some point this work party will be a party."

"It's no problem." Jade nodded. "I'll go find Jun and send him Eva's way."

'Thank you,' Michelle mouthed walking away.

No surprise to her, Jade found Li Jun at the bar, out of sight. She sat beside him in silence tucking her bangs from her eyes as the bartender placed another shot in front of him, the third in a row.

"Having a good time?" Li Jun asked, barely looking at Jade.

"Somehow I thought this would be more fun." Jade looked at him, ordering water for herself—trying to flush the Asian glow brought on by the long island.

"It's real fun if you come trashed. I'll never forget that year." He laughed.

"Look pull yourself together." Jade said, forgetting for a moment her sugar-coated 'self.' Li Jun took his last shot.

"She's really done with me, isn't she?" He sounded as if he were kicked, more a statement of fact than a question to be answered.

"Jun—"

"Okay, I understand. You're her friend. But she just walled me out. I don't even know what I did or what she thinks I did." He looked at Jade with injured eyes. "I'm trying to be the good guy."

"Stop trying. Be the good guy or don't." She said.

Li Jun stared at her for a moment, seeing something in her shift, as the lights dimmed further.

"Eva's looking for you." She stood, before walking away.

In the far-right corner of the ballroom a spotlight appeared on the stage and the music faded as Eva stepped out onto the platform.

"Good Evening everyone, I'm Eva Wong, here to introduce the last bit of tonight's live entertainment." Eva said in elegant Japanese. "Following our New Year's tradition, the Agency's newest talent, Michelle Yamato will perform." She smiled, and the crowd burst into applause. "I hope you enjoy it. Happy New Year," she said before walking off stage. The spotlight overhead faded as lights in the stage came on. A second spotlight illuminated, here Michelle stood with her back to the audience.

Just off stage, Victoria rushed to Eva's side. "Eva we have a big problem." Victoria jerked her by the arm. "What is it?" Eva questioned.

"A few drunken people got up to the roof. I told security—"

"Shit," Eva mumbled, moving toward and dashing up the stairwell to the roof. Victoria followed, a smile creeping over her face as she took a bottle of champagne up the stairs.

Eva opened the door and a gust of wind rushed in, slamming the door to the wall. She crept out, searching for the drunkards.

"Is anyone up here?" She asked, looking around.

A pair of cold hands covered her eyes from behind.

Eva tensed.

"I'm here." The voice said, sending heat rolling down her back in surges. "Do you know who I am?" He asked.

"Yu?" She questioned leading to her eyes being uncovered. Eva turned to him, a smile slipping through the cracks of worry. "What are you doing here?"

"I came to see you." Yu laughed, bringing light to his tea-colored eyes.

"There's no one up here is there?" Eva asked, feeling foolish. Yu shook his head. "Okay, its cold let's go inside." Eva grabbed his hand. "No wait," Yu stopped her, kneeling.

"Yu, are you okay?" She paused.

"I've loved you since we met eight years ago in Barcelona." He said, then paused to pull a jewelry box from his jacket. "So will you marry me Eva Wong?" Yu froze and Eva exhaled, a cloud blanking the air between them. "I'm sorry it took eight years to get back to you and realize I wanted you to be my wife." Yu paused, staring at her, his eyes glassy and shiny alongside the swell of his emotions.

"Ten—" the counting roared up from the ballroom.

"Will you marry me?" Yu asked again.

"—Seven—"

"I'm tempted to say no," Eva looked away from him. "Yes. I'll marry you." Eva nodded and Yu scooped her into his arms.

"One. Happy New Year," The ballroom burst into a cheer as Victoria popped out of the stairwell.

"Congratulations!" Victoria sung out, opening the champagne.

Game Changer
Tokyo, December 31st – (3 hours before midnight)

"Yes, Kazu!" She shouted, in the dark of her living room, the light spilling in from the surrounding buildings. Yu tried to catch his breath in the brief silence following her satisfaction. It was New Year's Eve, nine thirty-nine p.m. he saw looking at the clock on the oven.

"Kazu," she called still straddling him. "Asa made taizai." She stared into his hypnotizing eyes. Yu glanced at the clock in the kitchen again.

"Aiya, sore dekinai," he said as he stroked her face. "Ju-ji made yuaazuyo." (I'm yours until ten.)

Aiya Sighed at that. "Mou 1kai," She said digging her nails into his chest.

By Ten thirty-two, Yu picked up the cash Aiya left on the counter for the services rendered, and he left her apartment freshly showered. Once on street level he hailed a cab.

Slowly the taxi trotted in holiday traffic, bound for Shinjuku and Terada Fifteen-O-Seven. Yu glanced down at the ring in his hand, biting the inside of his jaw and nodding to himself. *To think this man who studied engineering, in Spain, just a few short years ago slinks from bed to bed now*, he thought of himself.

That's where it all began, but thanks to Dad's and grandpa's debts, we lost the mansion, the cars, everything. Everything. Find new footing, it can't be that hard, right?

It is. It is that hard and time hasn't slowed down for a second. The money was gone, so were the dreams— couldn't pay for 'em.

What happens to people like that in Japan, those who work harder than hard. They work three jobs, barely eat—barely sleep— because that's life, that's living. What happens when your only living parent gets Dementia while your half-brother is scraping to go to art school? Yu mused over his life as the cab came to a stop. He paid the driver and slipped out of the taxi.

He waltzed into the lobby with his famous golden boy smile. Yu flashed his pass to the guards seated in front of the elevators.

"Hiroshi-san yokoso," The guards greeted him. "Top floor, then up the stairs." One man said as the other held the elevator.

"Ms. Yang?" A man on the security detail upstairs, called pulling

Victoria aside. "There's a man by the name Hiroshi Yu, he's asking for you just outside the ballroom."

"Ah, yes." Victoria nodded, following the man to the front doors. "Where have you been?" Victoria stood in the doorway— the press uncharacteristically out of place.

"My flight was delayed and traffic was not on my side, then my phone died. Everything is still good to go, right?"

"Yes." Victoria glanced inside the ballroom for signs of Eva

"Okay good. Where's Eva?"

"She's attending to the scandals that won't make it to twelve." Victoria smirked, thinking of Beka.

Yu came into the ballroom. "Okay, we'll use that excuse then." He nodded back as he locked eyes with Seina seated at the bar. "Is that Seina Terada?" Yu asked, suddenly pulled from the conversation.

"Yes. He's here representing, something or other." She sighed, glancing over her shoulder. Seina waved to Yu, signaling that he come over.

"Weren't you friends?" Victoria asked in a delicate tone, waiting for him to fill in the gaps to the story. Yu looked away from Seina and turned his attention back to Victoria.

"That was a long time ago." He shook his head.

"Ah, Well I'd like to hear more on this once I'm Eva's VP.

"Yeah, sure. Thanks again, Victoria." Yu said changing the subject again.

"You're welcome," Victoria smiled, then the lights overhead dimmed and Eva appeared on stage. Yu nodded to Victoria then slipped up to the rooftop.

"Good Evening, everyone, I'm Eva Wong, here to introduce the last bit of tonight's live entertainment...I hope you enjoy it, Happy New Year." She said before walking off stage. The spotlight overhead faded as lights in the stage came on. A second spotlight lit up, here Michelle stood with her back to the audience, in a floor-length red dress. More stage lights flickered on, revealing musicians. Michelle turned to face the crowd alongside the building rhythms.

'Your love is a liar, So vividly I remember, how you wan-ted, to be, much more than a lover, to me.'

"Jade," Chris called, standing near the front entrance listening to the music. Jade turned to him, only a few feet away and alone. His bronze-like skin added a touch of mystery.

Jade walked over to him, arms crossed. "Hi, is something wrong?"

"So where is your date?" He grinned.

"Maybe he's servicing Korean Barbie while you're away." She looked at him, remembering her fingernails digging into his skin.

"Funny, she's on the phone with some investors."

'The thought of your touch or kisses, pull me, constantly, to memories, that haunt me, endlessly~, still I (try~, to forget)'

"Don't tell me you're here by yourself?" He asked, mockingly. "You know you're not fooling me with this good girl act you're putting on. I know bad girls."

"You want a gold star?" She scoffed.

"I'll swing by tomorrow instead." He whispered, "or tonight and tomorrow, if you're up for it."

"No, I'll pass."

"Need time to heal?" He smiled at her, jokingly.

"Go find fun bags, have her top you off and have a very Happy New Year." Jade sneered at him over Michelle's haunting melody.

"Are you jealous?" He asked, staring at her with a smile.

Jade scoffed.

Chris pulled her to him. "So, I guess you were chatting with my sister when you were asking about a place to fuck me?"

"Move," Jade stepped back.

"Make me," he said, looking her over before he kissed her.

It was the roar of applause that became the pin to their bubble. Jade pushed Chris back, both of their lips damp, then without a word she walked away.

With the performance newly ended and the band shifting to gayer tunes, Jade approached the songstress with a long island in hand. Michelle sat at a table off in a corner, disconnected from the rest of the room, swatting away the swarms of men seeking a quiet word.

"There you are." Michelle looked up still warding off the lingering hungry suitors. "I didn't know tonight was gonna be all work. If I did, I wouldn't have invited you"

"It's fine." Jade shrugged, pushing the drink over to Michelle.

"Did you have a little fun at least?" Michelle asked, her eyes narrowing with disappointment and fatigue.

"No." Jade shrugged. "By the way, I like that song. Who was it by?" Jade saw Seina moving in their direction.

Michelle sighed. "Me. Eva wants to push me in that direction." Michelle closed her eyes. "My head is spinning."

I imagine so, you lil-alcoholic, Jade thought, laughing to herself. "Are you okay?"

"Are you laughing at me?" Michelle opened her eyes, scoffing at Jade.

"Michelle we need to talk." Li Jun appeared quick like lightning as Jade stood and slipped away, to avoid the oncoming fire.

"Jun I'll pass." Michelle started for the bathroom.

Li Jun grabbed her arm.

"Let go." She said through clenched teeth, elbowing herself free. She threatened to break him as Jade sat watching the commotion.

"She said let go." Chris cut in, his eyes were like fire as he tightened his grip on Li Jun's arm. "You can't hear?"

Li Jun let go.

"Thanks Chris," Michelle walked away.

"Stay away from my sister." Chris stared Li Jun down, as he walked back toward Alyson.

Li Jun sat, finally giving up the idea of being heard. Jade sat beside him, placing a glass of water on the table.

"Here, drink up and go home." She said before walking away.

"Ten. Nine—" The crowd chanted.

"Eight. Seven—" Jade grabbed a glass of champagne from a passing waiter to survey the room.

"—Five—" Michelle watched Li Jun down the water provided by Jade, and moved toward the front doors.

"—Three—" Seina swooped in, with an arm around Michelle's waist.

"—One—" Jade watched as Seina grabbed hold of Michelle, pulling her to him and into a kiss.

"Happy New Year!" The room burst into shrill excitement. Confetti covered every surface like silver snow, leaving Jade to toast alone, and curse the existence of Seina Terada.

"To another bloody year," she mumbled, emptying her glass.

Outside the ballroom, Li Jun took Jade's advice and attempted to go home. Amidst the press storming up the stairs, Victoria swooped in to check on the wounded Li Jun. She pulled him to her, taking him into her arms.

"Let me get you home." She said, with no argument in return.

Back upstairs, a wave of flashes consumed the room—blinking lights beaming on silver confetti. The paparazzi finally charging in. Seina pulled away from Michelle with a smile.

"Happy New Year," his creamy voice echoed in her mind.

"Terada-san atarashii kanojo desuka?" A photographer asked as the camera lights blinked on and off, exploding like bombs. Michelle took a step back from Seina.

"Terada?" She questioned, turning away from the cameras, attempting to evade any further pictures.

"See you soon, Michelle." Seina said in a stage whisper. Michelle cut through the swarm of celebrities with her head spinning, until she nearly rammed Jade in her haste.

"I need to get the hell out of here," Michelle said, pulling Jade to the stairs.

"Yeah, *we do*," Jade agreed.

She and Michelle rushed downstairs to gather their things. While the photographers continued to shoot, Jade and Michelle moved toward the elevator with coats in hand. Finding the entrance gridlocked, they slipped into their coats and waited.

The press scrambled, snapping shots of posy celebs, artists and designers, while Michelle bored with the waiting, caught sight of Yu, staring at them. It was really a glance lingering a bit too long. Michelle saw in his face, he knew them— if not them, her. He looked away as Eva approached. But the thought lingered silently, then slowly resurfaced.

"Where do I know those eyes?" Michelle asked aloud a few minutes later, having met, if not seen the man on two prior occasions.

Jade, watching this, and hearing Michelle's question knew in an instant. She remembered their first meeting, the three of them, in September in Hiroo. Michelle glanced briefly at Yu, while Jade lingered on him. She saw the new ring on Eva's finger; *might destiny be stitching another path in her favor?* She wondered. Then the elevator chimed, their getaway car at long last.

3. The Tutor

Hiroo, Shibuya, Tokyo, September, (4 months ago)

"So, Jun says thanks to the captain." Michelle started again. She and Jade were seated in the shade of a small café, just off Meiji Dori Avenue. "Then Jun makes his way over to me. While I'm leaning on the railing, hot as hell, staring at this nasty green water. And, I'm pissed more or less and I'm trying to hide it." They sat having brunch overlooking the Shibuya-Furu river, Michelle recounting her recent trip to China. "Then he comes from behind and he wraps his arms around my waist." Michelle brushed her hair from her face. Jade nodded, then sipped her tea. The summer's humidity trailed into the beginning of fall with the nearby fan doing little to help.

"Then what happened?" Jade beamed with curiosity.

"I keep looking at the river and I'm like 'Jun, why are we here?' He says.

'This river has maintained power over the people of China for thousands of years.' Going on and on—you know how he does," Michelle rolled her eyes.

"I'm sure he was trying to impress you."

"But then he says, 'it reminds me of how my mother is hell-bent on controlling me and my sister's lives.' Then I hear something like, 'She has no place between us,' whatever that means. So, I deflect it, and squeeze him to make him let go. He pulls me in closer. And Jade, I swear the boat slowed allll the way down cus the breeze died. So, then I roll the dice. I look up at Jun and I say,

'Are you trying to say I love you?' Just to see, one, how he responds. Two, how he feels because he's been playing games for months, and three, to get him off me. Jun backs away then he looks at me. And I pile it on, 'I

44

know I said your family was crazy." Michelle said, hands and arms swaying as she told the story. "Especially your mother but, I think we can build a life together.'"

"And what did he say to that?!" Jade sat up, clutching her necklace.

"Nothing," Michelle crossed her arms. "I looked at him and he said nothing, like it didn't even faze him."

"Michelle he wasn't prepared for you to be so receptive."

"After all this bullshit about wanting to get together; Jun didn't say anything because he doesn't love anything."

"How did you respond to him after that?"

"I pushed him out of the way, then drove the boat back." Michelle laughed.

"Wow, Temperamental much," Jade said, laughing with her.

What Michelle will never say, or allow herself to remember, is how Li Jun grabbed her when the boat slowed down, how he pulled her into his arms and into a kiss then said,

'I thought you already knew that I love you. I just wanted you to know where I come from. That *we* came from nothing. My family's ancestral village is at the bottom of the three gorges dam and this is as close as I could get you.' And the silence that followed. How could Michelle say that she crushed a man in a vulnerable state with four simple words, and then kept on stabbing?

But Jade already knew this, or bits and pieces of the story having bugged her decoy's life from cell phone to suitcase early in their meeting.

One can never be too careful.

"Have you spoken to him since the trip?" Jade interjected.

"No. But he hasn't called either." Michelle lied, knowing he tried to talk to her, though she made herself unavailable on every front. Jade had already surmised that Michelle wanted to leave herself untarnished in this telling. Years later, she would realize Michelle simply wanted to avoid examining the true nature of the general she so often becomes in matters of the heart—but *every story needs a villain*, she thought in this moment.

"After that trip, I wanted to kill Jun." Michelle shifted her back to the wall of the café, crossing her bare legs to the side of the table.

"Kill him for what?" Jade questioned.

"I broke a pair of Gucci sandals I loved, then lost half my summer clothes in the swimming pool running from his crazy mother, plus, he broke my suitcase—"

"Michelle it's really not as bad as you're making it." Jade cut her off, her words attempting to mask the indifference.

"So you say, but it was the last of a five-piece, custom-made luggage set, Jade. Jun and I agreed if he pushed my career, I would help muscle him into a more powerful position at the agency. I hate to say it but you were right. He's just about messing around." Michelle sighed.

Jade quietly stirred her tea. "I think you should speak with him face to face, at least to repair the business relationship." Jade looked up from the tea.

"You really like Jun, don't you?" Michelle smiled.

"No. I just think you and Jun don't look terrible together. And that you make a good team."

"I don't look bad with anyone." Michelle scoffed.

"He-he, Michelle it's been a week, call him. But on to a different topic: how is your Japanese coming?" She took a sip from the cup of tea, changing the subject.

"Still bad, why?"

"Well, I came across a few jobs you might be interested in but you need to speak pretty good Japanese," Jade said. "I know you don't want this modeling thing to take over your life."

"I'll pass, besides I should keep a low profile." Michelle looked at Jade with a smile.

"Speaking the language is what would help you do that. Why not go back to the States if you don't want to learn the language?"

"I can't, unless I want to live hand to mouth as the daughter of an infamous killer." Michelle threw her hair over a shoulder.

"What exactly happened?"

Michelle sighed, "Euthanasia. My dad allegedly killed his business partner, who was already dying from cancer. And now that the deed is done, it looks like it was all over money or their practice or whatever." Michelle shrugged, glazing over the whole matter.

"Well why did you run?" Jade was interested in the finer points of her decoy's life but tried not to appear too interested.

"I had just graduated, and I wasn't financially independent, at all. Then my dad was one of two black men doing well in all of Newport and—" Michelle stopped. "Jade it was either this or deal with all that. And this is easier. Plus I thought it'd be a new start."

"That's fair." *So, she does have a soul*, Jade remembered thinking, *something beyond face, body, and hair*, as the story began to sound strangely familiar. "Well how have you not been found yet?"

"My mother's close friend is doing something shady."

"That's cool, in a scary kind of way." Jade paused. "And being a model isn't creating a problem?"

"Eventually, it will, hence, I just make money to get by until I find real work."

"Learn Japanese, blend in a bit," Jade placed her hand on Michelle's hand. "Avoid the sun, put on lots of sunscreen, and dress down."

"Easy for you to say, you grew up in Asia, and how many languages do you speak?"

"I don't know." Jade shrugged. "Four—five, I guess but not well."

"I still don't understand. You're Chinese. You lived in the states. You speak four languages, why are you in Japan with a job that's not making you serious money?" Michelle's brow furrowed as she stared at Jade.

"I'm Taiwanese, Michelle. And I love my job plus—" Jade smiled as a waiter walked up to the table.

"Excuse me. I couldn't help but overhear that you need a little help with your Japanese?" He stood holding an empty tray, a creamy tan good-looking man with bright tea-colored eyes, slightly draped by wavy hair. He was something like a skater boi turned man—clean cut in a way but still maintaining the jagged edges. The first thing Jade noticed was the unbuttoned server's uniform shirt and the lack of a tie, followed by the silver ring on his right thumb. Then the empty holes on his pierced ears. He caught Jade's eye, drawn in by his careless air of danger. His brown eyes cutting into Michelle, incisive, yet shallow. They were like green tea left to cool then forgotten. The top layer was clear— almost green; and the bottom, a chocolate brown. The result was a gaze that made one linger, while pained by doing so.

"Japanese people are supposed to be polite." Michelle looked up at him.

"What gave you the impression we aren't?" He asked with a smile.

"Well jumping into our conversation is a start." Michelle stared at him, unrelenting.

"I'm sorry about that." He smiled, graciously.

"You should be."

"Take him up on his offer Michelle." Jade looked him over.

"Look," Michelle glanced at the name tag on his chest. "Hiroshi Yu, I don't know what you're trying to pull here but I don't want anything you're offering."

"I'm just offering to tutor you?"

Michelle scoffed. "Tutor my ass."

"I'm not trying to come on to you. Honestly, I just need a little extra money. Like you." He shrugged, still smiling.

"Why don't you teach English? The whole country needs you."

"I guess you weren't talking to both of us?" Jade cut in. "I would love for you to be my tutor."

"I don't see how I could help someone who already knows enough Japanese to get a job."

"My problem is that I understand everything, but I have a hard time breaking things down." Jade said, somewhat earnestly.

"If you have the money and the time I don't see why not." He turned his attention back to Michelle. "The offer still stands."

"Pass." Michelle sarcastically smiled, narrowing her eyes to show the discontent.

"Okay." He turned to Jade. "Anytime, I'm yours. 4,000 yen an hour." He handed Jade a white card with his number scribbled down, glancing at the clock, near the café's kitchen door. "Have a nice day." He walked away from the table.

"You too," Jade watched him walk away.

"Ho, ho, ho. Look who's trying to pick up some game."

"What?" Jade placed the card on the table, near the glass of water next to her tea.

"I saw you, tryin' to flirt with the *buzz-boy*." Michelle laughed, brushing her hair from her face.

"You can read Japanese?" Jade smiled. "I thought you were illiterate."

"Whatever. I understand everything, but I have a hard time breaking things down." Michelle said, imitating Jade's voice.

"Shut up." Jade rolled her eyes, picking up the now wet card from the table. "Are you done? It's on you this time." Michelle stared at Jade as they got up from the table. "Are you going to leave him your number and pretend it's a tip?"

Jade paused, looking at the damp card. "What?" She turned to Michelle. "No, you don't tip in Asia, *Westerner*." Jade chuckled, as they stood up and walked to the register to pay the bill.

"So, are you still looking for a roomie?" Michelle asked, shifting topics.

"Yeah, I'm meeting with her today." Jade paid the cashier, nodded to him, and sighed.

They strolled out of the café in companionable silence.

"Well, Good luck," Michelle smiled, "I have some errands to run. Let me know how it goes."

"I will." Jade waved, and they split off.

It was only later, Jade remembered Yu Hiroshi, and learned his secret.

Woman in Red
Algeciras, Spain, December 31st – (7 hours after the New Year's party)

It was late evening, nearly ten time zones away from all the happenings in Tokyo. Naima, sat in her apartment by the sea. Better known by her nickname, Ari, she was a woman of a certain prowess and cunning. Yet she knew nothing of the waves of change headed her way, or the sly hand destiny intended to play.

Ari sensed something was wrong. *Seina always answers my calls.* She hung up for the third time in the last hour. *Maybe Tatsuya did something to him.* The roar of ocean waves and the sounds of a running shower filled the apartment. This is the age-old reflex, to protect Seina, her protector— at all costs. Ari glanced in the full-length mirror on the wall to her left. She took a long look at her golden bronze skin with its milky highlights, as she sat in her bedroom on the sofa, throwing the phone down beside her. She threw long brown hair that hung to her waist off a shoulder, considering her next move.

Ari and Seina had been inseparable since her move to Venice as a teenager. Going to university was the only semi-permanent divider, but Seina's decision to later work at Terada Industries and move half-way around the world drove another wedge in their relationship.

The ocean breeze rushed in from the balcony, leaving the red curtains swaying by the door. Ari heard the sound of the shower stop, then she walked out to the balcony into the darkness of ocean and sky. She stood against the railing, listening to the roar of waves, as a sense of calm washed over her. Pulling a cigarette from the pack on the patio's end-table, she sat folding a leg underneath her and lighting the cigarette. *Call him again*, she thought. *If there's no answer, I have to go check. I have to see if he's okay.*

"Who knows what Tatsuya could have done," she exhaled.

"Coming to bed?" a young man asked, standing in the doorway.

"In a minute," she took another drag, and smiled the kind of smile perfected over years of 'treatment.'

"You've been in a bad mood since you got back from Morocco." He crossed his arms.

Ari took a puff on her cigarette, her eyes locked with the ocean as her thoughts ran wild. For years she lived in Venice, Paris, Berlin, and now Algeciras, but not Mohammedia.

Never again. For that place remained far too painful, leaving a hole where so much hope once thrived. Memories of what was her childhood collected dust, and after being left unexamined, flourish, becoming more vivid, and more haunting than even the best actress would let on. Ari shrugged, noting that a storm was rolling in. Lightning ignited the sky like branches on a great tree, and thunder echoed like the voice of God. Few links remain of that world where her parents existed as more than a thought. *In truth, Samir is the only link left*, she realized. This search for him seemed to be costing her everything—her job, and now quite possibly her sanity.

"Are you still looking for that Samir guy?" The young good-looking man asked from the doorway. Ari sat in silence, taking a long drag on her cigarette. He was clearly trying to get her to open up, after the weeks of hook ups, but she would have none of this.

He shrugged for all his efforts. "Don't stay out too long," he said, going inside.

Ari got up to grab her phone. She walked into her bedroom with the man sitting on the bed in his underwear. Ari passed him, the smoke leaving a trail in her wake. She dialed Seina again, for the fourth time. It simply rang, five, six, seven times, as it had on her three previous calls. The standard greeting chimed in Japanese as Ari walked down the winding staircase and into the living room, puffing smoke with each step. She held the phone, pacing the floor of the living room, then pulled a suitcase from her closet. Ari hung up again, carrying the suitcase upstairs and putting it at the foot of the bed.

"Where are you going?" The man questioned, following her.

"Move," Ari put out her cigarette, then grabbed clothes from her drawers—meticulously folding them as she went.

"So, because you went to Morocco, and can't get in touch with some other man, you're leaving without an explanation?" He asked before putting on his clothes. Ari simply stared at him and the man left in silence. Ari followed him to lock the door, when the idea finally floated to her.

"Google him, of course. It's New Year's what was I thinking? He's got to be hung-over somewhere." Ari laughed, walking back to her room. She grabbed her laptop and clicked over to images, slowly pecking in his name. The first thing that flooded her screen were pictures of Seina kissing a woman in red, this piqued her interest.

"Who is that?" Ari mumbled, clicking on a picture. "Michelle Yamato? Let me Google this hefa," Ari scoffed furiously typing.

Michelle Yamato…Japanese-American model working in Japan born in Osaka…represented by the Eva Wong Modeling Agency…

"Michelle Yamato, rumors," Ari mumbled, still pecking away. "Twenty-two-year-old, model, Yamato was caught sharing a New Year's Eve kiss with Seina Terada." She read aloud. "The two are believed to have been an item since late May when Terada was spotted in London hiding a mysterious dark-haired woman." Ari scoffed. "That was me. Terada and Yamato went public with their *relationship* at the Eva Wong Modeling Agency's New Year's Eve Party. The pair was seen shopping at Kili Mono's boutique in Ginza." Ari reached for her phone, dialing Shahir, one of the detectives she keeps at her disposal.

Unlike the Shangs of Singapore who built their wealth in the 1800s, the Teradas were *newer* money. Think the 1940s, the whole world at war with itself, and here a Japanese immigrant in Brazil quietly amasses a small fortune smuggling anything from priceless antiques to ivory and drugs. This became Terada Shipping before they went legit. That's how it started with Seina's Grandfather, Masayuki.

Later, Seina's grandfather and father tried their hand at real estate, adding to the fortune. All of this would be irrelevant, but for Ari's adoption by her aunt and uncle— Seina's parents, thus entitling her to a sum in the Terada trust alongside Seina and his siblings. Never mind the small fortune left to her after the death of her parents. So yes, there is the desire to protect her cousin, but there is an even greater desire to protect his inheritance. Ari lit another cigarette, putting the phone to her ear.

"Shahir I need you to look into someone for me." She began in Moroccan Darija, before switching into standard Arabic. "Her name is Michelle Yamato, born in Osaka Japan and currently working for the Eva Wong Modeling Agency.

"A Japanese woman this time?" Shahir said playfully. "You're hitting' these ladies hard. Ten thousand dollars should be enough."

"Your retainer is three," Ari countered sharply.

"That last one you had me look for, Claudio kept eyes on her for a long time. It was a real risk confirming."

"You never told me where she was," Ari interjected.

"She was cremated. I don't know what happened to the ashes." Shahir said matter of fact. *That cruel bastard*, Ari thought covering her mouth. *How could Claudio do that to his son?*

"Alright, for ten I need everything you can find on this girl—anything I could use." Ari said glancing down at her nails. "Get a hacker on the case so I can start looking for someone to get close to her."

"Right on it."

"You have two days Shahir."

When Ari hung up, she closed the laptop and her phone lit up from a new message. She paused to read the romanized Arabic from the lock screen-

I found Samir, but not in Morocco - from informant three. *It's about time*, Ari thought. She replied quickly with blood surging and palms on fire.

In Dubai, the informant replied.

Extradition by Another Name
Ikebukuro, Tokyo, January 1st

The sun, bright and overly enthusiastic, woke Jade to bitter cold with her ears still ringing. It was midmorning, January first. Michelle lay stretched out beside her, deaf to the world as Jade got up, unable to rest soundly with the thing still left undone. She turned on the heat and crept to the bathroom.

Three years she's been like this, unable to sleep, unable to rest soundly. So instead, she used the restless nights to chat with Ah Fan, attempting to rewrite code, to plot logistics, and study layouts. This restlessness stemmed from a rogue privilege that moved about, seeking whomever it may devour; a privilege, along with her family wealth, dependent upon their manipulation of the developing world. Daily, Jade felt the weight of this privilege and all she was to inherit, along with the more than two million lives that are forever changed, every year.

After she washed her face and brushed her teeth, Jade moved to the living room. Back to plotting she goes with all of its sleepless nights. This was why Ah Fan told her to go to the source, to Robert. And that she has, though he is not the green-eyed monster she hoped for.

An hour or so later, Michelle rustled back to life, piecing herself together just as she was. Jade quietly cursed that seemingly effortless beauty, forgetting the hours of gym, and salon, and the pain Michelle so often speaks of. *She just springs to life, washing her face, unwrapping her hair and …beautiful. Who does that?* Jade sat on the sofa, her hair undone, in sweatpants, almost manly in comparison. *But then that is the trick, yes?* she thought. Jade's phone rang in the chair beside her and she glanced at the screen. Robert. She decided to let it ring.

"Thanks again for letting me stay with you and setting up the furniture delivery over at my place," Michelle walked into the living room, breaking Jade's train of thought. "-and letting me sleep in." She laughed, putting in her earrings.

"No problem," Jade smiled. "How did you sleep?"

"Not too good. It was hard to sleep on a good buzz. So, what are you doing today?"

"I have work to catch up on, like normal people." Jade chuckled.

"You know you are going to be so bored without me here." Michelle pulled some leftover take-out from the fridge.

"It's been nice having you around, but I'm looking forward to having my bed to myself," Jade said, getting up to get a glass of water.

Michelle closed the fridge, and paused to brush her hair back from her face. "Well, I'll miss you too, dear sister. If you had central heat in here, I would gladly sleep on the sofa. You know—" Michelle paused, changing the subject. "I think it might be a good idea for me to start looking for a publicist."

"Yeah, that is a good idea." Jade looked at her, crossing her arms.

"I thought about it for a awhile and I know it'll make things easier for me to deal with Eva." Michelle beamed as her phone roared violently from inside her purse. She dug around, ring after ring until:

"Hello," she answered before the last chime.

"Michelle, are you awake?" Her mother's voice cut in, the sound was a cool sensation, like a cold blade held to bare skin.

"Yes, why?" Michelle asked, thinking of the last time they spoke and the argument that followed.

"I have some news and I want to tell you before it makes it to the papers," Ms. Yamato, formally Yamato-Jang said.

"What news?" Michelle glanced in Jade's direction. Jade looked to be preoccupied, making her way back to her laptop.

"Your father was picked up in Kuala Lumpur, likely by men Madison hired," Ms. Yamato said with as much sympathy as she could gather. "His trial is set to start in March." She paused, turning her attention elsewhere. Words in Japanese floated from her mother, Michelle realized after a moment, the change so abrupt. After all those years in the Golden State, and season after season of French fashion, Michelle often wondered if her mother still spoke any Japanese. She heard something about Tanaka, goldfish room and Inoue, before. "Your brothers are planning to be there for the trial and I will be a witness. Will you be gracing us with your presence?"

"I'll do my best to be there," Michelle said, trying not to clench her teeth.

"I hope your father being on trial for his life isn't getting in the way of your modeling career."

"I don't imagine it will." Michelle said with the same cool tone, then she paused for a moment, the word, just one word, ringing in her ears— the one that started the argument. "Who's representing him?" Michelle asked, with her back to Jade.

Jade stopped to listen, suddenly intrigued as the pieces came together like a puzzle. The headline: surgeon, Miles Jang kills business partner – then, Chris Jang, Michelle Yamato—Jang. *Why did it take so long to see the connection?* She wondered, irritated with herself. Jade shifted back to eavesdropping.

"—Vanessa Lopez, a friend of the family," Ms. Yamato added to clarify.

"A friend of *our* family?"

"Yes, a protégé of mine. Well, I'm glad I told you before the papers got to you. I have to go now. I'll talk to you later."

"Bye," Michelle and Ms. Yamato hung up. Michelle paused as the word, one word, surfaced again—nearly jumping from her throat

"Something wrong?" Jade closed her laptop.

"Heartless," Michelle said.

"What?"

"My dad is being put on trial." Michelle paused.

"I'm so sorry. Are you okay?" Jade asked, leaping up and walking toward Michelle. "Why don't you cancel your plans and take the day to deal with this." Jade placed a hand on Michelle's arm.

"I can't." Michelle shook her head. "Thank you." She hugged Jade, to hide the standing tears. "I'm going to drop by Kili Mono's office," Michelle pulled away.

"I thought you were on a leave of absence?"

"It starts after Paris fashion week." Michelle nodded with a grin.

"Then what are you up to?" She looked Michelle over, trying to figure out the angle she was playing.

"I still have to secure some kind of income. Bills don't pay themselves, and Eva's cut seems to get bigger by the day." Michelle said, as her hair draped the sides of her face in the long-feathered bangs. "Besides, Eva forced me to go on leave after her mother tried to hit me with a chair." Michelle glanced at the clock. "I almost forgot, there's a gallery opening on Saturday. Do you want to come with me?"

"No, I have a lot of work I need to do."

"Okay, suit yourself." Michelle shrugged, closing the door.

"She got over that real quick," Jade mumbled, locking the door behind her 'friend'. Still her thoughts wound around the same question, *can one really put another at ease with no empathy? Can a person share feelings with someone like Michelle? Someone who when it serves her to be is both hot and cold; the empty—the scooped out—a pretty shell on a pretty beach. If Michelle were to have canceled her plans, and then burst into tears, what could be done? What words could be mustered and strung together? What can be said to the woman that cries at a chipped nail when the game is broken hearts and wounded souls? It's time to learn to play the game while injured.* Jade paused; suddenly thinking of the dress Michelle gave her a few days ago— the Gucci, then the words that came with it.

'Take it as the first step in becoming the woman you want to be. That dress was made for you, I just bought it.' The words echoed as Jade brushed the thought aside, turning back to her work. *I need control over the security system, then the power to start things off, but why can't I bypass these controls?* Jade sighed.

"Is breaking in from the inside really the only choice; but how?" She pulled a cigarette from a pack stashed under the sofa. *Eva*, the thought seemed to drop from the sky. *Use Eva, through the tutor to set up a meeting,* Jade sneered, lighting the cigarette, taking a long drag. "Good idea," she mumbled to herself.

Outside, Michelle hailed a cab in an effort to get to the salon, she already running behind for her standing eleven 'o' clock appointment—despite the holiday. After putting together, the address with the help of google translate, the driver nodded, closing the door with the press of a button and riding off.

Michelle exhaled, slowly letting her mother's news wash over her. Her truce with being in this country dying the quickest of deaths. *So, he was caught*, she reflected on that fact, *I could have gotten a job, could have stayed. If only I hadn't come. If only I hadn't—*

"Met Jun," she whispered, staring out at Tokyo, bathed in the radiant sunlight of a new year, the palette still grey. The sunshine dirtied somehow among the steel and concrete. People passed in heavy winter coats clouds of breath marking their trek from temple to temple, or from restaurant to show.

What surfaced then in Michelle's mind was a sweltering afternoon, just a few months ago, in late August. It was, 'The date': promised and postponed, canceled and rescheduled.

Michelle sat in Li Jun's bathroom flat-ironing her hair, when her phone rang. An unknown number. She answered the phone using the same accent Li Jun's mother was so fond of.

"Oh, Harro," she said managing to contain the laughter.

"Allo," the voice cut through the line.

She knew it instantly, the husky baritone passing a mouth of full pink lips. *He's been drinking*, she thought. *He knows where she is. He has her number,* it suddenly occurred to her.

"I needed to call you," he said, the French accent heavy from the alcohol.

"To say what," Michelle answered in a whisper.

"To hear your voice, Michelle I—" She hung up, and then walked away—out of the apartment, taking nothing.

As regret billowed from her memory, Michelle again realized she was alone in this city, in this foreign land. The Yamato-Jang's were spread so thin, they were like a light mist—present only in distance. That was why she was easy prey. This is why she had the general—the take no prisoners woman—the leave no witnesses war hero.

The tears returned to her eyes and it suddenly dawned on her how much power this lover still wields. How Seina Terada's affections reminded Michelle of his, of Adrien's. How one word could destroy the walls erected to protect her heart? How a simple Allo passing his lips, sank the hopes sailing on Li Jun's ships.

Li Jun waited for her. He told her, on one of their later dates. After unplugging all the things left on and finding her phone in the sink. He stretched out on the sofa, waiting for her to return. Thoughts of Mrs. Wong and the chair drifted to his mind.

Li Jun knew his mother meant to kill, if not maim, Michelle. Yet, in the moment, he still chose to leap—earning his long-sought-after date. What he also received was three month's leave, immediately from Eva, while Michelle's started in March. The purple bruises on his back accompanied by sharp pain along his spine were bonus factors.

When Li Jun woke on that sofa, light from the bathroom poured into the darkness of his apartment. The sound of rain was the only constant. He saw her, in the doorway to his room. The black bra and flimsy blue jacket stuck to her wet skin, hanging loosely from her shoulder. Ignoring his pain, Li Jun pressed against her as she leaned on the door frame. She said nothing. Her skin nearly burnt him as cold water dripped from her hair. She pulled him into a kiss. This kiss was but the first spark.

She was trying to extinguish a fever lit by an old flame. Li Jun was lost to the thrill of his desire. But of course, it wasn't enough for either. The flames burned too hot and the winds too strong for Li Jun's mere availability to drench the firestorm. While Michelle's pain and sorrow lacked the depth required to result in relationship and love. It was all too clear now. She laughed, remembering the two weeks she and Li Jun spent sick but together, though it pained her to. Getting out of the taxi, Michelle was reminded of this version of her and Li Jun, and for once saw the moment squarely as it was. At last, she caught a glimpse of the general in her true form.

Michelle knew now that Victoria was right, that she did take advantage of Li Jun, though not exactly in the way Victoria tells it. Michelle knows for a fact, she simply waltzed into Li Jun's life and broke his and Victoria's engagement. Though she told herself she had nothing to do with it. Then after having her way with Li Jun unintentionally, she left him. Like a discarded toy, she cast him aside not trusting or believing in his love. Did she even feel guilty about not loving him?

She was the monster—the villain—and he the victim. She used him to make herself feel something other than loss. Something other than hate, regrets, and despairs. These thoughts brought Michelle's mind to Adrien again and the influence he wields over her, even now.

Heartless
Asakusa, Tokyo, July, (6 months ago)

Some six months before New Year's Eve and the life Michelle now lives, she was holed up in Asakuasa— living with her brother. This arrangement came about after she graduated from USC, jobless, only to find out her life in Newport was no more. Her father had absconded, his cosmetic surgery practice, shut down. The house was sold, and her mother and brother were leaving for Asia. By that June, Michelle found herself living with Marcus, her oldest brother, and reeling from the loss of it all.

It was by chance that Michelle saw the stack of papers, amidst yet another attempt to avoid speaking to her mother. Ms. Yamato was sitting in Marcus' kitchen, casually having a mid-morning glass of wine. She was often in Osaka—doing what Michelle never knew or cared to ask about, so, it was more than a bit surprising to see her mother there. The stack of paper that sat beside the wine, surrounded by a sea of grey streaked white granite read: **Petition for Dissolution of Marriage**. Michelle raced to her mother, a fit of rage building, spurring her into conflict mode.

"You're still divorcing him?" Michelle was already on edge with the upheaval of their shared lives, but this was too much. "We've lost everything! And you're just trying to slide off into the sunset?!"

"This is not your concern," Ms. Yamato said, signing the document as Michelle watched horrified at her father's signature already there.

"Are you really that heartless?!" Ms. Yamato looked up.

"Heartless?" Her eyes burned like wildfire. "You think a heartless woman would have had you and your brothers without a penny to her name? Or worked to help pay your school fees while your father went to school?" Her voice began to pour out. "Your opinion is irrelevant, Sarah." Ms. Yamato said, quickly pouring the wine into the sink, she walked away.

Michelle hated when her mother called her by her middle name. It was her Eritrean grandmother's name, a woman Ms. Yamato never liked, and one who never like Ms. Yamato. Ms. Yamato walked into the other room, with Michelle meaning to give chase. By simple chance, Michelle's phone rang, a small act of God as they both welcomed the challenge.

"Hello." Michelle picked up.

"Hey, quick question," Li Jun said on the other end. "Can you be in Shibuya in about an hour? I need a model and it just so happens I know a girl with the skin for an ad I'm shooting." It was destiny on the line, this was what would become the billboard in Shibuya and Shinjuku among the neon lights.

"I'm not—" she began.

"Come on. It's not like you have something important to do."

Michelle paused. "Fine, but the first sign of trouble I'm leaving." She said and Li Jun laughed.

"Fair enough but, I am trouble. I'll send you the address. See ya soon." Li Jun hung up.

"And who was that?" Ms. Yamato questioned from the other room.

"Your son, the irritating one," Michelle lied as she walked out the front door.

Before Michelle knew it, she was in Shibuya, Li Jun stood at the front door of a high rise across the street. So, she tucked the phone into a pocket and walked to a crosswalk where a motorcyclist cut her off, stopping right in front of her. She stopped to look at him, but stared instead. Without fear, without hesitation, she lifted the visor, to find powerful deep-set eyes staring back at her, the color amazing—somewhere between hazel and caramel. *Caramel eyes*, she mused.

"Whatever you're about to do don't do it," he said.

"Who are you?" Michelle took in the well-defined jawline.

"A friend," he smiled.

"Might you be the friend that followed me from the airport? Or the friend that was tailing me the last time I was here? Or—" Michelle began with a smile; finally putting a face to the man she long ago realized kept tabs on her for Ms. Yamato.

"I can't say," his smile was beautiful and cocoa powdered skin rich.

"So, I'm guessing you're Yakuza?" He said nothing. "I didn't know foreigners could be in the mob. Does my mother know what I'm doing?"

"Can't say," he shrugged.

"You're enjoying this." Michelle smiled back, as Li Jun walked in their direction.

"What is there not to enjoy?"

"As my tail, is it okay for you to flirt with me like this?"

"As your tail, making contact means I'm off the job," he grinned.

"Okay, what's your name?"

"You can call me…Can't say," he smiled waiting for a response.

Michelle's eyebrow rose, involuntarily. "You really expect me to believe that's your name?"

"You're not supposed to."

"Well can't say, tell my mother I'm working and good luck in case I don't see you again. Now get lost." Michelle stepped back from the motorcycle as can't say revved up.

"Yes, Ma'am," he put the visor down and rode off.

"Who was that?" Li Jun had just crossed the street.

"A guy with an agenda,"

"There are lots of those." He took her hand.

"Yeah like you." She looked Li Jun over, pulling her hand away. He laughed.

Li Jun led Michelle across the street, into the building and up the elevator to a room buzzing with activity. From lights and backdrops to scenic views of the area, the room pulsed. Michelle had no way of knowing she would grace billboards, or that in this room, she would erase Michelle Yamato-Jang and create Michelle Yamato, the icon. This is what laid the foundation and helped cement Jade's decision to make Michelle the face of her plot in ways neither of them was aware of.

4. Sidewalk Bargain

Tokyo, January 3rd

"I was worried you weren't coming back." Yu teased, opening the front door for Eva. He was setting the table for the dinner with Eva's parents when she came, violently knocking at the door. Eva smiled as Yu closed the door to their apartment behind her. She rushed past the entryway into the kitchen, on her right, out of breath with bags of food dangling from her arms. Eva leaned on the counter catching her breath and Yu walked toward her. He took the food from her, laying it out on the countertop.

"I know-I-took forever—" She began, turning to wash her hands still out of breath. "The restaurant was packed-and they messed up my order."

"Did you run all the way back?" Yu chuckled.

"No, just four blocks." Eva took off her coat and Yu stopped to stare at her.

"*Only four.*" He mumbled, wrapping his arms around her trying to mask his confusion. *Why did she run four blocks?* Yu silently wondered. He took a moment to kiss the side of her neck.

"How much time do we have?" Eva asked, slipping away from him to unpack the food from their containers. Yu tucked a few stray hairs back from her face.

"They're running late, don't worry. Your mom just called to say they'd be here in fifty minutes or so. So, we have plenty of time." He said taking over the task.

Eva paused.

"Yu, did she say fif-tay?" Eva asked upward inflection pointing up, "or fif-tay?" downward inflection, pointing down. He considered. Eva's eyes widen, realizing another pitfall of not sharing their first languages.

"The first one?"

"How long ago was this?" Eva's body stiffened, wanting to curse her mother for all her craftiness.

"Maybe five or ten minutes," Yu shrugged.

"Oh my God Yu, maybe? Stop! Go get dressed. We can sling the food on plates afterward. Go!"

"Eva, relax." Yu took her hands. "You go get dressed. I'm ready." He giggled. He moved to pour the steamed dumplings into a dish dressed in jeans and an incongruous polo.

"Yu, please change into something more, business casual. My mom is vicious just-please." Eva ran from the kitchen to the bedroom. Yu stopped to wash his hands when he heard a crash.

"Eva, are you okay?" He walked down the hallway. "Eva?"

"It was just hangers, Yu. Seriously get dressed!" She yelled, pulling a grey dress over her head before stepping into a red one. Then Eva zipped the dress and ran into the bathroom. Yu grabbed a yellow and blue polo shirt from the closet, putting it on, sliding into a pair of blue slacks. "How do I look?" He walked to the bathroom door for inspection.

"You look good baby." She glanced back to the mirror to touch up her make-up.

"I'm going to finish the food transfer and get rid of the containers."

"Thanks soo much baby. I love you." Eva beamed.

"I love you too." He paused, "The ring, aren't you going to take it off?" He asked before walking back to the kitchen. She stopped, and turned to look him in the eye, reaching for an explanation. But there was none and by the time she turned, he was gone. Eva paused, *how did he know I would do that?*

Yu returned to transfer the food as Eva ran from room to room exchanging her décor for more traditional replacements. She took down her souvenirs from her travels, her pictures from parties, and the couple photos with Yu, for family photos, Chinese artwork and Confucian proverbs—all the things found in a dutiful daughter's home. That was when the doorbell rang.

"I'll get it," Yu called to her.

"Thank you." She shouted back.

"Who you?" Mrs. Wong's voice echoed into the apartment. She stared blankly at Yu with Mr. Wong at her side.

"I'm Yu, Mrs. Wong. Don't you remember?" He laughed at what he hoped was a joke.

"Ohh." Mrs. Wong turned to her husband. "Toe you she hab butlah and he japo-nese."

"Mom, you met him before," Eva beamed in yet another dress. She strolled over to Yu and her parents by the front door in a pale pink long sleeve sweater dress.

"Nice to see you, Yu." Mr. Wong extended a hand.

"Nice to see you again too Mr. Wong," Yu shook his hand.

"Come in," Eva said, stepping back from the door. Mr. and Mrs. Wong cautiously moved passed the kitchen and dining room to the living room with Eva and Yu following.

"When did you move to Chinatown?" Yu murmured, noticing the change in decor.

"My mother's here." Eva shushed him. A weighty silence fell like snow in the apartment, leaving Eva on edge. Still the two couples cautiously moved toward the living room.

The living room consisted of three sofas in a purple so dark it looked black in the dim lighting. The chairs were arranged around a larger grey and black marble-topped table.

"The food smells good." Mr. Wong took a seat on the sofa with its back to the window.

"Bought from our competition." Mrs. Wong spoke in hushed Cantonese to her husband. She stood by her husband all five feet two inches and she stared at Yu, drinking him in. Eva and Yu slowly crept into the room and sat opposite Mr. Wong with Eva on the arm of the chair. Mrs. Wong appraised the room but stopped and smiled when she saw Yu and Eva's phone's charging on the coffee table.

"I no lie him." Mrs. Wong said looking from Yu to Eva. "Why you wan Jap-nese. I wan Chanissa-in-low and Chanis gran-saa." Mrs. Wong crossed her arms and took a seat beside her husband "None of your sisters are having children anymore even the married ones and Li Jun is a mess. I want my Chinese grandson." She said switching from English into a rush of Cantonese. Eva blinked as if to change what was said.

"I'm sorry to hear that Mrs. Wong." Yu cut in. "But Eva and I love each other. If we were to get married soon, a grandson would be no problem." He said jokingly as both Mr. and Mrs. Wong stared at him.

"Shit." Mr. Wong mumbled turning his head, all too aware of his wife's impending dissent.

"Ohh, Eba." Mrs. Wong croaked, looking to her daughter while Yu quietly tucked the large tag hanging out of Eva's sweater.

"Oh, thank you—You speak Cantonese?" Eva stared at him.

"I only picked up a bit." Yu grinned a heartwarming smile.

Mrs. Wong moved to sit down beside her husband.

"Mr. and Ms. Wong, Eva and I like your blessing to marry. We love." Yu attempted in heavily accented Cantonese.

"Fine, you lil fucker—" Mrs. Wong began in English, dropping the accent.

"Stop it." Mr. Wong cut her off.

"Let's stop talking around it. I don't like you. You're not right—not good enough for my daughter." Mrs. Wong continued.

"Jing Chu!" Mr. Wong called, trying to stop her. She ignored him.

"Let alone my most successful one. Go back to whatever hole you crawled—" Mrs. Wong's speech was turning rant.

Mr. Wong grabbed her by her face, turning it toward him. "We will give him a chance." He said to his wife quietly as Yu's phone lit up on the coffee table.

Mrs. Wong glanced at the clock, then the phone, recognizing the number. *Six, one, seven, four. Just like that damn girl said*, Mrs. Wong, thought looking up from the phone, to Yu, then to Eva. "Fine," Mrs. Wong pulled away, she turned to Yu. "Your phone."

"It's okay, this is more important." Yu countered looking back to Mr. and Mrs. Wong. He placed the phone in his pocket.

"What do you do?" Mrs. Wong attempted a more civil approach.

Mr. Wong covered his face.

"I have worked the last five years at National Geographic." Yu smiled.

"Worked?" She questioned.

"I plan to quit once we get married—to be here for Eva." Yu took Eva's hands in his.

"Once," Mrs. Wong echoed sharply. "And then what?" She stared at Yu.

"I'll work freelance until I can find another job in Tokyo."

Eva hunched her shoulder, becoming increasingly uncomfortable. Mr. Wong sighed, crossing his legs then staring at his wife, thoroughly disappointed.

"You got A wife, an ex-wife?" Mrs. Wong turned to open her purse, bringing a cigarette to her mouth.

"Mom! D—"

Mrs. Wong exhaled two smoke rings before Eva could finish. She stood and took a seat on the edge of the coffee table across from Yu.

"A handsome boy like you must have made a few mistakes in that department." Mrs. Wong twinkled, tossing her shoulder-length-chemically-curled hair.

"No. I did okay."

"Since when do you smoke?" Eva was unable to hide her annoyance with her mother.

Ignoring Eva's comment Mrs. Wong blew smoke with a flourish and crossed her legs. Somehow, she suddenly appeared much younger than her sixty-one years. She took another drag.

Mr. Wong shook his head.

"Where is your family from?" Mrs. Wong's stare intensified and her eyes narrowed.

"Kyoto Prefecture."

"What do you like about my daughter?" Mrs. Wong glanced to Eva, then back, "Besides being rich?"

"She's messy, funny and driven." Yu snickered.

Mrs. Wong took a long drag of her cigarette, exhaling smoke in Yu's face. "Then what are you not telling her?" She asked glaring at him.

He paused for a moment. "Nothing." Yu stared at her, a slight smile forming with his confusion.

"He's hiding something." Mrs. Wong said, leaning back on her palms, still staring at Yu.

"The food is getting cold." Mr. Wong walked into the dining room.

Yu and Mrs. Wong remained seated, staring at each other. She took another drag feeling the chill behind Yu's eyes.

"Eva." Mrs. Wong dusted off the cigarette letting the ashes fall to the table. She stood, her bag lady persona melted away completely. "This boy is poison. Lose that ring."

"What ring?" Mr. Wong questioned.

Mrs. Wong scoffed. "I have eyes, on you boy." She looked at Yu, then to Mr. Wong. "I'm going home. I only dine with enemies I plan to kill." She said walking to the door, slamming it behind her.

Mrs. Wong walked toward the subway, fuming. *How did that girl know so much?*

Jade emerged from the shadows as Ms. Wong dialed for a cab. "Do you believe me now?" Jade glanced at her.

Ms. Wong pulled her phone from her ear. "Find out what he's lying about and bring it to—" She started.

"Or I could find out what it is and make him go away." Jade smiled. "Would you like that Mrs. Wong?" The two stopped and Mrs. Wong stared at Jade looking her over.

"How do I know you didn't plant him?" Mrs. Wong asked, cutting hawk-like eyes back to Jade.

Jade tittered. "I'm flattered, but eight years is a long time to plot and position a boy toy like Yu Hiroshi. Never the less, you want him gone and your daughter loves him. If you help me, I might even end this Li Jun, Michelle, and Tori problem." Jade said with brows raised, her eyes taunting the older woman.

Mrs. Wong stopped and stared at Jade. "Congratulations Satan. What do you need?"

"A white man will go missing, people may report it. You, the Ming family, and the Ho family will say he liked to drink, dealt drugs, and attacked someone in the Ming family, that he stumbled off after a beating, dark hair, green eyes, tall—got it?"

"Why? Why do you need me?" Mrs. Wong asked.

Jade grinned. "You have until tomorrow, yes or no. Good night, Mrs. Wong." She walked away and into the shadows.

"Yes." Mrs. Wong hissed in a hoarse whisper.

Jade stopped and turned with a twisted smirk.

"She warned me about you."

"Did she?" Jade giggled before turning and walking away, the clack of heels on cement growing faint, blending into the hum of the subway.

Terada at the Gallery
Tokyo, January 3rd

Michelle found herself in a dimly lit corner of an art gallery, with a glass of champagne in hand, bored, alone, and wishing Jade would have come with her. *God, I need more friends*, she thought with a sigh. She stood in a backless pink dress, her hair draped over one shoulder, looking up at a painting. She heard a rich-savory-tenor voice come from behind.

"Breathtaking." The voice caressed her shoulders.

"I don't get it to be honest." She swept the bangs from her face, with a smirk.

"I was talking about you," Seina smiled.

"I was talking about you." Michelle turned to him.

"I keep forgetting about your sense of humor." He stood beside her and chuckled, genuinely.

"I'll just keep reminding you then." She paused to look at him. "It wasn't enough for you to stalk me at Kili's store the other day?"

"I wanted to see you again. So, do you like this painting?"

"No. I hate it." She glared, sipping champagne. The painting was an image of double doors flung open to a breeze, where a patio overlooked the sea. Empty chairs sat at the edge of the doors as the sun either rose or set, blanketing the vista in reds, yellows and violets.

"Why?"

"It reminds me of everything I've lost." She emptied her champagne glass onto the painting.

Seina jerked her away from the painting. "What is wrong with you? Are you drunk? Why did you do that? What if someone saw you?"

"So what if they did?" She shrugged, pulling away. Michelle stared at him, draping her hair back over her shoulder.

"You're in a better mood than the last time I saw you." He said sarcastically.

"Forgive me if I don't like being stalked by you but—"

"What's wrong?" He inched in closer. She looked at him, caught off guard. "Nothing—It's none of your business."

"So, there's something wrong?" Seina's eyes changed from playful to concerned.

"Like I said—" Michelle began.

"You know, you can talk to me like a person."

"Seina!" A young woman called out to him.

Seina stopped, and grabbed Michelle's arm, to keep her from fleeing. Teresa, Seina's step mother, approached alongside a dark-skinned man, with long hair. He had the half-thrown together-art look going on. It was just the glimmer of a stare, but Seina saw a glance from the man looking from Michelle to her arm then to Seina. Seina loosed his grip and took hold of Michelle's hand.

"Teresa." Seina embraced her with a one-armed hug. The man's eyes were glued to their hands for five, maybe ten seconds, before shifting to Teresa.

"It's been ages since I've seen you. Why don't you visit? You've grown up so nicely, and handsome too." Teresa blushed.

"And you haven't changed a bit." Seina chuckled. Michelle grabbed another glass of champagne, trying to casually slip away but Seina tightened his grip.

"Stop it you liar. Oh Seina, this is Wong Li Jun. He shot my portrait last year." Teresa turned to Li Jun as he and Seina shook hands. "He made me look ten years younger."

"Hello." Li Jun smiled, before his glance drifted to Michelle.

"Hi." Seina grinned back, watching the exchange. Michelle was looking off in another direction.

"Nice to meet you, Mr. Terada."

"Likewise, and it's Seina. So, he made you look like a teenager? How did he do that?" Seina asked as Teresa burst into laughter.

"You're such a charmer, just like your father. You know I'm thirty-three this year. But who is this lovely creature?" Teresa shifted her gaze to Michelle.

"This is Michelle Yamato."

"Hi." Michelle leered.

"It's nice to meet you, Michelle. You be careful with this one, Love." Teresa pointed to Seina. "My Seina here is quite the heartbreaker."

"I've heard." Michelle smiled, trying to avoid eye contact with Li Jun while spotting the security guards closing in.

"Michelle this is my friend Wong Li Jun, the photographer," Teresa said extending a hand to Li Jun.

"Yes, we—" Michelle began as Teresa shifted her attention to Seina and started a new topic.

"Ah, Seina we all thank you for making an appearance at the party.

Kohana has been raving about today's magazine sales. Whatever you did keep doing it." Teresa laughed then turned back to Michelle. "Oh, what were you saying, love?"

"Clearly if you cut me off you didn't want to hear it. So, it's better we don't continue this conversation." Michelle sneered staring at Teresa before attempting walk away, jerking to free her hand.

Seina pulled her hand to his mouth and kissed it. "If you'd excuse us, Michelle and I just got back from friend's wedding in Rio and she's a bit cranky." He cut in, playing the hero. "It was good to see you again, Teresa, and nice to meet you, Li Jun." He wrapped an arm around Michelle, quickly directing her to the coat room.

"Hold on. Can we—" Li Jun started, but his protest went unheard.

"Excuse me, Mr. Terada." A security guard cut Michelle and Seina off just before they reached coat room door. "Your guest needs to come with me, please." He said looking down at Michelle.

"Hold on." Seina nodded. "I'll take care of it. Is the artist available by any chance?" He said to the guard.

"Yes sir, right this way." The larger man said with an arm extended toward a staircase on his left.

"Do you realize what could have just happened to you?" Seina asked Michelle, standing just outside of the coat room nearly an hour later. Rather than say anything, Michelle put on her coat, and dashed out of the gallery, taking long strides to get away.

Michelle kept walking, pushing past people to lose him in the crowd. This drew the attention of the press covering the gallery opening. Michelle cut through a crowded sidewalk with Seina barely two steps behind. When Seina caught her, half a block later, he grabbed her arm.

"Do you realize what could have just happened?" He repeated calmer, in a softer tone.

She jerked away. "What's the game? What is it you want?"

"I want you." He said—but too quickly. Michelle scoffed, and turned away, giggling. "You know I'm interested in you, right?"

"I know what you're interested in," Michelle quipped. She let out a deep sigh. "I don't need you drawing more attention to me or throwing money every which-a-way behind me. Thank you for getting me out of trouble back there. I wasn't thinking. I was angry and I will pay you back."

"Okay. But what do you need?" He asked, taking a step closer.

"What?" Michelle paused.

"If you need a friend, I'll be that friend, if you need someone to talk to, I'm here. That's what I mean. I'm here for you is that so hard to believe?" The two stood in silence for a moment, not noting the already alerted press. Michelle stared at him, the fleeting headlights adding a quick flash that lit Seina's eyes in passing. "I'm trying to get to know you. But you're making that *really* difficult." He grabbed her hand, an action punctuated by a camera flash.

Michelle pulled her hand from him. She turned a corner, away from the lights and the noise, down a dark side street, and Seina followed. Michelle walked down the street, with cameras also in tow. The photographer captured the scene*: Lovers, Michelle and Seina make up during moonlight stroll.* Michelle walked into a playground to the right with Seina following her to a bench. She crossed her legs.

Seina stopped in front of her. "Why were you so upset at the gallery?"

"My father was caught by his business partner's ex wife—" she began a trickle of thoughts that came to a point at: "I'm angrier at what we've— what I've lost, only for him to get caught a little bit later. I had a real chance, you know, to branch out before I came here."

"And modeling isn't a way to branch out?" He asked, taking a seat beside her.

"No." Michelle looked at him. "I'm tired, hungry, and sore all over. I am a glorified Barbie. I don't even get treated like a person and I haven't even been through a fashion week." Michelle stared at Seina laughing, somehow failing to notice the cameramen not ten feet away. "I'm serious."

"I know you are. What happened that you had to come to Japan?" He moved closer, while the photographers crept in for better shots.

"I couldn't find work to stay and support myself, and my mother, just so happened to be *seamlessly* planning to uproot and move to Japan."

"Wow, that's tough, but you can still have a future here, Michelle."

"I can get pieces of what I had. I want the whole thing back. I don't speak the language well, or know anything about Japan, yet here I am *stuck*, and hiding. I was living a dream before this."

"You had to wake up sometime. If you break the glass house you can never get all the pieces back. And sometimes dreams are shattered to accomplish bigger ones. You just have to fill in the cracks with the new."

"Like new houses and yachts, in your case?" Michelle said looking at Seina.

"Another money joke." He smiled at her, laughing. "How original."

"When I had money, it seemed like nothing. Now that it's gone it seems like the most important thing in the world." Michelle tucked her hair behind an ear.

"But here you are."

"Yes. Here I am: banned from working, banned from a gallery, sitting in a cold park, with some weird rich guy that won't leave me alone."

"It's okay. I'll keep him away." Seina nodded. "That just means you never needed the money."

"So says Mr. Moneybags." They snickered; Michelle still drawn by the light tugging sensation between them.

"You know my life isn't as great as you make it out to be."

"I'm sure when the typhoon hits your private island in the Pacific, it burns your toast that you have to go to Hawaii with all the regular people." Michelle said pulling the clip-ins from her hair. Seina scoff-laughed.

"There's that sense of humor again. We don't have a private island in the Pacific.

"Oh? Where then," Michelle questioned.

"Which part of the family?" Seina mumbled as Michelle threw the hip length clip-ins hair in his lap.

"What the—" He jumped.

"So much better." She sighed running her fingers through her hair, the waves slowly beginning to reclaim their shape in the damp air.

"You know, there are people that haven't gone to Hawaii, and people that will never go, and people that will never leave it." Seina glanced in her direction. "I'd give up almost everything to have grown up with normal parents in a normal family or for any children I have too." He paused here to look at Michelle.

"Of course, I know that." Michelle countered, following his logic. "I think about what other people have gone through. How I could be jobless or homeless," she paused. "—And I am thankful for this life every day, and somehow life is still beating the shit out of me and I have nothing to show for it." Michelle sighed, and the tears tumbled loose at last. She placed her face in her hands and the drizzle turned torrent, likely spurred by the alcohol.

"It's not over," Seina said as Michelle allowed him to take her in his arms. "Your life is still going, it's still moving forward. *You* just have to." He said as his embrace was immortalized in film from the nearby shrubbery. When the torrent subsided and a silence filled the space, Michelle cleared her throat, throwing her hair back from her face. "Are you okay?" Seina asked in nearly a whisper.

"Yeah, thank you. So, what's so messed up about your family?" She asked wanting to change the subject.

Seina snickered at the quick turnaround. "My family is old money messy."

"Meaning?" Michelle stood. "Let's go. I'm cold."

"Okay." Seina stood, then threw his coat over Michelle's thinner one. "My mom is my dad's fourth wife and they split when I was about sixteen." Seina slid his hands into his pockets, walking at Michelle's side toward the entrance to the park. "Now he's on wife five, Teresa, and I haven't seen him in about a year. So—" He began. As they rounded another corner back onto the quiet side street.

"I got it, daddy issues." Michelle smiled.

"No not daddy issues, princess." Seina said laughing

"Princess? Look, it's okay if you want to climb up on the pole. Most people with your issue do that." Michelle nodded, mockingly.

"Right, I'll keep that in mind." He added sarcastically. "So, your friend must have done something really great if he knows my step-mom."

"Friend is a very generous term," Michelle turned her eyes to the asphalt.

"So, what should I call him then?"

"Jun."

"And do you have any feelings for Jun? He seemed pretty serious about you, so I have to ask." Seina paused to sweep her bangs aside, staring into her eyes. "Your hair." He handed her the clip-ins.

"Thank you." Michelle broke the stare, as a flash bounced from one of the road mirrors up ahead. "Thanks to you I'm being followed again." She moved away from Seina.

"Let me take you out?"

"No." She shook her head.

"No? Why not?"

"I don't want to see you again." She called back to him pointing to to the paparazzi.

"Well." Seina whispered, unsure how to respond.

Michelle grinned then walked away. She stopped to look over her shoulder at him.

"How about I walk you home?" He called after her. She smirked at him before walking away and turning a corner.

To Dubai with Love
Dubai, U.A.E., January 3rd

Ari rode in a black town car, her niqab blending into the black leather interior. She glanced at her phone through sunglasses, as the car stopped in a parking garage. Ari continued scrolling through the old messages, re-reading them to find the strength she needs to be here, at last.

I found Samir, but not in Morocco – from informant three.

In Dubai, the informant replied.

She placed the phone in her purse, and gave the driver the door codes along with explicit directions in standard Arabic. Ari never asked his name, nor wished to know it. For this task, less knowledge was the best course of action. She saw the driver staring at her. The dark sunglasses masking her eyes, and she imagined how she must look to him, how this whole arrangement might appear; but shrugged away the thought.

They stepped out of the car, Ari's Abaya dancing in the increasing prevailing winds. She surveyed the parking garage, en route to the elevator.

When they entered the lobby, Ari was taken aback, walking across the marble floors, drifting past rich mosaics in turquoise, malachite, and chrysocolla.

The driver led her down a short hall, and pressed the button for another elevator. Ari collected herself, standing in front of the elevator doors, forcing her rage down, as it seared her insides. She glanced at the attendant behind the front desk who was dozing from an extra bit of something slipped into his lunch. All of her plans seemed to align with the help of her shadow dancers, the group of detectives and criminals kept on retainer to do her bidding.

Turning back to the elevator, Ari watched the numbers, her heart racing, as the elevator crept closer. She heard nothing of the people coming and going, only the pounding. *I want blood*, she thought as the doors opened and an Emirati family stepped out. Ari and the driver stepped aside, and slipped past the family. The driver yawned, pressed the button and the doors closed. He was ignorant of the danger made flesh in this woman as the elevator began its ascent.

If Samir were a beggar, or living in poor conditions to emasculate him would be fair, then leave him to die, she thought, as the pungent scent of gasoline wafted past her nose. The doors opened. The driver stepped out. As instructed, he turned down the hallway and took the stairs back to the garage. Ari continued on.

"Five-oh-six, five-oh-seven." Calmly she walked the hall. "Five-thirteen, five-nineteen," her feet carried her faster. "Five-twenty-three - Five-twenty-seven – Five thirty-one." Ari stopped.

She took a deep breath, then entered the door code to Samir's apartment. Pulling in another breath, she turned the knob which echoed like a gunshot.

On the other side, she found three white chaise lounges in what she knew was crushed suede. There were tall lush green plants growing in gold pots in the corners of the room. Fine pottery placed on the coffee table and end tables, and gold statues sprinkled about. Ari sneered at the painting of her father's parents which hung at the center of all this, framed on both sides by glass double doors leading to the balcony. She looked for signs of others that might be lurking. To the left of the living room, Ari saw the edge of a bed in the room just past the kitchen. Ari crept past a breakfast-nook on her right stacked high with pillows. She pushed the door to the room open with a gloved hand. Here, beeping heart rate monitor met Ari's pounding heart—a rhythm forming between the two.

Apparently, he has a bad heart, she thought grinning to herself.

She stood, looking at the frail figure lying in this king-sized bed, his arms and leg had shrunken from years of limited use. His skin had aged, his face had fattened, but his eyes were the same. Ari froze at the foot of the bed, with the heart monitor stationed to the right of it. Sunlight poured in through the glass door to the balcony adding an eerie aura to the room. It was then Ari heard Samir's voice, weak and trembling over the heart monitor.

"Who—" he started, but couldn't manage.

Ari opened her mouth to speak but the sound of a toilet flushing, broke the tension. She jerked her head in the direction of the bathroom door. The faucet came on and she moved to the small sitting area to the left of the bed, standing against the wall shared with the bathroom.

Complete with two chairs, and a coffee table there was no weapon but she decided to improvise. Ari picked up the potted bamboo plant from the table. The door opened and a woman stepped out dressed in a white lab coat. *Likely Samir's doctor,* she realized before hitting the woman over the head with the plant. It crashed to the floor, the earth and water seeping into the royal blue area rug. When the doctor turned to Ari looking dazed, she picked up the coffee table to finish the job. The woman fell to the floor, forehead bleeding and Ari dropped the table beside her and kicked the woman where she fell.

"What do you want with me?" Samir managed in Arabic. Ari threw her sunglasses on the bed. "Ah," he nodded, the heart rate picking up. Ari stepped closer, looking at the ghost. A mere shadow of the man, no longer beautiful but badly aged. Samir's heart rate raced along with Ari's as she crept closer.

"You've withered to nothing," Ari said standing over him, emptied of all inflection, as the mid-day sun grew strangely dim. "You were so strong, beautiful even." She continued in Darija, pulling a dagger from beneath the Abaya. The faint rays gleamed on Samir's face. His heart rate elevated again. He attempted to move his arms. "but you've done well for yourself, *Uncle.*" Smiling, Ari brought the dagger to his face.

His breath caught. Ari cut away at his shirt, leaning in over him. His legs moved frantically with panic. Samir's hand came up to slap her, to stop her. But he patted her cheek instead, too weak for her to do more than knock the hand away.

The excitement built up in her fingers as Samir stared at her, squirming. Ari dragged the blade down his chest slowly, leaving a shallow cut across the skin, and the heart rate monitor beeped violently.

"Even with you in this state, I can't give you mercy," she said, staring down at him.

Samir laid in his bed staring at her, willing his body to move. Tears welled in Ari's eyes and her lips began to quiver. Only when the blade reached his sternum, did the two lock eyes again. Samir saw the rage and the seething emptiness that possessed her. In all of this, the heart rate monitor drew a long note.

Ari stopped.

Samir's eyes rolled into his head. Her face went blank. Her jaw went slack and a tear fell to the body as she searched for a pulse. Her heart sank, as her hope for revenge simply slipped from her grasp.

"No." She yelled. She stabbed into his chest, once, twice, on and on. Ari paused, staring at Samir's body. *His corpse*, she realized. She closed her eyes. She felt lightheaded. Tears streamed down her cheeks, and suddenly she heard the faint tapping at the window. Ari followed the sound to find herself gazing at the clouds of dust tapping the glass.

Ari grabbed her sunglasses, and re-veiled herself. She flung open the balcony door. Dust flooded the room in waves, and Ari walked out of the bedroom, opening the rest of the apartment to the storm.

When the elevator doors opened to the garage, Ari rushed to the car. She got in and the driver turned to her.

"Go!" She said staccato, slamming the door. "Move over." She roared sensing his hesitation. When he moved to the passenger-seat she climbed over the seat then cranked the car.

It was by chance she made out a sign for Al Qusais station. *A straight shot*, she cackled, pulling the phone from her purse, and dialing. She came to a stop. Ari thought it simply luck, the sandstorm, and the forecast of it being the worst in a decade—and now this. The driver asked where they we're going, but Ari ignored him. The phone rang once.

"Hello," Darius' sultry voice rang in her ear.

"Where are you?" She asked in French.

"The old safe house in Du—" He started as she hung up, sliding the phone into a pocket, better wrapping her face in the cloth, she grabbed her purse and opened the door. The driver shouted after her, but she disappeared into the storm.

Ari walked past building after building, her feet remembering the way.

She ran to his rustic apartment building, a crumbling ruin away from all the glamour of Dubai—a horror left to the sand.

Gasping for air, she ran up to the third floor, knocking on the door. After a moment the door opened to Darius, caramel-eyed and shirtless. They stood in silence a moment watching each other.

"You still remember this place?" He asked.

"It's a place not easily forgotten." She walked into the very industrial space. The inside was bare, barely a dwelling, except for the leather sofa, the TV, and his bed.

"I was sleeping, sorry about the mess." He moved closer. "What are you doing in Du—"

Ari turned to him the niqab and abaya falling to the floor. She kissed him as she stood in a black bra and panties, pushing him to the leather sofa. "I leave for London in five hours."

The Roommate
Ikebukuro, Tokyo, January 5th

Jade sat in a café near a window, skimming the menu when her attention shifted to the world outside. She was simply people-watching when she noticed a tall Asian woman with long ringlets of orange-tinted-blonde hair. It looked like fire, the orange, red, and blonde threaded in the hand-painted-balayage fashion so many women often sport. Jade watched her in awe, in the knee length lavender formfitting dress and coat. The outfit was topped with a purple hat, fit for the Kentucky Derby, not the streets of Tokyo, long brimmed and tilted for a dramatic effect. *Her waist is tiny with boobs and ass for days,* Jade thought, turning her attention back to the menu, jealousy burning at the back of her throat.

"Sumimasen, Wang Jade-san de*suuuu*yo ne?" A gravelly contralto asked moments later. Jade looked up, and there stood the firey-blonde, pulling down purple rimmed sunglasses. "Ree, Soo Young de*suu*." Jade noted the accent instantly, attempting to rectify the sounds spilling from this woman's lips, with the story she knows of Lee Soo Young. Jade looked at Soo Young armed with a smile.

"Hai," Jade responded. "We can speak Korean if it's more comfortable." She said in Korean, already aware of Soo Young's limited conversational Japanese skills.

"You speak many language?" Soo Young exclaimed in Korean, extending a hand with a smile. "How you I not know Japan?" Soo Young giggled.

"You have a bit of an accent," Jade replied, finally pulling her focus from Soo Young to the situation at hand.

"Very bad?"

"No, not at all." Jade shook her head. *I would never believe you were Korean unless you told me you were born overseas,* Jade thought. *Better to bring that to her attention once I leave. That way her story can be more believable, paired with the Foreign Resident Card I'll forge.*

After months of looking for a roommate to share the financial burdens for her apartment, Jade would gladly take nearly anyone that could keep their mouth closed—with assurances, that is. That someone seemed to be Lee Soo Young.

From her research, Jade knew that Soo Young was born Ram Saetang and lived four years in Korea. For whatever reason, *he* became *she*, then came to Japan to work as a hair stylist—with a fake Korean passport. Jade never looked for a post alteration photo, and thus her awe. It was *this* set of confining circumstances Jade depended on to bind Soo Young to silence, given anything she might see or hear while sharing their space. Though, Jade framed the situation as having something to do with corporate espionage, Soo Young seemed genuinely happy to move into the old dusty apartment just minutes away from Ikebukuro Station.

"Last week when we chatted over the phone you said you own a salon?"

"Yes, its very good business." Soo Young laughed, emphasizing her words, in the throaty hawk heard in Korean dramas worldwide.

"Really?"

"Yes, very good. You?" Soo Young asked.

"Me? What do I do?" Jade paused for confirmation. Soo Young nodded. "I work at an advertisement agency."

"Ohh. Wow."

"So, what brought you to Japan?"

"Well," Soo Young laughed. "My *gum* left her salon for me and now I own." Soo Young smiled playing in her hair.

"Gomu?" Jade corrected.

"Oh, that's right, that's right!" Soo Young covered her mouth with a hand, "Yes, my father's older sister."

"I see. How long have you been in Japan?"

"About a *mouth*."

"A month?" Jade questioned.

"Yes." Soo Young smiled.

Well at least she seems nice, Jade thought, suppressing a deep sigh. *I just need the money for more equipment and help, that's all this is. It's not like we have to be besties.*

"Well would you like to see the apartment?" Jade put forth a friendly smile.

That evening as Jade lay in bed, drifting from consciousness, the enemy of all dreams appeared. It began softly at first, the tap of a knock on the front door, just audible in her bedroom. *Soo Young will get it*, Jade thought. The sound continued, moving from boisterous to just disrespectful. Jade pulled the cover over her head, deciding to ignore the knocking. *It was unrelenting.* Giving up the hope of sleep, Jade walked past the small kitchen and into the living room. She stopped to glance, across the seating area, to Soo Young's room. It was pitch black and silent.

"Who is it?" She grumbled standing at the door.

The knocking persisted. When Jade opened the door, she found Chris on the other side. "How did you find me?" She asked, shielding her eyes from the light of the covered walkway.

"We shared an uber ride once remember? You were pretty messed up so I understand if you don't."

Jade didn't find that cute. "What…What do you want?" Cold air crept inside as Jade's anger neared its boiling point.

"You wouldn't come to me, so I came to you." He smiled playfully.

"Seriously, you woke me up for that?! Go rub one out. You are such an ass. You couldn't call?" Jade dropped a hand to her side staring at him.

"I did. Are you going to let me in or what?" Chris said coming in and closing the door.

"I didn't answer. *Clear-ly* there was a reason."

"None strong enough to keep me away." He kissed her. She pulled away, wanting more of him. Chris lifted her, and her legs instinctively wrapped around his waist. "I'll be in Korea for a few days, but I had to see you before I left." He grinned. The sweet mint on his breath and the woodsy cologne were magnetic. The only source of illumination came as ribbons of moonlight from the balcony door.

"Get off me." Jade moved to climb down, pushing him away.

"Stop. Stop." Chris said almost whispering as he held onto her legs. He kissed her neck, slowly. Jade wiggled to the floor. Chris kissed her again. She passively attempted to resist but he paused for a moment, inhaling her, caressing her legs, thighs and hips.

"You need to leave." She said, trying to keep her composure, still wanting to give in.

"I'll leave, once we're done." He whispered. He picked her up again as Jade pulled his shirt off, throwing it to the floor.

On the other side of the living room, Soo Young watched Jade and this handsome stranger. She stood in darkness sipping a cup of tea, her eyes fixed on the moonlit silhouettes before her.

"My, my." Soo Young quietly admonished, grinning at the sight.

5. Hurt

In Transit, January 5th

There is nothing left in Mohammedia but ashes of what was, and what could have been. Ari woke in near darkness, to the hum of airplane engines, mixed with the faint whistle of metal cutting air. The cabin hushed.

She closed her eyes again catching her breath as it all swarmed back to mind. *What wasn't ransacked had been destroyed in the fire. At the end Samir took a small statue to the girl's head. The scars she bore suggested it was four or five times. But clearly it wasn't hard enough.* In her memory, *he tugs at her hair forcing her face into the rug—and tap-tap, it is done,* Ari thought making light of it. Those were the last moments. This was Ari's only firm memory of a life in Morocco, a thing burned into her existence. It was tied to *his* stench and the smell of gasoline. *But now, he is dead.*

Where am I, Ari asked herself feeling groggy, yet forcing her eyes open. *Going to London,* the self answered. *Ahh, right for the girl.* She remembered and sighed. Inky black hair draped her face, surprising her. *A new look,* she marveled— remembering next to nothing, but the storm, and the man in Dubai.

Following information that Michelle was in need of a publicist, a newly-job-less Ari, took this opportunity to look into the model. The intent was to do this by way of a trusted spy, of course. That was until, Ari reached the last person of somewhat-trustable, somewhat-shady repute, with the right skill set. After a buffet of 'no' and 'I'm not available', here Ari sat, in first class, on a plane to London.

Ari wiped the sweat from her brow and suddenly, without permission, the movie of her life played out in her head. *His ring, it glistens brilliantly in the heat and sun, a ring the girl's father gave him welcoming him into their home. His face so inviting, he is beautiful like only the deadliest of flowers. I went looking for him; only to find out how well he has lived these years, after killing my parents in some drugged out-rage.*

In the moments after Samir's death, Ari felt the rage boiling in her soul, take over her body. Only with Darius, in the still moments amid the sandstorm, did freedom spring from her being. Or what she thought was freedom. It was a freedom she knew would vanish at check-in, if not security. Two bodies in a high rise in Dubai, she wouldn't get away. She couldn't get away.

But here she was. A flight attendant appeared now, and placed Ari's food on the tray.

"What would you like to drink?"

"Red wine." Ari beamed, as the man poured.

"I'm not weak and I am not a victim," Ari mumbled.

"What was that?" The man questioned.

"I may need another soon, if it's not a problem. Flying is unnerving." Ari sipped the wine. *Would Allah crash a plane to simply bring the point home,* she wondered, *only killing her and allowing destiny to come full circle.* She closed her eyes, feeling this new freedom encircle her.

The movie began again in Ari's mind, *the father lays on the rug bleeding and dying— helpless— unable to stop his brother, Samir. The girl screams. Samir forces himself on her— inside, again and again— piercing soul with hot flesh, ripping handfuls of hair. The more she fights the more she suffers. She cannot give in— would die, rather than yield to his wishes. He is, her father's only brother. Buried in debt by his recreation of choice. She fights to get away from him, only to have the grip tighten.*

And like that he finished.

Sweat falling like summer rain on her back. The musk of his skin trapped in hair, on body, in clothes. He bears his weight down on her in his ecstasy. There are voices in the distance as his hands caress breasts, then hips. His scent is a mix of skin, sweat, and sun. Ari opened her eyes and downed the glass.

"I am free," Ari whispered, laughing. "And I just may make it to London."

In an act of mercy, perhaps to kill her, Samir hit her over the head. The flames surged, then another hit, then darkness. Ari woke forty-three days later, to her Aunt Daniele in Venice.

That was eleven years ago— eleven years, last week.

In the News
Ikebukuro, Tokyo, January 6th

Jade sluggishly strolled on her way to work, still exhausted from another night with Chris. She fumbled through her purse in search of the designs she put together as she passed a convenient store.

"Ugh." *I forgot it*, she thought. "I guess I'll make a copy," Jade mumbled glancing at the time. She turned and walked into the store with a thumb drive in hand. Cutting passed rows of magazines and ice cream. Jade walked down the aisle toward the copy machine but something caught her attention.

Terada Seina and Yamato Michelle Dating! one headline read in Japanese. Jade dropped her purse, rushing to the gossip magazines:

Terada's New Catch, another exclaimed.

Secret Terada Romance, a third highlighted alongside several more.

"I am going to kill Seina!" Jade said, grabbing the magazines.

If he draws too much attention, I can't use her. I need a distraction— a decoy, not a freakin' eclipse, Jade thought, using her emergency key to unlock the front door to Michelle's apartment. Jade tipped into the apartment, magazines in hand. She came to stand at the foot of the bed, covered in soft white and gold blankets, under a canopy of the same coloring. Jade cleared her throat, opening the curtains and dropping the magazines on the bed. Michelle barely stirred.

"Twenty-two year old model, Yamato Michelle caught—"

"Jade stop," Michelle grumbled under the covers. Jade turned to another page.

"Terada and Yamato," Jade continued "went public with their relationship at the Eva Wong Modeling Agency's New Year's Eve Party.

The pair was later seen at Kili Mono's boutique in—"

"Jade, stop it!" Michelle sat up.

"Michelle what are you doing? What happened to you keeping a low profile? And why in the world are you with this clown? Just the other day you were talking about how you didn't have a boyfriend, and you weren't working, that you should travel—then here you are splattered all over God only knows how many magazines with this guy." Jade sat down on the bed.

"Good Morning to you too," Michelle whipped the messy fog of flattened coils from her face.

"Here's the two of you on New Year's Eve and here you are New Year's Day and here you are at that gallery opening—" Jade started but paused. "So what's going on with this guy?" Jade crossed her legs.

"He's been stalking me. The Gossip is just gossip."

"Stalking you?"

"Not in a creepy way Jade." Michelle walked to the bathroom.

"What do you mean? Stalking is stalking." Jade shouted after her.

"You're really upset about this?" She stopped to look at Jade, grabbing her toothbrush and paste. "What's so bad about him?"

"Do you know who he is? Do some research on him, I guarantee you won't like what you find. He's a party animal."

"How do you know that?" Michelle stared at Jade, her voice muffled by toothpaste, speaking a mumbled language perfected by their living together.

"I can read." Jade stared back.

"Ha ha. Find something then."

"Okay." Jade stood up and walked into the living room retrieving Michelle's laptop from the sofa, pulling the information in a snap. "You ready?" She shouted.

"So, you really came over because of those magazines?" Michelle shouted from the bathroom.

"That and to get my dress and see how the place looks now you're moved in."

"Fine. Read it to me." Michelle stopped in the bathroom door way.

"Seina Terada, one of eight heirs to the multi-billion-dollar Terada fortune. He is the only son of Cláudio Terada and Ex-wife Daniele Alves. He has a younger sister April, grew up mostly in Italy with his mother and went to high school in Japan. Never been married, no children. He's twenty-nine. He has a B.A. in International Business and a M.B.A. from Columbia."

"They must hand those out after you give X amount of dollars."

"Ah, here we are. *The dirt*." Jade smiled. "Terada, known as the king of socialites and party goers, has come to be renowned for his lavish and wild parties. He—" Jade started

"A lot of guys are party animals til they get tamed." Michelle cut her off strolling back into the bedroom.

"What? You want to tame him?" Jade asked.

"No." Michelle scoffed. "I was hoping he was a jerk so I'd have an excuse to treat him that way."

"He and most recent ex-girlfriend, actress Selene Melendez, broke up in December of last year, after rumors of Terada secretly meeting current girlfriend, model, Michelle Yamato in New York."

"Eva is really going to be pissed," Michelle mumbled, changing her clothes on the far side of the room near the window.

"Did you meet him in New York?" Jade looked up at her.

"No. I didn't know him until the party. Besides, I've been in Japan since May, and last December I had finals."

"Maybe you met and didn't know."

"I was a blonde last year and spent all of December in Cali."

"Well they still called you his girlfriend and Michelle he's dated a lot of women."

"What's a lot?" Michelle walked closer to Jade.

"It looks like a database." Jade's eyes widened.

"You're joking, let me see— Jesus."

"I told you he's trouble." Jade smirked.

"Fine, I won't see him. Happy? Let's go to the paper moon. I'm hungry." Michelle had already slipped on a pair of jeans and a white fine-ribbed A-shirt over a black bra, when she plucked a sweater from the chair of her vanity table.

"There's more. The Terada family is also rumored to have hands in several Yakuza factions as well as ties to a number of cartels in Southeast Asia and Latin America."

"Okay Terada—bad—got it. Let's go." Michelle pulled the sweater over her head

"I can't, I have work." Jade closed the laptop.

"Okay." Michelle sighed, as the doorbell rang.

"Are you expecting anyone?" Jade froze.

"No." Michelle walked to the door then, stopped to look at the door camera. *'It's him.'* She mouthed to Jade

"Don't open it," Jade whispered. Michelle narrowed her eyes in Jade's direction.

"Michelle, I know you're here." Seina sang out.

"Not a stalker, huh?" Jade whispered far too loud for the acoustics.

"You probably led him here," Michelle whispered back. She put her arms into the sleeves, fluffed her hair and opened the door. "Hi."

"Hi— what took you so long?" He bore flowers and an irresistible smile that brought a sweet innocence to his playboy air.

"I had to put on a top." She said teasingly, brow raised.

"You didn't have to do that for me." He inched in for a kiss and Michelle moved away.

"I hate flowers. What are you doing here? How do you know where I live?"

"Well, you won't tell me what you do like and I hate to come empty-handed."

"Why are you here?" Jade heard Michelle say while she peeked into the living room.

"Your friend Victoria gave me your address." Jade saw Seina place a hand on Michelle's arm, before ducking back into Michelle's room.

"And why would she do that?" Michelle asked.

"I went to your agency to apologize for getting you in the tabloids, and Victoria slipped me your address after I said I wanted to apologize to you personally."

"Thank you." Michelle said coldly, deciding to play the kinder hand. "Is that all?" She asked.

"I still want to take you out, just less publicly, of course."

"Of course. Why?" She countered, staring back into his eyes for a second time.

"I want to get to know you. You don't believe me? The problem is I want to keep seeing you. And I know that's not a sexy response but here I am."

A surge of electricity filled Michelle's lungs. She sneered, noting Seina now *in* the apartment.

A newfound panic took hold of Jade. It was clear he was after Michelle, *but why so persistent*, she wondered.

"I leave for New York in the morning." Michelle lied. "How about I get back to you on that?" Michelle glanced at the door, signaling him to leave.

"Can I at least get a number to keep up with you?" He grabbed her hand.

"Why bother asking? Why not get it from Victoria?" Michelle gave the coldest expression in her arsenal, while pulling her hand away.

"I'll take that as a no, then, for now. Have a safe flight." Seina walked out of the apartment. Michelle locked the door behind him, shaking her head, and walked into the kitchen for a drink.

"He looks even better in person than in all the photos." Jade said, tauntingly. She walked out of the bedroom with her new dress in hand.

Michelle poured a glass of water. "What are you doing today?" She asked, changing subjects before bringing the glass to her lips.

"I have to go to work in about thirty minutes." Jade smiled.

Michelle smacked her lips. "You're no fun."

"Not everybody can live like you, Michelle. And not everybody can put Mr. Hot Ass on ice like you did either. Why bother asking? Why not get it from Victoria?" Jade mimicked.

"Stop trying to make me the villain." Michelle laughed.

"If you're not the villain, then who is?" Jade giggled.

"Very funny."

"See there it is again." Jade pointed. "You did the same thing to Jun before we left for the party."

"Well, Homeboy needed to chill out." She laughed.

Jade grabbed her purse. "Michelle, be careful, okay? I have a feeling about that guy. And don't get into too much trouble while you're gone. I'll see you when you get back."

"Yes, ma'am!" Michelle nodded, picking up her phone; she glanced at the time and stopped.

"What? What's with the face?"

"He has my number, and wants to go out tonight."

"Oh, I gotta go." Jade laughed.

"Bye." Michelle waved as Jade walked out the door.

Outside the apartment, Seina stood waiting for her.

"You knew I was here?" Jade was astonished.

"I heard someone in the back." Seina walked with her toward the elevator.

"I told you she wasn't going to fall for your shit." Jade turned to him.

"Maybe it's because you're always making me seem like a bad guy."

"I'm just the mirror. Plus, you're dating her, is only going to be a problem."

"Why is that?" His brows rose.

"There are things in motion. Things one can't undo." She smiled, pressing the elevator button. "Did Tori really give you Michelle's address?" Silence filled the air.

"Wouldn't you like to know?" He smirked. "I'll tell you if you tell me what you're really doing in Tokyo." They stepped into the elevator and Seina pressed the button for the lobby. "Last time I saw you was five years ago, and you were tight with—"

"If I tell you, I'll have to have you killed," Jade cut him off. "And as easy as it is, it's a waste of time."

"You are not the little girl I met in Switzerland." He smiled.

"At some point, we all have to grow up Seina, even you." Jade grinned back.

"And are you all grown up Lia?"

"Wouldn't you like to know?" The doors opened to the lobby. "Stop bothering her Seina." Jade walked into the lobby, the dress from Michelle waving over her shoulder as she walked out the front door.

Wine & Pepto
Meguro-ku, Tokyo, January 6th, (3 days ago)

After getting the runaround from Michelle following the gallery opening, Seina had his assistant call Hitomi, Eva's office manager. With the aid of a seventy-thousand-yen bribe, the assistant got Michelle's schedule. Armed with this, Seina began his preparations.

It was easy enough to get Michelle to agree to dinner with him. Yet, Seina knew the real challenge lay in making the dinner plan a reality. He got a town car and a driver. He blocked off the street Michelle took to get home from all traffic. When Michelle emerged at street level, he was waiting. Seina smiled and bowed as a few area residents popped up and uncomfortably went about their business. Michelle simply came to a halt when she glanced up from her phone.

In the middle of the street sat a tent set up for her to change clothes. Seina presented a smile, a simple green evening dress in her size, and Michelle knew she was cornered. Other than a string of no's there was little resistance she could find. He pulled a necklace from his pocket, placing it on her before she could protest. Following that Seina had whisked her away in a sleek black jaguar.

Now, they sat tucked away from the adoring press, and in Aoyama's Barbacoa Grill. Michelle looked up from the menu to Seina, staring at her, for what seemed like days. She felt uncomfortable. She looked out over the room taking in the ambiance, with the newly gifted pink diamond set in gold and dangling near her breasts.

"My God, you're beautiful." Seina smiled. Michelle turned to stare at him coldly, a step before looking past him.

"Why did you give me this necklace? I barely know you."

"After you cried, in my arms, in a park, what you said about losing everything stayed with me." He paused briefly. "So, when I saw that and thought of you, I got it." Seina stopped again, wondering if he should go on.

Michelle drew in a deep breath. "What about this made you think of me?" She asked and pulled a bottle of pepto-bismol from her purse. Pepto she thought she might need given the recent bout with Jade's attempt at making Brine-Soaked Duck.

"What is that?" Seina pointed with his eyes.

"Stomach medicine, flown in from the states. The Japanese stuff wasn't strong enough to deal with you." She brushed hair back from her face, stopping to unwrap a straw. "Please continue."

"You had that this whole time?" He asked. Michelle nodded with a smile and Seina continued. "Well I wanted to do something to make you feel better as a friend." He said watching Michelle place the straw in the bottle, noting the raised brow at the word *friend*.

"I don't feel like this is a friend gift." She said pointedly.

"Well, there's a Ulysse Nardin that you can get me for my birthday. I'll send you a picture." He reached for his phone, "But seriously, Michelle, I thought this might make you feel like you haven't lost everything by moving here. I also thought it might make you think of me."

"Interesting." She sipped her pepto. "So, what do you need? You want me to pose as your girlfriend, fiancée? Tie you up and step on your face? You rich boys are always into some weird stuff." Seina's eyes widened.

Not a jewelry expert herself, Michelle glanced at the rock and knew it was no small favor. A pink diamond, five or six carats she guessed, with that level of clarity and in that vivid color—it was a million easy. "Where did you—" She started.

"That's not what this is. I promise you. But, you know at some point we have to order." Seina said, changing the subject. "Unless you're on a pepto diet. I know you models types do—" He started.

"Order away, rich boy." She cut him off, smiling.

Seina called for a waiter and ordered, in Portuguese— from a secret menu, he told her later.

Then, once again *it* resurfaced, the push-pull of being with him. A feeling that something has changed, an opening. If not something broken open, something breaking open. Michelle wiped her mouth as the meal concluded and she looked at him. Not a glance, or a stare, but a look— taking in his features, for the first time since she saw him at the gallery.

"Do you want more? You devoured that food. I thought you'd like Brazilian." He beamed like a kid at Christmas.

"I love it but, I'm full." That was a lie. There was a beast in her belly, fueled from the endless workouts with that Nazi of a trainer Eva hired, fittings, and meetings. By then hunger and exhaustion were her state of being, then their were Eva's infamous weigh-ins to consider.

"Well, I see we both share a love of fine cuisine." Seina reached for the wine to top her glass off.

"No more, thank you. Please." Michelle covered the glass with her hand. "I've had quite enough."

"Of me?" Seina asked, exaggeratedly taken aback. Michelle laughed.

"No, the pepto is still working. I think I can stomach you maybe twenty more minutes." She smirked, half-jokingly. Seina burst into laughter.

"Good." He poured a glass for himself. "I like being around you. Especially like this." He said. "And I'm glad I got to see you before you rode off into the sunset. If you like I'll have the driver drop you at the airport tonight."

"How did you—" She began. Seina brought a finger to his lips. "Well, I had a good time." Michelle smiled.

"With me?" He moved back in mockery.

"Yes. Shockingly." She had laughed.

Michelle laughed again at this memory, a memory that has traveled with her from Tokyo to New York and now London, three days later.

Michelle got up from the bed of yet another hotel, basking in the twinkling glow of the city. She grabbed a bottle of water from the mini-fridge then stopped to stare at London, radiant, outside her window. At this juncture, her mind floated back to Seina, like a river to the sea.

Michelle beamed, remembering Seina's insistence to walk her up after the car had arrived in front of her building. Then, suddenly without warning her mind skipped forward to that kiss, in the hallway that took her by surprise.

They had come to a brief stop, standing in front of her door, Seina with his hands in his pockets, Michelle's in her oversized purse. She was saying 'good night' and trying to identify the right key. When she glanced up, he kissed her. Faint notes of the sweet wine flooded her senses, somehow still on his lips. Though Michelle would never admit it, this was the moment she felt the first tug to keep him around. The whole evening with Seina had, had a cinematic feel Michelle noted now, while her thoughts came back to London and the Waldof.

As though her mind were a Polaroid, an image surfaced—the color far too vivid—his touch too strong.

The Lover: dark hair and eyes, olive-oil golden skin and pink lips, the kind meant to be kissed.

Michelle shook the thought loose before drawing the curtains and going to bed.

Adroit
London, January 10th

After having secured an interview, two days ago, Ari had a friend of Shahir's delete the resumes of the more decorated candidates, while Michelle took on interviews in New York. One of Ari's minions found out where Michelle would be staying the two days she would be in London for fittings, so Ari booked a room at the same hotel. It was with a stroke of good fortune Ari acquired Michelle's schedule, and started pulling strings, to demonstrate her skill.

Presently Ari strolled down the hall to the cafe Homage, to meet the girl at last. The crisp cool of morning added to the tension. The goal was to shine, if not dazzle Michelle, and the outfit made that clear, a red dress by Dior and a tailored black blazer cut to leave her bare lower back in plain view. It was an enticing look Ari had taken on, her hair cut to her shoulders, asymmetrically draping an eye. The eyes powered by her trademark Arabic eyeliner.

In the hallway she passed a mirror, Ari stopped to gaze at herself, adjusting her jet-black hair. "Beautiful." She smiled, before walking toward the restaurant.

Restaurant? More an overdone café, she thought, catching her first glimpse of Michelle with the maître d' leading her to a table against the windows. Michelle stood and the maître d' pulled out a chair. Ari took the moment to assess, trying to warm up to the girl.

"Would you like a menu?" The maître d' asked.

"No. No, thank you, tea and an ashtray, please." Ari hung her handbag on the chair, her finger nails a glossy black.

"I'm terribly sorry. There's no smoking in this part of the hotel. I'll have your tea right away madam."

"Thank you." Ari nodded.

"Hello," Michelle stood extending a hand to Ari, her long hair in loose spiral curls framing her face.

"Michelle Yamato, nice to meet you."

"Ari, Ari Louien. Nice to meet you too." Ari beamed as they sat.

"Well, Ms. Louien—" Michelle began, in a poised manner. *Very refined— for an American*

"Call me Ari."

"Ari? Is that short for something?" Michelle paused to let their eyes meet. Her face remained placid, as if Ari were shooting her. *All of it staged, obviously.*

"It's my middle name, Arion, a gift from my father." Ari maintained her smile, drinking in Michelle's features. Ari was impressed, and pissed that the girl was as pretty as the pictures made her out to be.

"Ah, I see." Michelle beamed, warmly. "Well, I'm glad I could sit down with you." Michelle glanced down at a resume. "You come well recommended and—" Michelle looked up, then her brow knit together.

"I feel a *but* somewhere in all of this."

"Yes, thus far you've only handled a few minor European athletes then an heiress or two."

"Well, something made you decide to sit with me." Ari grinned playfully.

"Everyone I've talked to said the same thing, that you're talented like no other. That you get things *done*. I wanted to meet this talented woman face to face, just in case we might be a good fit for each other."

"Are you sure they meant to compliment?" Ari asked. The waiter sat the tea on the table. "Thank you." Ari said as he walked away.

"Even if they didn't, I need a sharp publicist on my team to help me take my career to the next level if that's where it's going. But if not I would like to keep a low profile while still finding enough work to live the life I want." Michelle said alluding to her father and the upcoming trial looming in the foreground.

"That I can deliver, but I can't pull a pig from the mud. My job is to keep the mud from splashing into the news. I put you with the right people, in the right places, at the right time. Nothing more— nothing less." Ari said with a disingenuous smile.

"Pigs and people aside, I need a bulldog, a shark— so that I don't have to be a panther." Michelle sat back in her chair.

Ari nodded, "That would be me." She shifted her attention to the pink diamond pendant around Michelle's neck. Ari handed Michelle a black folder, from her purse. "For *instant*, before this interview, I found out all I could about you. It took ten minutes to see you're drowning in relationship scandals, on top of your family issues. In this folder are discussions about you and that necklace from seven websites. People love or hate Seina Terada, but they like you less. There's claims the necklace is an heirloom from the Terada vault, last worn by Seina Terada's grandmother but reset for you." Ari's eyebrows rose and froze, staring at Michelle.

Michelle's face went blank. "Wow. Cyber stalking?" She scoffed, trying to keep a sneer off her face, her lips already dripping with poison.

"This was openly available info." Ari shrugged, sliding the jet-black curtain of her hair from her eyes. "I'm still calling contacts to see what else there might be." She crossed her legs as Michelle sat speechless. "I've been dodging scandals and making celebrities for the last five years and I'm ready to take my career to the next level. You've seen what I've had my hands in and I'm telling you I can do more. But my salary will be nonnegotiable."

"Give me a ballpark figure." Michelle pitched a tent of her fingers on the table.

"At least, a hundred and ten-thousand *starting*, plus a yearly bonus and we renegotiate in six months."

"What?" Michelle balked, with a laugh-scoff. "At that price what can you do, short of moving the hand of God on my behalf?"

"There's a statement in the folder. This thing with your father, win or lose, if it blows up you can write a book." Ari gave a sly smile. Michelle looked into the folder, pausing to read the statement. "By getting in front of the story, outside of Japanese or American media, you frame it. And make whoever you want come out however you want." Ari beamed. "That only works if you do this before the press gets wind of it being scandal material. It's already a small story in the papers but with controlling the story you shape all the characters. Hire me and I can have your story your way to all the major European publications within the hour." Ari lifted the tea to her lips.

"What makes you think I haven't already found someone for this job, at a lower price?" Michelle asked, her eyes narrowed. Ari could hear the wheels turning in Michelle's head.

"You have arrangements for more interviews tomorrow and the rest of the week, in Paris and Milan." Ari said flatly, then paused to let out a sigh. "Well, I don't want to take up more time, I'm sure you have a lot to do. I wish you well Michelle." Ari said, grabbing her handbag, before turning to walk away.

"Ari," Michelle called, drawn like a moth to a flame. Ari turned around. "You have the job."

"I won't disappoint." Ari sat back down, pulling a pen from her purse to write on a napkin. "This is the room I'm staying in. I'll draw up the offer letter to go over the terms, I also need your itinerary and I'll e-mail you any improvements for your approval." Ari lied quickly having already done the heavy lifting.

"First, I'd like to rework this statement." Michelle smiled. "I'll send it over to you once I have."

"Okay." Ari nodded, "I hope you're ready to run hard. I'll see you tomorrow." She said before walking away.

Unhinged
Ginza, Tokyo, January 11th

Back in Tokyo, Victoria strolled out of her favorite salon in Ginza and onto its crowded streets. January's chill was fresh in each step, cutting at her thin frame. Countless people rushed by, all in their own worlds, living warm lives as the winds sliced away at Victoria's thin ivory legs. She closed her tan fur coat, and found no relief. Her long, now-wavy hair and extensions flung into the breeze. It was a drastic shift from her blue-black pin straight tresses.

Victoria passed the window of a department store and stopped. She stared into the window at an almost unrecognizable self, a self she mistook for *another*. Only now does she see the spark that led to this impromptu makeover. Victoria stopped her shoulder bag from sliding off, staring, wondering who this person is, this woman staring back.

This is the woman she must become— the who and why still left unsaid. Yet, she knew. She couldn't let the thing out, and so wouldn't think the thought— let alone speak the name. Victoria knew she was a clean palate, a blank slate for the artist to play out the vision— nothing more. No charisma, no eyes that speak volumes, no skin that lights fires.

Victoria tugged at the thick black belt tied around her waist, still far too big after reaching the last hole. Her hands trembled with the cold. *You're not enough*, a thought whispered as she fumbled with the dense alien sea of chocolate wavy hair. She attempted to brush it back from her face. *You're not enough*. Victoria played with the bracelets and earrings in an effort to make them more becoming. She saw the dress, and hair— the accessories, but no trace of herself. *This isn't for me*, she thought, though she hates both the image and now the very woman looking back. *You're not enough*, the thought murmured again like a catchy tune. She turned from the window, wiping a tear from her eye, continuing down the sidewalk.

A single tear burst free and onto her cheek. She wiped it away, throwing her hair back from her face— an awkward motion. She could do nothing to stop the torrent that followed. Vision blurred, she sped up to escape the suffocating icy winds. Her breath was heavy. She gasped for air, and tried to incase the suffering flooding within. Victoria turned a corner, and sat sliding down against the wall, unable to see the surroundings. Her tears flowed endlessly as an ankle gave way. She hit the ground, and swung her arms in rage. In the silence her phone rang, her tears like rivers. **Zhang home** flashed across the screen. Victoria stopped, then cleared her throat.

"Hello." She said, erasing tears from her voice, with years of practice— employing the queen's English. "It's about time you got back to me Mr. Zhang." She paused to wipe her face. "I may have a lead as to where Jia Lang is." She sniffed.

"Good." His words echoed from the phone in a heavy Chinese accent. "and the other one?"

"I have something I need to take care of but, I'll be in Hong Kong in the morning. We can talk then. I know she's planning something." Victoria hung up, before standing to flag down a taxi.

"Akasaka hachi no ju no san ju yon, onegaishimasu." She said to the driver as the door closed.

渋　谷
6. Shibuya
Akasaka, Tokyo, January 11th

Dishes lay across the counter and piled in the sink of Li Jun's kitchen. Through his living room curtains, dismal sunlight peeked into the apartment. Li Jun stared at this light with steam rising off his body. He stood in the doorway leading to the bedroom, his hair long wet from the shower. He was surveying this, his apartment in all its emptiness. Though not truly empty, the apartment lacked what he never knew to seek out.

And what sparked that interest in Michelle? He wondered. The question skimming across his mind like a feather coming to rest on the surface of a pond. There was a time Li Jun would have been smart enough to cut ties once business and pleasure were thoroughly mixed. *Yet with Michelle, it just felt right*, he noted. *She was an equal, not conquest.* This is why Li Jun believed her when she told him he could run the agency, given his willingness to 'man up and do something other than the models,' or so she said.

But Li Jun knew that first night in Shibuya he wanted this woman, that *she* was something.

"This is Shibuya," he had said to her as they stood last summer overlooking the crosswalk. They had spent the day together and Li Jun showed Michelle the city— or as much of it as he knew. But Li Jun saved Shibuya for last. He thought it would impress her.

Michelle turned a bored scowl in his direction. "She-boo-ya?" she had repeated, her brows drawn together. "It just looks like an overcrowded square to me."

"You've never heard of the Shibuya crossing?" He baulked, and pointed to the mass of people jamming the street.

"No. *Obviously.*" She stared back at Li Jun, before moving to take a step.

"There's not enough time to cross, we won't make it." He said, stopping her with a hand on her elbow. She was clearly irritated but Li Jun couldn't figure out why. "This is the street you always see in movies when people talk about Tokyo." He paused as whistles roared and rushed people to the sidewalks stained by the neon billboards overhead. Then traffic started again like clockwork.

"I barely know anything about this country," she sighed, glancing to Li Jun as if to say 'next.'

"So, what brought you here?" He asked, genuinely curious. Here his eyes met hers, in a spark that spoke of the baser nature. That was the moment he knew he *could* have her. *That he would have her.* Michelle smiled, with what Li Jun would later come to know as an 'I'm changing the subject' smile. She moved forward with the enclave, leaving Li Jun behind.

The cloak of night in the east played out against the yellow-orange of sunset, tucked behind the One Oh Nine building. The thunder of ads and background noise blurred as a sea of unfazed natives marched onward to their destinations. Michelle reached the center of the crossing as the waves of people met and fractured. Li Jun rushed to catch up. In his hurry, he bumped someone. The someone, a tall caramel eyed stranger, looked at Li Jun with a hardness unlike any he had ever seen. It was a look he would never forget. Li Jun was no more than five feet away when Michelle, still moving forward, slammed into another person nearly making him fall.

"I'm sorry," she said, as the man stopped. "Are you okay? Daijobu?" She choked out leaning toward the man. His eyes were drawn to her cleavage. Michelle stepped back, reeling from the stranger's touch. She stared at him for a moment. Without warning, she kicked him in the groin. The man crumbled to his knees, grabbing the attention of passing onlookers, wishing to avoid the ugliness. Countless people stared and pointed, then pulled out their phones as Michelle hammered him with each kick. "Fucking asshole!" She shouted. Li Jun appeared and grabbed her, then bowed in apology.

The police were called over, but now that Li Jun thought back to running from the scene, it was all a blur. He only remembered the questions: What was that about? Why did you punch that guy? The two of them gasped for air on a narrow side street, out of view.

"That son of a bitch felt me up," Michelle sneered. She stepped aside as a group of club goers moved passed them in a hoard down the street.

"You didn't need to punch him or kick him." Li Jun leaned against the wall trying to catch his breath.

"I didn't need to punch him?" She stood up straight tossing her hair back from her face, with a devilish grin. "So, you're telling me if some lady goes for your junk you're just going to brush it off?"

"My junk?" He felt her breath graze his neck when she sighed.

"My God," Michelle mumbled. "Your dick!"

"That doesn't really happen here too much." He bellowed between breaths.

"And if it did? To you?" She moved closer, her chest to his, continuing in the rhythm of slow ragged breaths.

"I'd let it go." He shrugged, having found his wind and a smile.

"That's pathetic." She stroked his face and tucked his hair behind an ear, patronizingly. Then, suddenly, Li Jun saw him, again. It was that caramel-eyed-man. He was at some distance, but Li Jun was sure it was him. "So, you like being taken advantage of?" Michelle pulled his attention back to her.

"No one likes being taken advantage of." He said matter of fact, still feeling the caramel-eyed man's gaze.

"That's what your lips say." Michelle brushed her hair from her eyes as she gazed up at him.

Overlay
Akasaka, Tokyo, January 11th

Akasaka hachi no ju as it turned out was Li Jun's place.

And with him presently reminiscing about Michelle and Shibuya, he didn't hear Victoria when she unlocked the door. She stood in the living room watching him on the sofa for a few moments. Victoria waited for him to notice her, before calling to him— breaking Li Jun from his revelry.

"Hey." He turned to her, clothed in only his boxers. He didn't see the blatant change. The thick wavy hair hanging to her hips in chocolate. He didn't hear the gold bracelets lining her wrists or the earrings that chimed. He even missed the change from simple elegance to a nearly Bohemian style of dress. "What are you doing here?"

"I came to check on you." She sat down at the bar, looking at the dishes. "You haven't been answering my calls."

"I've had things on my mind." His smile faded.

"Right, you haven't been at work either." Sarcasm was the bassline as she placed her handbag on the bar. Victoria pulled Li Jun up by his arms. "We have to have a serious talk now."

"What?"

"Why is it so cold in here?" Victoria rubbed her arms, walking to the remote for the heater. Turning the heat on high.

"What do you want to talk about?" He crossed his arms.

"You need to let go of this Michelle thing. She's moved on. Why can't you? She used you to get a job. At best, she genuinely cared for you, got the job and moved on. It's time you do the same." Victoria paused, and Li Jun stared at her in silence. "Breaking our engagement for her is one thing, but enough is enough."

"I hear you."

"Do you?" She paused. "You're a great photographer, don't let this ruin you, Jun." Victoria said tenderly.

"Okay." He nodded, moving toward the bedroom behind her.

"Where are you going?" Victoria asked staring at his naked back.

"To bed, to clear my head. Lock the door on your way out." He said, before closing the door behind him.

"Is she really worth your career, because clearly, you're not worth hers." Victoria shouted after him.

Yet, she left an imprint. There was a feeling of lack, a hole in Li Jun's carefree life. Stretching out on his bed, Li Jun let out a sigh staring at the ceiling. His breaths slowed and his eyes became heavy, the warmth of his shirtless body seeping into the cool of his comforter. He began to drift, still thinking of Shibuya. Li Jun replayed those few moments in the coffee shop ignited by the aroma of hazelnut and espresso and like a wave, erasing the current circumstance, Li Jun was returned, to the Starbucks in Shibuya, with her.

He remembered sitting next to the wall of windows overlooking the crossing for the first time. Li Jun didn't bother to ask how she got the table. After beating a man for the world to see, he knew she was a wild card.

"So why didn't you stay?" He lifted the cup to his mouth— abruptly shifting the conversation.

"It was easier for me to leave, with no financial backup. My ex took everything." She had told him this lie with such ease.

"I see. Well, Japan's not that bad, just give it a chance."

"I've tried being that girl." Michelle shifted her eyes to the window.

"What girl?" His coffee cup halfway to his mouth. He remembered being taken aback by her words as he watched the neon lights bleed into Michelle's hair, skin and eyes.

"The kind of girl that only looks at the good things in life— it's exhausting." She paused. "I won't make that mistake again." Michelle downed the last of her watered-down iced coffee. "So, where do all these streets lead?" She looked back to Li Jun.

"They go to a lot of places— fun, love, sex, comfort, happiness, it's all here." Li Jun smirked.

"That's so corny," Michelle taunted. "Are you going to tell me about the crossing or not?"

"Okay, the best way for you to remember is to use your hand." Li Jun held up his left hand, and took Michelle's. "Your palm is the crossing—" He lightly drew a circle. "Your pointer finger leads to Dogenzaka. It's just hotels and clubs and that kind of thing. And this corner," he touched the area between her index and middle finger. "That's the One O Nine building.

"Uh-huh." She nodded and their skin tingled on contact.

"Your middle finger is Bunkamura, it kind of meets up with Dogenzaka. It's all clubs and hotels, then Sentagai." He touched her ring finger. "—Is mostly bars and restaurants and some clothing stores."

"Okay." She glanced up at him.

"Your pinky takes you to Omotesando and Harajuku, that's more shopping."

"Alright."

"And your thumb points in the direction of the bus station." He looked at Michelle, as a surge of electricity still pulsed in his fingers, electricity that betrayed. "So, where do you want to go from here?" Li Jun had asked, the spark from his hand already transferred to his eyes.

"Sentagai?"

They felt the need for a change of scenery, as one does with electricity and no words. The lights of the cafe dimmed— closing for the night, so Michelle and Li Jun descended the dark staircase leading back to the crossing. Li Jun glanced in Michelle's direction. Her hair draped the sides of her face as it dangled about her breast in loose curls. It was then, Li Jun pulled Michelle aside to kiss her. She pushed him back, and he stared into her eyes in the faint light.

Even as he tossed on his bed, some five months after the fact, he felt her as he once did. His hands moved up her body, from her hips, to her waist, to the kiss— a fan to the flames. She unzipped his pants and ran her fingers along the waistband of his underwear, black Calvin Klein— his blood rushing to the hands, fingers, and other extremities.

Li Jun remembered Michelle glance down between them. He even remembered the glimpse he caught of the Caramel-eyed stranger that watched them.

He heard Michelle say, "*It's not going to be this easy, Jun,*" as she once had. But there was no tug of the hair, no jerk to one side. Finding this strange, and remembering the real-life unhappy ending, Li Jun opened his eyes to the still mounting pleasure. *Tori?* Yet somehow this wasn't Tori, he noted for the first time. She was like Victoria but with longer, *waved* hair. Victoria grabbed a handful of Li Jun's hair. He grunted, uncontrolled, as Victoria gasped.

But, in the faded Shibuya memory, Michelle had pulled his hair, and stepped back from Li Jun, nearly exposing him to anyone that might pass by.

"What the fuck!" Li Jun zipped his pants.

"I asked you what you would do if some lady grabbed you by the balls." Michelle had crossed her arms and smirked. "Apparently you're the lay down and take it kind." Li Jun thought of the self-satisfied grin on Michelle's face. A smile, he saw only that once, *Had he been just a toy all that time? From then to now?*

Lights & Lovers
Paris, January 13th - 20th

Ari and Michelle chatted over drinks after the constant churning of fittings and go-sees since dark thirty when they first landed. This was Ari's intentional design of course. It provided her a chance to stress the subject only to create a respite, in which she would hammer at Michelle's vulnerabilities. Michelle sipped a vodka cider mix, sprawled on the loveseat in Ari's room, as Ari poured another drink for herself.

It was mapped out from the moment they boarded at Heathrow, contingencies and all. Tonight's contest began with Ari's simple suggestion, "*We should go out.*" Followed by a sweet, "*I know you're tired but its Paris*," in case of an objection.

She didn't object. Thus, Ari kicked off with, 'I want to take you to this bar. I know you'll love it.'

And she did, the two of them laughed, and laughed over drinks like friends for years, with banter and wit all their own, even as the trap drew closer.

The game was simple, since Shahir provided the background. Ari would bring forth the lover, trot him out and watch the sparks fly. It was a plot Ari put in motion almost immediately upon discovering the identity of Michelle's former lover.

A shame, Ari thought, slipping into a more devious self. *What a shame having to take down someone like this, someone I might like. Funny and sarcastic, entertaining but professional— like Lia, but more alive, more grounded in some way. I like this girl.*

This girl knows how to live, how to have fun, Ari thought as they walked still laughing, fully inebriated and en route to a club. It was a love of the soul, like King David and Jonathan— a love given a place to flourish outside of time— one always present, but suddenly kindled. Like the flame of one tree being carried onward by the wind, until the mountain was a glorious blaze. It was a feeling, Ari has never known— though she came very close, once, in boarding school, she recounted.

The next venue was a dive bar kind of club, set for a small concert, dark but inviting as the story often goes. Ari stopped at their table in the front, trying to contain her laughter.

"Is this our table?" Michelle glanced at her ticket.

"Yeah." Ari took a seat.

"This is a great table." Michelle looked to the stage not six feet away from them. She sat down across from Ari, with the stage chest high, to her left. "Ari, how did you get a table this good, so fast?" She leaned against the divider separating the walkway in front of the stage from their table. Then she continued surveying the room.

"An old friend, with boyfriend problems, and now here we are." Ari slid her bangs back from her eyes with a smile.

"Great friend," Michelle added. "By the way, what's the name of the group? I missed the sign when we came in." Michelle stopped, as a waiter appeared speaking French.

"Would you like something to drink?" He smiled; fair skinned with light brown eyes.

"Oui—" both women began at the same time. "I didn't know you spoke French." Ari turned to Michelle.

"My mother forced it on us." Michelle shrugged.

"Well, good woman." Ari smiled at yet another thing in common. "This round is on me, then." She turned to the waiter. "Two vodka cranberries to get us started," Ari smiled, her words slightly hurried.

"Right away."

"Nice choice Miss. Louien."

"Thank you, but not as nice as him." Ari pointed to the waiter as he walked away.

"I'll drink to him." Michelle's eyes drifted away from Ari to a man the color of milk chocolate, joking with a group of guy friends. "You see Morris Chestnut at nine o'clock? Grey shirt."

"I saw him when we came in," Ari said with a glance over her shoulder. He was standing at the bar when he lifted his drink to them with a smile.

"And he has friends," Michelle laughed, looking back to Ari. "I might need to put a French brotha on layaway if that's what they look like." They both laughed. "He's coming," Michelle whispered. Ari shrugged.

"Excuse me." He looked from Ari to Michelle. "My name is Andre." He shook their hands, speaking some form of erotic accented English that was difficult to place. "Can I buy you ladies, a drink?"

"Andre I'm sorry, tonight is my friend's birthday, we just came to enjoy ourselves." Ari lied, to keep the plan on track.

"Okay." He nodded, white teeth gleaming into a brilliant smile. "How about you give me your number, maybe we can get together later." They exchanged phones and typed in their numbers.

"See you around." Ari handed the phone back.

"I hope so." He smiled, before walking away.

"I'm impressed." Michelle chimed.

The waiter came a moment later and sat their drinks on the table.

Ari handed over a wad of bills. "Keep the change." She winked.

Michelle grabbed her glass. "To a great night."

"A great night." Ari raised her glass. *Now the waiting game.* She looked at her phone as a tall thin man stepped out on stage, speaking a whirlwind of French.

It wasn't until she heard the name that Michelle froze, and the applause thundered through the crowd, that she felt she was in danger. When the curtains opened, there stood *the lover*, golden olive oil skinned, dark haired, and dark brown eyed. He looked out on the crowd as he adjusted the microphone stand. He was more appealing than Michelle remembered, the body more sculpted, the look more rugged. If there were words, there were none Michelle recognized as the fans whistled and clapped. National Treasure of France, three-time Grammy award winner and recently divorced, Adrien Depaul was back, after a four-year absence.

Ari shifted to the paralyzed Michelle who appeared unable to think, let alone process all of this. Adrien caught sight of Michelle, just as Ari planned. Although he tried not to, he lingered. Ari pretended not to notice, secretly taking pleasure in Michelle's torture. Adrien turned to the band; microphone covered.

He shifted back to the audience. "Good evening," he smiled, perfectly tussled hair falling to his eyes. "I know you came to hear our old music, but this is a newer song, it's called Leila."

Leila? 'It,' not 'she'? No. Michelle thought, *surely not the girl he helped break—the one* he shattered.

Leila, was the name Michelle gave herself as a teenager. By pooling letters from her name, she created a new one, at an age she sought to reinvent a self she had yet to know. *Why did I ever tell him that?*

An electric guitar took hold of the room, then an acoustic joined, with the drums the last to chime in. *Sitting here, alone I think of you~, the wo-man, I just can't let go of. Even now I re-member, the sweetness of your scent, then your eyes, then your lips, then your face, and your smile. (I'm dreaming.)*

These, End-less dreams of-you, fill every-day. Ari sipped her vodka cranberry, still pretending not to watch Michelle. Michelle squirmed under Adrien's gaze, his eyes locked on her. She, willing her body to move. Regret, rage, sorrow and longing all warred for her to take action. *You, spoke to me, with eyes across a room, those eyes, pull-ing me closer-and-closer. You spoke my name, and-I just couldn't stop myself. Still I, have a girl and I want you, even as I sit here with her. My, passi-on has ta-ken the lead. Then the alcohol, Sweet-words-exchanged. Next~thing ~I~know~, I'm alone with you.* Michelle fought to keep tears at bay. *—I Long-to-be yours-again. Although, my regret doesn't reach you~. And I know that it's, my fault~. Is there a-way, I could still be-the-man, that you wanted~, that you needed~*

"I have to go," Michelle said to Ari looking as if she might cry, then vomit.

"What? Go where?" Ari questioned. *—Leila, my love, how can I take the pain back from you? To this moment my heart is yours~. Hopefully these words reach you.* A guitar solo ensued and Adrien walked down the stairs, and off stage. When the spotlight found Adrien again with security in tow, Michelle was still trying to escape. He was less than four paces from her. *Too late.*

Adrien crept closer and whispered into her ear, under the roar of guitars as the song whined to a close. He pulled away from her ear, before leaning in for a kiss. Michelle took a step back. Ari covered her mouth to hide her laughter. The flash of cameras capturing all of this.

"You *are* sorry," Michelle grabbed her coat and walked away. The guitarists and drummer continued to play as the audience stared at Adrien, still recording. Adrien simply focused on Michelle and the solo came to a crashing end. *Leila, my love, I know that I have only done wrong, Since the first glance, we took a chance. Playing, with your heart I lost the whole game. But I long to-be, yours again~. Al-though, my regret, doesn't reach you. Though, my regret, can't reach you. I still love you~*

The fans reluctantly cheered. Ari stood, slowly walking to Adrien's side. Security stopped her but Adrien motioned for her to come closer.

"I'm Ari, Michelle's publicist." She handed him a card from the hotel, then her purse. Ari grabbed her key card, then her coat, leaving the bag.

"What was that about?" Ari asked in the taxi Michelle had flagged down. Michelle sat with her eyes trained out the window, and tears silently falling. Yet, that was all it took to unhook the larger story resting behind the floodgates.

"Five years ago," she began.

Michelle and her mother visiting Paris, for the party of an unnamed designer. This was where Michelle met Victoria.

"So, you're in Paris just for this party?" Victoria had asked, seated beside Michelle. To Victoria's left, sat the infamous Adrien Depaul— the silent predator. Victoria picked up her glass of champagne, her eyes glued to the pretty American.

"Yes." Michelle nodded. "The head of the legal team went to high school with my mother and she invited us. My mother loves France and French fashion. So, she couldn't say no." Michelle shrugged, seated at a table with two of the original members of Depaul, and Victoria.

"And how old are you?" Victoria glanced to Davet, Adrien's band-mate, seated to Michelle's right.

"Seventeen." Michelle answered.

"Only six years younger than me." Victoria laughed, with a look at Davet.

"Way too young," Davet whispered in French.

"What makes you think you had a chance?" Michelle replied.

"There's no hope for you my friend." Adrien laughed.

"Tori that's the girl," Davet pointed with his eyes to a woman that passed the table. "Introduce me." He continued pleading.

"I barely know her." Victoria scoffed. Adrien looked at Michelle, with a lingering stare. Michelle stared back, sipping her champagne. Victoria excused herself to introduce Davet to his newest interest. Adrien paused and kissed Victoria before they left. *Then there were two.*

Adrien moved a seat closer, turning his full attention to Michelle.

She slowly cut her gaze in his direction. "Are you sure you should be looking at me like that?"

"I've wanted to be alone with you since I saw you."

"What would Victoria say if she heard that?"

"Do you really care?" His eyes were so incisive, so luring— he was so handsome, so famous, it was simply too deadly a match.

"I care, but not about what she thinks."

"What do you care about?" He asked, throwing an arm on her chair.

Michelle took off an earring and placed it on the table. "Maybe I'll tell you." She stood and walked toward a quiet hallway.

"So this Victoria girl caught the two of you together?" Ari asked, unlocking the door to her suite.

Michelle sighed. "I was undressing him, but she only caught us kissing, back then." Michelle plopped on the sofa. "But I met him again when I studied here, two years later." Michelle decided not to tell the rest.

"A kiss? That's it?" Ari stopped, alerted by the suite's phone ringing.

"I started dating him later down the road. He was my first."

"Hold on, hold on!" Ari dashed over to the phone. "Oui." She froze. "J'arrive tout de suite." Ari hung up.

Michelle stopped to look at Ari. "What is it?"

Ari winced, "This one is on me. I forgot my purse, and he's downstairs."

Ari went to the door to claim the bag, then took a seat in the armed chair facing the door.

"Hi," Adrien said to Michelle, slipping in behind Ari.

Michelle glowered at him.

"Tetsudai iru?" Ari asked, posted up like she might pull a pistol from the purse.

"Daijoubu. Kitemiyou." Michelle managed, Ari catching her meaning. Michelle turned back to Adrien. "Why are you here?"

"I've been looking for you. Victoria gave me your number after I asked about you." Adrien sat beside Michelle, placing a hand on her leg. Michelle knocked the hand away. "Gabriele and I are over." He said, in a low rumble. Ari's ears perked up at this.

"What do you want me to do with that?"

"I want to start over with you. Peut-on parler seul?" He whispered.

"J'etais sur le point d'obenir du pop-corn." Ari chimed with a smile.

Adrien sighed. "Michelle, my love, please." He begged, pulling her into his arms. At the placing of skin to skin, the body gave way. It sickened her, that her body would also betray, melting like candle wax to an open flame.

Michelle pushed him, hands and lips trembling. She back-handed him, "Don't touch me!"

Adrien clapped a hand to his face, feeling and tasting blood. Ari stood up, alert and ready to intervene.

"I deserve that." The anger and sorrow in his voice was unmistakable. "Forgive me." He said, it feeling and sounding more command than plea. Ari pulled Michelle away as she threw a punch.

"Get out! Get out! You son-of-a-bitch!" Michelle continued jerking and writhing to free herself. Ari pulled her into the hallway, taking the reins again.

After calming Michelle, and sending her to bed, Ari went back to work. She pulled her phone from her pocket and dialed.

"Hey, Natilie." Ari switched to French. "Can you draw something up for me? Oui, Oui. C'est parfait." She knocked on the door to her suite, as Michelle went to her room.

Adrien came to the door with ice in a towel to his face.

"Send it. I'll need it tonight." Ari ended the call and closed the door. "I understand that didn't go the way you hoped, but I tried."

"So Michelle knows you gave me your handbag, and the card with your hotel?"

"No, but she wouldn't believe you either way. So, unless you want a media circus you *will* obey me."

"So you lured me here." Adrien scoffed as his thoughts raced and he weighed the options. He went to dial his manager, then his lawyer.

Ari beat him to it. "Ms. Arion Louien for Kohana. Yes, I'll hold." She said into her phone. "You call for back up. I will summon an army. Cross me. 'Depaul woman beater' will be tomorrow's headline."

Magical was the word Michelle used for all of Ari's PR hoopla. With the aid of her shadow dancers, Ari put together a press conference for the cherished singer to apologize to his adoring fans. The official story was that Adrien's publicist hired Michelle to cause a stir during the concert, promising more buzz for Adrien's album with some added dramatics. The unnamed publicist was promptly fired after the stunt fell flat. And how did Ari explain the beloved singers bruised face, and busted lip?

Innuendo, placed by the press, on the estranged wife, given their quite recent and messy divorce. Checkmate. Never mind, there was never a publicist, or the surveillance footage of Adrien at the hotel, or that Adrien and Gabriele hadn't seen each other in months. Ari made it disappear. Simple facts, made to simply vanish.

The press ate up every word. Even the ones that weren't bribed. Michelle's fluent French and Adrian's presence, after decades of not doing interviews, made the tale sing. To seal the deal, Ari had an ironclad agreement drawn up, or so Adrien thought.

Thus, the duo slipped away, to Milan, through the fog of media speculation. Depaul, in turn, put the remaining rumors to rest. The additional clause stipulating that Depaul not contact Yamato-Jang was simply a bonus.

In Milan, run hard Michelle had. Ari made sure Michelle walked for as many designers as she could, despite all the press. With all this press placing Michelle in a not-so-great light, she knew hurricane Eva would exact her pound of flesh upon her return to Japan. Thus, Michelle was a husk by the time she and Ari split. She flying to Narita for an ill-timed string of photo shoots and Ari to Jerez de la Frontera to break camp for the upcoming move.

When Michelle landed, it was no surprise that there was an emergency email. It was for a last-minute meeting, with Eva, at eleven a.m. It was nine forty-one. So, Michelle freshened up, dropped her things at home, and dashed to Eva's office—like a good little flunky.

Just Business
Shinjuku, Tokyo, January 20th

When the elevator chimed Michelle's arrival at the office, it was eleven o-one. She raced down the lengthy row of cubicles lining the way to Eva's office. At the door she knocked, then waited, her chest still heaving.

"Come in." Eva called. "Close the door."

Michelle did, and took a seat. Instantly, she was transported to the last encounter in this office. For a moment, both Eva and Michelle paused, looking as if on cue to the chair.

"Are you crazy?!" Mrs. Wong had yelled as she stormed the Agency's conference room and into Michelle's meeting. She threw her purse down and before Michelle could find words Mrs. Wong had backhanded her. The client, a tiny Singaporean woman had backed away and stood mouth agape.

"You stupid whore! I'll put you in the ground for messing with my son!" Mrs. Wong yelled in Cantonese. The entire office had heard—though that was just the beginning.

It was Christine, Eva's secretary and the youngest of the Wong sisters, who alerted Eva and stepped in as the client collected her bag and simply left the office.

Later, Eva sat everyone down in her office. Mrs. Wong and a security guard on her right, Michelle and Li Jun across from her.

"Michelle was in the middle of a discussion with Lily Chang when Mom came in and slapped her." Eva paused to look at Li Jun.

"Backhanded." Michelle interjected.

Eva glanced at Michelle. "Now we've lost a client and the entire office saw the blow-up, all because of your relationship with yet another model." Eva stared at Li Jun, hands shaking with what Michelle thought was rage. "Mom, I don't care what you found at Jun's apartment—" Eva started again. Mrs. Wong rolled her eyes saying nothing.

"What the hell mom?!" Li Jun spoke for the first time. He looked between his sister and mother, incredulous. "What were you doing in my apartment? How do you even have a key?!" He shouted.

"Li Jun, shay no goo. Yo no can see." Mrs. Wong said sweetly, in that false accent she so often uses.

"Mother stop! We're lucky there are no charges being handed out." Eva turned to Mrs. Wong.

"Let that whore do what she wants! I can take her." Mrs. Wong said in Cantonese, staring at Eva. It was Michelle's turn now, and here she chose to make Mrs. Wong a lifelong adversary.

"Take me home." Michelle whispered. She stood and grabbed hold of Li Jun's hand. Perhaps it was the word 'home' and the sight of this 'whore' grabbing her son's hand, or maybe it was the way her son's eyes betrayed his feelings. Either way, the surge of rage broke loose.

Mrs. Wong punched the security guard in the groin, who doubled over in the chair. Michelle had just opened the door, with Li Jun following behind her. Then in a span too short for a woman her age, Mrs. Wong had Li Jun's empty chair in hand, and took aim. Li Jun took the blow across the back. Eva jumped to her feet. He and Michelle toppled to the floor, that was how Li Jun got the date— and an assortment of other consequences. Being pulled from her thoughts of the incident, Michelle caught Eva staring at her.

"I understand you're busy keeping my agency afloat but—" Eva echoed a phrase Michelle hurled at her months ago.

"I said that in anger, I'm sorry." Michelle said, her hands folded in her lap.

"I'm sure you did," Eva sneered. She took a moment to sit back in her chair. "Quite a few things have changed since that conversation. And to top it all off, you're splattered in gossip magazines from here to Paris." Eva stood tossing a handful of magazines into Michelle's lap. "All press isn't good press Michelle. And *I* don't do trashy, so *you* don't do trashy. Why can't you just play quietly like all the other pretty faces?" Eva asked through clenched teeth.

"I hired a publicist, to keep this from happening again." Michelle said hoping this might help.

"You hired a publicist? I'm still trying to get you into the studio and with producers and other songwriters. And you just tack on more problems. No one wants to work with a troubled foreigner." Eva's skin reddened, her collar bone length hair swaying with every angered word and gesture.

"I don't want to be a singer. Let me make money doing what I'm doing and as a team, we can decide on a direction *I* want to go." Michelle stared relentlessly at Eva.

"You can't play the sexy girl forever, least of all here. Few can, and fewer succeed." Eva scoffed, shifting back to the computer, a foot loudly tapping the carpet. "For the breach of contract, I'm fining you. You'll get it in writing. Now—"

"What breach?" Michelle interjected.

"Hiring personnel without consulting me." Eva smiled. "There's someone that wants to meet with you. Banana Republic heard you were available and came looking— in the conference room." Eva pointed with clipped notes.

Outside of Eva's office, Michelle took in a deep breath to calm herself and started down the hallway. *Strange, Eva usually sits in on all meetings*, Michelle mused, passing Yu on his way to see Eva. She looked at him, the face suddenly seeming familiar, but Michelle shrugged both thoughts away continuing to the conference room.

Yu walked to Eva's office and it finally dawned on him how he knew *that girl*, remembering her from the café, and his detest for her, but now another memory surfaced. It was from the cookout at the Wong's House in— *August? or was it September? Too long ago*. He remembered how she bumped into him by the bathroom. She had come down from the rooftop. The Wongs were having another of their barbeques in their rooftop garden. She was angry, not that she seemed pleasant to begin with. She walked into the kitchen and placed an empty glass on the counter. Then she stopped and opened the fridge trying to cool down. He stood in the kitchen doorway, and decided to make small talk:

"Looks like we're in the same boat," he smiled, with a chuckle.

"What do you mean by that?" Michelle turned from the open fridge to him in disgust.

"The Wongs don't seem to care for us too much." He strolled into the kitchen past her. Michelle closed the fridge with a bottle of water in hand.

"That doesn't matter to me." She shrugged. "I don't care for the Wongs."

"No?" Yu crossed his arms and leaned against the counter. "But you want their prize bull." He realized she didn't remember him.

"They can keep their bull and his shit." She turned walking out of the kitchen.

"That's anger talking, wooing mom and dad won't be easy. We could—"

"I don't woo." She cut him off. That was when Li Jun rushed down from the rooftop. She saw him and walked out of the kitchen, then out the front door—and of course, he went after her. There was something poisonous about her, Yu brushed that thought aside and knocked on Eva's door.

At the other end of the hall, in the conference room, Michelle stood, staring at Li Jun. He sat quietly watching her, a hand to his chin. His hair was recently cut, hanging mid-bicep, she noted, drawn more to his wounded eyes.

"How are you?"

"Fine, and you?" She said flatly.

"Good. I wanted to—" Li Jun began.

"What?" Michelle asked sharply.

"I needed to see you about work." He stood, walking toward her. "Just listen—" Li Jun started again.

He looks thinner, she thought. "Jun I don't want any more of this, just stop." She turned to walk away.

Li Jun grabbed her hand. "This is just business, Banana Republic wants us to work on an ad, together."

Michelle stormed to the door. Willing that he be heard, at last, Li Jun stopped her. He placed a hand on the door and slammed it closed. Michelle opened it again, and again he closed it, leaning his weight forward.

"I don't want to work with you." She turned, voice sharp, sharper than she intended. "Maybe in—"

"I'm bringing you money and you just treat me like trash!" The volume was building in his voice. "What did I do? Huh?"

"What did you do? You wouldn't take a no." She said as the tears burst forth, and her volume soared. "You can never take a no. From day one, you've always had it your way." She paused. "So, when I was feeling shitty about my life, and my past, and *everything* I lost, I threw you one. I told you I was sorry." Michelle looked at the table to Li Jun's right. "And I tried to walk away. But you wanted to *help* me." Michelle stopped to catch her breath. "We never worked, and this," she pointed from her to him, "—is completely fucked. I don't want to do this with you anymore."

"You pity fucked me?" He paused, staring at her in total disbelief. "And then you just kept doing it?" Li Jun stepped back. "I gave you everything Michelle, and I'm still trying to keep my promise to—" He trailed off, pausing again. "You know what, Fuck you! Fuck you Michelle." Li Jun pulled the door open "Fuck you." He repeated walking to the elevator, all eyes cast in their direction.

Inside the elevator, Li Jun leaned against the wall with his heart pounding. On the fourth floor, a woman wearing a blue blazer and skirt joined him, then Li Jun heard her voice again:

"You look good in a suit." He remembered Michelle saying about a suit in the same shade of blue. *Why did a compliment from this girl make him feel like a school boy?* He wondered. He even remembered the feel of her hand when she thwarted his kiss. His heart was pounding then too.

"What? Something wrong?" He had asked her.

"I'm going to stop giving you compliments," Michelle said with a half smirk.

"You think that will make a difference? We have chemistry." He smiled back. It was late October and they were in the lobby of a hotel, on the way to another of Eva's work parties.

"Why is this party so important?" Michelle asked as they strolled to the elevator.

"To push you to the next level, you have to get what all the seasoned models already have. That's our client's attention. This is a mixer for all of Eva's best clients to chat with the models and book them for big upcoming shows and ads. Eva does it to get a feel for how to plan out the year for each one."

"Why wasn't I invited?" Michelle questioned, when Li Jun pressed the button for the seventh floor.

"Eva hand-picks the ones that have promise and are loyal to her."

"And here I thought you were joking about helping me."

"I was at first," Li Jun said with a gleam in his eyes. He turned to her, to those haunting eyes focused on him as they stepped out on the seventh floor.

"Why do you want me to succeed all of a sudden? Why the sudden push to help me?" Even now, angry with her, Li Jun remembered the raised eyebrow as she searched him for answers. He paused and broke the stare. Somehow the question had caught him off guard. Then they paused by the elevators.

"I'm doing this because I feel like I took advantage of you. And messed up our business arrangement. I like this. Our team." He tried to bring his eyes back to Michelle's.

"You don't need to do this, it was my mistake." She looked away, likely thinking of the sex during the downpour, Li Jun realized. *How had he missed her meaning? Missed that she would kiss, and hug, and touch and love on him-- but not want him.*

"I want to Michelle." He had insisted, "to show you I meant what I said. I'll take you to the top and you'll take me seriously." This somehow left a foul odor between them. Li Jun paused. "Just go in and be your charming self." He smiled. "It's in Seven forty-three. I'll be right behind you. Trust me. I'm looking out for you."

Li Jun remembered how at that moment, in that hotel, he thought of them in another hotel. The cheap one, in Chongqing. He remembered how he thought Michelle would one day be his forever. Her head in his lap as she fingered the strains of his damp pony tail before tearing it loose. This was just before the leg on the bed broke, sending them both to the floor.

"That's not funny at all." She stood up trying not to laugh with Li Jun.

"I'm going to take a shower and eat and when I'm done, you better hope I'm in a better mood." She grabbed a towel.

"Come on, Michelle where's your sense of adventure?" He had joked, shirtless and beaming.

"I left it in California with my training bras and Barbie's. Besides, I'm still mad at you about your crazy-ass-mama chasing us *again,* and losing my stuff." She said from the bathroom doorway.

"Well, you know—" Li Jun lay against the tilted bed. "I could help you get into a better mood." He propped a leg up brushing his hair back with a wink, before placing his hand at the edge of the towel around his waist. Oh, how they laughed.

When Michelle entered the party in seven forty-three, she was enraged to find out that at Li Jun's instruction, she crashed a white party in all black. Yet it got her the launch Li Jun hoped for, some saw it as brazen, and others fearless, anyone who mattered said it was both.

"But I kept my word," he smiled, "and she became an overnight success." This is what Li Jun told himself as he made his way through the throng of people crowding his usual route to Shinjuku station.

7. Worlds in Collision

Chiyoda, Tokyo, January 24th

"A spa day, that was a brilliant idea." Ari smiled, sipping from a cup of fragrant chrysanthemum tea in a plush white robe over a pedicure. She sighed, melting into a white oversized chair following the one hundred fifty minute 'Aman Tokyo Signature Journey' massage she and Michelle had embarked on.

"Nihon yokoso." Michelle attempted, from an identical chair to Ari's left in a matching robe. The two young women at work on their feet glanced at each other muffling their giggles. Between Michelle and Ari was a small blonde wooden table set with a kyusu teapot and one remaining tea cup in charcoal. Blonde wood blanketed the walls, floor, and ceiling creating a sterile but calming effect.

"I'm glad we did this." Ari said, taking another sip of her tea.

"After you saved me in Paris, it's the least I could do to welcome you. And now that I'm nearly a thousandaire, I can *almost* afford it." Ari heard the laughter in Michelle's voice, without looking.

"Well thank you," Ari smiled.

"You're more than welcome, I want you to know I value you."

Ari beamed, dishonestly before leaning back in her chair and closing her eyes.

"By the way what are you doing tomorrow?" Michelle asked, reaching for the remaining tea cup on the table. "If you want, you can come to lunch with me and meet my friend Jade and her new roomie."

"I don't know about that. I'm still tipping around boxes." Ari said her eyes still closed.

"If you like them then it's nothing lost. Or Jade at least, the roomie is anyone's guess." Michelle shrugged. "From the way Jade describes her, the girl sounds interesting."

"What do you mean?"

"Jade said she's a six-foot Korean woman, with blonde hair and huge assets."

"Six-foot-blonde-Korean?" Ari repeated with her eyes wide. "*No.*"

"You know." Michelle nodded. "I hope she's cool," she took a slow sip of the tea.

"That's *interesting* at least." Ari smiled, and closed her eyes again.

The scent of eucalyptus, and sandalwood flooded her nostrils as she settled into the cushions of her chair. The firm warm hands of the pedicurist on her feet seemed to melt away with the aid of the steaming jets in the bowl.

In her mind, visions of a dark substance took hold of Ari, pulling her whole body down. Time faded away and in what felt like moments, or hours, rosemary bloomed in the air, and the heat from the water radiated up her legs as Ari continued to sink. Down. Down. Deeper. *Into sleep? Madness? Death?* Ari wondered, still sinking. A hand landed on her forearm. Ari lurched to life. Ready to fight.

"They're finished." Michelle jerked back, hands splayed. The younger of the two pedicurists, stood frozen in place behind Michelle. Sweat beaded at Ari's hairline as she tried to find words.

"Ogakusama-daijobu-desuka?" The other pedicurist asked slowly, standing to the right of Ari's chair.

"Hai, Sorry." Ari said in a whisper to no one in particular.

"It's fine. Are you okay? You're sweating."Michelle moved in closer to help Ari out of the chair. Taking her arm, Michelle noticed the rapid pulse.

"No need, I'm fine. You scared me that's all." Ari pulled away.

"Okay," Michelle said apprehensively. "I have a deep condition and a steam treatment next. What about you?"

"Just a facial." Ari climbed to her feet.

They strolled towards the door and the pedicurists bowed chiming a '*Arigatougouzaimashita*'. Michelle and Ari turned back to them and nodded briefly before moving into the hallway. In the hall, the blonde wood retreated to one wall, giving way to a floor to ceiling view of Chiyoda-ku, and Skytree off in the distance.

"You know Ari, I noticed you don't really talk about yourself." Michelle mused as they walked, the sun lighting her profile.

"What do you want to know?" Ari slicked her hair back from her face.

"Nothing in particular, it's just your name is Naima but you go by Ari. You're Muslim and speak French, Arabic, and Japanese, but you look vaguely Asian."

"Oh," Ari laughed. "I just understand some Japanese. From what I've seen you know more." She grinned.

"I guess I'm just trying to put the pieces together." Michelle shrugged.

"It's a long-*sorted* history." Ari sighed, cutting her eyes to Michelle and the view. "My father was Moroccan, I was named after his mother and he gave me the nickname. My mother was part Japanese." Ari said, spotting a male attendant at the other end of the hall.

"Wow, and the other parts?" Ari heard Michelle ask, as the attendant came closer. He smiled then neatly bowed to them. Michelle and Ari nodded in turn.

As Ari stood upright, she saw Samir lurking just behind the man. Not the shrunken troll she stabbed repeatedly, but the vibrant man— dark eyes and oiled beard standing tall and sneering at her. Ari came to a halt, closing her eyes. Strands of hair trickled down her face. The attendant went on about his business, down the hall and into the room left vacant by Michelle and Ari.

"Ari what's wrong?" Michelle asked. Ari took in a deep breath, and opened her eyes, grinning at Michelle.

"I didn't drink enough water." She chuckled, at this lie.

"Let's sit down." Michelle pulled her over to a set of chairs to their left. "If you need to, we can leave." Michelle knelt down, her hand on Ari's knee.

"No it's fine." Ari shook her head, her black hair stringy from the sweat. "What time is lunch tomorrow?" She abruptly changed the subject, shaking the chill left by the hallucination.

"It's at one. So you're coming?" Michelle asked with a raised brow, tucking her hair behind an ear.

"I'll try to— look stop fussing over me. I'm fine. Go get your hair done. I'll get my facial and we'll meet in the lobby." Ari patted Michelle's hand.

"Patronize all you want. You work for me Ms. Louien. I need you in top shape," Michelle stood smiling.

"I'll see you in the lobby," she said sweetly.

In the lobby, light from outside beamed into the floor to ceiling windows of a long narrow sitting room, brushing up against segments of lattice dividers, that bisected the room. On the other side of this divider, Ari sauntered down a wooden cat-walk walkway in search of Michelle, spotting her near the front door.

She stood with that trademark waterfall of black hair, magically extended to her waist, over a three-quarter sleeved white jacket with a clutch-sized wallet in hand and a slim-fitting black dress. Ari took a moment to assess Michelle's heels before moving on to the man Michelle stood chatting with.

She slowed her approach, taken in by his copper skin infused with golden olive-oil colored undertones, and his slim but muscular frame, cloaked in a black Adidas tracksuit. His hair was a brown-black like charcoal and chocolate, tapered on the sides but curly and slicked back from his face. He was incredibly cute, Ari realized, coming into ear range. There was the squared off jaw and dimples carved at the sides of his mouth that appeared every time his lips moved. His lips were so pink they brought to mind sweetness and bubble gum. There was the refined squared nose carved into his face and the hooded slits that formed his eyes.

"Wow, your accent— you almost sound native now," Ari heard

Michelle say, crossing her arms and looking the man over.

"I started studying English too while I was away. I don't sound British do I?"

"A note here and there." Michelle beamed, brushing those long-feathered bangs back from her face.

"So, I leave and you become famous." He said with raised brows, *flirting*, Ari pointed out.

"I'm not famous," Michelle shook her head as Ari appeared, cell phone in hand and purse swinging at her elbow.

"Excuse me." Ari said curtly.

"Oh-Ari. This is Hikaru." Michelle's voice went up a notch on Ari's name. "Hikaru, this is my friend and publicist Ari Louien," and this led to the story.

The last time Michelle and Hikaru spoke, it was a chance meeting at Asakusa Station. She was having trouble adding money to her subway card, and Hikaru acted as the good Samaritan. Later, on the subway, they exchanged names. Michelle used the broken Japanese while Hikaru relied on simple phrases and gestures. From that brief encounter, Michelle learned of his upcoming studies in England and his skill on canvas.

"So, you're an artist? Would I know your work?" Ari questioned, with a plot taking shape in her recesses.

"No," Hikaru shook his head, his hands retreating into his pockets. "I'm in art school." He paused; the intonation somewhat robotic.

"He's a fine art's major." Michelle corrected.

"You two seem to know each other very well," Ari said with some surprise.

"A little, she helped my English before I went to London." Hikaru beamed at her. "But I have to go. I have class." He bowed to them, "It was very nice meeting you," he said to Ari, with a blinding smile as he walked out the front door.

"He's cute." Ari turned to Michelle. "I hear that's what flies over here."

"Ari stop it." Michelle rolled her eyes.

"How many times did you *bump* into him?"

"I'm not a hoe, Ari." Michelle said, trying not to laugh. "He can really paint."

"You guys didn't *bump* anything else? Were you his muse?" Ari paused to look at Michelle, who was already staring at her. "I figure he's not your type but Michelle, cute boys like him, use women like you. He's what, eighteen?"

"Twenty-one,"

"Oh," Ari said, as if saying '*that makes such a difference.*' "Michelle, he wants you. And if there are any real thoughts in his head, he wants you to be his suga-mama. So, what was he doing here, dress like that?" Ari cut her eyes in the direction of the door.

"He's a trainer here."

"Oh, did you find out if he'd let you use his discount?" Ari paused to stare at Michelle as Michelle burst into laughter.

"No, I didn't. We were just catching up." Michelle glanced down at her phone, wedged inside her wallet. Feeling Ari's long cold stare. "Ari, I'll be careful—I'm sure he's a nice guy." Michelle said, with a smile.

"Yeah." Ari nodded. "Um-uh, danger often takes the least threatening of forms." She said as Hikaru walked back toward them.

"Here's my, keitai—mobile number," he said, handing Michelle a slip of paper. "Give me a call when you have time." He nodded.

"I will." Michelle grinned, glancing at the paper. And did: Call him, to lunch, in Omotesando, the next day.

Black Swans & Intricate Disasters
Omotesando, Tokyo, January 25th

It was the sight of white table cloths paired with overly stylish furniture that set Hikaru on edge. The atmosphere was stylish enough for a date but, casual enough for lunch between friends. Why had she called him? This is what Hikaru thought upon entering, just before a nervous glance at his watch—eleven fifty-three. When he looked up and saw her seated by a window.

"Long time no see," he said hesitant but jokingly, noting that the table was set for four. He took a silent sigh of relief as he sat across from Michelle. *But then again none of these tables are set for two*, he realized after the waiter took their orders. "So, what made you want to have lunch so sudden? And at such a nice place."

"Just to talk over really good food." Michelle shrugged. "My brother owns this restaurant. So, it's a bit like home. We can go somewhere else if you want."

"No. I've heard the food here is great." *From yelp*. He smiled, wondering if Michelle noticed he'd ordered the cheapest thing on the menu.

Hikaru and his family had been a part of the working poor since he was in middle school. This was a few short years before they lost everything his grandfather hadn't gambled away. So, when he was old enough, he had to get a job. School or not, debts needed to be paid along with the other bills, and then there was the chore of feeding oneself.

"Don't worry," Michelle said. "It's my treat, since I invited you." Michelle beamed, radiating warmth, with her casual kindness as she threw hair from her face.

"Thanks." Hikaru grinned, dimples in full view and bubble-gum-pink lips parting. Now every bite of the five-thousand-yen pork chop would be enjoyed.

Michelle and Hikaru knew they liked one another from their first meeting, but it was a question of quantity. Yet it was as if by magic, amidst conversation, large appetizers and entrees, that a kinship sparked between them again. *But were the feelings those of lovers, with a connection present from their first glance, or were they the stuff of legends and novels— the kind of attraction destined for friendship. Could they simply be two lonely strangers fated to more alone-ness and more abandonment, or were they designed for unrequited love and that assortment of endings.*

"I want to be a great painter, I just don't know what to paint," he laughed, Michelle smiling alongside. "I do landscapes and it feels wrong, I do portraits and I have to make them good looking. I'm still looking for my," he paused. "door?"

"Your niche," she added. "I guess I'm looking for mine too."

Waitresses zipped past the table, taking orders in the heat of the mid-day rush. Yet, the quiet surrounding Hikaru and Michelle was impenetrable.

"What do you *see yourself*?" Hikaru asked suddenly. Michelle paused, looking confused. "I mean *how*— how do you see yourself. I'm I saying that right?"

"Yes. A Californian," she shrugged, knowing that he meant, what they all mean. *Why do you stand out? What are you?*

"That's not what I meant."

She chuckled. "I'm American, I guess and that's convoluted in itself."

"Convoluted? What does that mean?"

"Intricate—um," she paused, to think. "Complex. People of color almost always feel the weight of that color. I only feel American going out into the world, or when I go back and get to go to a different line at the airport. But that's not the answer you were looking for either."

"You're right." Hikaru laughed, lifting a glass to his lips, eyes glinting as two birds flew past the window. His teeth gleaming into a smile, while he was trying to do the opposite.

"I am a minority, in a minority, in a minority. I am black and American but of the Nigerian-Eritrean variety, yet my mother is Japanese. I look Asian and speak only romance languages aside from English. I grew up well off and in So-Cal but was raised to be a princess of some kind."

"So, you have no connection to Japan?" Hikaru asked, the conversation turning interview.

"No, I don't. Not at all." She stared at him, feeling exposed.

"I can help you find where you fit here." He said, trying not to linger on her eyes, but doing so anyway. "I mean, I-can-help-you-find, *some interest* in Japan and Japanese culture," he stammered.

"I appreciate that Hikaru, but my father's parents went to America and they met as professors on a college campus. My mother's parents owned a restaurant in Osaka for generations until my mother met and married my father. My father and mother slaved to provide for me and my brothers while building my father's practice. So, I owe it to them to figure it out. The difference is they chose where they would make their mark, while I'm still searching. So, what do you see yourself as?"

"I'm both." He said almost laughing. "I am Japanese and Angolan, there is no *or,* but, I've never been." He shook his head smiling and staring at her— *intoxicated*, in a moment, with this near stranger whom he couldn't help but be drawn to. Despite this feeling, he couldn't seem to shake the notion that this was wrong in some way.

A figure came into view, just at the edge of Hikaru's periphery.

"I made it," Ari said with her purse swinging at her elbow. Hikaru stopped, the parade rained on, and out, as Michelle stood to hug her.

"You're fine. You remember Hikaru," Michelle said extending an arm. Hikaru stood to shake Ari's hand.

"You remember me?" He grinned.

"Yes," Ari said, coolly, tucking her bangs, leaving Hikaru to take pause before they all sat. "I see you started without me." Ari beamed at Michelle.

"We just started on an appetizer." Michelle lied.

"Considering you eat whole houses. I'm going to have to get a second trainer." Ari scoffed as Hikaru took a sip of water. "Didn't you see the email Eva sent? We need you to shed inches and stay there." Ari glanced at Hikaru, to ensure his discomfort, before turning back to Michelle. "So, where's Jade and the roomie?"

"I don't know. Jade told me she'd be here by one." Michelle shrugged.

"It's almost two-thirty." Ari looked to her watch, still watching Hikaru from the corner of her eye. Ari's eyes drifted to Hikaru, etched in black-winged eyeliner, alongside golden eye shadow— cutting eyes, threatening eyes.

Ari, the black swan, infamous, and threatening, he mused. *She who wields the most-deadly of aphrodisiacs, the kind of woman whose opinion becomes fact, whose word becomes law. She, who drips with raw, easy-to-harness, soft power— never mind the beauty, a different gift entirely.* Hikaru's eyes went back to Michelle and only now did he see those same *raw* characteristics in her—not yet budding, but present all the same.

"So sorry we're late." Ari heard a familiar voice say coming to the table. She looked up.

Ari stared at Soo Young with long swinging blonde hair, orange tinted at the roots and gradually fading into a gold color—*a nice look, for a video vixen.* Clad in a green Chanel jacket over a pink Marc Jacobs' dress, with pink and green Jimmy Choo's—all last season—and seamed stockings. *Oh my*, Ari thought, shaking her head. *She could be something, (pretty girl, nice figure, those long legs), were she not set on looking like Ronald McDonald in the Broadway production of the Devil wears Prada.* Soo Young's hair and clothes nearly muted Jade's line about something to do with the landlord but by then Ari was surveying this Jade character intently.

Jade looked over the table and found Naima Louien-Terada's eyes, locked on her. That was the moment she stumbled upon her fourth grave mistake.

"Jade this is Ari, my publicist, and my friend, Hikaru." Michelle said as Hikaru waved. Ari stared at Jade for a moment. A silent tension bubbled to the surface.

"Hi." Jade said smiling while Soo Young waved to the table." Michelle and Hikaru beamed at the introduction, exchanging pleasantries.

"Hello." Soo Young chimed.

The waiters expanded the table leaves. At this new circular table, Jade sat to Hikaru's right, then Soo Young beside her, and to Soo Young's right sat Michelle and Ari.

Later in the afternoon, as the food began to dwindle and the pleasantries faded with each glass, Michelle asked, "So why not go to Angola to paint?"

This caused Ari and Jade to both take pause. There being no prior mention of Angola or painting. All the while, Soo Young sat swirling the wine in a glass, trying to follow this new thread.

"I don't know anyone there." Hikaru paused. "But one day." He smiled, his dimples on display. Soo Young bit down on her lower lip as she watched him.

"You're Angolan?" Jade leaned in closer.

"My mother was." He glanced down at the table cloth not wanting to go further.

"I'm so sorry," Michelle said quickly.

Hikaru shook his head. "It's okay."

"I thou—" Jade began.

"I knew there was something about you." Ari cut in. She sat, a hand poised under her chin, the other beneath her elbow. "Something about you reminded me of home." She smiled.

Though Jade wasn't sure, she thought Ari glanced in her direction. Michelle felt the tension but wanted to know where this might be going.

"Home?" Soo Young chimed in, pouring a second glass. Her porcelain complexion was rosy from the alcohol. "Where are from?"

"Morocco," Ari said proudly.

"Ohh, but rooks so Asia. Are you Japan-s city?" Soo Young asked. Ari and Hikaru stopped to ponder what was said. Michelle turned to Jade, hoping she might translate.

"Nihon-de-umareta-desu-ka." Soo Young managed.

"Ah, hai," Hikaru smiled. "Boku wa nihonjin desu, demo kanojo wa—" He stopped and turned to Ari.

"Italia." Ari said. Soo Young nodded. "So, Harrison, you studied in London How long were you there?" Ari asked.

"It's Hikaru," he smiled. "It was just a semester. That's all I could save for." He answered, noting Ari's attention shift from him to Jade before he could finish.

"What about you, Jade? Have you been to Europe?" Ari posed the question as soon as Hikaru finished speaking. Michelle took pause, glass in hand watching Ari and seeing a different side of her come to life.

"Off and on, yes." Jade smiled; her hands folded in her lap meeting the heat of Ari's penetrating stare. Ari opened her mouth to speak but Hikaru intercepted, feeling Ari's intensity drifting to Jade.

"So, I loved London, but the next place I want to go is the states. Have any of you been there?" he asked, smiling first at Jade and then at Michelle, before a glance at Soo Young. Jade looked at him, almost shyly from the corner of her eye. She mouthed a *thank you* as she tucked her hair behind an ear, all of which Michelle saw.

"The U.S. is very big but one thing is very clear across the country." Ari cut in.

"What is that?" He questioned.

"You're blessed to be there, even more so for the brown and black people." Jade spoke up, her eyes on the table.

"There are no real relationships formed in spite of difference," Ari added, baiting the hook. "If so they tend to fade with time. Most countries have this problem but, it's also a bit different in every country." Ari sat back in her chair, eyes darting around the table.

Hikaru felt the conversation and the atmosphere begin to shift. He and Soo Young sat blanked faced trying to keep up as Jade interjected.

"I think what Ari is saying is that race relations *is* America's original sin," Jade said, then repeated in Korean for Soo Young. "I'm not sure how it is for you here, but when you make the choice to go to America, you become black. Don't argue. America doesn't care that you grew up in Japan or speak Japanese fluently. You become one thing and it's million other stereotypes." Jade said sweetly. Her eyes a chocolaty glow in the late afternoon light.

She's not flirting with me, right? Hikaru wondered, eyeing her dewy lips.

Ari raised a brow at Jade's response, a tug on the line. *Where have I heard that?* She wondered, as Jade continued.

"The U.S. was shaped in and by race and racism yet no one openly acknowledges that fact. It also doesn't help that the US is so young. Here, scars from the Meiji Era and all the Japanese occupations can still be found today, but because Japan has so much shared and recorded history it gets thrown in with all the rest. The US doesn't have that luxury and so the ugly parts of history are always staring you in the face as a minority. And with all these new movements popping up, history is being rewritten before our eyes, faster than ever."

"Japan is also very homogenous and group oriented." Ari scoffed, pulling her phone from her purse to look up that line.

"It's very insular too." Michelle sighed. Jade translated and Soo Young let a flood of Korean loose, bobbing her head up and down in agreement.

"How could I forget about that?" Jade turned to the rest of the table. "The landlord at Soo Young's salon and at the apartment gave her a very hard time when she found out Soo Young was Korean. That's part of why we were late."

"Well Japanese people only moderately like themselves, while tolerating everyone else." Ari laughed to herself.

"Ari!" Michelle exclaimed, hitting at Ari's arm.

"What? I'm not lying."

"That's not fair," Hikaru jumped in. "—and Italian's think they invented pasta but nobody thinks to get the Chinese or any Asians to weigh in on the noodle."

"Touché." Ari agreed, with a smile in his direction.

I didn't know she could smile, Hikaru balked.

"And why is that?" Ari asked, scrolling on her phone. Hikaru stared at her, his shocked smile going leaden. "Because they're white and western," Ari answered. "The west controls the narrative, while white is the lens."

Her eyes came to rest on his.

"But America can't be like that." Hikaru shook his head.

Ari moved back to her phone, then she looked at Jade, for the first time since the introductions. Though Hikaru couldn't put his finger on it he knew there was something left unsaid in that glance. *They just met,* he thought.

"Did you know anyone from North Africa or the Middle East, is automatically white on paper *in States.*" Ari said shifting the tide. She put the phone on the table, having found what she was searching for. So, a person from Iran is automatically white, while a person from Pakistan *become* Asian, while they have so much *shared history.*" Ari raised an eyebrow pointedly, looking at Jade.

"Where did you come across that piece of intel?" Michelle questioned noting Ari and Jade's mounting tension.

"Applying for a visa, it's on the census website. But that was years ago so maybe they got upgraded to white by now."

"Part of it is an effort to protect the purity of whiteness," Jade remarked. "The other part of it is to protect the secrets of the truly wealthy, with the old divide and conquer. But in the states, the first division, is race, then class, then religion, then political leaning and the system always operates as the shadow of the question you don't want to ask." Jade said as if she might go on for hours, until Ari interjected.

"To protect *whiteness?*" Hikaru repeated. "Growing up here, I thought it was just me being the brown face in all the sameness. I don't know what to say." Hikaru shook his head.

"You should still go." Michelle interjected. "There are good people and good places everywhere, you just have to find them." She beamed

"You know, Hunter," Ari paused looking at Hikaru. "— they're willing to screw you and your whole family, *literally*, but they need time to think about letting people like you become *citizen* or to have actual rights, treating you like an equal or God forbid a *friend.*" Ari shrugged, then paused to look at Jade. "It won't be as bad for you in states because you're cute, not dark and you still look Asiany." Ari said, smiling at him.

"Apreca is a big country." Soo Young chimed in, some six glasses in. "Ehjani zat's a city in Apreca?" She asked clearly not following the entirety of the conversation.

"No," Ari stopped. "Africa is a continent sweetie."

"Oh," Soo Young nodded to Ari.

"She's learning English," Jade interjected. "It's her third language." She stared at Ari.

"Afurika ga kuni de wa nai," Ari said speaking to Soo Young but staring at Jade. "Tairiku desu, Con-tin-ent eigo de—it's also my third language, while Japanese is a distant fourth," Ari spat the words.

By then Soo Young had shifted to Hikaru to get out of the crossfire. "So, you like chicken like heug-in or pish like Japan-s?" She asked brimming with curiosity.

Jade lowered her head. "I'm going to the restroom." She said, made to feel awkward by Soo Young's growing interest in Hikaru.

"Where are you from Ling Ding?" Ari cut in again.

"Kori-a." Soo Young smiled.

"No, Koreans can speak English, or at least Japanese. Where are *you* from? So we can start throwing some stereotypes at that."

"Ari," Michelle hissed. "I'm sure, she just has questions. Maybe Hikaru and I are the first black people she's met. And maybe you are the first people from the continent she's met. Yesterday, Jade told me she had to explain the difference between Taiwan and China."

"Same ting." Soo Young interjected. "jung-guk, jung-guk."

Michelle's eyes narrowed as she turned to Soo Young.

"Hikaru, dangsin jeongmal ippeuda. Na-Yeojachigu isseo?" Soo Young asked, all eyes and lips as she gave Hikaru the one over.

I don't like the bitch. Ari texted Michelle as a comfortable hush covered the table.

Who Jade? I can tell. Michelle winced, texting back, under the table.

Pick one Ari mouthed, with Soo Young and Hikaru chatting quietly in

Japanese. Michelle let go a deep sigh.

Meanwhile, Ari zoomed past a waiter carrying a large tray of appetizers, hot on Jade's trail. The scent of garlic and ginger wrapped themselves around her as she cut past the kitchen and the roar of its controlled flames, then table after table of people carefully devouring the food on their plates. Catching sight of the restroom symbol, Ari dashed to the bathroom, her black suede Gianvito Rossi pumps echoing on the white subway tiles. An elderly redheaded woman exited the ladies room and held the door for Ari.

"Thank you," she smiled. The woman nodded, and strolled back to her table. Ari stepped inside the bathroom smoothing her hair. Then she posted by the sinks, ankles crossed, waiting.

Two women came out of the stalls in quick succession looking at Ari in turn, somewhat confused at the sight of a woman waiting in a mostly empty bathroom, a rare occurrence if ever. Each woman washed then dried her hands and left. Ari was about to kick off a shoe and take a seat on the plush-looking bench by the door, when Jade stepped out of the stall. Her eyes were drawn to the floor before they slowly drifted to Ari.

"You scared—" Jade began with an animated smile. Her features and voice on a level of cuteness Ari knew only to be false.

"Don't. Last time I saw you was in Switzerland, at TASIS. No, it was the ski resort where *you left me*. What are you doing here?" Ari asked a hand on her hip.

Jade scoffed. "What gave me away?" her voice lost its pep as she moved to a sink, slowly washing her hands.

"There were a few clues," Ari crossed her arms, *suspicions confirmed*. "Your quotes from Americana for *instant*."

The bathroom door opened and a Japanese woman entered, moving past Ari to the first stall with a sneeze into a handkerchief. Jade dried her hands smirking.

"My mistake. I do like that book." Jade said, the smile gone now. "But that's why you kept the conversation on race and nationality."

"So, you disappeared with Oh Fan and what, rearranged your face to get away from him? Did he beat you?" Ari watched Jade carefully

"Yes, Naima. We got married, had five children and moved to Vancouver," Jade rolled her eyes,

"Then why did my only friend leave me stranded, no phone, no ID, no note? Then disappear?" Ari asked the cold edge to her voice melting away.

"I'm not doing this." Jade moved passed Ari toward the door. But the door opened again and Michelle stepped inside.

"There you are. Soo Young is making a play for—" Michelle stopped inside the door, her smile dissolving. Ari turned to the familiar voice as the woman on the toilet flushed, then opened the stall door. "What's going on here?" Michelle asked. The water at the sink came on, filling the sudden quiet before the fourth woman slipped past Michelle in a blur of pink.

"Your friend was telling me she got to see Sade live the last time she was in Europe." Ari lied. "The show I missed. She crossed her arms then stared coolly at Jade's back. Referring to plans they had, back before Jade disappeared.

"Oh," Michelle said, not looking entirely convinced, "Is that all? And here I thought one of you might pounce on the other."

"What?" Jade giggled, the warmth and sweetness coming back to her face. "Absolutely not. What were you saying about Soo Young?"

"She's making a move on Hikaru," Michelle sat down on the bench to her left, just inside the bathroom, looking between the two of them. Ari shifted to look at herself in the mirror and Jade completely focused on Michelle.

"Why are you telling me?" Jade's brows drew together, still smiling.

"He's cute. And I got the feeling you might like each other. So, I wanted to set you up."

"He does seem like *your* type." Ari added with a smile and some bite to the words. She exhaled and shifted her gaze to Michelle. "This afternoon was interesting. I'll pick up my tab and be on my way," Ari said moving to the door.

"Bye Ari. It was nice meeting you," Jade said in that cheery voice again.

Ari froze in front of the door. With the slow turn of the head, she glanced over her shoulder. "You too, Li—I mean Jade," Ari glared back at Jade before leaving the restroom.

"I take it you two don't care for each other," Michelle crossed her legs looking at Jade.

"We like some of the same music, that's about it." Jade smiled, pulling Michelle up from the bench. "So you think Hikaru likes me?" She asked strolling out of the bathroom.

Vulnerable Moments
In Transit, January 25th - 26th

After a long day of negotiations, Seina unearthed a quiet moment to be with his own thoughts. It was the single moment found after long hours on those most unrelenting of days. Now he was too tired to sleep and yet too sleepy to stand as he embarked on the short flight home.

He closed his eyes, for a moment, maybe longer, during takeoff. The roar of the engine was all too present to sleep. He opened his eyes to a setting sun in a sea of clouds, when Michelle flooded his thoughts. Seina let the thoughts of her linger, on his senses for a moment. *It's time to take action:* leaning his chair back and calling her from the jet's cordless phone, with a quick glance at the time. It rang, and rang— he considered hanging up, and then pulled the phone from his ear.

"Hello," Michelle answered, on the last ring.

"Ah, you picked up." Seina smiled, with eyes closed.

"I thought I blocked your number. You know my boyfriend doesn't like you calling."

"I paid that bastard to disappear." He laughed, placing a hand over his eyes.

"So why are you calling me?" Michelle asked smiling, to the point Seina heard this smile.

"Direct as always. I just finished work and thought I'd give you a call to see what you're up to."

"After I told you I don't want to see you again."

"What are you doing?" He shifted in his chair.

Michelle scoffed. "Eating dinner." She thought he sounded tender, almost genuine. He yawned. "Am I boring you? Is it past your bedtime?"

"Yeah, but I've been working nonstop since late last night. What have you been doing?"

"You work? I didn't know you had any workable skills." Michelle laughed.

"There's a lot I do, that isn't in the newspapers."

"Entertain me." She paused. "What kind of work do you do?"

"I just finished easing tensions at one of the Terada refineries. I also called because I thought we could celebrate."

"*We? Celebrate?*"

"Of course. It's a big deal."

"You mean a night on the town, right? Look, my trainer was brutal today then I got a little tipsy at lunch. I'm sore." She put him on speaker phone and typed a message. "Not to mention I'm still hungry and I had way too many empty calories this week." She sounded distracted as she texted.

"I could give you a deep tissue massage and have you good as new."

"Hmm, I bet you could," Michelle said sarcastically. "Well," She paused "—congratulations Seina. I'm going to take a bath," another pause. "Bye."

"Do you mind if I come over. I'll be landing in about two hours."

"You're asking me now?"

"By now I'm hoping you'll say yes. Now that we know each other a little bit better." He grinned.

Michelle took in a breath. "Rest well, I'll see you when you get here." She hung up, leaving Seina with his thoughts of her.

When she opened the door, he stood with two bottles in hand. She stood drying long limp curls with a t-shirt.

"I didn't know if you preferred red or white so—" Seina trailed off.

"You bought both." She shook her head laughing. "more empty calories," she sighed.

In time, the wine dwindled, and the feigned distances closed, once again. Seina and Michelle found themselves seated on the floor sipping the red. When Seina turned to Michelle, he smirked at her and they locked eyes. Seina placed his glass on the table, then Michelle looked away, to break the stare, taking the glass into the kitchen.

"You're staring." She said tucking long damp wavy extensions, then placing the glass in the sink.

"I was listening." He said sweetly. "So, your friend and your publicist don't get along. And your friend has a crazy roommate now?"

"Something like that," Michelle laughed, rinsing the glass, suddenly feeling Seina drape his arms around her.

"The factions in your friend group are very fascinating Michelle but, how do you feel about me?" He asked trying to mask a yawn. She turned to face him, leaning on the counter.

"I think you're smart enough to know I won't answer that with a drop of alcohol in my system."

"Fair, alright, two things then." Seina began, holding up three fingers, laughing. Michelle nodded, with a smile.

"Is it two or three?"

"It was a joke." He leaned in closer bracing his hands on the counter. "I'm not that drunk, and I like you, a lot," he smiled. "—and I'm not trying to buy you," he paused. "So, before you try to kick me out now or break out the pepto," he looked back to the coffee table. "I just wanted to say that."

Michelle turned his face back to her, pulling him closer. It was a peck destined for his cheek, but Seina jerked free at the last second, leaving their lips to cushion the blow. It became a kiss, with the push-pull of a current. Michelle instantly tried to pull back, she lingered, instead— the tide stronger than her reason.

Seina pulled away. "Wow." He smiled at her.

"I'm really tired." Michelle stared into his eyes, slipping his grasp.

"After three glasses? Michelle, what am I doing wrong here?" Seina paused to cross his arms.

Years later, when returned to this moment, Michelle will question: *why did it take so long, to see him, to see his intentions, his love?* And she'll be visited by the familiar feeling of having failed, of failing herself, again.

"Seina, I'm not ready for any of this," she said.Seina took a step back.

"Is it because you still love him—the French guy?"

"I hate him," Michelle said, staring at Seina, not moving or blinking. "I hate him." She repeated, as the rest came unbidden, how she met Adrien, again two years after their first encounter, and how they were smitten.

How she loved him— how he was married— and expecting the first child.

"Adrien told me about Gabriele after I told him I was going to stay to be with him." Michelle paused, looking at the blonde-coffee-colored wood of her kitchen floor, ashamed. She decided not to tell the rest, for fear of deepening the stain on her soul. Then the thing became clear to Seina at last, the scarlet A burned into her being. This was her last wine-soaked memory of that night, she was nearly in tears, when Seina took her in his arms.

Michelle woke to daylight and an alarm. She laid in bed on Seina's stomach. *I fucking hate wine*, she turned to free her cheek from his skin, her head throbbing. She sat up, reaching for the phone.

Every time Michelle, when will you learn to say no to w— Her mind went blank at the sight of him, sleeping, nearly naked, in her bed. *Did I have sex with him?* The alarm continued blaring. Michelle turned it off. She lifted the sheet. *Please don't be naked—Please do,* she amended the thought. *Didn't know all that was under those suits—focus Michelle! I'm sorry, it's the wine!* She battled her thoughts.

Awakened by the gust of cool morning air on his skin, Seina turned to her, "Are you hungry?" He threw an arm across her bare thighs, kissing one. Michelle looked at him at a loss for words and smiled.

"I—" she began.

"We didn't have sex," He beamed. "but we wanted to, til somebody passed out." Seina sat up to kiss her on the forehead. "If you're hungry I can go get breakfast." He paused to get out of bed. "Is there anything you want to eat?" He asked as she looked at her phone.

"Seina, I have to go. I—I have to get to work."

"I can take you." He laughed as the alarm sounded again. Turning off the alarm Michelle looked at Seina, not sure of what to say.

"You don't remember, do you?" Seina paused, taking a step back from the bed.

"Seina, I really don't have time to unpack all this." She said getting out of bed. "Let's talk later— okay? I have a shoot and a meeting to get to. I'll call you tonight."

"Wait—" he started as she dashed into the bathroom, closing the door, so he waited. He put on his clothes and he waited. When Michelle stepped out, ready to face the world an hour or so later, the cool silence welcomed her. The apartment was empty. Seina was gone.

8. Trapped

Akasaka, Tokyo, January 28th

Li Jun unlocked the door to his apartment, and was alerted by the scent of scallion and meat roasting—*is that duck?* He sighed, the dinner with his parents, he remembered.

"Where have you been? I called!" Victoria zipped about the kitchen with exhaustion draping her like a blanket. She was wearing Li Jun's orange apron—the one Michelle bought.

"Don't start Tori."

"I haven't yet." She looked up, from a wok with the oil just coming to a sizzle. "I call to ask you pick up some thing I forgot." She said speaking shorthand

"I'm sorry."

"So, because you didn't answer, I ran to every Chinese food store I could, to get everything need. Then some bloody idiot decides to off himself on my way back. So—" Victoria shouted, turning from the stove.

"Tori, I had a lot on my mind. I appre—" he started.

"*You?* You had a lot on your mind!? I am shooting a commercial tonight and here I'm cooking a traditional meal for four from your great-grandmother's recipes—*in traditional character and I can barely read it, Jun!*" Her fair skin flushed a shade of red with anger not fully rendered in the queen's English.

"I forgot I'm sorry," Li Jun said, putting his camera down.

"You forgot. Well, that makes it all better! Did you forget because you saw Princess Michelle?" Victoria turned to face him, a hand on her hip and eyes on the wok. "I know you met with her a few days ago."

"I forgot because I took a moment for myself!" He said, his lips curving into a snarl. "What does it matter to you? The only reason you're

149

here is to trap me. Because you and my mom got together and decided what I would do with my life." He walked away, toward the bedroom and Victoria grabbed his camera, hurling it across the room. Li Jun stopped. Then he turned to Victoria taking in controlled breaths.

"Look who thinks he's a god." She said coming closer. "I had everything I needed to trap you, your parents, your sisters, your child. Are you trapped?!" Victoria's hands flung out on her sides. "You showed up with Michelle while we were engaged. You took her to meet your family, you took her to China! You go to the ends of the earth for her. A woman that wouldn't even use you to wipe her shoe," Victoria yelled as the tears fell, like raindrops, pitter-patter down her face.

"My child?" Li Jun questioned, forgetting the camera, and Victoria's anger, and even the points she made. "What do you mean my child?" He inched closer.

"I was pregnant Jun. While you were fucking her, when you broke it off." Victoria scowled, as Li Jun grabbed her by the arm.

"Where is my—" He paused, unable to find the word. *Child, baby, kid?* He thought frantically.

"Don't worry she died." She spat, jerking away from Li Jun.

"When? Why didn't you tell me? You aborted my baby?" His face went blank, lips going slack, as he grabbed Victoria by her arms.

"All you think about is you. What *you* want, what *you* need."

"Did you abort my baby?" He repeated.

"You don't have a baby! You are one!" Victoria said tearing her arms free from him and unleashing a thunderous slap. "You chose your American whore."

"How could you kill my baby Victoria?!" He shouted creeping closer to her. Victoria pushed Li Jun back. Then she poured a pot of boiling water to the floor. Li Jun jumped back to the wall watching steam rise. Victoria threw the pot to the floor glaring at him.

"Since you think I'm trapping you." Air quotes. "—it looks like I made the right choice." Victoria lied, sneering at him.

"Why didn't you tell me?" His voice broke and his eyes glassed over.

"For what?" Victoria scoffed almost laughing. "You're irresponsible, flaky, and flighty, and most of all you don't love me, not the way I loved you. Nothing like the way you love her," Victoria said, taking off the apron.

"So you killed—" He paused eyes reddening and nose beginning to run. "—our baby?"

"Our baby?" She slapped him again, marching to the coat closet by the door. Li Jun grabbed her arm.

"Tori I don't love Michelle."

"I don't believe you." Victoria put on her coat, seeing the hurt in his eyes she added. "I lost the baby." She wiped a tear, then another. "I'm going home. Call your mother and tell her what you want." And with that Victoria walked out of the apartment, kicking the pot back toward the kitchen. As the door slammed, Li Jun slowly took a seat on the floor, trying to process. He sat on the wet floor among the sounds of the gurgling pots as the oil in the wok emitted a foul burning scent, feeling more trapped than ever.

Serenade
Tokyo, January 28th

Seina sat on a leather sofa looking out on the city from his living room, as he finished a glass of gin. He watched the sunset peer through the clouds, beaming from the windows of the high rise across the street. Sunlight and clouds danced, the rain pouring and lifting.

Seina grabbed a wine flute from the coffee table, and poured, spilling the gin on his white pants. He slammed the glass down and it shattered. Seina drunk from the bottle. The doorbell rang, and he grabbed a hand towel from the kitchen on his right pulling glass shards from the wound. He took in a breath and opened the door.

"So, you don't answer phone calls now?" Ari asked standing in the door. She leaned against the frame, her arms crossed with a white coat and black scarf folded over them. "Or are you just ignoring all my calls?" That black curtain of hair shone as she swept it from her eye with a finger.

"What are you doing here?" Seina asked, attempting to keep his hand out of view. She glanced him over, seeing the few drops of blood on his clothes.

"I saw you on the news and called. And because I didn't get an answer, I stopped in." She slipped past him. Seina closed the door.

"I'm sorry I had to cancel dinner last minute. Work has been a little hectic."

"What happen to your hand?" She leaned on the back of the leather sofa, throwing her coat and scarf down beside her.

Seina looked at the towel. "Nothing."

She knew he was angry from the limpness of his shoulders, the flat measured notes of his voice, and how he avoided her eyes. He glanced at Ari, and then returned to his seat at the window as she surveyed the condo.

"What do you think about my haircut?" She asked moving to sit beside him.

Seina said nothing.

"Why don't you tell me about it?"

"There's not much to tell." Seina looked at her, putting his feet up on the table.

"That's not what that glass is saying."

Seina stared at her. "I love seeing you but you don't pop up without a reason."

"If you would pick up a phone you would know. I got a job." She said her eyes gleaming.

"You got a job, here? In Japan?"

"Well in Tokyo to be specific, but yes."

"I'm not in the mood for this." The words roared from his throat.

Ari crossed her legs. "So, who's Michelle Yamato?" She kicked off black heels, folding her feet beneath her on the sofa. "You two are all over the place." Ari swept the bangs from her eyes to stare at her cousin-brother.

"Why are you interested?"

"I just want you to take your time with this one. Those last three were cries for help." Ari paused. "Have you been dating her since August?"

"No."

"And you gave her your grandmother's pink diamond from the vault?" Her brows rose, while Seina said nothing. He glanced toward Ari, or rather a blur of her jumping to her feet bounding toward the kitchen.

"So have you been spying on her?" Seina asked following Ari.

She poured a cup of a fruit beverage and Seina drank from it, before placing it back on the counter. "No." She smiled. "But did you know she speaks French, fluently?" Ari asked, turning to pour more into the empty cup.

"So, you have been spying." He walked back into the living room and Ari filled the glass a second time.

"I just told you I haven't." She came back to the living room. "But Seina, you can tell me now or I can find out later." Ari brought the glass to her mouth. "That's a good batch of break-up juice." She looked at Seina, her eyes glowing. "I'm just concerned for your liver. She must really be something if you're drinking like this, during the day."

"Break up juice? *Really*?" He stared at her.

"You make it every time you break-up with someone." Ari shrugged. "—break-up-juice."

"This is about work."

"Work makes you drink like this?" Ari turned to Seina resting her chin on her hand. "What's the problem then?"

"I'm working at the company."

"Isn't that a good thing?" Ari shrugged. "Securing your what—5 billion?"

"4."

"Right-right-right." Ari nodded, before taking a sip.

"No matter what I've done, or how many projects I've managed it's not enough. I thought he wanted me to work with him, to get to know me. But he just wants a successor."

"Claudio Terada one oh one, but go on."

"He's testing all of us out. Meanwhile I'm—" Seina stopped.

"Meanwhile what?"

"Nothing." He shrugged.

"It's about Michelle." Ari laughed. "You obviously need help. How do you know she's not all smoke and mirrors? That she's not after you for your wallet, instead of your heart." Ari turned his face, making him look at her. "What kind of cousin-sister would I be if I wasn't here for you? You already have April and she's the shiftiest sister ever."

"You know somebody even wrote a song about Michelle."

"A song?" He questioned. Ari nodded. "What kind of song?" Seina turned to her, Ari shook her head.

"This girl has some ins and outs that need to be looked at, before she really gets her hooks into you." Ari sat her cup on the table. "I don't like the bitch, but then again I kind of do." She mumbled. "Give me your blessing. I will try to stick to all the proper channels, but things can become very illegal, very quickly."

"Will you stop it? Don't do anything, especially if you're going to use Shahir or his shady agency to help you." He crossed his arms shaking his head.

"Shahir and I built that agency with our blood, sweat and tears." Ari said feigning outrage. She chuckled as her phone chimed. "Shahir just got back to me about that song." Ari paused awaiting Seina's response. "So the artist wrote it four years ago, couldn't finish it and went through six versions before he released it. Four years to write a song." Ari shook her head.

"Give me the phone." He extended a hand over to her.

"Here." She handed him the phone.

"You know I can't read Arabic!" Seina said through clenched teeth. He threw the phone on the sofa and stood.

"Seina." Ari called, softly. He stopped. "It's called Leila and it's on Adrien Depaul's new album, Serenade."

"Leila?" Seina paused.

"Yep," Ari nodded. "These hoes be international." She sang out. "Well I have to go," Ari said stuffing her feet back into her heels. "See you Tuesday for dinner." She grabbed her scarf and coat, clicking to the door

"Bye." Seina called after her as the door slammed.

After gauging Seina's response to the news about the song, Ari decided to remove the metaphorical gloves. So, as she sat in her town car, black Manolo Blahniks kicked off and massaging her feet, she called Shahir.

"Shahir, change of plans." Ari said in Arabic, with a slight glance from the middle-aged Japanese man driving her. "You remember the package I asked you to put together on Michelle Yamato?"

"Got it right here," Shahir echoed back.

"Make a copy." She paused. "Forward one to Victoria Yang at The Eva Wong Modeling Agency, send the other to me." Ari said hanging up without another word. The rain picked up as Ari watched the city go by in swirls of muted colors, she bound for Jingumae. When the car came to a stop, almost without warning Ari slipped back into her coat and shoes, smiling graciously at the driver.

"Arigatougozaimashita," she said before closing the door, buttoning the knee length white coat.

"She speaks Japanese too." It was the familiar voice of caramel-eyed Darius. He stood behind her on the sidewalk, umbrella in hand.

"She does a lot of things," Ari blushed, reaching up to hug him, taking in the rich musk of his cologne. "Good to see you again," she pulled away to look at him, dressed in all black.

"I hope Indian is okay," His gaze locked on her.

"You know I love Indian food," she said as Darius led her along the sidewalk smiling.

Sister
Shibuya, Tokyo, January 29th

It was early morning, before the sun. Jade was asleep after another liaison with Chris had run longer than anticipated, following her drinks with Robert. In the pitch black of her bedroom, her phone lit up violently vibrating across the nightstand. *It's too late for all this,* she thought, reaching from beneath the covers. **New message**, the screen read.

Meet me at the Starbucks in Shibuya or I'm selling you out ~Tori
How did she get my number? Jade wondered. "Shit." She grumbled. Victoria knew she was here. Jade got out of bed, making her way to the chest of drawers on the other side of the room. She put on sweatpants and a coat, loosely tying her hair in a ponytail. She walked into the living room toward the front door.

"What, ah you *doink*?" Soo Young asked from her room. Jade jumped back with a scream.

"What is wrong with you?! You can't sneak up on people like that!" Jade shouted. Soo Young, stood in shadows beneath a green facial mask. The white of her eyes the only visible feature aside from the pink scarf in her hair.

"Oh sar-ri. Where ah you go-ink?" Soo Young pulled her pink robe tighter, and stepped from the shadows

"Out." Jade turned back to the door.

"Out where?"

"To a place, Soo Young! Mind your business!"

"Do some-*tink wid* a *certaint* man of *evenink*?" Soo Young laughed, trying not to crack the drying face mask.

"I'm meeting Michelle."

"So rate? Sound like pooty call."

"A what?" Jade snapped.

Soo Young repeated.

"Oh my God," Jade said under her breath. "Look, Soo Young go to bed!" She replied in Korean.

"Fine. Sorry. I just wanted to practice witty banter in English." Soo Young walked into her room. "Don't bring any presents back." She sang out.

"Siao wah lah!" Jade mumbled, moving to the door to slip on her shoes. She turned to lock the door behind her.

"What are you doing up?" Chris asked standing at the door.

"Why are you still here?" Jade replied..

"I got food and condoms." He stepped closer.

"I have to go. Don't be here when I come back." She said rushing to the stairs.

Jade briskly moved down the sidewalk; her arms folded to keep out the cool air. She weaved through the dying crowds trolling the streets and spotted Victoria, alone, at a table near the front window of the coffee shop. Jade watched her, saddened, yet sickened by the sight of her sister. She was likely on her way home when she texted, it occurred to Jade.

Victoria seemed much older and somehow less vibrant, than the girl she once knew. Jade strolled passed the crossing, watching Victoria. She was staring into a cup of coffee, sandy brown fur coat and long curled hair. *Beautiful. But so blind*, Jade thought preparing herself for a battle.

At this juncture, Soo Young appeared hopping out of a cab on the other side of the street. She watched Jade enter the coffee shop, lowering her sunglasses to get a better look. Soo Young was dressed in a trench coat and matching Carmen San Diego hat. She spined, ducking behind light poles, creeping toward the shop.

Inside, Jade sat across from Victoria in her sweatsuit and, black coat.

"You look nice." Jade said, an effort to break the ice. The scent of cigarettes and alcohol blanketed Victoria's fur and lingered in the air.

"Just finished a shoot. What took you so long?" Victoria spoke in clipped Mandarin.

"You're angry? You're the one who wanted to meet *me* at three in the morning. You'll wait as long as I want pulling that kind of shit." Jade responded in Cantonese, each girl speaking the language of her mother, though they were forced to learn both growing up.

"She finally shows her teeth." Victoria scoffed. "What did you do to your face? You look like an Albanian street walker. You were cute *once*." Victoria said, in English with a slight smile. That was the moment Soo Young crept into the shop, sitting down at a corner table.

"Is she *lesbin*?!" Soo Young mumbled. *That Chris can't cure you girl? I'll show you what to do with him.* Soo Young pretended to look at the menu, a wild puff of orangey-blonde hair peeking out from behind it.

"How did you know I was here? Jade asked, switching to British English.

"I saw you, at the party." Victoria said flatly.

"So what do you want Tori? Did Jun kick you out?"

"Jia Lang, this is about you."

"What do you want?" Jade repeated.

Victoria raised an eyebrow with a twist of a smile, sitting in silence. Jade got up.

"Jia Lang wait." Victoria paused. Jade turned back to look at her. "Baba wants you to come back. Zhang Yong is offering you clemency if you stop trying to destroy the company and just come home. Baba misses you and Zhang asked me to pass on the message."

"So, you haven't told him where I am?" Jade tilted her head.

"Not yet."

"Why now?" Jade sat down. "Why not just put that in a text?"

"Baba is in love," Victoria sat back in her chair, crossing her legs and arms, in one fluid motion. For a second Jade thought she misheard. "He misses us," Victoria said cryptically with that blank far away expression Jade could never read.

Meanwhile Soo Young watched them trying to make out the conversation by reading their lips, not knowing they were code switching.

"Baby I miss you and-*something*." Soo Young mumbled aloud, "*Something, something*-told you who I am. No. Why now, why not say *at* then." Soo Young gasped. "*Something* in love. I miss us." Her eyes widened.

"And if I say no, to coming back?" Jade said, shooting Victoria a lopsided smile.

"He'll come looking for you himself. He—" Victoria began Switching seamlessly back into Mandarin.

"Did Zhang say that?" Jade scoffed.

"If you come back, He's offering a pardon for trying to expose the company." Victoria leaned in closer with both hands clasped around her cup.

"There's no proof. And what does that matter to me?" Jade said almost laughing.

"There *is* proof." Victoria retorted. "And you going 'missing' the last four years only makes it more damning." She lifted the cup to her mouth.

"Are you threatening me?" Jade questioned, a full smile sweeping across her face.

"Why are you like this? Baba has been looking for you ever since you left that boarding school."

"Why didn't he look for Cole? Why did he send him away?"

"Cole is a different story." Victoria brushed the long chocolate curls off her shoulder, shifting back into English-outraged by the statement. "He's not a part of our family and his mother was something Baba dragged in." Victoria's nose wrinkled at that.

"Coal is different-something. His upper hours family *something* attic?" Soo Young murmured still trying to follow the conversation. *What kind of kinky mess?* Soo Young shook her head while sipping her coffee.

"Stop being simple. Cole is just as related to you as I am." Jade spat back.

Victoria crossed her arms. "Jia Lang you're ba-ba favorite, you've always been. Do you—"

Jade cut her off. "I really hope you realize your father sees us as pawns."

"He stopped being my father the day he let more people die just like my mother, knowing it would happen—knowing that Yang Wei was killing them from the inside. I came to him Tori and he did nothing to save those people. Almost two million every year," Jade paused, then in a whisper. "After he lost his wife to the same thing, he chose the money." She shifted her gaze to the window on the verge of tears, speaking clinically now. "Do you realize you haven't suffered half as much as your mother, or mine," Jade shifted back to Victoria. "—or even Cole?"

"What do you know about my mother?" Victoria shouted across the table.

"She was poisoned and as she lay dying in a foreign country, he carried on. After she died, your father made three decisions. Where to have her buried, where to send his only son and how to propose to my mother."

"Stop this." Victoria shook her head.

"I did the research," Jade paused, noticing Soo Young watching from afar, in yet another stylish but ridiculous outfit. It was then Jade switched into Cantonese. "As your sister I wish you all the happiness in the world. I hope you'll wake up one day and find yourself in the world you dream about. But as long as you help that man, I will curse the ground you walk on."

"Is that so?"

"It is." Jade nodded, just once.

"Jia Lang, our father's greatest wish is to bring his family back together."

"Then where is Cole?"

Victoria huffed, "Have it your way, Jia Lang. I'm done trying to talk to you. Don't say I didn't warn you. Zhang will come looking and he will kill you." Victoria said standing.

"And you think he would dare do that without *Liam Yang's* okay?" Jade scoffed, trying not to laugh.

"You've all but backed us into a corner. So, what would you expect? Baba has loved you thr—" Victoria, started leaned in over the table.

"So, your life—his life is worth two million other people's every year?" Jade quipped. Victoria stopped and just stared.

"You have all the answers, don't you?"

"I hope you don't get hurt in the crossfire." Jade stood. "I'll see you soon enough." She said slipping past her sister.

"Come back here!" Victoria shouted after her. Not understanding the words Soo Young leaned in, watching intently, as the few patrons and employees turned toward the commotion.

"Who do you think you are?" Jade turned to face Victoria. "Never mind, you don't know." The words came smooth and as constant as a babbling brook.

"What is that supposed to mean?" Victoria tensed, her voice lowering.

"You need others to give you an identity. That's why you *were* a good model all those years. But you're weak." She whispered, adding salt to the wound. Victoria slapped her, leaving the imprint of all four fingers

"You little bitch." Victoria raised her hand again.

Jade stopped the second blow. She flung Victoria against the window, brown curls and fur swirling past her face, a hand on Victoria's throat. "Careful, Tori. Even real sisters kill each other, from time to time." She whispered. "I let you slap me and I said that to hurt you. I'm sorry. But you deserve better than what you keep settling for." Jade let go, taking a step back. Victoria saw the manager on the phone. *Likely the police*, She realized.

"Okyakusama daijoubu desuka?" Jade heard an employee ask she rushed out and she strolled toward a line of cabs.

In her haste she called Robert.

Generals & Patrons
Tokyo, January 30th

Michelle's phone rang deep inside her purse. She locked the door to her apartment and glanced at Jade standing beside her.

"You gonna answer it?" Jade asked on the third ring.

Michelle already had a feeling who was calling, and fishing the phone out of her purse, she answered.

"*Hey*," she felt the guilt puddle at the back of her mind. "Sorry, I didn't call. I just forgot."

"Yeah?" Seina questioned on the other end. "It's good to know you're alive. You hurt *all* my feelings," he said playfully.

Michelle could feel him pulling away, could feel the distance forming and oddly she wanted to pull him closer. Jade led the way down the hall to the elevator with Michelle lagging behind.

"Look you're sweet, with the carrying me to my room and all that," Jade heard Michelle say as she stopped in front of the elevator.

"So, you *do* remember?" Seina fired back. Jade popped in her headphones deciding to listen in on Michelle's phone call.

"That's beside the point," Michelle avoided Jade's gaze.

"What is the point?" Seina asked, kindly but with *some* bite.

"I think it's best if you stop trying to see me." It came out in one seething rush as Michelle came to a stop in front of the elevator. Silence covered the other end.

"Do I stink?" He asked a moment later.

"No."

"Have bad breath?"

"No," she laughed softly, tucking her lips to stop herself.

"Then what; where is this coming from? Earlier this week *you* undressed *me* then passed out. Sex was on the table and it could have happened— but that's not who I am." His words drummed on Michelle's guilt and shame as she looked at Jade, patiently waiting for her to get off the phone.

Numbly the words shot out, with no warning. "My life is a mess right now with New York fashion week on the horizon."

"I gather that." Seina said, pointedly.

"So come," Michelle said, throwing on that emotional armor and quietly declaring war on Eva. "I'm not that big a hit in New York. So, *I'll make time for you*," she said throwing her hair back from her face.

"You want me to come to New York?" Seina asked obviously thrown by her words.

Jade's face went blank. She shook her head, willing this to be a joke, a cruel roundabout way of Michelle getting her point across—*whatever it might be.*

Michelle turned back toward her apartment. "I understand if you can't," She tilted her head looking down at her feet clad in calf length 'riding' boots, "But I won't be back until early March and even then I have family stuff to deal with." Michelle said thinking of her father's trial.

"Okay," he said briskly.

"You'll come?" Michelle smiled.

"Yes," Seina paused. "I could get one of the jets and take you. Like a work-date-vacation." He laughed. *Or is that a scoff*, Michelle wondered. "So, I'll clear my schedule as much as I can," Seina paused again, "*to be with you*," he added, the words sweet but a bit cloying.

"Michelle," Jade called, seeing a bashful grin splash across her face. "We're going to be late for Hikaru's show."

"Okay." Michelle nodded. "Hey, I have to go." She said in a husky whisper.

"I'll, talk to you later. We'll handle the details then."

"Okay, Bye." Michelle hung up.

"So, why do you suddenly want me to go to New York with you?" Jade pretended not to know the answer as they rode in a taxi.

163

"I would love for you to be there." Michelle smiled.

"Your publicist is coming and you know how I feel about *that* creature." Jade stared at her blankly. "Does this have anything to do with the phone call?"

"Jade—yes, I was on the phone with Seina."

"I know that." Jade scoffed. "No, I'm not going." She smiled before shifting her gaze out the window.

"Come on, Jade."

"Why are you pushing me on this?" Jade turned back to Michelle.

"Seina is flying me on his jet."

"Oh?" Jade said with mock surprise. "He just so happens to be pulling out the jet to take you to New York?" Jade nodded. "And it's not a commercial or a company jet but, *his*? I wonder what Ari would say about this?" Jade questioned.

"How—" Michelle started.

"A birdie told me." Jade sneered. "His voice carries. But anyway, I'm not getting involved with this." Jade shook her head and the cab came to a stop. Michelle turned to the driver and handed over the fare.

"You're moving like grandma today. What's going on?" Michelle said watching Jade get out, moving at a glacial pace. They stood on Meiji Dori Avenue near Aamteras, in Ikebukuro as cars zoom past them in the afternoon rush.

"I slipped in the tub and it hurts like hell. But I'm fine." Jade said, jokingly, taking to her lies more easily than one should. "I really don't think you should go," she said pausing to stand up straight on the sidewalk.

"With Seina, why?" Michelle stopped, letting Jade set the walking pace.

"Ari, for one, she's not gonna like it and I know you know Eva is going to flip too. If not just have an aneurysm." She turned to look at Michelle. "You like him." Jade paused. "I thought that was all lip service on the phone." She stared at Michelle for a moment.

"Stop." Michelle protested. "I think he's attractive."

"He'll hurt you." The words came, taking on a prophetic tone. The two women slowly made their way across the wide avenue.

"No, he won't." Michelle offered. "I can't let him be what he wants to me." She said ambiguously. Jade said nothing to this, though years later, she would wonder why Michelle had said it and why she never pried further on the topic.

They walked in silence for the next few steps, strolling away from Kiraboshi Bank northward, their destination in plain view. Michelle spoke again. "But since you brought Eva up, there's something I want to ask you to look into for me." She said not looking at Jade.

"What?"

"I think Eva is stealing money from me."

Jade paused, and turned toward Michelle.

"The checks are just weird, the fees don't add up, and they're not consistent," Michelle stopped to look at her "—but if she's stealing from me it makes me wonder if she stealing from others and—" Michelle trailed off.

"—And if so, what is she doing with the money." Jade nodded.

"Exactly. I've seen what you can do on a computer outside of ads."

"You have?" Jade felt her stomach tighten.

"Yeah, you do coding and all that nerdy stuff. So, will you help me?" They both stopped walking.

"I don't know, this might take a long time. I might not be able to find proof that would hold up to the law even if I find any at all." Jade protested, buttoning her coat.

"All I need is proof Jade. I'll pay you for it too. Ten percent of the money she's stealing from me." That sweetened the pot.

"I'll—" Jade started as her phone vibrated, she glanced down, **Robert** on the screen. "Let me take a look first, okay? Hello." Jade answered the phone.

"*Thank you,*" Michelle whispered.

Jade nodded, waving for Michelle to go into the gallery.

"Hey. No, I'm on my way to an art gallery with a girlfriend. Oh, I can swing by later. Okay. Alright. Bye." Jade smiled.

"What was that about?" Michelle crossed her arms.

"A friend." Jade was still smiling.

"The friend who has you walking like that?" Michelle joked.

"I told you I fell."

"No need to lie." Michelle giggled, taking Jade by the arm.

The gallery, as Hikaru put it, was a garage filled with student art. He said it was a student run showing, but this was not what was expected from one of the premier art schools in the country. Brick walls, concrete floors, exposed piping, and sliding garage doors. *Very urban industrial,* Michelle thought, straggling behind Hikaru and Jade. Looking at the various installations, and then to the couple walking arm in arm, Michelle's mind drifted to Seina and the prospect of New York. Could she really handle a fling? *Yes certainly.*

But he wants more than your body, a quiet voice whispered.

"Oh look at that one." Jade pointed to a sculpture of what looked like the David but with long locs shaded in life-like skin. Jade and Hikaru came to a stop.

"That one was done by our professor's favorite, her work is hard to miss." Hikaru smiled, looking from Jade to Michelle.

"The pieces here are pretty incredible." Michelle added, brushing her hair back from her face. "Where's yours?" She asked looking around.

"I can't tell you that," he smirked. "Just point out the ones you like." Hikaru said with a lingering stare. Jade, feeling awkward, let go of him and drifted down a few paintings ahead.

"I will." Michelle nodded. They stop, not noting the pause, until bumped— Hikaru slamming into Michelle, knocked by the over-zealous art professors showing the fruits of *their* labor.

"Sorry. You okay?" Hikaru asked as Michelle reeled from the blow.

"Yeah." She sighed, rubbing her shoulder and along her collar bone.

"I'll live."

"By the way, I might know somebody who could work as your trainer. I asked around after Ari brought it up at lunch," Hikaru walked alongside Michelle.

"Don't worry about that. Ari was just looking out, because I've been dragging my feet." She flashed him a smile.

"You know, I've been thinking for a long time—" Hikaru started but stopped.

"About what?"

"Quitting school. I can't pay for it—I'm not as good as—" he stopped again. "I don't know if my heart is in it anymore." Hikaru shrugged.

"But you have talent, Hikaru you can't just quit." Michelle placed a hand on his bicep, her hair draping the sides of her face, lips dewy. Hikaru wanted to kiss her. She was inches from his face. "Karu, where ever this is coming from, it'll pass. You can't let doubt snuff out your promise." And just like that, he had missed the moment, again.

In the corner at the far left of the gallery, Jade stood eyeing a painting that dominated the wall there.

"Wow," she said aloud, without realizing.

"Subarashii desu ne." An older gentleman stood beside her.

"Kandoushite imasu, totemo." Jade nodded to him, suddenly feeling tears and the swell of loss. It was this piece that stopped her, pulling Jade away from Hikaru and Michelle. The scene that arrested her was of a snow coated bay and a raven-haired beauty. Her Afro was bejeweled with snow as she looked out to the sea, watching ships crash along the rocks. It called something forth in Jade, as she would later discover all of his works did.

"The artist should be here." The man said in English, after hearing Jade's slight British accent through the Japanese. "There he is. Blue jacketo. Nandemo dekiru, kare ga." He said with pride. "Sadly, he will no longer be a student here, school's cost raising, scholarships falling and patrons not as many." The gentleman said, before glancing back at Hikaru and Michelle. "Hiroshi-kun." The man signaled for Hikaru to come closer.

"Tanaka kyoju. Konbanwa." Hikaru bowed, then glanced at Jade, seeing her wipe tears away.

"Hiroshi-kun kono—" The professor began.

"Is this your painting?" Jade asked, still wiping her eyes.

"Oshiriai?" The professor asked looking from Jade to Hikaru and back.

"Ah hai. Tomodachi desu." Hikaru paused turning to Jade. "Yes, it's mine."

"This is your mother," Jade paused, "isn't it?" She managed to ask, overwhelmed by the loneliness of Hikaru's work. She looked at him, the black hair draping along her eyelashes and Michelle saw the sparks for the first time since she'd known Jade, Michelle saw the *woman* in possession of Jade's sweet alluring eyes, rather than a girl.

"Your gifts have made room for you," Jade whispered as Hikaru caught sight of his brother storming out of the garage.

"Yu!" Hikaru called, causing Jade, Michelle, and the professor to turn. Hikaru waved a hand. Yet, the figure kept walking away. Jade turned back to Hikaru

"No, you won't quit." Jade said, trying to stop the tears. Her eyes meeting Hikaru's. "I'll help you." She smiled.

"You can also come on as my trainer, if you want," Michelle threw an arm around Jade, rubbing her shoulder.

"Fushigi desu ne, unmei ga." The professor chimed, laughing and patting Hikaru on the back.

"Sou desu ne." Hikaru smiled, with a slight bow to his professor.

9. After the Morning After

Harajuku, Tokyo, February 1st

"Sorry I just popped up at your place last night." Jade said to Robert as they strolled through the streets of Harajuku on the heels of brunch.

"Well I'm glad you showed up, and was overjoyed you stayed. It's been awhile." He smiled, throwing an arm around her waist, nearly blushing at what they'd done. Jade smiled back before glancing at the sidewalk then at Robert again.

"My new boss is crazy. She's just stressing me out."

"I will be your stress reliever, then." Robert laughed in her ear. He was smitten— and why wouldn't he be, after nine months of seeing her. Better yet, two months of Jade reeling him in, with lunch dates and coffee, then a month and a half of just holding hands and kissing, followed by five months of what Robert called mind-blowing sex, on an irregular basis. He was her's to do with however she wanted.

They were steadily sailing down the course Jade plotted out, and now she had access to his apartment and by extension some of his unclassified work. Though, Jade had to divert a few confessions of the L word, her work was finally budding, no matter how exhaustingly elaborate her façade had become. He trusted her, and now the only thing that eluded her, was one complex set of access codes in a format that sprung from the imagination of one Robert Harris.

Just one string, of letters and numbers, placed side by side in a *particular* arrangement. This is what kept her coming back to his bed, and living this lie.

"You know, I-I would like to see you more often," Robert said, hinting at a more serious step in the relationship.

"You see me almost every day, lunch, dinner, and now breakfast,

169

besides who told you to go live on Yokota?" She looked at him as a couple of teens shoved past her. "By the way, I still have to go home and prepare for my New York presentation," Jade lied. She planned to use Michelle's invitation to stoke Robert's fire for her.

Jade also hoped to set up an emergency meet with Ah Fan in person to help her glean, *something*. In the 23 times she had been to Robert's place she found nothing, and the limited hacking skills she possessed still got her nowhere. Jade was tired, she suddenly realized as she and Robert came to a crowded street corner.

"How the heck do you deal with all the pushing and shoving here? It's not like this where I live."

"You just do." She shrugged. "Do you mean Yokota or Oklahoma?" Jade asked as the cross-light changed.

"I'm proud to be a country boy, ad queen, so tell me what's the most popular design you've ever done?" Robert looked at her genuinely curious.

"That commercial for Kat-tun's re-launch album." Jade laughed.

"You did that?" He laughed. "That's so horrible."

"What about you Mr. Engineer?" She tucked her hair back from her face, as they walked to the other side of the street.

"That's classified."

"Oh, so you ain't done shit?" Jade looked him over.

Robert stopped by the curb. "I love you." He grabbed her hand, turning to look at her. She paused, looking into his big green eyes then ran her fingers through his hair.

"I love you too." The words cut her throat. He smiled, and she kissed him in broad daylight, for all to see.

Later, on the train ride home, Jade would think of this moment and reflect on the fragile nature of humans, feeling like the scum of the earth. *So delicate, that a mere three words can change the depth of our existence.* But for now, in this instant, she threw Robert's arm around her waist—pulling him deeper into her web.

"What time do you leave, again?"

"Tomorrow at eleven." She said smiling as Robert pulled her closer. "How about we eat a big meal then go back to my place?"

Hesitating, Jade rolled her eyes.

"Come on you're going to be gone for four weeks."

"Well, four weeks is a long time." She smiled.

Departure
Tokyo, February 2nd

Jade spotted Michelle and Ari just passed security. The two were clearly in a standoff, visible even at this distance— luggage off to the side, Michelle's crossed arms and Ari's tapping foot. It was a war waged in near silence, with eyebrows, and double-edged meanings. Still Jade marched into battle.

"Sorry I'm late," She said, continuing to play the young novice. "So Ari, are you looking forward to this flight with Seina?"

"Oh, you told her?" Ari cut her eyes at Michelle.

"You didn't tell Ari?" Jade turned to Michelle, shock and a touch of terror on her face.

"No, I didn't, it slipped my mind." Michelle lied.

Ari cut her eyes to Jade, then back to Michelle. "So, I take it she's with you?" Ari asked. Michelle nodded. "I expect to be better kept in the loop in the future."

"It took forever to find you guys," Hikaru beamed, walking into the tension, not realizing until it was too late. Each woman glared at him in silence. "I see I came at the perfect time." He cleared his throat, pulling his rather large duffle bag off his shoulder.

"Morning Heidi. I thought Jade was going to keep you company. Looks like you're going it alone today." Ari said briskly.

"What?" Hikaru asked, looking at the three of them.

"I'm in First Class, you're in economy, they're—" She stopped. "So, why are *we* flying with him?" Ari asked, flicking her bangs aside.

"*Him?*" Hikaru paused. Ari waited for Michelle to answer. Michelle sighed while Jade looked down at the floor.

"You set this up didn't you?" Ari looked at Jade now.

"Careful," Jade whispered back.

"Jade and I are flying with Seina," Michelle answered Hikaru's question, then to Ari. "Ari it just happened this way. Can you let it go?"

"I'm sure it did," Ari sang out.

"By the way Michelle," Jade cut in. "I got an invitation for Jun's—" she started.

"I'm not going," Michelle cut her off, glimpsing a pilot walking in their direction.

"Who's Jun?" Hikaru turned to Ari.

"You're not going to his exhibition? But I already said yes!" Jade exclaimed.

"Jun is Michelle's ex," Ari whispered, before jumping in. "I told Michelle it would be in her best interest not to go."

"When did we decide this?" Jade's eyes bulged.

"Around the same time, *we all* agreed to this trip to New York with Seina Terada," Ari spat. Jade said something in a rapid-fire response as Michelle pulled Hikaru and her suitcase to the left of the group, away from the two bickering women.

"Me? You could have given a heads up." Hikaru heard Ari declare as he and Michelle moved away from them and their clamor.

"Sorry." Michelle rolled her eyes, letting go of both Hikaru and the suitcase. "I won't ever let these bitches be in close quarters again," she sighed. "But will you be okay with her?"

"They are who they are. I wish I could say I understand." He shrugged. "Don't worry about me." Hikaru said, hearing Ari again.

"I didn't know you were here until that lunch." Ari said in a hissed whisper, suddenly noticing that Hikaru was listening.

"Please, nothing is a mistake with you." Jade scoffed in the same tone.

"Yeah," Hikaru responded to something Michelle said—half listening but focused on Jade and Ari's conversation. Ari quietly said something before she walked away from Jade to Hikaru and Michelle.

"Come along, Hilton," Ari muttered, inviting him to accompany her, red carry-on in tow.

"*Bitch*," Hikaru heard Jade almost belch as he and Ari, walked past her. Jade grabbed her suit case and wheeled it over to Michelle mumbling something along the way. "I told you she was not going to like this."

"That's why I forgot to tell her."

"Then why did she already have horns raging when I pulled up?"

"I told her to give Hikaru my room and that you and her would be sharing." Michelle looked at Jade grinning. "Unless you were planning to share a queen with Hikaru." She winked at Jade.

"Ms. Yamato, I'm George. I'll be your pilot today." A pilot appeared on her right. Michelle turned. "You and your party can come with me. Mr. Terada is already on board."

"Yes of course." Michelle smiled. "This is my friend Jade,"

George nodded at Jade. "Right this way. The pilot smiled leading them away from the security checkpoint.

Seeing Michelle and Jade stroll away from him and Ari, Hikaru stopped to wonder what he may have gotten himself into.

Swain
In transit, February 2nd

Post take off, Jade reclined in a massage chair eyes closed and mouth agape. While Michelle sat at a table across from Seina, looking out at the clouds. A stewardess cleared the table but, left the drinks. Seina glanced from Jade to Michelle.

"Where are you?" Seina asked pulling Michelle from the scenery.

"In the clouds."

"You know, I like your hair wavy like this." He said changing subjects. "You should wear it like this more often," an infectious smile stained his lips, slowly revealing teeth.

"You seem a lot happier than the last time we talked." Michelle answered, crossing her legs.

"Was I that different?" Still smiling he glanced at his drink. He could feel Jade watching him in silent judgement.

"Different enough." Michelle countered, throwing her hair off a shoulder.

"Let me show you something. Come on," Seina stood, taking Michelle by the hand and leading her into the cockpit.

"Asshole," Jade mumbled as the pilot, George, switched with Seina, taking a seat at the table across from Jade with a smile.

Inside the cockpit, Seina sat down placing his hands on the controls, resting the headset on his shoulders.

"Buckle up," he said to Michelle. "I won't bite, I promise."

"I'm not worried about a bite." Michelle laughed taking a seat.

"What are you worried about, then?" He looked out at the sky.

"You."

"Me? I'm harmless."

"Says the spider to the fly," Michelle grinned. His profile was lit up by the afternoon sun. *He looks like Godfrey Gao,* she thought wanting to kiss him. To taste those lips.

"Give me a little credit here, I just wanted us to be alone," he stared at her for a moment.

"And here we are." She stared back at him.

"Yes, here we are, after you barely responded to me and buff all my advances."

"I told you I don't want to make a mess." She looked at him with her eyes a glitter.

"Okay. I'm attracted to you and you know that. You know I'm into you. So what's stopping us?"

"Seina, what is *us*?" She brushed her hair back from her face, leaning in closer.

"That's what I want to discover, with your consent." Seina grinned.

"Hey! Hey! Hey! Eyes on the sky," she shouted.

"Sorry! I'm not driving," he laughed, as Michelle sat blank faced, but irritated. "It's sort of on cruise but I make corrections every so often. I just thought you would like this view."

"Way to scare the shit out of me." Michelle hit him.

"By the way, how did you and Jade become friends?" Seina tried to change the subject.

"That's a long story."

"It's a long flight." Seina smiled.

"Answer my question."

Seina cleared his throat. "I'm drawn to you." He held her gaze, with a smirk.

"Oh, and here I thought you were just a stalker." Michelle laughed.

"You don't get to do that," Seina pointed at her. "your turn, a real response this time." He said with raised brows.

"My life is too complicated for all of this right now, and though I am attracted to you, I don't know that we want the same things."

"I can help un-complicate things, or I might even understand them. I've been told I'm a very good listener." Seina turned to her resting a hand on his chin. "And how does one get to know another, if another is always avoiding him?"

"Slow and steady wins the race." Michelle said smiling.

"That, I can work with that." He chuckled. "So, tell me what exactly happened with you and Jun, if you don't mind me asking?" There was a touch of tenderness in the eyes.

"We had a work relationship and," Michelle paused. "I let it become more than that and it blew up in my face." A silence fell on her, wiping the smile from her lips and the glint from her eyes.

"What's on your mind."

"You." Michelle smiled, playfully patting his leg.

"Now you're making fun of me." He smiled back.

"Yes," she giggled. "And you like it."

"Are you this hot and cold with everyone, or just me?" He asked, glimpsing at her before his eyes returned to the sky. Michelle unbuckled the seatbelt.

She grabbed Seina by the chin, looking into his eyes. "That's who I am, Seina." She bent to kiss him, he tasted of mint, expensive vodka and the scent of roses—something she never had a taste for.

Seina pulled her down guiding her into his lap. He brushed her hair aside, his hand resting at the nape of her neck. Michelle pulled away.

"Before we left, I gave my room to a friend," she said with knowing eyes. "I hope that's not a problem." She stood.

"No. Not at all," he stared at her as she walked out of the cockpit in silence.

"That was quick." Jade commented when Michelle walked past her. "Was it not good?" George watched Michelle finish her and Seina's drinks in smooth succession.

"I'm going to sleep." Michelle said fanning, before walking to the small bedroom and further away from the cockpit.

Seina appeared, a moment or two later—face flushed. He placed a hand on the pilot's shoulder. "Thanks George, it's all yours." George nodded in silence, before walking back to the cockpit.

"Where is she?" Seina turned to ask Jade, wiping his lips.

"Oh, now you have something to say to me." Jade crossed her arms.

"You were the one playing stranger. I'm not getting caught up in a lie."

"Shut up." Jade sneered.

"We need to talk. Jade you have things you'd like not to be known, well so do I."

"Go to hell Seina. Why did you choose my friend, after I asked you not to?"

"You're friends?" He asked.

"Yes!" Jade said adding a question to the tone.

"You don't make friends." Seina stared at her, his brow wrinkled in disbelief. "Just let me tell Michelle about everything, in my time."

"You want me to help you lie to her. Why?"

"No not lie. Just give me some time, help me out." He pleaded.

"Time? If she asks the right questions, I can't help you."

"She's that good of a friend to you?"

"You're nosy."

"And you're diabolical. So what's really going on?" He stared at her, eyes narrowing.

"I can't tell you that." She said smiling. "No worries Lover-boy your new princess won't get hurt, not by me." Jade stood and walked to the bar at the head of the row of seats. Seina turned in time to see Jade pour a shot.

"But who does, since we're on the subject?"

"No one," Jade knocked back the shot, "Ideally," she smiled, looking at the bottle.

"What does that mean?"

"It means the more you know the more problems there'll be."

"Fine," Seina nodded. "so what's up with this publicist? You've met her right?"

"Yeah we've met. She's a fucking bitch," Jade beamed. "Why?"

"I want to meet the whole team."

Jade scoffed. "Team Michelle is all of four people as of now: Michelle, her agent, Eva, the publicist and the trainer."

"And the publicist is a bitch? Worse than Eva?"

"The kind with horns and a tail." Jade nodded.

"That means a lot coming from you. What's her name?"

"*Ally*, I think it's short for Allison." Jade lied, hoping to prolong Ari's game for her own entertainment.

The Big Apple
Manhattan, New York City, February 2nd

A black town car stopped in front of the Waldorf-Astoria, as the press swarmed the sidewalk, cameras readied. The door opened and camera flashes bounced here and there against the cold night air. Jade was the first to step out, her eyes covered with a hand, zipping to the lobby as the press zeroed in on Seina.

"It begins." She said, watching from the lobby. Michelle stepped from the car, cloaked behind dark sunglasses and Seina took her hand.

"What are your plans for Fashion Week?" Jade heard a reporter shout, the lobby door closing behind another guest. She saw Seina whisper into Michelle's ear. Jade turned away. *I can't use her anymore,* she thought suddenly. *I need another out, another decoy. At this rate the world will know who she is before I can get her to the front door.* She drew in a breath as Hikaru approached from the elevator.

"Hey, here's your room key." He said, coming to stand at Jade's side. "Ari told me to give it to you."

"Thanks. Where is she?" Jade said with her eyes still on Michelle and Seina

"She said she was meeting a friend." He shrugged.

"*Shit,*" Jade mumbled. "Well, how was the flight?" She shifted from the door to look at him.

He laughed. "Not bad."

Jade glanced to Michelle and Seina then back to Hikaru. "Are you hungry?"

"A little," Hikaru shrugged again.

"Good, your first meal in the city should be something amazing." She smiled, grabbing his hand.

Jade whisked him away to a cab and Hikaru, like so many before him, became lost to the city— to the pace and feel of Manhattan, stunned by the grunge, glitz, and glamor. Down Park, they rode into the haze of the city lights to dinner, on Broome in a quiet vegan restaurant, then the tourist shopping, as Jade called it, on Canal. Followed by the mad dash to a cab, that Jade jumped out of.

It was nostalgia that led the way for Jade, all the same places unchanged in some ways and vastly different in others. The city went on, without her. So, nostalgia played its hand, preying on her emotions. How else did Jade drift down Park, through glamor and grunge from:

"I gave Ari the name Ally just roll with it when Seina's around." She said this coldly—covering her tracks, in the taxi, en route to the restaurant. The softening along the edges, came later, over Teriyaki Seitan at Wild Ginger, with stories of high school and living alone in this ever-stirring city.

"Last time I was here. I was about to leave New York." Jade said sweetly, the unripe tears brimming. She huffed. "I was dating Min Jae." Jade mumbled but a bit too loudly.

"What happened?" Hikaru pried, suddenly very interested in her life.

"Huh?" She questioned shifting back to reality. Hikaru repeated the question.

"My Father, he pulled me out of school, and sent me to finish the year in Switzerland."

"Why?"

Jade tucked her bangs back from her eyes blue-black in the lighting. Her eyes lit with a sorrowful glee.

"I meant what happened with Min Jae." He laughed. "And the leaving." Hikaru added, with a smirk.

"You're flirting with me?" Jade narrowed her eyes at him.

"I'm curious," he said, picking up the check. It was the softening in this moment that made Jade forget the reason for coming to lower

Manhattan. This would become Jade's fifth grave mistake, the one that linked the previous four along with the two still waiting in the wind.

Now, as they strolled down Mulberry, Hikaru glanced at Jade every now and again. The city brought her to life. She glowed, the lights, in her hair, on her skin— vivid Jia Lang shining through Jade's dull coating.

"You don't want to tell me about you and Min Jae?" His pulse quickening.

"We got drunk on soju." She looked at him, then shifted her eyes further down the street. "I told him I loved him and that I was leaving."

"Why so hard?" He said unable to find the right word.

"Ijiwarui ne?" Jade looked at Hikaru, smiling but wounded by her own words. "We're inching into Chinatown, you can buy a lot of souvenirs, if you want. We might as well get the tourist shopping out of the way." She responded, changing the subject. "Maybe I can find soju or baijiu," Jade mumbled again too loudly, as they came to a corner.

"You're not gonna leave me too are you?" Hikaru laughed turning on Canal.

Hikaru strolled the sidewalks aimlessly among the dying crowds eyes a glitter, drawing the hungry vendors. Jade suddenly feeling protective, intervened in rusty Cantonese, thus saving a lamb from the slaughter, while inquiring about her contact, Ah Fan. That's how she missed the woman following them—pixie cut and dressed in all black.

"Could you get any more touristy?" Jade shook her head laughing and eyeing Hikaru's bags. He smiled, turning to a vendor, an older Chinese woman with greying hair pulled back into a bun.

"Where can we find soju?" He laughed in that sweet giggle that made Jade think of babies at the height of their elation. Jade smiled along with him, as the woman in black moved to watch from across the street.

The vendor said something in Cantonese, and then handed Jade a stuffed dragon about the size of both Hikaru's spread hands. The vendor glanced past Jade and Hikaru with the jerk of her head. The woman watching them, snapped a photo, while Hikaru continued browsing.

Hesitantly, Jade turned and made eye contact with the woman across the street, before she disappeared in the push-pull of people passing. Understanding the danger, Jade grabbed Hikaru. She paid the vendor. Dashing down Centre to Lafayette, Jade hailed a cab.

"Jade what—" Hikaru began as she shoved him, got inside, closed the door.

"Madison Square Park!" Jade shouted and the driver pulled off.

"What's going on?"

"Nothing." Jade looked down at the dragon, then to Hikaru. "Do you know the way back?" She paused. "Never mind, I get off, you go back in taxi," She said in a clipped accent, *slightly British*, Hikaru noted.

"Why?"

"Doesn't matter!" She snapped then closed her eyes, calming the sudden rage. She opened her eyes, then looked to the dragon, ripping the stitching she pulled a note out.

Zhang knows you're here. We'll find you, without a shadow. Here are the HEXD in case we can't meet, written in Ah Fan's hand.

Inside the dragon, Hikaru saw red, black, and blue marble-like spheres, before Jade closed the dragon up. The driver's music was the only texture to their silence, M.I.A's 'paper planes' adding to the tension and anxiety. Twenty minutes they rode, like that, in the livid hush of the taxi, until the car stopped. Jade handed the driver the money.

"Take him to Waldorf Astoria." She said getting out, handing Hikaru more money. She slammed the door, then walked into the park.

"No need." Hikaru bellowed, getting out. He followed her. "Did I make you mad with the soju thing?" He called to her while following. He continued along the stone paths, deeper into the park. He was no more than ten feet behind, when she sprinted, around the monument, into the dull darkness, where, like fog, Jade vanished.

10. Friend, Foe or Frenemy

New York City, February 2th – 3rd

"So early," Ari sat on her bed by the window as Jade closed the door behind her.

"I thought you would be still meeting your *friend*." Jade sneered, walking a bag of soju and soda to the desk across the room.

"I was. But I'm sure he's worn out," Ari laughed to herself. "I have work in the morning." She returned to painting her nails. "Were you with Hiroshima all that time? Midnight is a bit early for you, alley cat."

"I had something I needed to take care of if you must know," Jade mixed the three bottles of soju with pineapple Fanta. She paused to pull her laptop from her bags, placing it on the desk by Ari's bed, then she shifted back to the alcohol stopping to take a sip. Ari watched her all the while. *Naima has never been one to hesitate, she is a woman of action, rarely ever this much talk*, Jade found herself thinking.

"Is that pineapple Soju?" Ari asked knowing the answer. "And your not going to share?"

"You want to drink and paint your nails?" Jade responded.

"And do my eyebrows." Ari grinned.

"Fine." Jade poured a cup and sat it on the nightstand between the beds. Jade took a seat on the other bed with her laptop, shifting out of Ari's view.

"Push it close, please." Ari pointed to the cup. Jade rolled her eyes and handed the cup to Ari. "Okay honestly, I'm looking out for Seina. Why are you here?" Ari took a gulp and drifted back to her nails.

"I'm righting wrongs," Jade said, uninterested.

"Oh, that all? So *principled*." She cleared her throat. "That *is* good. Just like the old days. You know I miss—" Ari began.

"Let's not stroll down memory lane," Jade cut her off, placing an earbud in one ear.

"Fine." Ari put her cup on the nightstand, continuing to paint. "Seina is like my brother. I can't let some bitch just come in and ruin him or his money."

"That's not your decision," Jade mumbled, wondering why Ari remained so involved in Seina's life, and quietly at that. Then, she thought of how Ari suddenly became Michelle's publicist: packing up her life a whole world away at the drop of a hat. *Wasn't she living in Germany just a year ago?* But Jade dare not ask, for to ask demanded an answer, answering for disappearing midterm her junior year in boarding school, some five years from then to now.

"What happened with Michelle and Eva's brother?" Ari asked, capping her nail polish and lighting a cigarette.

"Michelle and I weren't that close then. I know she went to China with him, they came back and it was basically over." Jade paused, considering whether to go on. Ari nodded, taking a long drag. She exhaled, placing the cigarette in the ashtray on the nightstand between them.

"She told me that she never dated him." Ari paused to blow on her fingernails.

"Obviously, he didn't know that."

"So, she used him?" Ari lifted the cigarette, prompting. She glanced at Jade, trying to clarify, her questions leading to more questions.

"More or less, like I said we weren't close," Jade retorted, feeling the conversation turn interview, and not wanting to get caught up with Ari's scheme. Sensing this, Ari took another puff, and walked over to her luggage grabbing tweezers and eyebrow scissors.

True, Ari felt a kinship with Michelle, both: beautiful, well-traveled, with similar interests. They were like two sides of a coin, seductive and mysterious, fun and dangerous, *but blood is blood*, Ari thought. Jade took a gulp of pineapple soju watching Ari as she sat to pluck her eyebrows.

"And now you two are close. You act like sisters. I think you really like each other." Ari took a gulp from her glass.

"What is so special about her? That you are going through all of this?" Jade asked, her eyes still on the computer screen.

"All of what?"

"You moved from Europe to become her publicist." Jade said flatly, cutting her eyes in Ari's direction.

"I didn't know you were keeping tabs on me. Nice to know I'm still loved." Ari said sarcastically. "Seina has never pursued anyone this hard. I thought she might be a plant by Kohana or even Subaru but I see she's not." Ari put tweezers and mirror down, then spoke staring absently at the foot of her bed. "I can't read her. I don't trust her. Seina is delicate where she is not." She snapped back with a smile. "What are you doing? Drink up! I need you drunk so we can dance to Arabic music!" Ari threw her finger in the air, slightly moving her shoulders signaling a dance.

"I'm in the middle of something." Jade scoffed, just now feeling the third bottle added to the pineapple concoction.

"With what, you're always clicking on that damn computer."

"I'm editing a piece," Jade closed a command prompt, in fear of Ari's probing.

"What kind of piece?" Ari hobbled over. "What is that?"

"These are people dying from plastic and rubber poisoning."

"Why are you looking at that?" Ari clutched a hand to her chest. "We're having a good time and—" she trailed off, sitting down on the bed.

"It's a project of mine. And it's important," Jade stared at her in silence.

"What kind of freaky project?"

"It's bringing awareness to the issue. These people aren't using these products they're making them." Jade stopped, feeling a surge of heat overtake her face. *Funny Ari* thought, *doesn't her father have something to do with*—she paused mid-thought.

"Lia, when did you grow a heart?" Ari asked, playfully, "You used to be so distant, so detached. Like Wednesday Adams with a drinking problem."

"When did you lose your warmth?" Jade questioned, voicing words she never meant to say aloud.

"What does that mean?"

Jade froze not wanting to go further. "You used to be so much more than you are now, as a person." *More unneeded honesty*, Jade thought trying to contain the leak.

"What do you mean by that?" Ari stood up, arms crossed. She was irate, her eyes glimmered with a sudden burst of it, as her brows drew together, one slowly raising. "What the hell you tryna say?" She questioned. An untouchable past between them, now unexplainably violated.

"You're carrying something you didn't have the last time I saw you." The leak spreading, and the dam collapsing. "I don't know what it is and we may not be friends Naima but, we were never, not ourselves around each other. You're walled and dammed up in some castle and—" Jade started.

"You did that." Ari stared down at Jade unflinching. "You left with my I.D. and no warning. You left me stranded and then fucking disappeared from my life. You, friend. You expect us to go back to like it was?"

"No." Jade shook her head. "And I don't want to. But you asked and I'm tired of finding *other* answers."

"For me? Or you Lia?"

"For the world." Jade closed her computer, standing. "Good night." She walked into the bathroom, slamming the door.

Interruptions
New York City, February 6th

Seina opened his eyes to Michelle, asleep at his side as the faint rays of sunlight leaked into the room. He watched her, there, lightly snoring and in this moment, he was seized by the urge to kiss her. She wore his silk pajama top in navy blue, and green panties— the bra resting on the carpet.

"Morning breath," she grumbled, pushing him back.

"You caught me." He laughed. "Most women like it when I kiss them."

"I'm not them." She opened her eyes, pausing to wipe the sleep from them.

"None of them complained."

"They were more interested in your money," Michelle laughed and slid to the edge of the bed. Seina stretched out on his back with his hands behind his head, as Michelle stood, tying her hair up.

"Where are you going?" He grabbed her by the arm, pulling her back. "Let's have breakfast in bed."

"I've spent more time in this bed than the one in my apartment," she sat up on Seina's stomach, rubbing her fingers down the length of his torso and over his chest.

"What's wrong with that?" He stared up at her, pulling Michelle down to lay on top of him.

"I have work," she slipped from his grasp, her fingers again finding the long twisting scar on his left arm.

"What about me?" He shifted to his side.

"You can take a shower and get dressed," she smirked. He sat up, pulling her into a kiss. That was when Jade appeared in the doorframe of the bedroom.

"Good morning," she called, throwing Michelle's itinerary on the bed. Michelle turned, to grab the sheet of paper. "Ally made a few changes," Jade paused.

Seina sat up in bed, looking her over, wondering why she was in heels and a cleavage bearing top at six a.m. "Jade do you need something?"

"Just my friend," Jade said curtly. "Michelle can we talk?" Jade used a pitiful tone. She moved toward the bathroom and said no more. Michelle followed.

"What is this about?" Michelle's brow furrowed.

The tears poured from Jade's eyes as she hugged Michelle. "Jade what's wrong?" Michelle closed the bathroom door.

After ordering breakfast, Seina's suspicions began to get the better of him. He picked up a glass and crept to the bathroom door.

Listening.

"*He's into some bad shit, I know it,*" he heard Jade say. "*Drugs, guns, both- who knows.*" She exclaimed.

"*Do you know this for a fact?*" Michelle asked. Seina shifted the glass against the door, missing the next string of words.

"What's going on in there?" He knocked vehemently on the door.

"*No and I don't know, Michelle,*" Jade still crying.

"*Okay. Okay, don't worry about it. Everything will be fine. Hold on a second Seina,*" Michelle called. Seina dashed to the other side of the room.

"Where's breakfast?" Michelle asked, stepping out of the bathroom followed by Jade, red-faced from crying.

"Just ordered it, it'll be right up," he came closer, leaning in to kiss Michelle.

"Alright, I'm going to take a shower." Michelle walked over to her suitcase, while Jade tried to slip out of the suite unnoticed.

Seina nodded to Michelle, following Jade into the sitting room. "What did you just say to her?" He grabbed hold of Jade's arm. The water from the bathroom filled the background.

"Are you worried I didn't keep my end of the bargain?" She smiled, wiping away the false tears. "What's the problem? Seina you and I both know Michelle can't weather your family's power struggle. Besides that, you know her father's trial is coming up. And he doesn't need you bringing the press with you to trial. Not to mention she's already in hot water with Eva all the time, partially because of you."

"But what is your stake in all this?" He stopped and Jade smiled. She opened her mouth and a knock came from the door.

"We're not done here." Seina turned to get the door, where Hikaru stood on the other side.

"Hey, I'm Hikaru," he extended a hand. "Michelle's personal—" Hikaru managed before Seina cut him off.

"I remember. Come in." Seina waved him inside.

"Thank you, I'm looking for Jade. Is she here?" Hikaru stepped inside, surveying the entryway of the suite.

"Yeah, she's here. But I haven't seen much of you. So what have you been up to? Michelle told me it's your first time in the Big Apple." Seina said, trying to make conversation.

"It is. I've been taking in the sights mostly," Hikaru replied, as they walked into the sitting room.

"That's expected. So you've been hitting the clubs and bars—that kinda thing?" Seina took a seat.

"Restaurants and museums mostly," Hikaru said unsure whether to sit or remain standing.

"Nice! So, you really are a cultured man. Michelle said you are an awesome artist." Seina nodded to himself, distracted. Hikaru sat down. "Well my mother and two of my stepmothers love art. If you ever need a few buyers give me a call."

"Thank you," Hikaru smiled, looking vaguely uncomfortable.

"Oh, I'm sorry." Seina stood up. "I'll go get Jade."

"I'm here," Jade walked out of the second bedroom, behind Hikaru. The blue pointed stilettos, announcing her. She sat down in the arm chair near the window, directly across from the front door and Hikaru. Then Jade crossed her legs and the tension suddenly made perfect sense, to Seina. The eyeliner, and sensual red lipstick— their was attraction in the air. Hikaru watched her carefully as Jade looked from him to Seina and back.

"So, you were looking for me." Another knock on the front door sliced through the tension. Jade paused to look at Seina and Hikaru turned.

"Room service." An attendant called from the hallway.

"You're not going to get that?" Hikaru asked.

Seina smiled. "I'll leave you kids to your messiness." He went to the front door.

"So, what happened the other day?" Hikaru opened the conversation.

"I said too much, the last time. Just forget it." Jade shook her head.

"You ran away from me, in a park. That's hard to forget—" Hikaru started.

"Then leave it where it is," The bounce in Jade's hair was amplified by the rigid tension of her body.

"And here I thought we were friends." he stood. "Ally says to stay away from them today."

"What do you mean? Where is she?" Jade stared at him.

"At the control panel," he left a piece of paper at the end of the table before, walking away.

"Hey Hikaru," Michelle smiled, walking into the sitting room in a bathrobe in search of Seina and breakfast. "You're up early."

"Yeah," he smiled, and walked out the front door, causing Michelle to shift attention to Jade. Jade said nothing.

"Okay," Michelle nodded.

"The food is here." Seina called. Michelle walked over to the cart at the far left of the room, and picked up a slice of bacon.

"What did Jade say to you?" Seina whispered as Michelle came closer.

"Some trouble with her boyfriend or ex-boyfriend. I was too hungry to hear what she said." Michelle gave him a kiss, "What just happened?" She whispered back, grabbing another slice of bacon. Seina shrugged.

In the sitting room, Jade scoffed at Hikaru's exit, then shifted to the slip of paper: Three East Fifty-Second street, 11:30, it read in Ari's handwriting.

Tatsuya
New York City, February 6th -7th

Number Three East Fifty-Second Street turned out to be a restaurant as Jade discovered, La Grenouille. Upon entering Jade knew why Ari chose this place. *Just as pretentious as she pretends to be,* Jade thought.

It was as if Paris had thrown up one of its prized fine dining establishments in Manhattan— this deeply irritated Jade in ways she had no words for. The recessed ceiling was lined with yellowed lights, matching the shaded wall-lights between the tables. The booths and chairs were a rich red covered in an intricate woven design, on the backs of which stood tall vases with white lilies and long blooming branches of cherry blossoms. It was stuffy, like Eva's party, but French.

Jade gave Ari's name, and was taken to one of the best tables in the renowned French family restaurant.

"What is this about?" Jade's eyes narrowed, almost scowling when she sat.

"Tatsuya," Ari smiled placing a napkin over the plate.

"That's your brilliant plan? That's an act of war. You know Tatsuya hates Seina." Jade shook her head.

"I know." Ari smiled.

"Then don't call him!" Jade exclaimed.

"It's already done, we had dinner last night. I warned you by way of Howard out of respect. Now I'm telling you as an invested party, Tatsuya is going to stir the pot."

And that he did. By way of page six – Seina's typical form of New York headline, but Radio-One-Asia *herself* heard it first. Ari employed Tatsuya and innuendo, for the page six sighting—this requiring much less investment in a real story. The baseline: two mildly famous strangers, a man, and a woman, chat backstage at a fashion show, where a photo was snapped.

The dimensions came later, citing that Tatsuya Terada (older brother to Seina), posed backstage with *supermodel*, Michelle Yamato. By the time

AsiaOne and Tokyohive picked up the story, it had taken on a life of its own. Enews only bothered writing about the incident after Rihanna dropped in to talk with Tatsuya, while he and Michelle chatted over lunch. All of which was posted alongside circumstantial photos—photos that left a certain pot thoroughly stirred, and boiling over.

So that evening, as Seina walked into the suite, he was heated, despite the cool of the room. There were notes of perfume floating in the air alongside music— 'Kiss of Life,' playing faintly. Seina called to Michelle, but there was no answer, and wandering deeper into the suite, he found her, waiting on a bed of roses in a black bra and panties, in front of the fireplace.

She poured a glass of champagne from a bottle sitting in an ice chest— one Seina had failed to take notice of. He stretched out beside Michelle, then clapped his hands to turn off the remaining lights overhead.

"What made you do all this for me?" He asked.

"It's our last night here, in this room. I thought I should take full advantage of you." She took a sip from Seina's glass. "We can stop if you want," she joked. He said nothing, allowing the room to fall silent, Sade the only whisper. "So, your donation dinner," Michelle began, changing the subject and feeling some strain from him. "How did that go?" She ran her fingers through her hair, then through his.

"Did you have lunch with my brother today?" An accusation, not a question.

"No. I turned him down." Michelle inched away. "Why? How do you even know about that?"

"I read about it and saw pictures of you two just chatting it up." He said, staring at her.

Michelle sighed. "Pictures?" She questioned grabbing her robe from the sofa. "You saw pictures and decided to come question me? What— You think I want your brother now?" She put the robe on speaking coldly, clinical as she tied it and moved to the sofa. "Where is this coming from?"

"Why were you with him, after the show?"

"Answer my questions dammit!" She cast the cool tones aside. "Where did you see these pictures?"

"They're all over the internet Michelle!"

"Great," she sighed, then covered her face. Seina sat on the floor staring at her. Michelle's hands fell to her lap and they sat in silence. Five seconds past before Seina spoke.

"Why were you with him?"

"Your brother came up to me, while I was changing, being all kinds of friendly. So that must be a family trait. He asked me to lunch, I said no, and then he just showed up where I was, Seina. Then Rihanna popped up out of nowhere too." Michelle scoffed, then stood, walking toward the second bedroom.

"Look—" Seina started out, following behind her.

"No, you look!" Michelle turned to him. "I'm not playing twenty questions with you. Either you trust me or you don't. Either you want me or you don't. Clearly you need to go back to the drawing board. But I'll be gone in a few hours so don't worry about it."

"I just—" Seina started again.

"Just save that. I don't care. Don't call me," she said before closing the bedroom door. Seina knocked and she didn't answer.

"I don't trust Tatsuya. I'm wondering why he came to you. This isn't about me trusting you, Michelle." Seina shouted through the door to be heard.

When the door opened Michelle stepped out, in jeans and white shirt, a calf length black coat and thick red scarf.

"Hold on. Did you hear what I said?" Seina asked hands splayed. Michelle looked at him, pulling her hair out over the scarf.

"Same difference." She rolled her eyes, wheeling her suitcase to the door and leaving Seina to Sade and the fire.

Heathrow
London, February 8th

They stood, in silence around a baggage carousel at Heathrow
Airport, Hikaru, Michelle, Jade and Ari, jet lag beating all conscious
thought away. Jade sat on her carry-on, closing her eyes to the violent
florescent light overhead, trying to stay awake. Ari checked e-mails, but
finding the words too fluid she just scrolled, eyes closing, head, nodding.
Hikaru stared blankly, at the carousel in a haze, too sleepy to focus, too
wired to sleep, until a stranger appeared at Michelle's side.

While in a stupor, Michelle yawned, bringing a hand to her face, when
she saw *him* in the corner of her eye. She found this figure familiar, and her
eyes met his caramel-eyes. Hikaru was the first to see it, the chemistry, the
first to hear their airy banter and sense the air of danger that shrouded this
man.

"We meet again." Michelle stared at 'Can't say,' Hikaru taking note of
the man and his dazzling good looks, searching for flaws.

"We do." 'Can't say' laughed, tucking a Japanese passport in his
pocket, shifting to keep the other in his hand.

"And do I get your real name this time?"

"That I can't say," he smiled, as the luggage track moved forward.
Michelle pulled the remaining passport from his hand— the wrong one,
the real one.

"Cole Hale, interesting," she laughed. "To what pleasure do I owe this
chance meeting, Cole?" Michelle sneered, looking up from the passport.
Hikaru continued listening on the lookout for his bag as Jade continued to
drift. "That's a better name than last time," Michelle laughed, the sound
pulling Ari to attention and to caramel-eyed-Cole.

"That's a fake, my name is Darius and the pleasure is work." He lied.
"What about you? What are you doing in England?"

"The same, strangely enough," Michelle smiled, unconvinced of the
coincidence. Darius surveyed the surroundings catching Ari looking at
him. Their eyes locked. He nodded, then glanced to Jade, then back to

Michelle. Three points of interest, alongside three of contention, here in these women. Jade tried to open her eyes taking in deep heavy breaths. Hikaru grabbed his bag still watching this movie unfold.

"Well I have something for you, Michelle." Darius beamed, pulling an envelope from his coat pocket and handing it to her. "It's from your mother."

"You're still entangled with that one?" She sighed, stuffing the envelope into her carry-on.

"Friends of the boss I'm afraid," he winked. Michelle spotted her suitcase on the carousal. "Later then." She nodded to him.

Ari waited until Michelle went to retrieve her suitcase to make a move, swooping in on Darius like a hawk.

"Are you following me?" She whispered placing, a hand on Darius's lower back.

"Yes and No." Darius grinned. "It's good to see you again," he said when Hikaru passed, bag in hand.

"So, you know Michelle?" Ari questioned

"We met once in Tokyo," Darius watched Michelle haul her suitcase to the floor. Hikaru stopped within ear-range of them as Jade opened her eyes.

"I assume it was work," Ari asked as a statement.

"It was." He replied, leaving to retrieve his duffle bag. "I'll see you later," Darius whispered, walking to customs. Michelle appeared with her luggage, silently at Ari's side.

"Do I need to avoid him?" Michelle asked, the two of them watching him. Ari smiled until suddenly, she and Hikaru made out a hand-signal from Jade to Darius.

"Sorry what—" Ari turned to Michelle.

"You seem to know him. Do you have a claim?" Michelle asked smiling.

"What do you think?" Ari asked playfully.

"Who was that?" Hikaru questioned, inching toward Jade.

"I didn't get his name," she turned sharply. "Do you want it?" Jade rolled her eyes walking to the baggage carousel.

"But you know him," Hikaru said to her. *Lil Monet is sharp*, Jade thought, standing her suitcase up, *—too sharp*.

11. All Too Familiar

London, February 11th

"Is it me or is she different?" Jade asked, watching Michelle take the runway from backstage. She was attempting to break the silence between her and Ari. The silence having traveled, from their suite in New York to here in London, along with the lack of restful sleep. "It's like she's—" Jade began.

"No, it's not you." Ari cut her off. She shook her head watching models peel off clothes. "I can't believe there's two more weeks of this." She mumbled.

Jade scoffed. "You really hate Michelle enough to sit through two more weeks?" Jade smiled, tossing her hair.

Ari cut a look at her. "I meant to tell you, how nice it is to see you back in your slut-uniform. I'm glad you found style again."

"Thank you, fashion police. These are things Michelle got from the designers. I hope she's getting a real check too, or are you taking that for yourself?" Jade glared. "I'm off to the bathroom." She said without another word, pushing past, Ari.

"Fuckin bitch." Ari mumbled.

Down the hall Jade strolled, patting herself on the back for the clever comeback, that was until she realized she was being followed. Jade moved to the bathroom, to empty her full bladder, knowing she might have a fighting chance in close quarters. Here, she noticed her new shadow must be either very polite and, or a man since he did not follow her in. It was a thought that gave her no solace. She returned to the hallway, necklace in hand to use as a weapon. She saw Darius waiting across.

"What are you doing here?" Jade whispered, putting the necklace in a pocket and giving him a hug.

"Here," he handed her an envelope.

"What's this?"

"It's your way out of London," Darius said. Jade peeked inside. "At ten there's a—" he started.

"No." She protested, looking up from the plane ticket.

"What are you talking about no? You got spotted, Zhang is coming to find you."

"I'll take care of that. But how do you know?" Jade crossed her arms.

"Your guy, Ah Fan, he said he couldn't contact you. So, he found me." Darius said guiding her away from the bathroom. "Just walk away from this Ja."

"Ah Fan promised me something where is it?"

"What's on them?"

"Rent money, now cough it up," she said extending an open palm.

Darius sighed, then handed her three-thumb drives from his pocket. "You need money this bad?" He asked hesitantly.

"Untraceable money. Yes." She replied matter of fact, hand extended. Her face made up in the smoky colors of a glamazon.

"So now I need something from you," Darius said and Jade scoffed.

"Sure." She smiled. "But you owe me and I'm going to have to cash in that favor right now." She smiled.

Darius sighed then agreed as applause erupted from the direction of the runway.

Jade slipped Darius backstage, bringing him directly to Ari and Hikaru, away from the chaos.

"Look who I found." Jade sang out.

"Hello." Ari smiled, with notes of jolly surprise Hikaru stared at Jade then Ari in disbelief.

"We ran into each other in the hallway. He was looking for Michelle." Jade added.

"She'll be here in a moment," Ari flung her hair from her eyes.

"Hi, I'm Hikaru, nice to meet you." Hikaru extended a hand.

"Darius." He replied

"I thought it was Cole?" Hikaru said.

Michelle walked over to the group, fanning herself. "My feet *are on fire*." She hissed to Ari, then Darius turned to look at her.

"Do you have a minute?" He asked, before pulling her away from the group. "I need that answer before I leave." Ari heard him say. She eyed Darius and Michelle suspiciously. Hikaru was attempting to pry information out of Jade, which Ari found uninteresting, except for Hikaru's mix-up with the names. Yet, in her irritation, at the sight of Michelle with Darius, Ari's mind began to drift to a similar setting in Germany.

It was a graduation party for Ari's classmate, Halima, another Moroccan living abroad. They toasted the future with Moroccan food, music, and dance. Alcohol and smoke clouding the room with the music calling Ari to the dance floor— as it always has. Halima playing matchmaker, brought Darius Ari's way. Back then he went by yet another name. Halima introduced him in Arabic, raving that he was fluent—and that he spoke Moroccan Darija best of all. It was a lie of course. He spoke standard Arabic, and Japanese in addition to English but Ari indulged him.

Darius and Ari laughed for hours. He loved her Egyptian-Arabic imitations, and the mystery lurking in her eyes. By then, Ari's Darija, was a mix of French and it enticed Darius even more, or so he said. He leaned in closer, placing his fingertips on her thigh, licking his lips before a kiss.

"Let's get out of here," he whispered. She had smiled and sipped from her glass before agreeing. Surfacing from the memory, Ari moved toward them without thinking.

"Yes," Michelle sighed. "Let Vivian know, I'll be at the trial. I can't believe she sent you for that." Her nose wrinkled and she shook her head.

"That's part of the reason." Darius gave Ari a sly glance.

"You work too hard." Ari smiled, causing Darius to smile back at her.

"I'm also here to invite you guys out. Celebrity parties might last all night but there's no guarantee they'll be fun." His lips fanned out into a smile.

"Well there's the after party, we have to go," Ari said.

"That can be the warm up," Darius replied.

"Aren't you tired?" Michelle looked at Ari as Jade and Hikaru continued to argue.

"No, let's go." Ari smiled.

Disappearing Acts
London, February 12th -13th

It was after eleven when they started, this after party then another, until Darius took the reins. In a surprising corner of London, Michelle, Ari, Hikaru, and Jade found themselves amidst the sway of the Caribbean, where electrifying rhythms of dance hall and West African music pulsated. Ari stood at the bar a drink in hand, hips, and thighs rocking to the cadence, she knew Darius was watching her. She liked that he was. He watched taking a sip from his Jack and Coke. Hikaru, stood chatting over a drink with a rather nice gay man, unknowingly being flirted with, and enjoying the conversation.

Jade sat further down the bar, in her zone. It was the spot closest to the DJ, yet still close to the bartender. She leaned against the bar, took a shot, mouthing the words to every song. She was searching the crowd when her eyes met a blue-eyed stranger across the room. She flung her bangs aside, wiping a finger across an eyebrow, the stranger smiled. *Not him.* Jade cut her eyes away and continued to examine the crowd. She caught the bartender's glance and ordered. Jade shifted back to the crowd, body swaying intoxicated by the rhythms.

Michelle came out of the bathroom and some guy got her attention. *A smooth talker by the looks*, he smiled saying something flattering and Michelle laughed shaking her head. The bartender placed the drink beside Jade. Jade sipped as she watched Michelle. *So free, not a care in sight it would seem.* Jade shifted to Ari with Darius beside her.

"You look really good tonight," Darius whispered to Ari from behind.

Ari sipped her vodka tonic, "And the sun comes up every morning." She looked over a shoulder at him. A bartender slipped her a shot. *'Thank you.'* Ari mouthed.

The man nodded.

"I see you're not pleased. What is it?" Darius finally asked.

Ari knocked back the shot. "Nothing," she smiled, turning to him, flinging bangs aside. "You know, you're hovering. Go put those hands to good use," she said pointing to her fellow club goers.

"What number you on?" Michelle appeared and whispered to Ari.

"Five," she smiled. "Wait, six I just took a shot. How many have you had?"

"Five." Michelle nodded. "Jade said she lost count," Michelle pointed with her eyes. Jade was cracking jokes with an Asian man and a different drink in hand now.

"Look, old rodeo boy tryin' to chat me up while you and that *hefa* havin' a great time," Ari rolled her eyes, biting down on her straw.

"Who, Darius—I'm sorry I got the feeling he wanted to talk-to-you not t-a-l-k to you. Let's just go make a new friend," Michelle said taking Ari's hand.

"Hey, where are you going?" Darius stopping them.

"To meet people," Michelle replied all eyes and eyebrows.

"Hold up," he said.

Ari sighed. "I'll be back, Michelle."

"Ari—" she started.

"I'll be back." Ari looked up at Darius then led him to the open-air deck where the smokers gather. She turned. "What?" A blank stare swept her face, Rotimi's 'Want more,' bleeding to the outside.

"Are you angry?" He asked,

"About what?" Ari tucked her hair.

"I don't know."

"What's with you and her?" Ari pointed with her head.

"Her?" Darius prompted. "As in Michelle? I was tailing her,"

"I'm sure you're giving her a good *tailing*," she stared flatly. "This isn't about Michelle. I've known you for almost two years and I know next to nothing about you."

"I told you lying is part of my job. You said okay."

"I know I did, but now I'm saying never mind."

"Naima—" he started.

"We can do this all night. What do you do? What are you *doing* here?" She asked.

Darius bit his lip.

"Assassin, ninja, ninja-assassin?"

"Naima, I understand you're angry but, if I die or go to prison, which happens a lot in my line of work. I'll disappear. If I get shot right here in front of you, and die in the hospital, the minute I leave your sight I become a shadow. So, does it really do any good to know my name or what I do?"

"Yes, because I don't know you," she stared, waiting for a response.

"Naima, I can't tell you unless I know your all in." His eyes pleaded. "And even that's a risk for me."

Ari nodded, "And your real name is Cole? So we're three names deep."

"I go by Darius, that's what I said when I told you who I was."

"You also said you wouldn't lie to me." Ari moved to walk away. Darius stopped her. "Do you have something to tell me?" She asked, only now noting the fresh outlines of a Japanese style tattoo creeping onto his wrists.

Minutes later, Ari blew past Hikaru and his friend in search of Jade. She saw Michelle and the handsome guy—the smooth talker.

"A club rat if I've ever seen one," she mumbled. He and Michelle knocked shots back at the bar, and then she pulled him to the dance floor. Michelle's hips rocked to another pounding beat with the smooth talker dancing against her from behind. Ari walked over, his tattooed arms wrapped around Michelle's waist, the hands, on hips and thighs. Michelle whispered something to him after seeing Ari, then she grabbed Ari's arm.

"A shot and a drink," Michelle walked Ari to the bar. "What's with you and Darius," She asked getting the bartenders attention.

"We hooked up a while ago," Ari said tucking bangs back from her eyes.

"And?"

"And we never stopped," Ari shrugged. "Have you seen Jade? She disappeared."

"She was just at the bar." Michelle glanced to the place Jade had been seated.

"Yeah?" The bartender looked at Michelle.

"Two shots of your best vodka and two vodka sodas."

"A Long Island and a Captain and coke too," Smooth talker, cut in with a smile, handing the money to the bartender. "What's your name?" He said to Ari.

"Ari," she smirked.

"Ari, this is my man, Nate." Smooth talker pointed to a taller man, the color of German chocolate, who nodded with a grin. "Nate this is Ari, and Michelle."

"Girl, you fine as hell. Let me talk to you for a minute." Nate chimed looking at Ari.

"*Mmm*," She moved toward Nate, intrigued.

"You didn't have to buy us drinks," Michelle said shifting from Ari and Nate back to the smooth talker, pushing away thoughts of Seina.

"I wanted to." He licked his lips. "Aye, you remember my name?"

"Alex?" Michelle questioned, trying not to laugh. "Garfield? I know your name, Gabe."

"And what do I do?"

"Oh, we talked about that?" Michelle stopped to look him over.

"We did. Um just tryna see if you fucked up, you had a lot," he said, his plump lips moist. The bartender sat their drinks down, handing Gabe the change.

"I know," Michelle smiled, handing Ari her the shot. Michelle and Ari knocked them back in unison, chasing with vodka soda. Michelle downed her drink and turned to Gabe. "Let's dance doctor Gabe," she pulled him back, leaving Ari to her own devices.

It was only later, around last call, that Ari suddenly remembered what she wanted with Jade.

"Michelle," Ari shouted near her ear, the girl still dancing with Gabe. Michelle stopped. "Where's Jade," Ari asked.

"I don't know she was talking to Gabe's other friend a while ago," Michelle looked around the club.

"Okay, maybe they hit it off." Ari shrugged, knowing that not to be the case. Gabe came to retrieve Michelle, already in his coat, with 'last call' echoing all-around.

"I'm gonna go." Ari said in French to Michelle, motioning to Nate discreetly.

With Nate,' Michelle mouthed.

Ari nodded. Michelle grinned at that as Ari walked away in search of Jade.

"Hey, where'd your friend go with mine?" Michelle asked turning back to Gabe.

"I don't know," he tried to kiss her again. Michelle turned her face, and he got cheek.

"Aren't you sweet." She laughed.

"Uma show you how sweet," he licked his lips, turning her face to kiss her. The baritone voice resonated with her, *he meant that,* she thought, pulling away. Michelle looked at Gabe, throwing hair over her shoulder.

"I just got out of some—" she said looking into his eyes.

Gabe licked his lips and cut her off. "But this is you and me. Come back to my place," he took her hand, pulling her closer. "We both know you want to."

Michelle smiled, then shook her head. She kissed Gabe again and backed away, joining Ari and Nate.

Ari spotted the Asian man she saw Jade drinking with at the bar earlier. He was seated at a booth with another woman now. She stepped in.

"Sorry, do you know where my friend went?"

"We left together and she buggered off," he said with a heavy British accent.

"Of course." Ari's face tightened just realizing the happenings, *Darius and Michelle, the party, then the club, the alcohol, and so many other distractions. They were in this together*, she thought. "She's gone, again," Ari said to herself, she walked past Hikaru again, still with his new friend. "Hayden we're leaving." She announced. "Where did Jade go?"

"I thought it was Hikaru?" The other man asked.

"It is," he shifted to Ari. "Yeah, Michelle told me." He sipped from his beer.

"You know ol' boy wanna fuck you, right?" Ari whispered completely shattering her polished façade. She looked the man over, and then walked away. Hikaru watched her slip into her coat.

"So, you want to get out of here? Go back to my place?" The man asked sweetly.

"What? I—I'm not gay," Hikaru stammered, "I have to go," he gulped down his beer and followed Michelle, Ari and Nate. Ari grabbed her phone to check the time.

Hey, I'm off with this guy! See you when I see you, night-night! —Jade, from over two hours ago. A weak cover story.

The *Safe* Choice
Tokyo, February 15th

Jade slumped down on her sofa, exhausted from the journey back to

Tokyo. Her suitcase stood at the door with her shoes as she closed her eyes, drifting to sleep—still in her coat.

After escaping Michelle and Ari in that club, Jade collected her things. Using the banking credentials Darius provided, she put together funds, and fenced a few weapons. Upon her return to the hotel, Jade turned her sights to the classified documents delivered as payment for acting as the go between. It was then Jade did something reckless. She took a standby flight, London to Dubai. It was the furthest going east, and leaving within the hour, with a seven-hour layover.

She loved Dubai. It was one of her favorite places, and she had to buy perfume. Coffee beans in one hand, like dice in a gambler's, she sifted through countless perfumes: Rosewater, Bonjour l'amour, Pink play for her. One after the other, she was a mad-woman doped up, in her element.

Now, in Tokyo, Jade woke herself snoring in the dark of her apartment as the sun's rays played out on the horizon. In her lap sat a pile of tests and studies. Jade knew these, alongside the documents she acquired in London would silence the guilty conscience that has plagued her for as long as she could remember. Only at the cost of fencing weapons on the black-market— something Jade swore she would never do. *But the tally of sins will only grow from here,* she thought sitting up to answer the phone ringing in her pocket.

Two missed calls, a voicemail, and a text message the notification icons announced. Jade listened to the voicemail. She was fired as of a week ago, so she dismissed the missed calls from work and opened the text message from Robert.

When do u come back again? I miss you.

Jade smiled as she typed her response. Grabbing her suitcase, she wheeled it into her room. She closed the door behind her, with plot shifting into high gear.

Stepping from bathroom to bedroom in a towel, Jade dried light honey blonde hair. Then turning the heat on, she sat down on the bed in front of a mirror. Jade crossed her legs gathering her weapons. She began by searching for and finding an old tube of Arabic style eyeliner— a gift from Ari in years past. Briefly Jade glanced at Arabic words she almost remembered.

With the outfit decided, she stared at a more recognizable self. The blonde hair, dark eyeliner and red lipstick reminiscent of the woman she always wanted to be. It was at this juncture, Jade opened her suitcase looking for her scent. A spray of Rose Water, Davidoff for her chest, at her wrist Pink Play. Lastly to her thighs, and the sweet nectar there between, she added a splash of play, Givenchy.

Jade exited the subway at Shinjuku station floating up to street level like a balloon. She spotted him— tall, dark haired and green-eyed Robert.. He stood, waiting for her, continuing to search the crowds as she walked past him. Red heels, dark jeans, and a black corseted top paired with a red scarf and a black peacoat.

"Are you lost?" She called to him. Blonde bangs over smoldering, smoky eyes.

"Jade? Wow. You look—" He paused, but trailed off.

"Good to see you too," she went in for a hug, pressing her breast to his chest, her hands on his shoulder blades. Her scent gripped him whole—with no warning. A hoard of people split and moved around them when they parted. "Are you hungry?" Jade pulled away holding him at arm's length.

"Yeah, really hungry."

Clearly, for more than one thing, she thought.

"How do you feel about Chinese food?"

"I like American Chinese food." Robert took her hand. They strolled further away from the station.

"Have you ever had Chinese-Chinese food?" She questioned walking hand in hand. "I mean Chinese food real Chinese people eat."

"No, I guess not," he laughed, looking her over again. Jade flung her bangs aside, smiling at him. Robert punctuated this with a kiss. Jade bit his lip when he tried to pull away, looking from his lips to his eyes.

"Come on. I know a place."

They sat down in a bustling restaurant, with dim lighting, the kind romantic enough for a date but still trendy enough to double as a lounge. The restaurant carried with it the feel of Shanghai in the twenties, despite the constant flow of Mandarin spilling over from the kitchen.

Robert took off his coat, making himself more comfortable in their booth.

Jade reached across the table and ran fingers over Roberts thick stubble. "I wish you weren't military. This beard is sexy on you."

"Koban wa—" the waiter said, appearing with menus in hand. He stopped, to stare at Jade and the *excess* exposed skin— cleavage and shoulders bare. Jade turned to him without pause, playing with her necklace as Mandarin poured from her. Robert watched her, point, smile, specify in detail, from what he could tell. The waiter nodded, taking pen to paper

"Robert, do you like spicy food." Jade asked, sweeping blonde bangs from her smoky eyes.

"Yeah, I can do spicy," he smiled.

"Okay. Thank you," Jade said in Mandarin, handing the waiter the menu. "Sorry that took so long, my tones are off and we had to switch to Cantonese," she lied. "Guess I'm getting rusty," Jade beamed.

"You're amazing," Robert said, though smitten, he truly meant it.

Jade, both touched and caught off guard by his words, decided to kiss him. "You're sweet," she smiled.

"I'm serious. Does no one tell you that?" Robert grinned back, staring at her. "You're amazing," he took her hand. "That's why I can't get enough of you." The sincerity in his eyes, cut Jade to the bone.

Were she not the rebel seeking to destroy her family company and he a conveniently good-looking piece of the puzzle, she could settle with this man, and lead the life of a military wife. *Pop out a kid or two, and tie up the old tubes, then grow old, with this* safe *choice.* But Jade laughed at this thought as the waiter returned, helping to reinforce her plan. The waiter placed shot glasses in front of each of them, then sides, alongside a bottle of Baijiu. Jade poured a glass and took a sip.

"What's that?" Robert asked.

Jade just beamed. "If we're more than friends, bottoms up," She poured a shot into his glass, trying to cover the amitriptyline-sertraline powder in the glass. "If not just take a sip."

"Okay," Robert took the shot and Jade moved to sit beside him.

She smiled at him, before kissing him again. "Robert, I need something from you." She took a second shot without pause.

"Really? What?"

"The H.E.X.D. program codes."

"What—" Robert started, pulled away from her by the topic. "What are you talking about? I don't know where—" he flew into cover up mode.

"I know what can happen, and if you help me, you can deny ever knowing anything." Jade went on, the air suddenly stale, and his image of her cracked. "I'll have a ticket for you within the hour to any country that doesn't extradite, *just help me.*"

"No," Robert shook his head.

"I chose you, Robert. If you help me, I can get you almost anything you want."

"You—you—" Robert started on what Jade knew would become a rant, a rant that came to a point at: "You're playing with my life, and my career, and my work. What is wrong with you?!" He asked, giving Jade the outburst needed to elevate the situation.

"The owner of this restaurant is looking out for me. He'll say whatever I say. Like one of your drug deals went sour, then your commander will have reason to search your place and find the evidence I planted," she bluffed. "Help me, and your life can stay the same or completely change for the better. I don't want any more people to die because you wouldn't help me." she said sounding miles away. "Let's go." Jade stood, glancing to the man at the register, who nodded back.

"I'm not going anywhere with you!"

Jade grabbed Robert's coat and her jacket, without so much as glancing at him. "You *will* help me." she said only loud enough for Robert's ears.

Robert leapt to his feet, sluggishly. He smashed the bottle of Baijiu and grabbed Jade, holding it to her neck.

"Don't move!" He shouted to the room, jerking her toward the front door. The patrons, froze watching him.

"Let me go!" Jade protested. "Taskute! Korosu tsumori!" She screamed to murmurs and horrified gasps.

"You were using me." He hissed, his eyes growing heavy.

Jade elbowed him in the groin. Missed once, then twice. It was then the elderly mother of the owner, appeared like a ghost, breaking a toddler-sized bottle over Robert's head. He let go of Jade and slammed the old woman into the wall. Robert stumbled, then slumped to the floor. Jade walked back to the counter and a wave of Mandarin spilled forth in apologies. Jade handed the owner money, bowing before him.

"No," he waved a hand. "This is for my sister," he said. Jade bowed again, and his aged mother touched Jade's head.

"Avenge us," the woman said in Mandarin.

"Follow my wife." The owner tried in broken Cantonese. "My sons will take the man." The old woman nodded at his side. Jade bowed again, following the owner's wife out of the restaurant.

Unveiled
Milan, Italy, February 21st

Drifting from the usual ambiance of yet another gala, Seina glanced at his phone re-reading Ari's text, when he spotted Michelle on the other side of the room. She wore a long purple gown with lace along her waist, form-fitting at her hips before falling heavy to the floor. Seina knew she was in Milan, and that he would see her again, at some point, *soon*. Yet he hoped not *so soon*, and not with proverbial egg still on his face. Or at least not while still feeling the sting of slyly calling her integrity into question— then having everything she said confirmed by a stranger. *Too late.*

The source of the sting, however indirect was another model Seina slept with his first night back in Milan. Said model heard from a stylist in London, who got wind of a whisper from one of the make-up guys, who had lunch at the restaurant mentioned in the papers. The unnamed make-up artist, claimed Tatsuya came in after Michelle. That she was surprised at how Tatsuya sat down flirting and just *'doin' too much,'* before *'flagging down Ri-ri'* to the table for an all too brief chat.

Incomprehensible.

She wasn't lying, about any of it, he thought, blindly blowing past all the secondary questions like: why would Tatsuya bother with one of his girlfriends, or how did he even know where to find Michelle.

Seina's work-friend, and plus one pulled him from his thoughts, as he excused himself. So, Seina took the opening.

"Good to see you again," he said, walking over with a glass of champagne.

"Where did your date go?" Michelle asked texting Hikaru and Ari. "I hope it wasn't me that turned you gay." She looked him over. Seina laughed, in that scoffing way Michelle always managed to pull out of him.

"My *colleague* went to the bathroom," he sipped, admiring her, and that her hair was curled—albeit loosely. *So she took the complement to heart.* "I see you're here solo. Where's the team?"

"Ari and Hikaru are here somewhere, looks like I lost them. While Jade bailed on us in London, apparently she flew back."

"*Ari?*" He questioned.

"Oh, yeah. Jade was playing some kind of joke Ally is Ari, her real name is Naima. I'll introduce you once I find her."

He paused, the picture suddenly becoming clear, all too clear, along with the reason for Ari's message. All the irregularities suddenly came to a head, then the thought dawned that Naima was here, *lurking closer than imagined.*

"I hear you attacked a stylist today," he smiled, changing the subject and trying not to chuckle.

"Attacked is a strong word. He burnt me with the curling iron, so I snatched it from him and motioned to hit him with it." Michelle glanced at the floor and laughed. *Odd*, she thought, *to be here talking with Seina* and laughing like they didn't just storm off like children less than two weeks ago. "I guess that's why everyone is snubbing me."

"Are you okay?" He was trying not to show too much concern.

"I'm fine," Michelle adjusted her hair over the burn on her neck, as she glanced up from a text message.

"How big is the burn?"

"Don't worry about it." Michelle hit his arm. "Wow, I see yo mans is keeping you in shape," she laughed, trying to avoid any deep conversation.

"Michelle, stop playing," Seina gazed at her, their eyes locked, for the first time since they parted. "I jumped to conclusions," he felt a growing sense of shame. "I'm sorry," he glanced down at the floor briefly, then looked back to her. That was when he saw Ari. She was trying to stay out of sight, by slipping into the foyer of the ballroom.

"I-have-to-go." Michelle turned.

"Michelle," Seina stopped her. "Let me know when you have some time. I need to talk to you about some other things I should have said earlier."

"Oh?" She asked sweetly, lips curling into a smirk. "Tell me."

"It's not a good time or place, right now."

"I'll check and get back with you—" Michelle trailed off. She saw Darius near one of the giant swan ice sculptures stationed protectively by the buffet of alcohol. He smiled, picking up a glass of champagne, then waved to her. She waved, and Seina turned to see what pulled her attention away.

"Seina, I'll be right back." She said walking over to Darius. "What are you doing here?" She beamed after crossing the room. "Have you seen

Ari? She disappeared on me."

"I had work, in the area, and I was just looking for her when I saw you." Darius grinned with a look at Seina.

"So, what's the story with you and her? I figure since you left us in London too. Something—" Michelle began.

"Michelle, I know you mean well but, I got this."

"Fine, then tell me what's up with you and Jade." She stared at him smiling.

"Are you trying to figure me out?" He laughed. Seina watched them from across the room, jealousy beginning to bubble in his chest.

"A little bit." Michelle laughed.

Laughing, why is she still laughing, Seina thought watching Michelle and the tall cinnamon colored man walked into the foyer. *Nothing in the world is that amusing.*

"Jade is a whole other thing." Darius grinned, with a hand on the small of Michelle's back, while Seina watched them leave.

"But there is something there. Is this a love triangle? You show up, she leaves us with a weird message and then you disappear too." She leaned against a wall, her arms crossed, as she stared at Darius for a long moment waiting for a reply.

"Jade is trying to stay off the radar. You and Seina Terada put her back in the limelight. So, she had to go."

"What are you talking about?" Her eyes narrowed more intrigued by this.

"That's cute. You think I'm going to tell you," Darius' grin grew. That was when Hikaru appeared, walking toward them, and looking uncomfortable in his tux.

"Hey Cole," he interrupted. "Michelle we're about to go."

"Where have you and Ari been? I was looking everywhere." Michelle stood up.

"I was keeping the slagathor company," he joked.

"Of course. Well, lead the way," Michelle followed Hikaru with

Darius in tow.

"Hugo, I asked you to bring Michelle, just Michelle." Ari said ending a phone call.

"It's Hika—" He began, before seeing the light switch off and her attention shift to Michelle.

"Michelle what's with the cryptic text," Ari said avoiding eye contact with Darius. "It's too early for you to be that drunk."

"Sorry I was talking and texting. Tomorrow can I squeeze in dinner or lunch with a friend, between a show maybe?" Michelle questioned with a smile.

Ari shifted to her phone and paused. "You have maybe an hour at four and that's cutting it close," She slipped the phone back into her clutch, looking out for Seina.

"Okay great," Michelle nodded.

Ari glanced at Darius who stood, silent and handsome. He caught Ari looking at him, and Ari shifted her attention back to Michelle.

"Michelle that's one hour, going, sitting, coming back, going to the show," Ari stressed.

"I understand, I'll go somewhere nearby."

"Don't be late," Ari flung her bangs aside, reaching for her phone again.

"I won't be." Michelle sang out. "Hikaru let's go." She grabbed his hand leading him over to the alcohol inside the ballroom, leaving Ari and Darius in silence.

Darius cleared his throat. "You look amazing. Red and Black have always been your colors," he smiled. Ari scoffed. "You have a good friend in her."

"We're not friends." Ari cut her eyes at him, only to see Seina walking in their direction.

"Looks like trouble," Darius whispered.

"Tell me you're not here doing what I think you're doing," Seina said before pausing. "Sorry, excuse us." He said acknowledging Darius.

"I'm not here doing what you think I'm doing?" Ari shrugged. "You know I don't lie." She said flatly.

"Naima I told you to leave her alone and here you are—" Seina started.

Darius cleared his throat.

Seina paused to look at him.

"Hi, I'm Darius." He cut in. "I was in the middle of talking with your sister, Seina."

Seina paused. "You were also just talking to Michelle. Who are you?"

"Darius," he said in quick reply.

"Seina I'm, protecting you." Ari cut in. "She loves Adrien Depaul, the man that wrote seven songs about her. He just called—" Ari started and Seina cut her off.

"Naima I want you gone, you have three days. Not three and a half, not three and a quarter. I mean it, quit and find another job that has nothing to do with Michelle. Got it?"

Darius' brows rose at that. He waved to Ari and walked away in silence.

"Fine," Ari said to Seina while watching Darius leave.

"Who was that guy?" Seina asked, motioning to Darius.

"If you don't want me prying in your life, why would I welcome your prying in mine?" She shot back quickly. "Why are you looking for Mich—" Ari changed the conversation as she saw Michelle and Hikaru approach, drinks in hand.

"Oh." Hikaru said to himself, trying to change the trajectory, after seeing Seina and Ari exchanging words, *too late*.

"Wow!" Michelle announced to find Seina and Ari talking. "You two finally met." The two couples came closer.

"He was looking for you." Ari glanced back to Seina.

"Really? I told you I'd be back." She grinned at him. "Seina, this is my publicist, Ari Louien. Ari this is Seina Terada."

"Publicist, huh?" He chuckled, looking at Ari then smiling at Michelle.

Hikaru stood with Michelle at his side, caution ringing in his ears. There was also the long-withheld belief that Ari and Seina knew one another.

"What happened with Darius?" Michelle shifted to Ari.

"Nothing. I'll see you in the car. Excuse me," Ari mumbled to Seina and Hikaru, then walked toward the exit.

"She's moody that one." Seina scoffed.

"She's still a good person," Michelle said, avoiding his eyes.

"Guys, I'm going to go check on Ari." Hikaru cut in. "Nice seeing you again, Seina." He said excusing himself.

"Thank you Hikaru," Michelle whispered, placing a hand on his arm.

'No problem,' he mouthed back.

"How long has she worked for you?" Seina asked.

"About three months?" She shrugged.

"Watch out for her, yeah? You never know what people are really after. So, about that chat," Seina switched topics while a steady stream of guests, began to pour out in the foryer.

"Four o'clock, in Paris. I'll send the address and I'll be at the bar."

"I'll be there," he nodded.

"I'll text you if anything changes," Michelle turned to walk away, as the ballroom emptied.

Downstairs, Ari ended a call to the driver when she was stopped by Darius a mere three steps from the door to the carport.

"I had to see you before my job here ended," he said.

Ari snatched her arm away, her earrings clanging. "Let's stop this. You can't be honest. So, I don't want to do this anymore. Good night, and goodbye." She took the three steps to the car without so much as glancing back at him. The door closed, and dumbfounded, Darius stared at it in silence.

12. Headliners
Paris, February 23rd

Michelle rushed to a restaurant down the street from her hotel clutching her coat closed. The Parisian winter winds howled at the mess of waves that adorned her head, cascading down her back. She was wearing a grey sweater and jeans, Seina noted, more casual than he had ever seen her. He watched Michelle from across the street between two buildings. He had watched Adrien enter this same restaurant, moments before. This was likely Ari's doing, he realized, but he had to be sure.

He had to see them *together*, to be certain. Seina turned the corner, making his way to the small eatery, not knowing what to think, he prepared for the worst. He moved along the busy sidewalk trying to keep his hurried stroll from shifting into a sprint. It was a quiet voice that urged him to go earlier, to wait, and a good thing he did. Seina knew Ari *would not* go quietly. That was too easy. So after Michelle sent him the address, he felt in his bones something would be waiting in the wind.

He was about to step into the crosswalk, but stopped. Seina saw Michelle storm out of the restaurant. Adrien gave chase. The older taller man grabbed a handful of loose sweater— just enough to stop her. Seina froze. Though firm, Adrien was loving with her, yet Seina wanted to see Michelle's response. He needed to—to be assured, once and for all, that Adrien Depaul held no sway on her. Still, the photographer at the other end of the block just wanted the next scoop. The one Ari promised.

"No!" Seina heard Michelle shout, pushing Adrien. *Click*, went the camera. "I don't care what you want!" She continued, dropping her coat, still trying to separate from him. Pedestrians slowed to watch, but dared not intervene. *Click*. Michelle broke free, ripping her sweater. Seina came now, dashing across the busy street and nearly taking a car full on. *Click*.

"Aye! Back up Frenchie!" Seina shouted, giving Michelle his coat and stepping between her and Adrien. *Click.*

"Who the hell are you?!" The photographer heard Adrien say as he lunged forward.

"I said get back," Seina shouted, then to Michelle. "I'll meet you in the lobby." He was still standing between them.

"Who the fuck do you think you are?"

"The man that's gonna break your face. Back up off my woman." Adrien's eyes moved from Seina to Michelle and back.

That was the moment Seina swung— better still, chin checked Adrien.

Adrien threw the second blow— *perfect landing*, Seina's nose.

Blood stained Seina's shirt and trickled onto the sidewalk. *Click, click, and click.* Adrien hammered him again and again although Seina managed a blow here and there.

"Stop it Adrien!" Michelle screamed as the larger man prepared to swing again, but stopped to look at Michelle's horrified face. It had unfolded quickly, as only the most charged fights do.

Michelle swooped in and whisked the bloodied Seina away, before managing to grab her coat. Adrien stood, not surprised but hurt all the same. *Click.* Each of them saw the photographer and each knew this scene would grow into a tale, adding to the story reporters spun about their lives. Still, each chose to *act* from the heart, rather than from beneath the façade.

So be it, they would be one of tomorrow's headlines, perhaps even the front-page story. So be it. The couple zipped through the lobby with Seina holding his nose and Michelle's sweater coming apart. Still a touch concerned about being seen, she decided to forgo the elevator, opting for the stairs instead.

"So much for being a hero." Seina said trying to grin.

"Are you okay?" Michelle asked as the stairwell door closed behind them. "I have to leave soon. I'm so sorry all this happened. I was running late and he was there waiting for me. But why did you punch him?"

"I care for you, so I had to step in, otherwise you'd never believe me,"

Seina stared at her, blood dripping down his chin. He took a deep breath, "And there's something I need to tell—" He started.

"Believe you about what?" She stared at him, wiping the blood from his face with her torn sleeve. "Look we don't—" Seina cut her off.

"I'm—I'm in love with you," he said in a confessional tone. "That's why I was such an ass back in New York. I thought maybe my brother sent you to seduce me, or that you were using me to get to him—I don't know! I was irrational because I don't—" He said in one visceral rush, then paused. "I never wanted to spend my life with anyone, but—" He licked his lips, wanting to go further, but Michelle stopped him.

"We don't have time to talk about this. I planned for you to come to the show with me. But we can't have this conversation right now. I'm on the second floor. Let's get some ice and get you to my room." She could see the swelling beginning to deform his nose. Michelle motioned up the stairs. Seina grabbed her hand stopping her.

"Right now, Ari is trying to mess with your life because she wants to drive a wedge between us."

Michelle glanced at the time on her phone, then to Seina. "Why would she want to do that?"

Seina took a moment to answer. "Because she's my sister and—"

Michelle cut in again, letting go of a breath she didn't know she was holding. "Okay, we unpack the rest later. Come on," she motioned up the stairs, clearly not absorbing all the information, dialing Ari as she climbed. When there was no answer, she hung-up and focused in on Seina.

"So your sister?" Michelle asked suddenly with Seina trailing behind her out of the stairwell and into the hallway.

"Adopted. It's complicated but—"

Michelle held up a hand. "Here's my key. Room 2102, ice is just down the hall," she handed him the card and moved back toward the stairs. "I'll be back, just stay put this time."

"I'll be here." Seina nodded.

Michelle left and Seina looked down at the key card in his hand. He slipped it into his pocket, then called Ari.

"Where are you?" Seina barked as soon as she pickup.

"4105."

Where Delusions Prevail
Paris, February 24th

Ari looked out the window, a lit cigarette in hand with 'the city of lights' at dusk stretched out before her. The door to her room was left ajar. It slammed into the wall behind her.

"I told you to leave and instead you start a fire?"

Ari exhaled, shifting from the pink-stained cigarette-butt to Seina. "It turns out, I only needed one more," she smiled, her smile fading as she looked at Seina. "You look like hell."

"I know you sent Depaul to that restaurant and Tatsuya in New York. Why are you fucking with her? With us?"

Ari nodded, and brought the cigarette back to her mouth, then exhaled. "I won't pretend to be sorry about it. You really think she can handle Claudio? We both know your father would do much worse given the chance." She walked to her suitcase by the bed. Seina ran a hand over his face, careful of his nose, the other hand on his hip as Ari took a seat on the bed.

"How do you see this as something not to be sorry about?" He stared into dull hardened eyes. Ari put the cigarette out.

"I spared her, Seina. I could have outed her for her affair with Adrien Depaul or for aborting his kid while he and the wife struggled to have theirs. But I chose to let her hang herself. To let her behavior, show the world her character. She doesn't love you. She doesn't even see you"

"What the hell is wrong with you? I care about her. Did my family twist you up this much?" Seina asked, outraged.

Ari listened unfazed, then her attention shifted past him.

"So you just wanted to ruin me?" Michelle asked. Seina turned and tried to cool the flames beginning to spark in her voice.

"Adrien told me he wanted to start a new chapter with you. I also thought you would destroy Seina's life."

"You don't think that was Seina's choice?" Michelle scoffed. She turned to Seina. "You knew what she was doing here? Then why play along?" Michelle threw up her hands. "Never-fucking-mind!"

"Hold on—" Seina started, to no avail.

Michelle turned to Ari, sitting on the bed, with her legs crossed, staring steadily back. Then, without pause, without flinching Michelle spat, the saliva landing squarely on Ari's chest.

"Bitch." Michelle said, the voice dropping an octave. She turned to walk away. Seina followed her and she fired again, hitting him squarely in the face. "Leave me the hell alone, both of you," she shouted, slamming the door behind her.

Ari laughed, uncharacteristically. Then she stood, and removing the blouse, she exchanged it for another. "I have to go now. Call me when you get over this."

"You won't just walk away from this." Seina said eerily, wiping his face with the blouse on the bed. He stared at Ari for a long hard minute and she said nothing. Suddenly, he sprinted down the hallway. Ari sighed, putting on her coat, and stepping into five-inch stilettoes, before walking out of the suite wheeling her suitcase behind her.

In the town car, en route to the airport, Ari laughed though she didn't quite know why. She kept laughing, harder and louder as tears slowly began, a trusty flask in hand. *He is angry*, the tide of her thoughts spelled out, *but it will pass, in some weeks, if not months*. Yet, Ari could feel the logic thinning, and the taste of bitter betrayal swept her tongue.

Not angry. Seina is furious, but why, Ari thought suddenly dawning armor. *I was protecting him. From himself. From her. From Claudio. He falls for the same girl every time. Smart, pretty, at times even interesting.*

He may hate me, was the next thought to wash ashore. *And what if he actually* loves *Michelle,* was the next pounding wave of questions. The thought had occurred to her. Though now it seemed the only answer. Ari took another swig from the flask. *Seina, could very well be in love, with a woman I have come to like—and would have befriended under other circumstances. What if he's actually in love with her,* she questioned replaying his reactions in her head.

It suddenly dawned on Ari, that Seina had gone after the girl. *That if Seina was serious, he would pursue, and all Ari's efforts to quell the budding love would be for naught. But then Claudio would step in, like the last time.*

Ari sipped from the flask again. *No doubt the old fox would be more heavy-handed. Claudio would destroy them. If not Michelle, just to hurt Seina.* Then another thought appeared like a wave building on the horizon, *but I was the one who hurt them. I hurt Michelle. I hurt Seina. I inflicted the harm, over the Terada trust, over Seina's life, over Claudio's wrath.*

I am the monster. So that she will never meet the true creatures of the night, Ari thought, stealing herself against a sudden chill. Then she thought of Darius, dismissing him in the same breath.

"I was protecting him." She said aloud as the driver gave a sly glance in her direction. *I thought Seina would thank me. That Michelle would return to Adrien. That Seina would be happier knowing who she was, and what she did. That he would leave—hurt and bruised—but not by Claudio. Alive, though unhappy. Alive, dammit! That in spite of Michelle Yamato-Jang he would still be whole* enough. This was her plan, the thing now warped, cracked and shattering. The whole plot stretched out on the black leather interior, of this 1947 Rolls Royce. Ari sat in silence, seething, unsure of everything, but her wrongs, once again.

Midnight City
Paris, February 24th

Victoria strolled into the chaos of backstage-fashion-show preparations. She slipped through the bustle of the grand salon turned dressing room, on her phone, acknowledging familiar faces as she went. Victoria was overseeing the details of a new property, gifted by her father, and so took one of the few open seats in her hurry to get settled. She hung up, only to realize she was seated next to Michelle. A make-up artist applied dark eyeliner and Victoria cut her eyes away from the sight.

"Good to see you again Tori." Kelvin, the make-up artist, said adding the final touches to Michelle's face. "Heard you got the spot as VP with Eva Wong. Congrats."

"Thank you," Victoria smiled, stiffly. Michelle prickled at the mention of Eva.

"And when do you start?" Kelvin paused capping a bottle of mascara.

"Sometime in May," Victoria replied, the sparkle of her bracelet pulling Michelle from her Ari-Seina induced daze.

"Congratulations," Michelle chimed in a touch too late to seem sincere.

"Thank you," Victoria responded. She glanced from Michelle to her reflection in the mirror. "I heard Adrien is singing tonight, to another God-forsaken Midnight City remix. Is this another stunt in your saga?"

Michelle scoffed, then stared at the other woman in the mirror, her eyes daring Victoria to go further.

"Something wrong? The attention whore doesn't want anymore?"

"Are you still mad Adrien wanted to screw me while you two were messing around?" Michelle asked point blank. Those around them stiffened. Heads turned, and ears perked up. "You have a whole planet or at least a small country of men falling over you and you're still stuck on that? *I was seventeen, Victoria*, and I didn't even sleep with him, *then*. *You* were the grown woman in that situation. And, again, I'm sorry. I'm sorry I've hurt you on both counts." Michelle said, alluding to Li Jun. "How many times do I have to say that? You want me to apologize every time I see you?—That's not gonna happen. It's time for *you* to grow up." Michelle cast a lingering stare at Victoria.

"I see you still love when all eyes are on you, *attention whore*," Victoria stood. "Otherwise you wouldn't have been after Jun or Adrien in the first place. And you wouldn't be here making a scene. Low class whore." Victoria spat storming away, throwing her purse on her shoulder. She left in a whirlwind of rage, blowing past the various people that pause to listen. That rage reached for vengeance as it led the heiress and veteran model into a quiet hall. Victoria was looking for the sound technicians when she pulled a flash drive from her purse and spotted the sound booth. "Hey," she called.

"What's up lovely," a man asked from the booth. His west end accent was apparent to her the moment he spoke. He wiped his nose once, then again. Victoria took in his enlarged pupils and spoke.

"If I score you some good stuff will you put this on near the end of the show?" She showed him the flash drive.

"What's on it?" he asked, eyes narrowed.

"How about three thousand euros, no questions and you forget who I am?" Victoria said curtly, head tilted.

"Okay." The man agreed, taking the drive.

"Give me an account," Victoria pulled her phone from her purse.

Sometime later, out near the runway, Ari spotted an empty seat beside Hikaru, one of the two she had reserved. Shocked to see her, Hikaru stopped to stare at Ari. She sat down beside him, dressed in red head to toe.

"Can I help you, Hunter?" She avoided looking at him, crossing her legs in the red pant suit, the black camisole cut to enhance her cleavage.

"I heard what you did," he crossed his arms, looking her over.

"Should that mean something?" The eyebrows displayed her indifference.

"Don't let this nice guy rou—" He started.

"Down boy," Ari smiled, noting his horribly tied tie. "I come waving white flags." Ari turned to him untying the tie. "I know you have feelings for Michelle," she began re-tying, jerking him with each twist. "And I know you're not man enough to make a move. You might protect her, but you will never *have her*, Hikaru. She'll destroy you not even realizing it." Ari smiled, patting him over the heart. "Learn who you're dealing with, then their weaknesses. That's the only way to make it and do well in life." Ari looked him over again. "It's called an Eldredge knot, looks good on you," she said, turning to the runway.

"Were you born evil, or did it just grow on you?" Hikaru asked in a gruff whisper as the lights dimmed.

Ari sighed, and steeled herself in the darkness. "I'm here to make peace," she repeated.

A hush fell over the crowd and one by one, lanterns lit the edges of the white diamond shaped runway. Snow and rose petals fell and the runway lit up blinking on and off to the rhythm of a heartbeat. Boom, boom-boom, boom, boom-boom. At the back of the runway, videos of neon-lit-cityscapes played out to the left and right of a set of gigantic glass-paned double doors. Here two white-gloved men in black tuxedoes opened the doors in unison.

The music began, then slowly the sound of the heartbeat faded. Victoria emerged from the doorway, looking angelic in all-white. She wore a beaded top with a high collar over a lacy-camisole. The wide-leg pants echoing the sway of her hips with each step.

Adrien appeared at the center of the room, amidst the falling snow. Victoria passed him reaching the end of the runway, then posed, one, two, three. *She was beau-ti-ful~ an in-cre-di-ble vis-ion~. Dream-of-my-dreams~. You-were sim-ply a-maz-ing~*

Michelle approached on the other side, in a floor length black dress flecked with gold along its edges.

Ari and Hikaru unconsciously held their breaths Adrian grazed Michelle's thigh. High on the excitement of this world, the lights, and the music Michelle ignored it. *Prada-and-Dior~, that's-the-world she lives-in~. A dream-like place~, that she rei-gn-s over. A beautiful girl~ (beautiful girl) turned into a stunning wo-man~, reaching for a dream~ (~reaching for a dream~) here-in-the-city at~mid-night.*

Another model materialized from the doorway in a white coat dress styled with fur and diamonds down the front and along the cuffs. While the model after her, wore a black three quarter-length pantsuit. The blazer embellished with three beaded chains across the front, a black satin draping the shoulder, and across the back before trailing to the floor.

En route to the dressing room, Michelle and Adrien's eyes met—his rage to her outrage. Still, he stared at her, and obviously so. Michelle moved onward, but Adrian's eyes remained on her.

I knew her as a girl~, starry-eyed vis-ion, she-was, the-beau-ti-ful girl~ now-a stun-ning wo-man~. We-were both fools~, (~foolish~) we-were so care-less,

We-were in love~, and-still-I-fail~ed you~

Vision in my dreams~, Leila I truly miss-you~.

The screen displaying the picturesque cityscapes on the sides of the doors changed. Photos of Michelle and Adrien appeared. The ten or fifteen pictures placed Adrien on dates with Michelle kissing and holding hands, alongside photos of him and the wife. Ari jumped up and ran backstage to stop the slide show. Yet Hikaru, like all the other viewers stared at the photos, losing sight of the clothes.

Ari reached the back hallway and barged into the technician's box, pushing past the technicians themselves. She pulled the flask from her blazer pouring the contents out.

Three seconds. That's how long the image of Michelle leaving a back alley 'clinic' remained on the screen. Following the images of her massively pregnant, clearly in her second trimester. In that last picture, she was grey, barely alive as the figure of an unknown individual towered over her, pulling her along. All of this, staged after a handful of candid photos of Adrien and Michelle. All of them were dated, as Ari would have it no other way. The screen faded to black, the music died, and shouting backstage ensued.

Eva and the Busboy

Tokyo, February 24th

As late morning waned, in Tokyo, Jade slowly made her way to Eva's office, tucking blonde hair behind an ear, as she walked in five-inch black stilettos, and a matching dress. She approached the assistant's desk with a smile.

"Good Morning, Christine. Is Eva in?" She sweetly inched toward the door, draping a black coat over an arm.

"Yes, she is but, she has a ten o'clock."

"Yes, I'm her ten o'clock." Jade smiled.

Christine stopped. "Does Eva or Hitomi know that? It's under Michelle Yamato."

"She will." Jade smiled, continuing toward the door, forcing Christine to walk her in. Christine tapped on the door frame with the back of her hand.

"Come in." Eva looked up from her desk.

"Ms. Wong, Jade Wang, your ten o'clock is here," Christine entered the office and quickly slipped away.

Jade stepped into the office.

"Jade? I was expecting Michelle. Is she running late?"

"Actually, I made the appointment in her name. After all, Michelle is still in Paris." Jade placed her purse on Eva's desk, allowing the tablet inside to pair with Eva's computer, unnoticed.

"Then what is this meeting about?" Eva noted the purse as a sign of blatant disrespect—one to be dealt with, in a moment.

"Michelle has hired both a publicist and an assistant in order to help keep the workload from piling up. So, I'm here as her assistant to liaison and do whatever you need Michelle to do if she can't." Jade drew on pad and pen.

"Excuse me?" Eva paused. "I'm supposed to be notified before she hires anyone, then *I* confirm whether or not *you* get the job, especially if you expect to *waltz* into my office like you just did."

"I'm sorry, I thought you were notified. I haven't officially started yet but I'll alert Michelle of your concern. Is there anything else we need to discuss?"

"Alert Michelle to the fact that she goes on *indefinite* leave as of March first, making her *contractually obligated* to stop modeling." Eva spat.

"I will do that. Is that all? I was expecting a bit more." Jade smiled, further irritating Eva.

"Until you're actually confirmed for the position, it is. Now I—"

A knock interrupted Eva, and Yu opened the door, before he paused in the doorway. "I see you're busy, per usual." He smiled. The look shifted to a cold stare when he glanced at Jade. "Should I come back?"

Jade traced every inch of him, thanking heaven for sending such a wonderful opportunity, *again*. She had completely forgotten about him.

"I'm sorry time got away from me." Eva genuinely smiled.

Jade noticed the visible softening of Eva's countenance.

"You mean you forgot?" Yu beamed back, crossing his arms and shaking his head.

Right, the busboy fiancé, it dawned on Jade. A glimpse of his name tag from the café flashed through her thoughts, *Hiroshi Yu, that was his name.*

"Yu, this is Jade. She will potentially be an assistant to one of the models." Eva extended her hand.

"Nice to meet you." Yu was cordial, as though meeting a stranger. *Does he not remember me?*

"Nice to meet you too." Jade grinned back— playing the role of an eager intern or the like, her attention drifting to his watch. "Well if that's all you have for me—" Jade stood up.

"Thank you, so much." Yu cut in. "She'll be here forever if I don't get her now."

"It's no problem. Have a nice day." Jade grabbed her purse and walked to the door, before glancing at Yu's watch, again.

"So, how much time do you need?" Yu asked closing the door.

"Her Prince came," Christine said in Japanese, watching Yu close the door.

Jade stopped in front of Christine's desk. "Doiu imidesuka?" Jade asked.

"Kanojo no Fiancé," Hitomi, Eva's office manager said standing over Christine's desk. She was a thirty-two year old divorcee, with Yamada Yu-esque beauty. "Hachinen mae Supein d e aimashita. Ima karera wa kekonshitai. Lucky, ne." She pouted.

> Eight years a g o t h e y met in Spain Now they want t o
> get married

"Ah, Totemo." Jade agreed as they gossiped for a bit, before she walked back to the elevator.

New Territory
Tokyo, March 1st -12th

Drenched in scandal from Paris to Tokyo, and with her leave of absence already in play, Michelle began to distance herself. She said nothing to Ari before or during the flight, but shared a brief but heartfelt goodbye with Hikaru at Narita. After touching down Michelle was fined and berated, *again*, by Eva, but simply took it.

"Are you retarded?" Eva had asked standing over her. Michelle shook her head, looking down at the floor in front of Eva's desk. The dismal light from the window and the overcast day, greyed everything in Eva's office. "or, are you just simple minded?" Eva retorted, crossing her arms.

"No," Michelle said in a whisper. Eva came to stand beside her desk.

"So, you *are* an attention whore. Because I have yet to find one publication, or news channel that isn't talking about you, Seina Terada, Adrien Depaul and/or the baby *you murdered*. If you weren't under contract, or made me any less money you'd be out. *Pathetic*," Eva spat under her breath as she shifted her gaze out the window. "I don't want to hear your name before my vacation from you is over. Do you hear me?" Eva glared back at her.

By that point, Michelle had no fight in her, it was as if she were a balloon following its collision with a bullet. Head on, dead center. Not just deflated but shattered— in pieces, again. Like she had been when Adrien appeared at her apartment all those years ago and let his wife drag her to that clinic. *Saying nothing—doing nothing.* But he wrote a song for her. He loved her. Just like Li Jun who never made her feel like his one and only. He never made Michelle feel secure in his love, only bringing questions to their status with flirting and playful winks, at other women— in spite of being a great manager.

Once locked away in her apartment, Michelle dodged phone calls from everyone, not wanting to put forth the effort 'to be alright.' Of course, there were tears. Like when Seina left voicemails.

"Seina Terada calling for Michelle Yamato, update number four. I miss you." A whisper, as if just realizing it himself. "I could swing by with food and copious amounts of alcohol, or just sweets, whatever you want. I just want to see you. To make sure you're alright. I know you're probably still angry with me but let me explain. I owe you that," he said looking for the right words. "Just call me back Michelle. I'm here for you." At this, the quiet sobs overflowed. Raining tears down her cheeks, in her lap, on her sheets, for days.

Michelle had always regarded models and fashion shows as a dirty but necessary evil business. The likes of which fueled by scarcity, fads, jealousy and obsession. But in Paris, on that stage, she came to understand why these people pushed through the pain and fatigue, and continued to put themselves through the horror. It was this very realization amidst this natural high, paired with the irrefutable evidence of her lifelong shame that nearly destroyed her. Michelle was unable to gather the pieces. She ate next to nothing the three days she laid in bed.

So, needless to say Michelle's search for answers – (a) for Jade's disappearance and (b) for her disappearing money were knocked off her radar, until Jade showed up at her apartment, laptop in hand.

"Come in." Michelle said tucking her hair behind an ear, the curls running rampant, bigger than Jade had ever seen. "Let's go to my room,"

Michelle led Jade past clothes strewn about.

"So, I think you were right about Eva," Jade took a seat on the bed in the darkened room as Michelle closed the door. "I'm going to check a little more and flush it out but it looks like the money is being funneled to a few offshore accounts. I can't—"

"Do you have anything on her?" Michelle suddenly cut her off.

"Not yet," Jade smiled, stiffly. "—but what I find won't hold up in a courtroom."

"I don't need it to." Michelle said with no inflection.

"So, are you okay?"

"Irritated, mortified, all the emotions," Michelle smiled as the tears began of their own volition. "I'm tired of crying about this," Michelle said gasping for air as tears ran like waterfalls

Uncharacteristically, Jade took the crumbling heroine in her arms, allowing her tears to fall, until Michelle fell asleep in her lap.

And why did I do that? Jade wondered. *Why did I comfort the downcast-supermodel in her hour of need? We're not friends. And to what end?* Jade asked herself repeatedly even a week later, as she waited at the Paper Moon for Michelle to arrive. The Paper Moon was one of the first places she and Michelle frequented after becoming acquainted, ground zero if you would—neutral territory.

Michelle arrived, in armor—the hair straightened, five-inch heels, a peach body dress and a black floor-length coat paired with dark sunglasses. The norm, *but something was different. Calmer? Cooler? More assured?* It was as if a light switch were turned on, the kind of switch that appears to do nothing but is left off just in case. Michelle sat and ordered water with lemon, no ice, before asking:

"So, what really happened in London?"

This threw Jade. She expected to talk about Eva, about missing money and account types.

"I had to go Michelle," Jade began with the first of several artfully drawn lies.

"Darius said it had something to do with staying off the radar."

"My mother was killed," Jade began knowing Soo Young was listening on the other side of the partition, as Soo Young had every opportunity she could since she and Jade became roommates. "The man who killed her works in media." She said spinning in some abstract version of the truth. "Being around you and Seina may have drawn his attention. So, my boyfriend, Robert, got me a ticket back. So, I would be safer."

"Wow," Michelle mumbled. "Why didn't you tell me? You didn't have to lie."

"I just wanted to enjoy myself." The tears came now with no effort, seamlessly slipped into the conversation.

"That's the kind of thing friends tell each other. I wouldn't have asked you to go if I knew." Michelle whispered on the verge of tears herself.

"I didn't think I could trust you with that," Jade wiped her eyes. The tears trickled forth, slow at first, then a downpour in moments. Though Jade didn't know it, this was the moment she would remember, seated on a beach with the sun glinting brilliantly on the waves—the sky…the sea…as far as the eye could see.

When the downpour lifted, Michelle, Jade, and even Soo Young wiped their eyes, neither able to give words to what just happened.

"So, there's a boyfriend," Michelle laughed, pulling her sunglasses from her hair.

"Yes, Robert." Jade beamed, sweeping aside her blonde bangs.

"Sounds like you like this Robert guy," Michelle wiped her eyes. Jade smiled, fighting back the thought of Robert's toenails at the end of her pliers.

"Yeah, he's an officer in the Air Force and he is gorgeous." Jade's stomach turned.

"Really?"

"Yeah, and this is new territory."

"New territory?"

"He's white—" Jade giggled. Soo Young covered her mouth. "green

231

eyes and these big lips!" Jade said, falling out in her seat.

"Oh my God Jade. Slow down," Michelle laughed. "Is he the reason for this color change?" She ran her fingers through Jade's hair.

"Partly," Jade shrugged.

"Well, it looks good on you, way better than your roomie's." Michelle laughed then glanced at her phone. Soo Young scowled at that.

"Oh, I'm sorry, I've got to go. I have to meet Hikaru for tango class." Michelle stood, rolling her eyes.

"Tango class? Why are you going to a tango class, and with Hikaru?"

"So I'll be a great dancer by the time we shoot Alex and Andrew's music video in Barcelona." Michelle, grabbed her purse. "You should come with *assistant*," she winked, before putting on her sunglasses.

"I'll think about it," Jade called after her.

13. Caught

Shin-Okubo, Tokyo, March 13th

Yu sat in Shin-Okubo, on the curb of an empty back street, under a street light, in a tuxedo. It was just minutes after one a.m. He lit a cigarette, reeking of Chanel and Patron. It was his version of drinks with the big clients. *But it's over*, he thought smiling. He inhaled, the cigarette glowing orange in the dim light. *The contract is up. I'm done.*

Yu exhaled with a smile, relishing what he somehow knew would be a fleeting moment. He stood, pulling his phone from a pocket, before taking another puff, then he dialed in.

"Owarida. Kaeruyo," he announced, exhaling smoke.

"Not so fast Kazuki," his handler's voice rang back. "I told you earlier, you have a VVIP. I'm sending the address." Tina hung up.

So not quite *free,* he thought, the moment soured. The text rolled in.

"How the fuck did I do this to myself?" Yu muttered walking down the quiet street in near darkness, the crunch of stray pebbles under foot. He knew he chose this life, *and* the why of it. His father's dementia was the first thought that suddenly spooled forth, unbidden.

Those old ladies went as far as taking shots off me, Yu remembered with a scoff, expelling smoke and finally feeling the Patron. *To think, those women have kids my age—if not older,* he snickered, trying to shift his attention away from his past, away from *his* choices—but there was no escape. The question had been asked, and God had answered.

Not that Yu Hiroshi believed in God or anything other than money. Money was his God. Even as his mind circled away from this thought he wanted to avoid, the notion patiently, waited to be examined. Its fingers drummed loudly on his temporal lobe. Its nails dug into the creases of his hippocampus. Yu's phone lit up again with another text. **Hikaru** appeared on the screen.

Yu ignored *that* text and slid the phone back into his pocket. He walked onto an off shoot of Okubo Dori—near Shin-Okubo station, a much busier street, ambling toward a seven eleven. There, Yu finally allowed the pestering thoughts in. *My Father had an affair while my mom was devoted to him. I got over it,* he thought, walking down the aisles of the store. *From the affair, I got a brother.* He grabbed a sandwich. *I got over it.* Yu picked up a bottle of mouthwash, and a pack of baby wipes, before walking to the counter. *I even got over the little* imp *coming to live with us—after a few years.*

I went to school for structural engineering, in Spain. No one would believe that now. Thanks to Dad's and grandpa's debts, two and a half years in, that ship sank and we lost everything. Nothing else worked after that. Dad got Dementia, and Hikaru wanted to go to school, for fucking art. Not something that could help us. Nothing that could help me.

In the taxi, Yu showed the cab driver the address on his phone. He opened the bottle of mouthwash. Then rolled down the window, swishing, and gargling. After spitting out the window, to the driver's annoyance, Yu took baby wipes to his previously Patron-soaked body parts.

The car came to a step. Yu paid the driver, and into a hotel he went. *I'm not angry about my life. I'm pissed.* He stopped outside the room, pausing to adjust his clothes, slick back his hair. *And I can't get the person I was gonna be out of my head.* He knocked on the door, bad-boy persona readied. It opened, he paused.

"Kazuki almost suits you, Hiroshi-san," Jade said, smiling up at him, bright red lipstick amplifying the ambition that cloaked her. She was in a sheer red blouse, her lacy black bra in plain view, and a black pencil skirt. She walked away from the door to a small bar backed by the window across from Yu. Atop the bar, where Jade had clearly been sitting, was a bottle of vodka and several mixers. She was waiting for him. *Waiting. For. Him.*

"Close the door," she crossed her legs. Yu went blank as he closed the door, his thoughts going into over drive.

Jade grinned, at Yu's shock, marveling at how well he channeled the fear into feigned confusion. Even in the poor lighting, his tea-colored eyes seemed lit from within. This along with that creamy skin tinted to the color of sandalwood, made Jade wish she were here for an entirely different purpose. Yu's heavy-lidded eyes shifted from cold, to colder as he came closer.

"You look nice," she beamed. "Sit. Have a drink. We have some business to discuss." Jade turned back to the bar and her drink.

"Business, I think there's been a mistake." He tried, with a polite smile.

"Of course there's been a mistake," Jade's voice dropped to a low rumble, "—if you really think that's going to work," she laughed, flinging her blonde bangs aside. "Come, *sit down*."

Yu walked through a tiny sitting room toward the bar, where he could see the bedroom to his right, just a few feet behind Jade.

"I was told you guys don't get paid unless your client calls in satisfied for the evening," she looked him over.

"What do you want?" He asked, siting.

"We can do this one of two ways. Deal, no deal or cat and mouse." She finished her drink. "Do you want one?" She asked, mixing vodka and tonic water.

"I don't want any problems."

"I know," she paused.

"What exactly are you trying to get out of me?" Yu stared flatly at her.

Jade grinned. "Do you love Eva? Or better yet, would you be okay being a liability for her?" She sipped from the drink.

"No, I wouldn't."

He picked an empty glass from the bar making a drink.

"I'm after the money." Jade sipped from her glass. "Contracts and financial documents that's what I want."

"And if I don't *help*, you'll expose me?" Yu questioned sarcastically.

"Not just you," she laughed.

"What do you have on Eva?" He poured a long shot of Patron.

Jade shrugged. "Her crimes are a bit more Martha Steward-esque."

"And how do I know you won't expose us after you get what you need? Or that you really have *anything* other than our current misunderstanding?" Yu smiled, almost giggling at her flimsy attempt to strong-arm him.

"Because, I give you my word." Jade drew an X over her heart.

"I'm supposed to just trust you?" Yu sat back in his chair, knocking back the shot.

"A few months ago, you were working as a busboy, how could you suddenly afford to be Eva's man? Unless you're doing something illegal. Yes, Eva could be your *sugar* mama, but she's not the type. But you know what wouldn't leave me alone Kazuki?" She looked into his eyes as she reached for his hand, "—your taste in watches. How can a busboy, newly wealthy or not, afford a four-thousand-dollar watch? You had an even more expensive one on at the New Year's party,"

"A gift." Yu smiled.

Jade scoffed. "Not from Eva. The other side of that card you gave me at the café was blank, *until it got wet*."

"And now you're all wet." Yu smirked, inwardly cursing his carelessness. "Well, the doctor's here." He said to her, staring, and removing his blazer, placing it on his chair.

Jade stretched toward him, placing her hands on Yu's shoulders. "I called—we'll call it your office." Jade's hands glided down to his chest, along his abs, and into his lap. "Aiyoh, if you know how to use that thing it'll pay for itself." She laughed, turning to sip from her drink.

"So, you came here just to blackmail me and feel me up?" Yu asked with a slight smile.

"I'd go further but, Eva hasn't done anything to me and, you're still just a hooker." Jade watched him visibly dim his irritation at that. "So why should I take her fiancé to bed?"

"But it's okay to blackmail us?"

"Sounds like you want to be bedded." She grinned.

"You paid for it," he inched in closer.

"Did I?" Jade scoffed.

"So, you called my office, then?" Yu prompted.

"Yes, I registered and opened an account with *your company*, Delights Bakery. As a new member I got the premium menu with all the specials and there you were, Kazuki. Bright eyed and one of the most expensive flavors."

Yu leaned close, the nearness of which startled Jade. "And?" He asked, in a husky note.

"Since you were a limited time offer, I indulged," Jade smiled stroking his face. "Or Eva's credit card did," she beamed.

"And here I am." Yu beamed back. "Now what?" He kissed her, surprising even himself. His hands moving to her buttons and zippers. Though Yu spectacularly managed the rage building inside, Jade noted a single vein along his forehead that told the story of his distress. She let him kiss her, moving to her neck, then her collarbone. Jade had difficulty reconciling this man with the wild careless one she met back in Hiroo. The wild wavy hair was gone, slicked back and combed to one side. The Skater-boi-jagged edges dulled to one smoothed polished layer.

"*Yes*, here you are," Jade pulled away looking him over again, "at my mercy."

"How much did you spend?" Yu stared at Jade like he might devour her.

"You don't know how much you cost?"

"I have a ballpark figure of my usual number," he whispered, pulling her into his lap. "But I'm retiring and tonight is my last night."

"You really love Eva?" Jade wrapped her arms around his neck.

"With all my heart," Yu kissed her again, slowly unzipping her skirt.

She pulled away, relishing the kiss. "Your heart isn't half the size of your dick," she laughed. Jade zipped the skirt then kissed him on the cheek. "Gotta go."

"We're not finished."

"We are for now." She nodded. "You have until April first to get me what I want, *Kazuki*." Jade walked to the door, hand bag and jacket in hand as she closed it.

That Hiroshi is some good stock. Jade absently thought. She stood fanning, and pressed the button for the elevator a fourth time, when Yu's voice came from behind her:

"You're really going to leave without saying good-bye, *the right way*?"

Jade turned. "This is not goodbye—" she started.

"This is." He kissed her, again, long and passionate, pressing his body to hers, hands tracing over back, hips, and thighs. The elevator sensor lit up and the doors opened.

Jade pulled away. "Good night." She stepped into the elevator, pressing the button for the lobby.

"Don't leave." Yu held the door open.

Jade smiled. She hit his hand with her purse, allowing the doors to close. Jade leaned against the wall, trying to clear her head, when she saw a couple staring at her.

"What are you looking at?!" She snapped. Jade sighed, then pulled Yu's wallet into plain view, along with a microphone from her bra.

"Old habits," Jade shrugged, counting his money.

形　見
Katami
Tokyo, March 14th

Evening fell as evening does in Tokyo, in winter—creeping shadows of a setting sun at four, then promptly dark, by four forty-five.

By six, Michelle found herself stretched out on her bed, fresh from a hot bath in a pink robe and her hair drying. She was searching for valid reasons to move, or not to. It was then Ari walked into the apartment and into Michelle's bedroom, carry-on suitcase en tow.

"What are you doing?" Ari closed the door. "The party is at nine," she said as nicely as the words could come across her lips—without sarcasm.

"What?" Michelle walked to her dresser, failing to return the pleasantry.

"The magazine party," Ari walked over to the vanity, on the far side of the room, near the window. She sat and unpacked her dress, perfume, and make-up from the suitcase. Michelle looked at the clock on her nightstand—six nineteen.

"There's plenty of time," Michelle grumbled, grabbing a bottle of lotion from her dresser, sitting on her bed then applying it to her legs. "I'm going to take a nap."

"We don't have time for that," Ari turned from the mirror fingering her hair. "And since you haven't given up on finding a new publicist, I've arranged for interviews while we're in L.A. for the trial. But you'll never find one as good as me," she smiled.

Michelle stared blankly at Ari. "We shall see." She said as her limp curls began to frizz.

"Looking at the applicants you're pulling, there's a lot to be desired, D-list celebs and celebutantes." Ari chided.

"Says the girl who worked for one heiress and two semi-pro European basketball players," Michelle scoffed grabbing a keratin mist and blow dryer from the bathroom.

"I never did that," Ari turned to her. "My resume was made up. Whether you realize it or not I'm *overqualified* for this job."

"What did you do before? Work for the mob?" Michelle pumped the mist time after time and slathered it into her hair, staring at Ari all the while.

"I was a partner at a PR firm in Madrid, but that's beside the point," Ari stood, changing the subject. "Jade's here, and so is Harold." She grinned, "You know he's going to be a train wreck."

"*Hikaru*," Michelle rolled her eyes. "And give me my key." Michelle wiped her hands.

"You know he can't wait to see you. So, you should hurry and get dressed," Ari smiled with some sarcasm, handing Michelle the key. "Did you, screw him? He's cute but not screw-able cute."

"No." Michelle sneered, taking the key pushing up her sleeves and applying lotion to her arms and hands, before placing the lotion bottle on the floor.

"Just because you didn't sleep with him doesn't mean you didn't mess with him in some other way."

"What are you implying?" The heat picked up in her voice.

"That I just can't believe you didn't already corrupt little Harry. I'll go get Jade, then see to it Hector gets dressed," Ari said walking into the living room.

"I thought I was the only one that liked that show," Ari heard Jade giggle walking into the living room. Jade sat on the sofa with her back to Ari as Hikaru stood beaming at Jade.

"I can't get over Yamada Yu's character. I just laugh non-stop, you know?" Hikaru said, their leftover tension from New York began to dissipate. "By the way, I like this new look."

"Thank you." Jade blushed, absently touching the blonde hair

"Jade," Ari said, sweetly, "we don't have much time. Hagar, there's a bathroom over there," Ari pointed. "Come on Jade." She walked back into Michelle's room.

"What is with her?" Hikaru mumbled. "I can't tell if she likes me or hates me."

"She only really likes her reflection. If you get a mirror, you can distract her for at least an hour," Jade stood up and Hikaru burst into laughter. "or tell her how beautiful she is. It's sickening how happy she gets." Jade beamed. "Let's go before Slagathor comes back."

Hikaru snickered "See you later."

Jade froze in the doorway for a moment, reading the tension.

"Wednesday at eight am was the earliest flight I could get to LAX."

Ari finished as she sat down at the vanity.

"Fine, and what do you plan to do while I interview applicants?" Michelle came from the bathroom, now in bra and panties. It was tense, but no more than she and Ari, Jade realized.

"Testing them, to show you how green they are." Ari called, pinning her hair to start on her make-up.

Jade put the tote down and closed the door. Michelle turned on the blow dryer.

"You won't find another me, but clearly you want something close." She called to Michelle still facing the mirror.

"So, you're leaving for the trial on Wednesday?" Jade asked, inching into the conversation. Michelle nodded.

"So, Jade what do you think about Hamilton?" Ari chimed in, zipping a mauve color cocktail dress, before sitting in front of Michelle's vanity again.

Michelle turned to Ari and turned the blow dryer off. "You know, that is not his name," she stared at Ari from the bathroom as Jade sat on the bed.

"I don't care what old rodeo boy's name is. They were '*hittin*' it off from what I saw," Ari beamed in the mirror dabbing small dots of foundation on her face.

"He's a nice guy." Jade cut in. "Why?"

"I know you like *those types*," Ari looked away from the mirror to Jade. Michelle, rolled her eyes and turned the blow dryer back on to finish straightening her hair.

"I barely know the guy." Jade said flatly.

"Beggars can't be choosers," Ari mumbled, still talking in the mirror. Jade cut her eyes in Ari's direction. Blending her foundation Ari spoke again. "Well Jade its better you don't like him." She pulled out a tube of eyeliner.

"Why is that?" Michelle questioned, putting the blow dryer down. Ari dabbed her eyeliner in silence. "Huh?" She glanced up from her reflection, quickly returning.

"Why shouldn't Jade like him?" Michelle repeated, stepping into a lacy red cocktail-dress with a squared off neckline, her hair a massive puff.

"His eyes are on you, Michelle," Ari said applying her Arabic eyeliner, one eye, then the other without pause, and then she winked to herself, "Beautiful."

"Are you talking to yourself?" Michelle tried not to laugh. She added heat protectant to her hair, ran the flat iron over it, then placed heated rollers in section after section. Michelle's skin was glowing and eyes narrowed in disgust at Ari. It was that moment, Jade realized she would miss this Yamato girl and that she might one day want to remember her for her kindness.

"Only the truly self-absorbed talk to the mirror," Jade said looking in Ari's direction, deciding she would acquire a keepsake from Michelle, to help curtail the loss. That was when Jade saw the set of thin gold rings, three of them, sitting on the night stand near the bathroom, her *katami*. This, the first of many small keepsakes she would come to acquire.

Hikaru sat on the sofa nodding off, in his tux, his head drifting ever so close to his chest, before he jerked back, snorting himself awake.

"God, what are they doing?" He stood, walking over to the bedroom door. After knocking, he waited for a moment. Ari opened the door, her eyes lit by an alluring force. She spoke, the words echoing unheard.

"What do you want?" Ari repeated.

"Are you guys finished?"

"I'm not. Are you two finished?" Ari called.

"I'm helping Jade," Michelle shouted from the bathroom. "We're almost done." Michelle walked into the bedroom, grabbing one of Ari's make-up bags when she paused. "You look good," she smiled, reaching for a pack of facial wipes on the nightstand.

"Thanks," he beamed. "So do you."

'*Thank you,*' Michelle mouthed with a grin, the long loose waves cascading around her. She went back into the bathroom, as Hikaru watched her in the mirror for a moment.

"I knew that's what you wanted to see." Ari smiled. Hikaru stared at her.

"Jade it's fine. You look great, stop." Michelle walked out of the bathroom again a moment later, putting an eyeliner pencil away. Hikaru still in the doorway paused as Jade walked out of the bathroom. He, watched her fling hair off a bare shoulder.

"It's cold Michelle, and you send me out in the shortest dress you can possibly find."

"Well, I knew if you looked good in that other, you'd look great in this one.

"From the bride of Frankenstein to a supermodel, that blonde really saved you," Ari laughed. Hikaru simply stared. "I hope you didn't pull the hoe in her out too," Ari turned to Michelle.

"How does she look Hikaru?" Michelle asked, ignoring Ari.

"Beautiful," He nodded, taking in the sight of her in an off the shoulder long sleeve black cocktail dress, its neckline curving down to Jade's sternum.

Later, amidst yet another party, it occurred to Michelle that perhaps the pain from weeks of walking runways in shoes far too small might still be taking its toll. This came to her as the heels she chose bit into the back of her ankle for the thousandth time while she made polite conversation.

She made note of this, again, and her attention wondered from the conversation with, Ari and the editor-in-chief of *something* to Jade, sitting on the far side of the party with Hikaru. *She seems so different. The smile, even body language,* Michelle thought, *nothing like the girl I first met. It complements her,* it dawned on Michelle, *she fits here, in more ways than I could have imagined.* Observing Michelle's boredom, Ari shifted away from the conversation.

'*Do it,*' she mouthed to Seina on the opposite side of the room.

"I'm going to freshen up my drink," Michelle said excusing herself.

"Okay," Ari nodded with a smile.

"Take your time. There's lots of eye candy on the way," The editor laughed. Michelle walked over to the bar, further away from Jade and Hikaru.

"Toasted Almond," Michelle turned her attention back to Jade. "She's a completely different person," She mumbled, the girl playfully touching Hikaru's leg while she laughed along with him, her intent: far from unsheathed, in playful whispering eyes. The bartender sat the drink beside Michelle. *Has this girl been playing me the whole time?* Michelle wondered, the wounds inflicted by Ari's betrayal throbbing for her attention.

"Everything okay?" Seina cut in, pulling her again from her thoughts. She glanced in his direction.

"I really don't want to talk to you."

"I'm sorry to hear that your father is going to trial."

"Me too," she took in a deep breath. Seina paused at the sharpness of her tone.

"It's been a while. Level with me, how are you?" He asked sitting beside her, his disarming words and eyes already at work.

"It's been what? A month since I talked to you?" She sipped from her glass.

"More like two weeks since you started ignoring my texts and disappeared somehow. Three weeks since I've seen you face to face because you pretend not to be home."

"Anger must make time pass faster," Michelle smiled. "I asked you to stay away from me. *Remember, in Paris*, with your crazy cousin." Michelle's brows rose and Seina sighed. "See, you do remember. Well, I'm going to go back to my riveting conversation," Michelle moved away with a smile both sharp and false.

"Are you going to keep ignoring me?" He placed a hand on her arm, a halting motion—tender but firm. "Just let me talk to you, to explain," Seina said as a question.

"No." Michelle shook her head.

"I need to at least let you know why all that happened," his eyes locked on her, peering into her.

Michelle looked away, letting out a sigh. "And you just won't take no for an answer. Seina I'm tired, my feet hurt and I don't care what you have to say. You brought Ari into my orbit, now I have to get rid of her," she said shaking her head.

Silence spread between them, as Michelle stared steadily back. She knew there was a story, one that he and Ari likely concocted in the wake of this mess. One that exempted each party of all fault. Yet she wanted to move past it, to resume her life, before Seina Terada and Arion Louien. *But can my life be the same?* She wondered, shifting from his eyes to his lips, wanting to punch him, wanting him to have chosen her, rather than trying to help Ari creep away in the night.

"Let me explain and I will leave you alone, if you want."

"No."

"No?" He echoed, disappointment and surprise in his eyes.

"I have family things to take care of." She sighed. "And the sooner I get rid of shifty-ass," she motioned to Ari, "the sooner we'll have a chance to talk." Michelle walked away.

Veiled Truths & Futures Lost
Newport Beach, Orange County, California, March 18th

Michelle sat in the hush-hum of the court room nearly ninety-six and a half hours after seeing Seina, with a pang in her chest, pulling her in three directions. There was her father's freedom fluttering in the breeze. There was the faint scent of betrayal, liken to burnt hair or popcorn, still lingering in her nostrils: two parts lover, one part friend. Yet her mind wandered. She wondered whether her existence would ever be the same; whether it could resume its natural course, after the upheaval of her life here in Newport. *How do I move on? What do I move on to?* Her thoughts moved along this line of inquiries.

"Better late than never." Chris broke her from these, and *other, darker* thoughts. He returned with the rest of the onlookers from recess as day-six of the trial moved onward. "I was beginning to wonder if you were too busy in the headlines."

"I came as soon as I could," she stood to hug him. This drew Ari's attention. Chris took a seat beside his sister, seeming a bit on edge.

"Can you believe it?"

"Believe what?" Michelle brushed her hair back from her face and crossed her legs.

"After all we went through," he whispered, "disappearing, moving to Japan, the fake identities. Dad still got caught." Chris shook his head. The sounds of people talking and taking their seats again took away from the quiet.

Michelle scoffed. "Nosey white women always find the killer, especially when money's involved." They both snickered, trying to ease the tension.

"But seriously, are you okay?" Chris turned to look at Michelle for a long moment.

"I'm fine, Chris. Where's Alyson? I hear congratulations are in order." She shifted the topic.

"I asked her not to come."

Michelle looked at him confused. "If you're going to marry her, she should know the shit show of a family she's marrying into."

"Who's that? Your girlfriend?" Chris changed the subject, pointing to Ari with his eyes and a sly grin.

"Oh, this is my publicist, *for now*—Ari," Michelle said fighting the urge to say something witty and cruel about the girl. Ari looked at Chris then nodded. He smiled his sinister-heart-breaking smile. "Ari, this is my brother, Chris."

"Christopher Jang, nice to meet you, at last." Ari extended a hand, returning the smile. "I've heard a lot about you from a friend."

"A friend other than my sister?" He stared at her.

Ari watched him, saying nothing as Michelle uncomfortably

scrutinized the exchange. Ari just grinned and retracted her hand.

At the front of the courtroom, the attorneys conferred with their clients, orchestrating the next phase of the battle. At the far end of the bench. Vivian Yamato-Jang sat in a bone-colored knee length dress, matching blazer and four-inch heels. Her black and chestnut colored hair pulled into an elegant bun, slicked back from her face, from Michelle's face, but oval and shaped in porcelain. Michelle's oldest brother, Marcus, sat one row ahead, his curly black hair pulled into a pony tail. He was enthralled with the proceedings, the blonde former-mistress of Miles Jang's deceased business partner took the stand.

Before the Yamato-Jangs washed ashore in Japan, and just weeks prior to Drew Taylor turning up dead in his hospital room, Taylor and Jang were named in a malpractice suit. It was a life threatening infection, damaged breast tissue following a routine augmentation. Taylor and Jang lost the suit and the private practice. That was when Drew Taylor opened up about his cancer. They had been sitting on Drew's patio, drinking cheap beer in silence, looking out on the Pacific. The setting sun beamed orange and red on the cold blue water's surface.

"I have multiple myeloma, Miles," Drew Taylor had said out of nowhere. "Stage 4."

"What?" Miles looked up, still grappling with the day's loss—too wounded for another. Jumping past his fury, as a lifelong minority is always taught to do, Miles Jang shifted into concern for his friend. The rage came later.

"Does Kayla know?" Miles asked. Drew shook his head and broke down. "What about Madison, or the kids?"

"You know." Drew said.

That was the story Michelle had pieced together, after being 'banished' to what she called 'asialand'. Ten weeks later, Drew was dead. Madison, the ex-wife, was in Mexico with the kids. The mistress-turned-girlfriend, Kayla, was at his bedside. The best friend, Miles Jang, had vanished.

Madison only came into the picture when she heard of the remaining four million following the liquidation of the practice, after discovering she had been written out of Drew's will. At Madison's insistence, an autopsy was performed, which helped uncover the final syringe of heroin with its *two* sets of fingerprints. When the report was filed mentioning air pockets in Mr. Taylor's veins, Madison had all she needed to take what she wanted. Nine months later Madison's thugs caught Miles in Kuala Lumpur, bound for Andorra, and still working as a cosmetic surgeon.

As a little girl, Michelle thought her father was famous when she saw Ernie Hudson in Miss Congeniality— Chris was the one to bust that bubble. Even now she could see the resemblance, that debonair slickness, that she was always drawn to in any potential partner. It was painful to see him here fighting for his life like this. Beside her father stood, Venessa Lopez, Miles' Attorney notepad in hand with long hair and long legs.

Slighted from her wielding justice by her marriage to Miles Ms. Yamato poured not only money, but time, into children the system works against. Children of every hue. She took especially to the girls. Girls like Vanessa Lopez whom she had mentored from high school to the bar, keeping close tabs every step of the way. The same Vanessa Lopez that swooped in to save the un-savable Miles Jang, knowing the risks—to aid those who had aided her.

"In 2004 you were in a car accident. Can you tell the court what happened?" Lopez began.

"Objection." the opposing counsel, Mr. James Park, stood. "Your honor, what does this have to do with the case?"

"Your honor, I'm establishing a pattern of behavior." Lopez retorted.

"Overruled, I intend to give her the same latitude I gave you. Make it brief Ms. Lopez." Judge Barns sighed.

And brief it was, drawing upon the sealed records of the young woman's past: 2004, attacked another driver who left the scene needing fourteen stitches— 2010, threatened and beat a bartender, broken-bottle in hand when police arrived— 2017, threw 11 soda cans at an unidentified man in a Wal-Mart, all unprovoked. Better still, all the victims were minorities. Circumstantial, *yes*, but interesting nonetheless.

"That has nothing to do with this." Kayla Miller mumbled but too loudly, too sharply and through gritted teeth.

At this break in character a smirk crept across Ms. Yamato's face. Michelle and Ari took note of this as Ms. Lopez changed course. She began her line of questioning like a spider spinning a web; slow and graceful— steady and disarming. Four or five questions later, the rhythm changed, and the bottom fell out.

"On the day you threatened the defendant, Miles Jang's life in the presence of," Lopez glanced at a notepad. "Five nurses and two doctors, there was an argument. What was it about?" The question seemed to surface from thin air.

"We-That's-Drew was asking for drugs," the young woman began to clarify, but Lopez killed the opportunity.

"You and the defendant had a disagreement. What happened during that incident?"

"The nurses left and Miles told me not to give him the drugs."

"So you were alone?"

"Yes," the witness glanced at Madison, the plaintiff.

"And then what?" Ms. Lopez turned to the small courtroom audience.

"He took the syringe from me."

"The same syringe you left when you fled the crime scene?"

"Yes, I think so." Kayla sighed. "Drew was alive. I went to—" the witness tried to explain. Lopez cut her off.

"Earlier, you said you provided drugs to Mr. Taylor. How long had you been doing so?"

"The last two weeks he was alive, just for the pain. The doctor's wouldn't," Kayla said, the tears starting.

"How long had you and Madison Taylor been paying the nursing staff to look the other way? Surely it showed in his blood work."

"I don't know. I never paid anyone."

"Who were these drugs obtained by? How often did you cook up the smack? When you administered the drugs how did you measure the dosage? When you shot Drew up, that last time did the plaintiff tell you to *'take care of him?'*" Lopez's questions were endless. She undid nearly all the coaching done by opposing counsel, giving the witness only enough time to further incriminate before another question surfaced. "

"No! I didn't kill him," the witness shouted.

"You were the only one in the room, weren't you?!" Lopez continued, this time allowing no answer. "You were there right before he died. What was he doing? How did he get air and cocaine into his bloodstream? How much was the plaintiff offering you?"

"I didn't do it!" Kayla shouted, leaping from her seat, "I didn't kill him. I loved Drew!"

"Objection!" Mr. Park, Madison's lawyer stood. "She's badgering the witness!"

"Sustained." Judge Barns ruled. "Ms. Lopez you'd best tread lightly from here on."

"Yes sir. No further questions your honor," Lopez replied, but Michelle saw the triumphant glint in her eyes.

"*She bad.*" Ari said in a hoarse whisper.

The Judge then turned to the witness. "I warned you, Ms. Miller. You may step down. Bailiff place her in a cell," Judge Barns said before the bailiff came forward. "Ms. Lopez, Mr. Park this is a court of law. I will not allow either of you to continue badgering witnesses. Is that clear?"

"Yes, your honor," they said in unison, then the judge glanced at the time.

"Good." Judge Barns dismissed Ms. Lopez to her seat. "Mr. Park, call your next witness."

"The prosecution calls Vivian Yamato-Jang to the stand," James Park said smiling. Michelle glanced at Chris reflexively.

"I don't know what she has planned," Chris shrugged.

Ms. Yamato glided to the witness box. Upon taking the oath, she glanced at Miles remembering how with a *'yes'* and the slip of a ring the foundation of their lives was poured out.

"I do," Ms. Yamato grimaced, taking her seat. Her first act was to waive spousal privilege as planned with Park pre-trial. This allowed Park to get to the heart of the matter in a mere eight questions.

"Will you describe for the court how the defendant confessed to having a hand in killing his business partner?"

"I'm not following," Ms. Yamato's brows knitted together, uncannily like Michelle's. "Miles never confessed anything to me," she lied, looking at the judge then to Park, completely at a loss with feigned confusion. Vivian Yamato knew to take the stand for Miles's sake; she would be best cast as the angry ex-wife. She stared through the prosecutor as she veered from the facts that landed her the spot as his star witness. Yet Vivian also knew in taking on this, she will confirm for Michelle the woman she knows her mother to be. The woman Michelle hates.

"I'll rephrase," Park grinned, with his hands on his hips. "How did you, help your now ex-husband flee the country after learning of his involvement in Drew Taylor's death?"

"Miles left of his own volition, taking most of our liquid assets with him." Another lie. She pushed him to leave, to cancel the commercial tickets in favor of a private flight. They told no one, not even the kids— *not even Marcus.* Yet how can even the greatest legal mind escape the facts that establish perjury?

The answer is simple, and rests with the stenographer— Anna, who currently sat just to the right of the judge's box. Young, strawberry-blonde, sweet, unsuspecting Anna.

It began in December with a man, good looking, well-dressed— a man of Darius' caliber. He had close cut hair, and a matching beard. He was the kind of dangerous that made him only a bit unapproachable. But he moved in on Anna with dark sunglasses and a killer smile. There was flirting and a touch of what seemed like odd conversation in hindsight, mixing code words and light coquettish laughter. They chatted over coffee, exchanged numbers, and promised to meet again. The whole event was caught on tape, unbeknownst to Anna.

In the months leading up to Ms. Yamato's deposition, Anna discovered 5 large sums deposited in her account. Each was just a dollar shy of $10,000, then the terms came via a letter. That was when the situation became clear.

Change Vivian Yamato's deposition transcripts to match the sample provided or lose teeth. -- lose limbs.-- lose family.

Each letter provided a promise of new harm as it arrived daily. The video was sent as a warning shot, a way of making Anna look like a part in some larger plot. Sadly, the funds and letters were untraceable. After trying to locate the source of the money, the threats became more pointed. They began to appear with photos: a lock of her mother's hair along with an image of her sleeping. Her sister's dog killed in cold blood and wrapped in the sister's favorite sweatshirt, the very shirt that went missing days earlier when they spoke.

Anna had been cornered. So, she called the man with the killer smile and begrudgingly agreed. Thus, following Ms. Yamato's deposition the unchanged transcript was sent to Park. While Anna edited the version sent to both Lopez and the judge, leaving James Park's copy as the only one of its kind.

"Your Honor, permission to treat the witness as hostile?" Park requested, shifting gears. Judge Barns nodded, losing interest. "Why did you and two of your children flee to Japan after your ex-husband?" Park asked standing in front of Ms. Yamato.

"I planned to go back to Japan months before Drew died, before we sold the house. My two younger children weren't financially stable so I brought them along."

"But you went to the Philippines. Why?" Park came, and leaned on the edge of the witness box.

"I went to meet with each of the schools and orphanages Miles and I supported to let them know we could no longer donate," Ms. Yamato said as if thrown by the question.

"Your ass is mine Vivian," Park whispered then moved away from the stand, pacing. Ms. Yamato's attention shifted to Marcus with his honey-caramel complexion and his strong chiseled features. Beside him sat Devina, dark sepia skinned, with long hair and haunting green-blue eyes. They sat on the second row looking on nervously, when Ms. Yamato's head started to spin. A cry echoed from the depths of her memory. These spinning headaches are how all of her hallucinations began as of late.

"But on today of all days," she whispered, briefly closing her eyes.

"So, you deny any and all knowledge that you knew the defendant was in Japan," Park asked. "I'd like to remind you, you're under oath," he raised an eyebrow at her.

"I found out Miles was in Japan two weeks or so after I arrived, in the middle of the divorce. That was as I was starting construction on my restaurant."

"Ah, yes. The restaurant. How much would you say your restaurant is worth?" Park asked with a smile.

"It was appraised at about Fifteen million dollars," Ms. Yamato didn't see the trap forming. With the growing tension, a memory surfaced without permission. Ms. Yamato suddenly remembered waking face down among the immense puzzle pieces of what was a street, houses toppled and crumbling before being shifted back to reality.

"How were the funds for this restaurant procured?"

Ms. Yamato cast a piercing hot gaze in Miles' direction. "The restaurant was built using the savings I kept, *separately*," Ms. Yamato said, as Park paused to grab a sheet of paper next to the plaintiff, Drew's ex-wife.

Michelle shot a look to Chris. "Told you yo momma was shiesty," she mumbled and Chris snickered cracking a smile

"Your honor, I would like to show the witness a receipt labeled exhibit F," Park proclaimed to the courtroom.

The cry pulled Ms. Yamato's mind back. The sound, had led her to stumble then fall, as she searched, limping through Kobe's ruined streets.

This was a route she had walked daily, now unrecognizable. Yet Ms. Yamato could not ignore, that cry rumbling up from a muffled place, or the sirens that had deafened her to it.

"I've never seen this before." Ms. Yamato looked up from the paper, still able to hear the sirens that once came from every direction.

"That is a transfer receipt and final balance for an account you claim was for charitable giving. One you placed seven million dollars in last February, right before the funds were moved again and the account was closed five months later. That was about the time construction started for your restaurant. Could you read the final balance for the court?" Park asked, as Lopez objected.

"Relevance, your Honor, how does this relate to the case?"

"Over-ruled, Ms. Lopez. Go on Ms. Yamato."

"$47,852,900 and 78 cents." Ms. Yamato said, then stared at Park. Chris' eyes widened in utter shock, and Michelle's mouth fell open as she looked at her brother.

"How the—" Michelle trailed off.

"Ms. Yamato, did you intend to give 47 million dollars to an orphanage? Park asked as Ms. Yamato cut her eyes at Miles again.

"I used this account to make sure the malpractice suit didn't wipe us out." She lied, covering this error on Miles' part, knowing that must have been his intent.

The cry echoed in her mind again. This time it was much closer, it was the lion-like roar of a baby. After several long desperate moments of searching, Ms. Yamato had traced the source of the wailing. What she found was a crushed table under a partially collapsed wall where a young woman laid clutching a large pot.

"So, how much did you give to these orphanages annually, if not the forty-seven million?" Park asked.

"We usually donated a million between a number of orphanages and schools in and around Manilla," Ms. Yamato nodded, still remembering the blood on her coat as she knelt down and climbed under the crushed table. When she peeked inside the pot, there lay the source. A baby, red-faced with a cloud of spiraling curls about his head.

"Why orphanages in the Philippines, Ms. Yamato. "Did you have someone handling the money there?" Park asked, completely unprepared for the one of two half-truths in Vivian Yamato's testimony.

"When I was still living in Japan, a Filipino woman saved my life, in an earthquake. That woman died with four children in the Philippines," she said, making the words shine *nobly* in another lie of omission. She failed to mention the fifth child in the pot, the joyful boy that she raised. What newspaper would cover this story? The headline:

Bright young woman, studying law, dating gangster, finds baby in earthquake.

The story going on to say how she married an American, Miles, moved to the states, California. Raised the child adding two more to the set, thrown in a world of charity functions and galas, of appearances and performances. In spite of all that, in spite of all the becoming, here she sat, divorced and sick and lying. Lifting the veil of her life before a room of strangers.

"What help did you provide the defendant in entering Japan without the authorities being alerted?" Park quickly changed the tide, moving to catch Ms. Yamato in another lie.

"I didn't. By the time we met he was already in the country," Ms. Yamato lied solemnly. She sought out the Yakuza in secret, prior to Miles' brief tenure in Japan, and even his new life in Andorra la Vella. She arranged her meeting with Shinoda in a taxi. Shinoda agreed to provide asylum *for all*— no questions asked. This was a testament to the brotherly love between their fathers, Shinoda the Yakuza leader, and Yamato the restaurant owner, both men of long-ago "erased" Korean descent.

"So, you deny any dealings with Junichiro Shinoda, and the Kobe Yakuza syndicate?"

The money came later, 4.5 million or so, pulled from the sale of the house and the remains of the practice. It became the payment for relocation, new identities, and the works. It was only during this process, Ms. Yamato conceived the idea of providing the Yakuza with the same services the Yamato clan of Osaka was long renowned for.

"No, Junichiro was a high school acquaintance who I met again after the restaurant opened. Since then, we have become friends." Ms. Yamato had grown bored with this game and the familiar tension. She could feel Park beginning to wind down as she had all but bested him in altering the golden testimony out of nowhere.

All of these ins and outs, James Park knew, thanks to the original deposition. The *single* unaltered one. But with the unwilling help of Anna, the impending perjury charges won't stick, if there are any. *For the testimonies will match, and any shred of evidence to contradict it, will come at a high price.* Yet, Ms. Yamato was prepared to go all the way, having already furnished Lopez with her medical records. Thus, allowing her state of mine to come under question, if need be. The 'disease,' yet unacknowledged.

Ms. Yamato shifted to more comforting thoughts. She paused to imagine how James Park's day might unfold after leaving this court of law, as Lopez came forward to cross-examine. It would likely begin with two voicemails: first, the wife informing him of the break-in at their home.

"Honey," she might say, breathless, while clutching her baby, tables and chairs overturned, glass shattered everywhere. "James, we're going to spend some time at my parent's house. A guy just kicked in the door. Call me when you get this." She would say, her nerves torn to bits, as she notes that her husband's laptop and hard drives are missing.

The second voicemail will be from Park's assistant, to tell him there was a gas leak at the office, which resulted in an explosion. One *only small enough* to take out his and the adjoining suites. But what Vivian hopes, is that before James Park calls anyone back, or checks his voicemail, that he'll walk to his car, find it unlocked, with a book bag wedged under his seat, and a cool million inside, recognizing it as the hush money it is.

"If not, he can be taken care of," Ms. Yamato muttered to herself.

"Has the jury reached a verdict?" The judge asked, a mere three and a half hours later.

"Yes, your honor." The forewoman stood to read off the ruling. "We, the jury find the defendant, Miles Jang—" She began, and just as simple as when people leave rooms, justice slipped out of this Newport court, slung over the shoulders of one Miles Jang, and Vivian Yamato-Jang. Though not scot-free, the villains slipped away, off into the sunset, to fight another day.

Ambitions
Tokyo, March 20th

Eva sat in her living room on a new red and white designer-sectional. She and Yu bought it on a whim, and since then *her apartment* was beginning to feel like *their home*. When Yu surfaced from the shower, Eva was watching TV, in white silk pajamas over red wine, huddled up under blankets. She watched the steam rise off his body as he threw on a shirt and walked past the TV.

"How was your day? You haven't said a word since I got in." Eva said.

"It was fine," he kissed her, then sat down beside her.

"It doesn't sound like it was fine, Yu-boo," Eva smiled, touching him with her feet.

Yu raised an eyebrow at her and smiled. She moved closer to him, and then turned, placing her head in his lap. He grinned at her again, then shifted his attention to the TV.

"So, what did you do today?" Eva looked up at him, her dark brown hair shining in his lap. "Did you find your wallet yet?"

"Not yet," he shook his head, his eyes still on the screen. Eva watched the light from the TV fall on his well-defined jaw, neck, and Adams apple. Though she would never say it out loud, there was something dangerously compelling about Yu Hiroshi. Something, Eva still found herself desiring:

in him, with him, from him. This was why she let him pursue her all those years ago in Barcelona, and again here in Tokyo—despite their year-long romance and the subsequent six-year gap. *It felt like destiny when Victoria bumped into him at a Tsutaya over in Ginza, then invited him and Eva to dinner at Li Jun's place when Victoria and Li Jun were still in item. It was like no time had passed*, she and Yu simply picked up where they had left off.

"I think you should report it." Eva said suddenly. "You did cancel all your cards, didn't you?"

"Yeah, I did. Don't worry. It's been taken care of," Yu grinned, shifting his gaze to her, "I just hope the wallet itself shows up."

"Is it your dad's?" She asked, sitting up to face him.

"It's the one you bought me in Spain," Yu looked over at her, eyes glinting.

"You still have that?" Eva asked genuinely surprised, touched that he kept it these last eight years.

"Yeah," his grin bloomed into a smile. "It's not like it was fifty years ago."

"Still, it's been almost a decade," Eva motioned to stand, but Yu grabbed her.

"You're not getting away from me," he laughed, fighting to keep her in his grasp. He pulled Eva closer tangling the blanket between them. "The more pressing issue is, when do I get to call you Mrs. Hiroshi?" Yu grinned impishly.

Eva released a sigh. "We have a lot to work out before we can even think about that," she said diplomatically, before she pulled away.

"That's what wedding planners are for." Yu chuckled.

"I'm talking about before a wedding," Eva looked at him squarely.

"Like what?" Yu asked, searching her eyes for some hint of a joke.

"Well Yu, my parents are very traditional. They only came here after they couldn't get citizenship in the US, or the UK, France, Germany, Korea—" she went on, "Pretty much anywhere else."

"Okay," Yu nodded, struggling to follow where this was headed.

"In their minds they lost face by coming here. When they left China for Vietnam, the Japanese were the enemy. And when my father left for the states they planned to live there. Coming here was the ultimate defeat. They would have gone back but we were prospering here. So, for me to want to marry you, let alone date you, it's a problem for them."

"Eva that's the past. Why can't they just see that you and I are in love?"

"Okay history aside, what religion will we practice? What language do we teach our kids? Yu, I haven't even met your dad or your brother."

"None of that matters. We'll be true blue agnostics, you speak to the kids in Cantonese, I'll speak to them in Japanese and on their tenth birthday, I'll start speaking only English to them. My family doesn't exist without you."

"It's not that easy, Yu. And I'm Buddhist, so are my parent's—my whole family is."

"Okay I can give on that one," Yu grinned. "Buddhist we shall be."

"My mother hates you. And not just a little bit. She really hates you." Eva deflated as she looked at him.

"I'll grow on her. Your dad likes me." Eva shook her head. "What do you mean no?" Yu's tone shifted from playful to concerned. "He was over here a few days ago laughing it up with us and playing board games."

"He wanted to give you a fair chance, without my mother interfering," Eva's gaze drifted to the red cushions of the sectional.

"And what did he think?" Yu questioned.

"He likes you as a person." Eva paused. "But he doesn't think we're right for each other."

"*Wow, Eva.* Thanks for keeping me in the loop."

"I'm keeping you in the loop, by telling you now," she tucked her hair behind an ear, as it grazed her shoulders.

"Why does their approval matter so much?" Yu asked, suddenly becoming defensive. He turned the TV off and shifted his entire body to face her.

"Because I love my family, we are family oriented. You think I employ two of my siblings just because? *We* stick together. And my father doesn't believe you care enough about your family to be a part of ours," Eva paused, trying to soften the blow.

"So, what if they never approve of us?"

"Don't say that," she moved closer to him.

"I'm still young, healthy, good looking, I'm not poor. I speak Chinese or understand ninety percent of what they say. Fine, I'm not Chinese." Yu's rambling turned rant.

"They weren't too happy when I told them your father was ill and that you don't look after him, either," Eva mumbled, adding fuel to the fire.

"Because my dad is dying, they want you to have nothing to do with me? Are those the only problems they have with me? Or will they not like me because I have a black brother too."

"Yu, I don't know why they don't like you!" She placed her hands on his cheeks, looking into his eyes. "But what I do know is that three people I love, refuse to meet in the middle. You, just have to win them over. Show them you are the man for me," she kissed his nose. "Did I ever tell you how much I love your eyes?"

"It doesn't matter, your parents don't like them," Yu mumbled, turning the TV back on.

"Yu, what would your parents do in this situation?"

"Nothing after I told them we were engaged. But I still wonder how your mom knew if you didn't tell her," Yu said pulling away. He walked over to the balcony door, looking down to the street.

"Yu," Eva followed him with her eyes. "Yu-boo."

"It's fine I'm over it—Tori called again."

"Don't be like that."

"She sounded pissed," he said in a distant tone, glancing over a shoulder.

Eva gasped. "I forgot to call her back. I'm sure its work drama." She stood, and walked over to wrap her arms around Yu as he stared out the window. The faint orange of the street light creeping across his face.

"You know I like her and she's your oldest friend, but she's selfish and really needy," Yu said.

"No, she's not," Eva protested.

"Today she called me four times in a row for you with no thought to what I was doing," Yu turned to face her. Eva sighed, bringing a hand to her forehead.

"Then it must have been serious. I mean, we've been friends since we were in college and—" Eva trialed off, sitting to write herself a note.

"Most people outgrow those friendships," Yu added.

"Okay, let's talk about us."

"You've made it clear there is no us until mom and dad like me," he said taking a seat on the floor.

"Come on, Yu," Eva griped.

"What happened that Tori needs you so much?" Yu asked.

Eva sighed, moving to sit back on the sofa. "Tori ended up being offered a job with Michelle." She said with pointed distaste.

"The same girl from your parents' party last summer? The rude girl that came with Jun, right?"

"Right," Eva nodded "Tori was given the lead but, now it's being shared."

"Tori is old news, she can't be the lead in everything forever. She's been modeling for what ten—fifteen years? They wanted the other girl, they got her, business is business."

"No, Michelle is savvy and when it comes to work she knows how to charm. This job just fell in her lap. That's why I need to knock her down a few dozen pegs, but poor Tori."

"Did you miss something or did you look the other way?" Yu asked, almost laughing.

"I missed it completely. She got them to pay for everything, plus a really good commission for the agency. And right now, she's bringing in so much money. Everyone wants her because everyone wants her," Eva said.

"Build up more models to put her in check, and then put her on a probation." He sat down on the coffee table facing her.

"I did, then she landed the big fashion weeks, then she was offered a job with Kili Mono to be the face next season—the face!" Eva exclaimed, moving to the floor and closer to Yu. "And now Victoria Secret wants her.

"And they're still recovering from that scandal a few years back." Yu nodded to himself. "So, you need to knock her off her horse before she turns around and bites you."

"You're mixing metaphors but yeah." Eva nodded, laughing with him. "Yu, she might help me expand outside of Asia, to be a permanent presence."

"At what cost, Eva?" He paused, staring at her. It was in that instant he saw her dreams fanning out before her on the back of Michelle. Then it all became clear— the real reason for all her hesitation. Her sudden talk about meeting his family, getting to know Hikaru, all of it. "You just said she's out of control."

"I know and I'm trying to reel her in." Eva objected, still dreamy eyed.

"And what if you can't?" He asked searching her eyes, noting her dimmed excitement at the thought.

"I don't know. But I've been trying to take this agency further for years. If I lose Michelle, I don't know if this chance will present itself again. I've never sent anyone to one of the big four, let alone all of them, and she fucked it up with Adrien Depaul and Seina Terada." Eva rolled her eyes. Yu bristled at the mention of Seina. "The problem is Michelle knows she's an asset." Eva shook her head.

"If you can't control her it doesn't matter what she can do for you. It won't work Eva."

"This is my dream," Eva said, which caused Yu to take pause.

"That's why you won't set a date." The realization dawned on him.

"What?" Eva balked.

"That's why you're slow walking our engagement. You're not going to take time to start a life with me, not if you expand. Not if you become a permanent presence overseas," Yu stood as the realization washed over him more strongly now. "How do you think all this expansion is going to affect us with you flying here and there for this and that. How are we going to get married even if I do manage to win your parents over?" Yu's eyes narrowed now as his brow folded over.

Eva scoffed. "You're jumping to conclusions," she stood. "I'm bringing Tori on, in a few months to handle just that. So I can be here with you."

"Eva that still means more work— more meetings— and late night texts from Hitomi about things that *just popped up*. I know you know that." He stared at her still in disbelief.

"We'll handle it Yu. Besides, this was in the works way before you popped up again." Eva said more sharply than it was meant to sound. "I'm still trying to balance us and work. We can figure it out together. That's what marriage is," she smiled, throwing her arms around him, trying to make him hug her back.

"Why didn't you tell me you had these plans before I proposed?" Yu asked, flatly.

"Because they didn't seem real or even possible then." Eva looked up to find his eyes colder than she had ever seen.

"And now they are?" He questioned. "We're supposed to share those hopes," he said cutting away at her defense. "—so what time frame do you see us getting married?" He prompted.

"Three-four years maybe," Eva winced as the words came.

Yu stared at her, his mouth open. "I'm going to bed. Good night."

"Yu," Eva called after him. He slowly walked away. "Yu!"

"I love you. I'm going to bed," he shouted back.

"We're talking here," she yelled, to the sound of a closing door.

Tales from the Spanish Village
Tokyo, March 26th

Afternoon dawned in Tokyo once again, and Jade walked to the Bakery across from Eva's office to have lunch with Hitomi, as she's done since becoming 'Michelle's assistant.' She waited at their usual table when Hitomi floated across the street, smiling. She had a slender nose and a round but still angular face. The heavy bangs cut across her forehead shielding the eyebrows from view. She was beautiful but, in a cute way, her long brown hair curled perfectly at the ends.

"Hitomi-senpai." Jade called beaming back, waving and feeling the need to turn on the 'cute'.

They sat over fusion French-Japanese pastries discussing boyfriends and workloads in a wave of girl-ish Japanese, until Jade dropped the bait she hoped would lead into a bit of gossip. "Senpai, atarashii baito iru yo." She said, pouting.

I need a new part time job

"Koko ni kinasai. Eva wa—" Hitomi stopped.

"Eva wa nani?" Jade asked, swearing not to tell a soul.

Although for weeks she and Hitomi had gossiped over croissants and coffee, there was never any real information. Sure, there was Eva's schedule which Jade controlled remotely. And true it was much easier to change meetings through Hitomi's phone as a proxy, at lunch across from the office— so that any ugliness wouldn't directly tie back to Jade. But the moment Hitomi uttered *Rebranding meeting,'* Jade lit up like a Christmas tree.

Thus, Jade shifted Eva's calendar a bit more, moving the rebranding meeting and the talks with Victoria's Secret as a parting gift of sorts for Michelle.

She also set up a meeting with Yang Wei Rubber's President, Liam Yang, while moving and canceling a few meetings to make it look good on paper. As Hitomi's lunch hour came to an end, Jade slipped tickets to a

Maxwell concert in Hitomi's wallet, to help with the boyfriend troubles, they said their goodbyes, then Jade went on to the next phase of her plot.

Eight hours later, in Spain, the Barcelonan sun radiated overhead, scorching Victoria's milky skin. She took in a breath. Then she and her dance partner, Elias, took their places in the town square of the Spanish Village to shoot her scenes for the Alex and Andrew music video. Victoria glared back at Michelle, who was looking on from a distance. She sat underneath a tent and a row of trees, her portions already shot aside from their joint segment and this one remaining scene with Elias.

She may as well be the face that launched a thousand ships, or the beauty slithering from a rug, Victoria thought, of the woman cloaked behind dark Aviator sunglasses—the daughter of the new O.J. Simpson. *The sun here embraced her, by contrast.*

Victoria took her stance behind her partner battling those thoughts. The music began, the sound of the Spanish guitar and a haunting contralto filled the square. Victoria stepped out from behind Elias, her hands on his shoulder, and his hand slipping down the length of her body. Victoria stepped around him, turning to face the man, and then she turned her back to him. Ari and Hikaru watched with Michelle, as the camera man zoomed in on Victoria and Elias.

"She's gotten better." Ari smiled, pulling the sunglasses from her eyes to wipe her face. The blaring distorted music, worsening her headache. "I don't get it, it's not usually this warm here," she said to no one in particular.

"I just hope Victoria doesn't fall again." Michelle mumbled to herself, pausing to drink an entire bottle of water. She was in a foul mood, *again*. Her father's 'not guilty' verdict and Chris's fast approaching nuptials both soured, by her inability to replace Ari with a competent publicist.

In scenario-based interview after interview they all proved to be inexperienced as Ari promised. Even the seasoned ones provided lack luster solutions to Michelle's abstracted everyday problems with Eva, Li

Jun, Victoria, and even Seina, which infuriated Michelle even more. Now, there was the addition of Seina's continued attempts to reach her. On top of all that was this unbearable heat.

"After seeing her fall so many times, I hurt." Hikaru added, trying to lighten the heaviness of the Ari-Michelle stand-off.

Michelle looked down at her phone. Ari watched Victoria and Elias in silence, the booming music the only constant.

"So, what are you guys thinking for lunch?" Hikaru asked, looking at a map of the village.

"That's fine," Michelle said, throwing dampening hair off to one shoulder, before shifting back to the phone, completely uninterested in her surroundings.

"What are you talking about?" Hikaru looked at Michelle, his eyes narrowed and cheeks puffed in forced cheerfulness. It was then Ari shifted to peer at Michelle's screen. **When will I see you again? –Seina**. Michelle put the phone face down almost hearing the question in his voice.

"I thought you were done trying to intervene?" Michelle looked over her shoulder at Ari. "I don't know what's going on with you Teradas but you need to find someone else to fuck with."

"I've been apologizing for months now. When are you going to let up?" Ari questioned as Hikaru noted the seriousness in their voices.

"A month! Singular! And *bitch*, you said I'm sorry. *That's it*. Oh, I'm sorry I tried to destroy your life. I'm sorry I pulled your ex out the woodwork, but you were dating my cousin-brother, or whatever fucking Addams family bull-shit you niggas tryina pull. You can't fix betrayal with a fucking band-aid, Ari!" Michelle said, turning to face her. Hikaru stepped away, his frozen smile melting before falling to the ground.

"I'm sorry, Michelle." Ari came closer, standing at Michelle's side. "It felt right. And it was before I realized how much Adrien hurt you but, by then it was too late. So I'm sorry for hurting you, but not for protecting Seina," she shook her head.

"So, did you dig up that shit for the show?" Michelle watched Ari searchingly, her face tense and her skin damp with sweat.

"No, but why would you even believe me at this point?" Ari asked point blank. "For those pictures to even exist someone had you in their sights before I showed up." She narrowed her eyes at Michelle. Michelle opened her mouth to speak but that made her think.

In the courtyard, Victoria crossed her legs at the ankles and paused. Elias stepped around her, his foot catching hers. He dragged his foot, rotating her entire body. He turned her, again and again, and then a third time. Victoria twisted to shift her footing but, tripped over her shoe, pulling them both down to the cobblestone street with another deflating thud.

"Cut!" The director shouted, "Alright. Let's all just take thirty minutes for lunch." Victoria's tiny assistant, Quinn, rushed over to help, ponytail bobbing.

"This is the fourth time we've shot this!" Michelle rolled her eyes.

"She's threatened by you. You have that effect," Ari said before Michelle stood and walked away. She grabbed another bottle of water, before slamming into Hikaru.

"Sorry," she grumbled.

"You okay?" Hikaru stopped her.

"Fine," Michelle said while Elias carried Victoria to a shady place along a line of trees.

"Why are you being so mean today?" Hikaru asked.

"It's a lot of things, Hikaru. Look, just give me some time to myself," she said. Before he realized it, Hikaru was watching Michelle walk away. He took a step, feeling the urge to follow her, but he was struck by the sense not to.

Ari scoffed at him. "What? Can't make a move?" She asked, watching Michelle approach Victoria. Hikaru cut his eyes to Ari but said nothing.

"It's just a scratch. Are you okay Elias?" Michelle heard Victoria say as she approached.

"Are you okay?" Michelle inched in, looking at the bruise blooming on her knee.

"What do you care? As long as I can't get it, you're the star," Victoria put ice on the bruise and Elias stood in silence.

"I just wanted to check on you," Michelle said flatly.

"To rub it in my face that you're better than me?" Victoria asked.

"No, because you're taking blows like an NFL player." Michelle sneered "But if you don't want my concern that's fine."

"No, I don't want your fake concern you barren cunt." Victoria chucked ice cubes in Michelle's direction and smiled.

Michelle rushed Victoria and backhanded her with the full weight of her body. Hikaru and Ari stopped and looked at each other wide eyed. The sound echoed.

"That could have been you." Hikaru said smugly. Victoria froze then spat out blood, her face already swelling. Elias was stunned.

Michelle continued away from the group in silence. She moved toward the narrow white-washed corridors with Ari following after her.

"Michelle," Ari called, barely three feet behind. "Seina is the closest thing I have to a brother in the little family I have left." She began in her monolog, "I saw you as poison, and tried to cut you out. Knowing how Seina feels for you now and seeing the two of you together, now I know I was wrong."

"I understand that Ari." Michelle looked into her eyes as the pace slowed. "But we became friends, and trust doesn't rebuild itself with an 'I'm sorry' and well wishes." Michelle spoke clinically, from a place of distance keeping her eyes on the street. "I trusted you even when there were moments of doubt, and you cut me open. In what world does someone lay you out bleeding, say I'm sorry and you go back to braiding each-others hair? I don't trust you or Seina. And both of you just keep prodding me like I'm going to give in after a while. Leave me the fuck alone, stop trying to be my friend, and prove you're worthy of my trust, then you might keep your damn job," Michelle said still walking. Ari stopped.

A chill took hold of her in the early heat of Barcelonan spring. Ari knew it well, had dealt it a thousand times over. It was a thing comprised of so much, but changed next to nothing, *on the outside*. It was the force capable of taking away the sweetness and bitterness of life, bringing them to a cool, tasteless, neutral, blocking the fruit of the spirit. It was a thing as thick and transparent as it is often unbreakable. *I am Samir. I am Lia*, Ari thought hearing Michelle's footsteps echo on the cobblestone streets. The sound seemed to ricochet off the white-washed villas, in the oppressive heat, in that narrow corridor, of the Spanish Village. *I am the very thing I meant to destroy*, the thought reverberated, the thing, had come full circle, ending, at the beginning, or so she thought.

The Deal
Tokyo, April 2nd

Eva unlocked the door to her apartment with evening playing out on the horizon. She struggled to grip the bags of food bought from Yu's favorite restaurant. She turned the doorknob, walking in and managing to lock the door behind her.

"Yu?" She called stepping out of her shoes. "Yu-boo, where are you?"

"In the kitchen. Okaeri." Yu peeked out with a smile.

"Tada ima." Eva laughed, walking passed the kitchen and into the living room. She sat the bags down on the coffee table and walked back into the kitchen to kiss him.

"I got dinner." Yu pointed to the kitchen table.

"What? I bought dinner." Eva pointed to the living room.

"I thought it was my day. I got your favorite from the Mexican place up the street." Yu smiled.

"I went to that Moroccan restaurant by the office." Eva grinned, bringing a hand to her face.

"Let's just eat both." Yu shrugged, pulling her closer. She leaned in to kiss him. Yu half heartily gave her a peck, but held on to her.

"So, where do you want to eat?" She asked, stepping back to assess him.

"The living room's fine." Yu grabbed the plates of food from the kitchen table.

"You read my mind. Let me get changed first and I'll help you set up." Eva dashed off.

"So, I called your parents today." Yu moved the bags of food, beginning to set the table in the living room. "And I set up a brunch for the four of us."

"Really? What did they say?" Eva shouted back.

"Your mom said no and to go to hell along with a few other choice things." He finished setting the table. "But your dad said that they would be there," Yu took a seat, propping his feet up on the coffee table.

"When?" She called from the bedroom.

"The seventeenth," he replied, stacking food on his plate

"The seventeenth," Eva paused. "I can't do brunch on the seventeenth; I have a standing meeting with the rebranding team."

"That's impossible." Yu protested, sitting back on the sofa. "I checked with Hitomi this morning and this afternoon."

"Hold on, let me check," Eva walked into the living room to pick up her phone.

"I'm telling you Hitomi said you had no meetings that day," Yu looked up from his plate.

"Hitomi is the best office manager but, even she makes mistakes every now and then." Eva winked. "Just don't tell her that," she whispered. "See I have a meeting, on the seventeenth from ten to twelve. And before that I need to do a little last-minute prep." Eva said showing Yu her calendar. "Did you already make reservations?"

"Yeah, I did." He nodded, taking the phone.

"What's wrong with you tonight? Are you still mad at me?"

"No."

"You're not being warm and fuzzy. I'm sorry Yu-boo. She must have made a mistake." Eva sat on the arm of the chair while Yu scrolled on her phone. "If you get a smart-phone I could just add you to my calendar, and you could always slip in a surprise or two."

"Eva it's in red. It's been moved to the Twenty-ninth, see click on it." He said, smiling at being right. "I asked her to double check before I booked anything."

"Why would it be moved?" Eva questioned.

"The food's getting cold." Yu piled more food on his plate.

"You set the table without me? And you're eating?" Eva hit him playfully.

"You were taking too long." He chuckled. "Sit down, let's eat." He smiled, pausing to kiss her. Yu pulled away and Eva rolled her eyes but sat beside him.

"I still don't know how my meeting was moved. That makes no sense," Eva grumbled scrolling on her phone. "And since when do I have a meeting in Hong Kong with Tori's dad on the thirteenth? What could they want with the agency?" She mumbled. "I have to do some research." She said, doing just that. Yu sat in silence for a few long minutes, then Eva glanced up. "I'm sorry-I'm sorry-I'm sorry!" She put the phone face down on the table. "I'm all yours Yu." She grinned, making a plate for herself.

"So, you think brunch with your parents is a good idea?"

"Yes. I'm so glad you're trying to reach out to them." Eva placed her hand on Yu's arm. "That's why I love you." She kissed him.

"I love you too," Yu said back, the words feeling hollow for the first time.

"You know if this marriage thing is really gonna work out one of us has to learn how to cook." Eva chuckled looking at the food on the table.

"I'm up to the task," Yu said, picking up a taco.

"My hero." Eva beamed at Yu, finding a sweet smile paired with sad eyes. "Yu what's wrong?"

"I'm just thinking."

"About what?" Eva asked.

"Us." Yu bit into the taco then locked eyes with Eva. "I love you Eva," he said after swallowing.

"I love you too, Yu-boo. I—" She started, not knowing where he might be going with this.

"I've loved you for a long time now. And I know your company is what matters the most."

"I'd choose you over—" She started again.

"No, you wouldn't." He beamed, looking into her eyes. "I love you too much to lie to you, anymore. I'm-we're being blackmailed." Yu paused.

Eva stared at him her face expressionless. "What are you talking about," she blinked, her head shaking, "by whom?"

"You and I are being blackmailed by Jade," Yu repeated.

"Jade, as in Michelle's wanna be assistant?" Eva questioned. "What does she have on *us*?"

"I don't know what she has on you. But she's after your financial documents. She said if I got those that she would forget all the dirt she has on us."

"When did this happen?" Eva crossed her arms, her brow wrinkling with the question

"About three weeks ago."

"Someone threatens to reveal something if they don't get my financial documents and you tell me a month later?" Eva was outraged. "What did you say?"

"It's the same thing you did with your dad. I thought I could handle it. But she walked off with my wallet."

"So that's what happened to your wallet." Eva put her plate down. "Well, what could she have on you?"

"A lot," Yu stared into Eva's eyes. "life changing things."

"What do you mean?" Eva's brows moved together a deep valley forming between them. "What does she have on you?" Eva inched away, the voice making up for the distance.

"I was an escort for the last three years and a host before that," Yu put his plate down and wiped his hands. His eyes met hers.

"You were an escort for three years?" Eva repeated, staring at him.

"No one knew, not even Hikaru."

"But she does, somehow. How long ago was this?"

"Was what?" Yu asked.

"Your escort days?" Eva stared at him.

"Up until three weeks ago," Yu said. Eva stopped and closed her eyes, moving off the sofa, away from him. "But, I quit and I planned to quit months before I proposed to you." Yu looked at her.

"The entire time we've been dating. Even while we were engaged!" Eva shouted, her ring glittering in the light.

"Yes. I was under contract and when we ran into each other a year ago, I couldn't say no. I was enamored." Yu's hands flung open.

Eva placed a hand on her hip and covered her mouth, looking at the floor.

"Eva—" Yu started.

"So three weeks ago you were having sex with random people for money, and Jade comes up and threatens to out you?"

"Yes." He said in a whisper.

"How did she find out?"

"She became a client and—" Yu tried to explain, but Eva cut him off.

"You slept with her? How many women-how many people have you slept with?" Eva asked trying not to shout.

Yu stared at her. "I don't know." He paused, choosing to forgo the goodbye speech pledging love. "But Jade plans to reveal this and more if she doesn't get something from me."

"Why are you telling me this now?" Eva sat on a bench on the other side of the room, with tears welling in her eyes. "I was just starting to believe in this dream you created for me." She stared at the coffee table covered in food. Yu stood and walked over to Eva kneeling down to comfort her.

"Eva, I know—" Yu began again.

Eva started to chuckle. "So, my parents were right," a smile swept over her face. Eva's eyes shifted to Yu, the tears ripening and pouring softly down her cheeks. The smile remained. "I really loved-you," she whispered, looking into Yu's chestnut-colored eyes again before she stood and walked into the bedroom, locking the door.

14. Curiosity
Tokyo, April 2nd

Jade sat cutting news articles about Liam Yang in her bedroom. She glanced at the clock on her nightstand, knowing Soo Young would be home soon. Jade walked to the kitchen, sprinkling articles here and there en route to the trash. She rushed back to her bed, to place the remaining loose articles in her notebook.

Soo Young flung the door open, back from work, right on time. She kicked off her shoes hobbling across the living room as Jade jumped up, almost frantically throwing the notebook into a lockbox. Jade saw Soo Young watching, pretending to have lost something in the living room and now looking for it. For weeks Jade's done this, collecting articles, acting a bit off— piquing Soo Young's interest. Jade glanced at the clock again, grabbed her jacket, and out the door she went, forgetting to lock away the notebook. In her haste, Jade dropped a few clippings by the door, leaving Soo Young with the tingling sense of wonder.

Soo Young went to the door to lock it. Drawn like a moth to flame, she picked up the story there and read it. Soo Young found herself in the kitchen humming, the curiosity still ringing bells and setting off alarms. It was then she saw another clipping on the floor, then another.

She read them, made coffee, put them down, glanced at the time. She sipped her coffee, glanced to the door, then read again that the President of Yang Wei Rubber and Plastics, Liam Yang, was to be presented an award, and in Tokyo, tomorrow. Soo Young put the article down again, and wonder's bells chimed once more, shifting Soo Young's interest to the notebook. She eased the door open, surveying the room. Soo Young heard the unlocked lockbox call to her, and so opened it. Abandoning all pretense, she was on the hunt to piece it together now. *Who is Liam Yang to*

Jade, she wondered?

Jade slowly made her way back up to the apartment, still watching Soo Young from her phone. Soo Young was thumbing the pages of the notebook, each page littered with articles on the one man, Liam Yang, and going back eight or nine years. *Who is this man?*

"Soo Young what are you doing?" Jade appeared in the doorway of the bedroom, snatching the notebook from her.

"Mimianhae—" Soo Young stammered, caught off guard.

"Get—" Jade started.

"Who is this Liam Yang?!" Soo Young countered, holding up a picture. "Are you in trouble?"

"No!" Jade shouted turning away from Soo Young.

"Why are you obsessing over this man?'"

Jade sniffed, then wiped her eyes with the palms of her hands, her back still to Soo Young.

Soo Young placed a hand on Jade's shoulder. "Look, I know we're not close but, people should help look out for each other. And to do that, you have to be able to trust the people in your corner. You don't have to carry this alone." Soo Young said, meaning every word, offering what Jade knew could be friendship. But Jade chose the dark path, again.

"He killed my mother." The words trickled from Jade's lips as the notebook fell to the floor, her abstract story another lie of omission. "Then he kept on killing," she paused. *"and walked away to still live his life."* A whisper. The tears roared free, at last, her perspective clear and the story framed. "I want justice."

Soo Young took Jade in her arms and another torrent came raining down and spilling forth, through Jade's weakening facade. Though tears were unplanned, the moment was perfect. As Jade intended, she, with a new decoy eating from the palm of her hand.

"Help me understand honey," Soo Young said in English—dropping the accent.

Revision-Rebuild
Kita-ku & Nakameguro, Tokyo, February 8th - April 3rd

The idea for Li Jun's exhibition came to him in February, as he sat in Asukayama park. Though the concept wasn't revolutionary, it was eye-opening for Wong Li Jun, a way to deal with his grief, yet to be *truly* recognized.

It was a cold day, far too cold for spring to even seem like a faint possibility but there they were, a Black man and two little boys: one Black, the other Asian. Save the four of them the park was empty in the mid-day thaw. Li Jun had been sitting on the raised cement planter surrounding a tree, looking for inspiration. Li Jun sat, dejected, watching the two little boys chase each other. They wound around the slide with the elephant base, then the monkey bars, as the man— the Black boy's father, Li Jun presumed, watched the two boys run and scream with wild delight. It was an odd sight but, not so strange that Li Jun lost sight of the moment.

The man had a wide grin of straight white teeth as tears came to his eyes, slow at first, then a river of emotion running onto the man's face, in silence alongside his beautiful smile. The image both disturbed and moved Li Jun so deeply, he took a photo. The man stood chocolate skin, with broad shoulders, in a black pea coat and hat, and white jeans. None of the other photos Li Jun had taken in the last three months tore at his heart the way this one had. Li Jun had been so absorbed in capturing the image in all its raw intensity; he didn't notice the woman watching him.

She came up from behind, convenient store bag in hand. "What are you doing?" The woman had asked sharply. Li Jun looked at her crying and she stopped. The gleeful laughter of the little boys cut through the playground.

"Sorry." Li Jun cleared his throat, wiped his eyes and sniffed. "I'm Li Jun," he extended a hand, then paused. Li Jun was completely floored when their eyes met. She stood with elbow-length locs pulled from her face, and draping her back, large gentle eyes heightened by eyeliner, and a wide nose with wide full lips painted red. She was awe inspiring, *so very beautiful*. "I'm a photographer." He had sniffed. He snapped the photo of the woman.

"Uchechi!" The man shouted coming toward her and Li Jun.

"I'm fine." Uchechi said in Igbo. Then she looked at Li Jun. "Let me see it." She looked to his camera her eyebrows pulled downward and together at their center.

Li Jun showed her the camera and she flipped through picture after picture, looking for the perverse. "Sorry, I thought you were some kinda freak." Uchechi sat down where Li Jun had previously been sitting, crossing long thick legs in grey slacks.

"I found out I was about to be a father but—" Li Jun broke off, pouring out but not intending to. He covered his face to stop the tears. For a long few moments, Li Jun and Uchechi sat in silence, drinking heated cans of apple cider.

"His name is Okechuku," Uchechi began out of nowhere. By then, the other man was chasing the children and roaring, the boys laughing contentedly. "That's Caleb and Kenta," she pointed, her entire face folded into a smile, and then the smile faded. "Oke was dating Kenta's mother when they all moved to the states. When she died, Oke adopted Kenta. Two years later Oke and I met in DC through our sons." Li Jun snapped more photos of Okechuku as Uchechi watched the three of them. "We got engaged, then married, and now we're expecting. It took us some time to get back to Japan so that Kenta finally met his grandparents but, we made it." Uchechi added. Li Jun snapped a series of photos of her, then put the camera down.

Uchechi flung her locs off a shoulder unsure why she felt the need to share. She wasn't moved by Li Jun's pain—though she felt it, knew it intimately after losing her husband in her last trimester.

"I'm sorry for your loss," her words seemed to hit Li Jun in the belly, and stay there, making *the lost* more real. "Losing a child is heart

278

wrenching." At this, his unexamined hurt finally retched forth, uncontrolled. How could he have known losing someone that had never drawn breath could break him, a man's man, the man he believed himself to be. Uchechi rubbed Li Jun's back as it rose and fell with his tears.

"From this suffering, life will take you places you thought you might never be able to go again. It's up to you to find the good in your life and move forward." She said at last.

When the depth of his loss was made known to him, and the tears had dried up, Li Jun paid Okechuku and Uchechi for becoming his model's. That was the beginning of Li Jun's Revision-Rebuild exhibition. Or so Victoria paused to read, in the brochure at the showing, alongside the masses.

Victoria fought against the raw intensity found in Okechuku's tears, and dismissed the beauty of Uchechi watching Oke play with the boys. She wrestled the tide of every image as she moved through the gallery, shielding herself from Li Jun, and his emotions, with the aid of her white fur coat. Despite the constant emotional assault, Victoria felt at home in the space, the knee-length silver dress, against the galleries glass walls, polished concrete floors, and the exposed track lighting. It felt like a shoot. She tussled with her long-chemically curled hair, and it was then Victoria stumbled across the image that broke the spell.

It was a photo of a breech birth. The child floated above the nurse's hands facing the lens as its head slowly slipped from the vaginal canal, hanging into the world. The new born kicked and flailed as if still in the womb, and yet in the high definition of the image's excitement and chaos, this moment was silent. **Between Worlds**. That was the title.

Victoria stood in silence thinking of her lost child. It didn't matter that there were two or three images of children and babies shot just as powerfully, just as beautifully, this one was haunting.

Had little Hua lan, for somehow she knew it was a girl, *looked something like that when she was sucked away, then placed in some lab, or some vaccine, some fast food burger, or*— Victoria couldn't continue down that line of thinking. Then she thought of the other child she lost, the one in New York. Victoria turned and walked toward the exit when she saw Li Jun.

He stood behind the reception desk, his coat draped over his shoulder while he talked with, *'a shapely little black girl.'* She couldn't be more than twenty, Victoria realized. Li Jun laughed with her, wearing what Victoria knew had to be bespoke. It was a double-breasted suit, black with gold buttons, cut slim, *with no shirt. It's freezing out, for heaven sake*, she thought.

"What was he thinking?" Victoria walked closer to the desk on her way to the door.

She tried to ignore the growing detail, like his hair pulled into a half up style, the rest hanging in a textured curtain down to his biceps, or his warm tan skin, tinted copper. She looked at the floor. Victoria didn't want to be reminded of the definition between clavicle and sternum, let alone see it. Nor did she wish his eyes to meet hers. She moved toward the door, nearly home free, when she heard her name. Victoria paused, the sound of dress shoes on concrete, flooding her senses, then she felt Li Jun's hand on her arm— through the protection of her coat.

"Victoria." Li Jun repeated, slowly turning her to face him.

"Oh, hello." Victoria said with British O, plastering on a smile—like women the world over are taught to do, in *tough* moments. She attempted to avoid his eyes.

"I didn't-I wasn't, sure you'd come." He said hesitantly. Victoria kept her eyes down, remaining on his bare ankles and chiseled thighs, in those tapered pant legs. She hated the style but, *wah lao, he looks good.*

"Jun, I'm not feeling well I need to go." Victoria found the courage to glance up. An elderly couple came in the door, then a string of artsy-hipster types. Li Jun and Victoria stepped aside, his hand on her elbow.

He let go. "Victoria, do you love me?" Li Jun asked, his eyes on the floor. Then suddenly she found his eyes on her. She stared at him blankly as he rocked back and forth gently with his hands in his pockets.

Victoria turned toward the door but Li Jun grabbed her hand.

"Why?" He asked looking back to the polished concrete floor. "Why do you love me? After all these years, why do you *want* me?" Li Jun fixed his gaze on her waiting for her answer.

Victoria inhaled, then exhaled. "I fell in love with your work. When I first saw it in New York." She paused. "From there it was fait accompli." She said in a whisper, looking down at her hands. "I thought someone with so much love in his work could love like no other. Then we met, and you were so enchanting and we were in New York, so I fell, in love—with you." Victoria said. This sight caught the eye of an elderly woman, snow-white haired and dark-blue eyed, who was about to enter the building, but thought better of it. She watched Li Jun and Victoria for a moment, from outside.

"And I broke your heart." Li Jun said staring at Victoria.

"You did. More than once." She agreed, looking away from him to wipe her eyes.

"I wasn't trying then, Tori, even though I knew you were. When we got engaged it was because my mother wanted it more than I did."

"We would have worked if you could keep it in your bloody pants and stop flirting with everything that has a fucking snatch." Victoria said in that sharp British tone with tears leaking from her eyes. She turned to walk away from him and Li Jun grabbed his coat, draped across the reception desk.

"I want us to work," Li Jun opened the front door for her, stepping out into the cold. He threw his ankle-length black coat over his shoulders, fighting to hold the door open. Li Jun paused, and extended a hand to Victoria. "Ràng wǒmen chóngjiàn" he tried in Mandarin.

It was then our elderly onlooker intervened, and came to stand in the doorway beside Victoria. "Now, I don't know what he said but, he seems pretty sincere, honey." The old woman said in a thick southern drawl, every syllable stretched. Then just as quickly as she cut in, the older woman walked into the gallery.

Victoria looked at the older woman's back, then to Li Jun. "Why now?"

"Because now I see you, and the love I've taken for granted, and all the things you've lost because of me. I see you Victoria. And I love you."

Victoria stared at him, holding the door open. Slowly, *pensively*, she took Li Jun's hand. He pulled her into his arms, and kissed her, for all to see. Together they left, walking down the Cherry blossom lined Meguro river canal toward Nakameguro station. They strolled hand in hand, coats and hair swaying in the breeze, along with the branches of cherry blossoms beginning to bud.

At this juncture, the elderly woman walked out smiling alongside the girl from the reception desk. They went in the opposite direction as Li Jun and Victoria, and turned the corner toward Yamate-dori where Jade stood with Mrs. Wong at her side.

"How'd it go?" Jade asked the two women.

"Jumped in just in time, she was about to say no." The older woman said smugly, dropping the accent.

"I called when she showed up and it happened just like you said it would." The younger of the two women added. "But they just left together." The girl crossed her arms.

Jade looked at Mrs. Wong with a smile, flinging blonde hair from her eyes. "Told you. I know my sister, I also happen to know your son." Jade grinned at Mrs. Wong, as she handed each actor an envelope with cash.

Mrs. Wong eyed Jade when the two women walked further down the street away from them. "And I know there's a special place in hell just for you." Mrs. Wong shook her head, before walking away.

Proof in hand
Tokyo, April 3rd

Later that evening, while Jade slipped back into her clothes. She considered how easy it was to pull Soo Young in, and deceive her sister.

These were the kind-er of her countless betrayal's. *Perhaps Mrs. Wong is right*, Jade thought, pausing to lean against the door, putting on her shoes.

"Where are you going?" Chris asked, stroking himself through the sheet. He lay, propped up in the bed of a love motel, as she was trying to slip out. "I'm not finished with you." He smiled, grabbing her.

"I'm meeting a friend for dinner." Jade pulled away. "Bye." She threw her blonde hair to one side and zipped her black dress, while glancing at him over a shoulder.

"Your friend can wait." He wrapped an arm around her waist and pulled her back to bed. "I have some stuff you've got to take care of." He whispered, kissing her neck.

"*He* can't wait." Jade attempted to push Chris away. Jade stared at him, and they froze.

"You got some nigga on the side?" Chris asked smiling.

"Yeah, *you*." She cut her eyes at him, throwing on a grey sweater coat.

He kissed her, taking off her shoes. "No need for the other guy, now that we got the boring stuff out of the way."

"Shut up," Jade ran her fingers down his chest. "The only reason I keep seeing you is cuz you're a good lay."

"Really?" He threw her legs over his shoulders.

"And I thought you liked me."

"You're way past expiration." Jade glared at him.

"Tell your friend traffic was really bad." Chris smiled, slowly moving closer to her center.

Now, after the hellish swell of Tokyo commuter traffic and the even more daunting task of hailing a cab, Jade sat, thinking of Chris, not meaning to—just doing so, all the same. She looked at the drink menu, in yet another chic restaurant as she waited for Ari—her handsome Moroccan, fresh from Spain. Grave mistake number six waiting to devour her—seeds and all. When Jade looked up from the menu she spotted Ari at the door. Ari slipped past the hostess then the sign for the smoking section, to Jade's table in almost feline-like movements.

"Sorry the flight was delayed." Ari crossed her legs, flinging jet-black hair from her eyes. "March in Barcelona was so beautiful but hot. I miss it already. So why did you want to meet me so badly?"

"Before you go back to your lair and sharpen your talons, Slagathor, I needed to talk to you." Jade smiled.

"Again with that name?"

"I've always called you that." Jade sneered, Crystal Kay's 'Last Kiss' playing overhead.

"Whatever hefa, can I smoke here?"

"We're in the smoking section." Jade stared at her. Ari pulled a cigarette pack from her purse, searching for the lighter.

"Anyway, you've been hella secretive lately. What's going on?" Ari smiled bringing cigarette to mouth. "You want one? *From States.*" She pulled the lighter from her purse. Jade paused as Ari sat back and exhaled.

"Give me one." Jade caved.

"I knew it." Ari handed Jade the pack and Jade stopped to take in the scent. "How long has it been?" Ari expelled smoke laughing.

"A long time," Jade fumbled to pull a cigarette from the pack, smiling as she lit it. "you didn't tell Michelle about meeting me, did you?"

"No. Why?"

"Good. I have some dirt you'd probably like to know. Here," Jade handed over a sheet of paper. "You want a drink?"

"Sure." Ari nodded, then glanced to the paper. "What's this?" Ari stared at Jade, who smiled. Jade brought the cigarette back up to her lips, then pulled Yu's wallet from her bag.

"Sumimasen," Jade called to a waiter. He came rushing over. She placed the drink orders, then turned back to Ari, continuing after the waiter walked away.

"That's the receipt for the new "cyber protection" Eva's Agency installed as of Monday. On the back is the access codes to Eva's computer. And if necessary the code in red can take out the whole encryption, *quietly.*"

"What am I supposed to do with this?" Ari questioned, brows raised and black nail polish shining.

"Just listen," Jade thumped her cigarette over the ashtray. "After I hacked Eva's computer. I planted a seed, with her fiancé."

"Interesting." Ari tapped her cigarette on the ashtray.

"Eva beefing up her security means he told her, and she's trying to cover her tracks. In doing so, she showed me what I was looking for."

"Okay. And what were you looking for?"

"This." Jade pulled a hard drive from her purse. "These are financial records. If you show them to an accountant, they'll confirm that the money is being funneled. I don't know where, I'm not that good." Jade drummed her cigarette on the ashtray, glancing to the waiter, bringing their drinks.

"Omataseitashimashita." He placed the drinks on the table. "Manhattan—Gin tonic— Chocolate Cake. Goyukuridozo."

"Arigatougozaimashita." Jade nodded to him.

"Now I have questions." Ari smiled, leaning back in her chair, venom dripping from her lips. "What did you do with the fiancé?" Her eyes narrowed Ari stirred her Manhattan then put out the half-smoked cigarette.

Jade grinned. "I found out he was an escort." She nodded. Ari's mouth fell open, and she put her drink down. Jade sipped her Gin tonic. "And before that, he worked in one of the really big host clubs in Osaka."

"Does Eva know?" Ari asked. The atmosphere shifted from restaurant to bar, with the dispersing of the dinner crowd under the influence of Thelma Aoyama's 'I'm Sorry.'

"I don't know. Just wait another week or so before you spread that fire." Jade cut into the cake. "Since he didn't bring me what I asked for, you can go public with the info and strong-arm Eva." Jade sat back in her chair.

"Fine." Ari nodded, her eyes drifting to Yu's wallet. "Why are you telling me this?" She paused. "Michelle asked you for this, didn't she?"

"Once you strong-arm Eva, you can also get a piece of the pie—I'm sure Michelle will." Jade changed the topic. "Then you can take the credit for helping me put the pieces together."

"How nice of you." Ari sang sarcastically, "What else did you plant on Eva's computer? What are you plotting?"

"Ari, stop being—" Jade started.

"You've been acting *way* too shady, lately. What-else did-you-plant on her computer? It's a simple question." Ari paused. "We're on the same team."

"No. We're not." Jade said, with British O.

"Oh, Okay." Ari looked to the window. After a few seconds looked back at Jade. "Lia, you should know you are the closest thing I have to a sister. You're also my oldest friend."

Jade scoffed.

"So, what do you want me to do with all this information?" Ari picked up her Manhattan and took a sip. Jade took the last drag of her cigarette, before putting it out.

"Hold on to it, tell Michelle in a couple of weeks. I need Eva to do somethings."

"What things?" Ari asked holding her glass by the stem, one arm across her stomach.

"I'm working on something. So that hard drive and receipt are probably all I can do to help you." Jade took another sip of her drink.

"I'm sure it's good enough." Ari glanced at the receipt, and the hard drive, placing them in her purse.

"By the way," Jade changed the subject again, "Victoria's Secret wants to sign Michelle."

Maybe it's nothing, Ari thought, finishing her drink. *But pieces are moving. Where and how I don't know.*

Jade continued. "—Eva doesn't want Michelle to get the contract. So, she's meeting with one of the representatives on May seventh at two."

"The fact that you know this lets me know you have something else on that computer. You have to push the meeting, Michelle will be in Osaka."

"Why?" Jade questioned.

"She's going to the rehearsal dinner." Ari shifted to her phone. "My mistake, the dinner is on Wednesday. The weddings are Friday and Sunday. But she'll go at least a day in advance."

"Weddings? As in more than one?" Jade asked, her brow wrinkling.

"Two, actually one in Osaka, the other in Busan. The girl Michelle's youngest brother is marrying is some Korean heiress. Her family wants a Korean-wedding, in Korea."

"Chris is getting married?" Jade mumbled.

"Yeah." Ari paused, seeing the seed take root. "You know him?"

"I've met him. I just didn't think he was the marrying type."

"Michelle said he's a hoe." Ari laughed. "But he's been engaged to this Korean girl for nine months or something like that."

"You want another drink?" Jade asked, getting the waiter's attention.

"How long have you been screwing Chris?" Ari cut her off.

"How do you—" Jade stopped.

"I didn't." Ari grinned. "After paying Soo Young for a little info, and meeting him at the trial, I just put it together. *You* confirmed it. Plus he's your type, *too*." Ari chuckled, alluding to Hikaru.

"Like Darius is yours, frienemy-sister." Jade smiled, and Ari glanced to the table, with nothing to say.

They both paused, letting the noise of the restaurant fill the space— *I'm sorry, so sorry*, the song chided.

"I'm sorry, about Chris." Ari finally said.

"Save it. We were never together." Jade said, realizing how much that sounded like Michelle. The waiter appeared; pen poised above paper.

"Mou hitotsu onegashimasu."

"Watashi mo," Ari added.

"Hai," he nodded putting the pen and pad away.

"Did you know you were the other woman?" Ari started first.

"No." Jade shook her head.

"Fuck Chris he's—" Ari began.

"I just did." Jade chuckled, before they burst into laughter, until smiling Ari said:

"Let's go out and have a good time, like the old days."

"That sounds like a horrible idea." Jade beamed back before relenting. This was her sixth grave mistake.

Red Flags & False Starts
Hong Kong, April 13th

"Good morning, I'm Eva Wong, here to see Mr. Yang." Eva beamed at Mr. Yang's secretary, after making her way to the 61st floor of the Hong Kong high-rise.

"Morning," The secretary smiled back. The office buzzed with the sound of phones and idle chatter. "Mr. Yang should be wrapping up a conference call." The young blonde said, then glanced at the flashing light on her phone. "As soon as he's done, I'll see you in. I'm so sorry for the wait."

"It's fine. I'll take a seat." Eva sat, looking out on a hazy Hong Kong, then she turned on her laptop to do last minute prep. She ran through model profiles, stats, and figures, given the unclear nature of Mr. Yang's inquiry. This was the very thing Jade was waiting for, as she sat in a restaurant a country away.

Not recalling this meeting, Jennifer Martin, the overzealous secretary, double checked the appointments, with a glance at Eva, then an exchange of smiles, only to find the meeting, *There*. **Eva Wong, 9 to 10:30.** *Strange*, Jennifer thought. Meanwhile Jade pushed through the system, using Ah Fan's tools to corrupt Yang Wei's anti-virus software, remotely, through Eva's computer and a local printer. As the moments ticked by, Jade ventured deeper in the network, unlocking Yang Wei's secrets over

Dakgalbi, Yakisoba, and Honey Toast, favorites from a fusion restaurant she loves.

At Yang Wei, Jennifer led Eva to Mr. Yang's office, the computer still on, the remote access tools still working, striking both the headquarters and its extensions in Singapore and Seoul. Eva and Mr. Yang shook hands, exchanging pleasantries as Jennifer placed tea on a table between them. Eva took a seat. Liam Yang was handsome with his silver crew cut and goatee, along with the black mustache and matching thick black eyebrows.

"That will be all, Jennifer." Mr. Yang said and Jennifer left, still eyeing Eva.

"It's wonderful that you could make time to sit down with me." Eva opened her laptop, placing it on the sofa beside her.

"Well if you can save me on my overhead, I would be a fool not to sit down with my biggest supplier." Mr. Yang crossed his legs, grinning at Eva. "And such a beauty in my office is a rarity" he grinned.

Eva paused, not hearing the rest, taking a moment to consider. "I think there's been a mistake. I'm Eva Wong, from the modeling agency—a friend of your daughter." She stared at him. Mr. Yang was staring at her screen, to a video of Jade asleep, and just barely visible at his angle, *dated today.*

"You have her? Where is she?" He asked in a cool tone. "Where is Jia Lang?" He suddenly demanded.

"What do you mean? She's missing?" Eva gawked at him, wondering where this outburst came from.

"Why do you have a video of my missing daughter? Are you here for money?"

Back in Tokyo, a smile took hold of Jade's face. She sat cross-legged in front of her laptop over her feast—the last barrier falling to the sheer might of her tools, thanks to good old Ah Fan. Jade shifted to the last scraps of her meal as the intrusion came to a halt. She glanced at the screen, the command prompt completely stopped, password prompting— a final fail safe.

Though she uncovered the password almost a year and a half ago, it enraged her to recall its meaning, and then to type it, letter by letter.

Lhy20gy.CH97ch.myJLY.JM, they spoke to her.

Meanwhile in Hong Kong, Eva walked out of Mr. Yang's office. She got into an elevator with security alerted to follow her.

"He is out of his mind." Eva scoffed, brow wrinkled and arms folded once the doors closed.

When the doors opened to the lobby, security seized Eva. For hours the police questioned her about Jia Lang. The investigation going in circles, with neither answers nor real leads as to the girl's whereabouts—aside from Tokyo, perhaps, which forced them to free Eva at the insistence of her lawyer.

The unintentional interrogation granted Jade an opportunity to fully corrupt the anti-virus software, and then not so quietly enumerate the network of all three locations, a bonus she hadn't planned on. Yet the password still longed to tell its story.

l.h.y.—Leihua Yang, the first wife—Victoria's mother, who he met at twenty, then g.y.—Guang Yang, Victoria. C.H.—Catherine Hale, the love of his life as some have said, who was taken by a drug overdose in nineteen ninety-seven, followed by C.H.—their son Cole Hale, not Yang. Then M.Y.—Mia Yang, Jade's mother, and J.L.Y.—Jia Lang Yang, all there, in the order received.

But why, Jade still wondered, staring out a window from her table, in the bustling restaurant that she loves. *All his tools present and accounted for, but why? And who is J.M? Is this a joke?*

"What a joke." Eva grumbled, getting into a cab and slamming the door, as Mr. Yang watched her leave from his office.

15. Summoned

Tokyo, April 16th

When will I see you again? –Seina, from March 26th

Back on 13th maybe then

Michelle had lied, and left it at that. It was radio silence from there, until:

Sending a car tonight, driver: Kaneko. Dinner at 9. You choose. –Seina, 5:11 pm

It was 7:41, after a long day of photo shoots, with Kili Mono, despite the endless drama of Paris. She would go, Michelle decided. So, with time working against her, Michelle showered and skipped the flat-iron, throwing a set of heated rollers in her hair while she dressed. She slipped into a thick strapped black cocktail dress, pairing it with a heavy red shawl, and then she positioned the long loosely curled locks to drape her left shoulder.

Stepping out onto the street, Michelle spotted the car, with the Terada logo on tiny flags. She walked toward the car and the driver got out then quickly opened the door.

"Kaneko-san desuka?" She asked in her best Japanese.

"Hai, kochira e," he smiled, motioning to the open door. A man came forward pulling Michelle into the car. The driver closed the door, hopped into the driver's seat and drove off.

Now, Michelle stood silent, bathed in warm white light, listening to the roar of an elevator as she rode up. One of the straps from her dress was ripped and her hair, disheveled. The shawl was tied around her waist like a leash, linking her to the burly man from the car. The doors opened to the top floor of this unknown building and the man beside her

291

motioned for Michelle to step forward.

They entered a dark office lined with fish tanks and a spotlight by the window, the city down below. The man from the car grabbed Michelle and she punched him in the groin.

"Let go you asshole!" She fought with all she had. H e threw her over his shoulder. Michelle elbowed him in the nose. "I will kill you!" She said through clenched teeth. The burly man, bloody nosed and limping, walked Michelle deeper into the room, passed tanks of exotic colored fish to the desk by the window with an empty chair. He dropped Michelle into the chair, depositing her shoes in her lap. "What do you want?!"

"That's enough Miss. Yamato," said another man wheeling past her in an electric wheelchair, taking his place behind the desk. He paused. There was something familiar about that nose, she thought. Thick wavy silver hair slicked back from green eyes. He looked at her something like a cat eyes a mouse, the predator to presumed prey. "You've put on, quite a show, breaking windows, beating my man," he paused to catch his breath, with the aid of an oxygen tank and Michelle saw it, *she knew him*. The same tone of voice, the joking manner—although quite serious. Then she looked to the window and realized where she was. Apparently, this showed on her face. "Call my son. Tell him you can't make it," he gasped. "I trust you can lie," he said in a heavy Portuguese accent.

"I don't have my—" Michelle began. The bloodied-nose guard flashed his gun and presented her phone, with the number dialed and ringing, on speaker

"Hey are you coming?" Seina asked.

"Hey, *love,*" Michelle said forcing a smile. "I can't make it. I'm sorry. My mother showed up wanting to *help* plan *our trip to Spain*. She's so excited for us. I think it's going to be a late night."

"Okay," Seina paused, thrown by her words. "I love you, Michelle." He said it firmly—*surprisingly*, "Whatever this is, I want you to know that." Without knowing quite what, he knew something was wrong.

"Bye," she squeaked and the guard hung up, putting the phone away.

"Good," Claudio smiled. "I'd like you to stop seeing my son," Claudio's green eyes glowed, like a beast of legend, alongside his thick gasps.

"Why?"

"Because I have a check for you," he stopped to breathe in, writing out a check. "In fact, give me a number. I'm sure I have it in my safe," he grinned, turning to open the safe on his right.

Years from now, thinking back on this moment, Michelle will only recall hearing a click come from the guard. She will remember looking up, closing the cold silver briefcase that seemed to have appeared from nowhere. She will recall feeling sweat at the nape of her neck and the base of her spine, as she tucked hair behind an ear and then nothing. Fade to black.

Vicissitude
Tokyo, April 16th -17th

"Hello." Michelle answered, sounding out of breath.

"Where are you?" Jade asked, trying to mask her panic, en route to a taxi. She had just left Chris in her bed, alerted by a call from Seina, who asked Jade to intervene on his behalf. "I called three times. Look, I just got a weird call—" She started, but Michelle cut her off.

"Terada Industries." Michelle paused. "I'll call you back." She hung up.

After riding on pins and needles, waiting for Michelle to call back, Jade got out of her taxi in front of Terada Industries. She glanced down at her phone, throwing a large messenger bag over her shoulder and getting out of the cab. When she looked up at the ominous building, she saw Seina approaching, in her periphery.

"Did you hack the cameras?" he asked breathing heavily.

"It's not magic, Seina." Jade hissed. "Give it a few more minutes."

She said trying to comfort him. Jade pulled the laptop from her bag and squatted on the sidewalk to check. After a few dozen keystrokes, "I have access. Go!" She chimed, unlocking the front door via the security system.

Once inside, Jade stationed herself behind the reception desk. She placed the cameras on a loop before turning her sights to the security feeds from the last few hours. Seina went to the elevators. His heart racing as it climbed, knowing Claudio, he half expected there to be hookers strolling about, offering blow jobs to kids—his fifteenth birthday, or even alcohol and weed, like his tenth. When the doors opened, Seina heard the whistle of wind coming from the window at the far side of the room. Though the office was dark, per usual, there was something ominous in the air.

"Michelle," he called, slowly moving toward his father's desk, the fish tanks chilling the atmosphere even further. "Michelle are you here?" Seina called again, seeing his father's bodyguard lying face down in a pool of his own blood, drenching the charcoal grey carpet. "Michelle," he repeated, moving around the desk. It was then, Seina saw his father.

He was turned out of his chair, *wheezing*. A still spreading red spot over Claudio's abdomen spilled onto the carpet. Claudio's eyes were closed, a pained expression gripping his face. The window whistled from the gunshot-hole there, pulling Seina from the sight of his father. He looked to the open safe, standing as tall as him. It was filled to the brim with cash and what he could only assume was cocaine or heroin. Removing his coat, Seina covered his hands with it, searching for a bag of some kind. What he found were a series of boxes, and files.

Downstairs in the lobby, Jade glanced at the time and sighed. In the eerie silence, her phone rang and she quickly pulled it from her pocket. **Michelle Yamato**, flashed on the screen.

"Hello," Jade paused. "Ah hai," she listened intently, "Dare -sama? Ah, hai naka yoshi desu. Demo, sono keitei ga doko ni sagashimashita ka kana?"

Back in Claudio's office, Seina stared at his father as his breathing slowed, when the elevator chimed— breaking him from a chain of dark thoughts. Jade stepped out onto the floor, quickly moving toward him.

"What the hell!" He turned to face her. "You scared the shit out of me."

Jade noted he was breathing heavily, again. "I didn't want to call again in case our phone records were called into question," she paused, surveying the room, the messenger bag on her hip. "I see I was right to do so."

"I'm glad you're already a criminal," Seina said, looking her over. Never one to miss an opportunity, Jade pulled a hand-held cloning device from her bag along with her laptop.

"What are you doing?" Seina's brow furrowed.

"You didn't think I was going to help you for free," she asked as a statement. Seina shook his head and Jade stepped over Claudio.

She pressed a button on the desk unearthing the desktop housed within. "I'm cloning his computer," Jade hooked up her laptop and the device to the desktop. "It may be obvious to an investigator, so I'll clone it several times and place them strategically. I assume since you've been up here for a while you were *busy*?" Jade paused, glancing at the open safe and the one brick-lined shelf of drugs still remaining.

Seina stared at her in silence, sweat glistening at his temples. "We all have secrets," he shrugged with a half-smile.

"We do," Jade echoed back. "I just got a call. It was some guy that found Michelle's phone at a family mart near Shinjuku Station. He said Michelle looked like she was going toward Akebonobashi."

"Akebonobashi? Why?" Seina asked, wiping his forehead.

"I don't know," Jade pulled a vial from her pocket, dropping several hairs, and other fibers on the floor, while Seina wasn't looking. "We have to get over there." She made a show of wiping down the computer, the button, and the desk, then paused to pick up her bag before walking toward the elevator.

"You're leaving your computer?"

"The data will go to a safe place, and anything on it will lead people on one hell of a chase." She paused, looking Seina over. "I hope you wiped down everything you touched," Jade moved past him to the elevator. She pressed the button calling it to the office. Seina moved toward his father, but after taking a step, he thought better of it.

"I didn't touch anything." Seina mumbled, following Jade with the sudden realization that this was *a crime scene*. The thought that his father might die never crossed his mind. The indicator chimed and Seina followed Jade, she pressed the button again. They rode the elevator in silence, until the chime alerted them they had arrived at the lobby. Seina walked out first.

"The cameras are on a loop from the last four hours." Jade's small voice, seemed to echo in Seina's ears, in the vast emptiness of the deadly silent lobby. "Only DNA and footage from other buildings can tie us to this place."

"And our cell phones." Seina said not looking at her.

"Michelle said she was here, we were looking. What I'm saying is you can go say goodbye to him," Jade was well aware that Seina was unloved by his father, and it was no secret to the wealthy inner circles that he was the least favorite of the Terada children. Yet it was his answer that truly broke her heart.

"He's dead to me Lia," he kept his back to her, but she heard the tears just below the surface. "—has been for years," Seina paused, "He was going to make Michelle disappear. I have to know she's safe," Seina pulled his phone from a pocket and dialed Michelle's number, while staring at the building's address.

In the thirty minutes it took Jade to pinpoint the phone's location, she and Seina met with the man who found the phone. He claimed, Michelle left in a hurry with a muscular foreigner. The older Japanese man handed over the phone and gave the general direction they went.

Nearly an hour and a half later, Jade spotted Michelle as she and Seina roamed the streets of Ichigaya-Honmuracho. Michelle was walking past another Family Mart en route to Ichigaya Station. She looked like a mad woman—hair nearly horizontal, shawl dragging on the sidewalk from her hand, shoes in the other, and a split torn into the back of the dress. Seina grabbed her by the hand, but Michelle's skin was icy to the touch, not just from the cold. He pulled Michelle to him and took off his coat, throwing it over her.

"Michelle look at me," Seina turned her face to him. She sounded like she had been running, taking quick jagged breaths.

"Thank God," Jade doubled over, after running to them. Michelle said nothing. She had no phone, no purse and no indication she knew where, or who she was. Jade took Michelle's shoes, patting her on the back.

"Let's go home." Seina swept her into his arms. Michelle laid her head on Seina's chest trembling. Jade hailed a cab.

Michelle opened her eyes to a ringing silence. Mid-morning sunlight flooded her bedroom. She sat up, with memories of a gunshot brimming from the depths of her mind while Seina slept beside her.

"What happened?" She woke Seina.

He looked at her his eyes blood-shot but smiling. "Hey," Seina sat up, "how you feeling?"

"I asked you what happened?" Michelle repeated, moving a tangle of curls behind an ear.

"I'm not entirely sure, but I do know my father took you."

"Yeah! Kidnapped! How did I get here *Seina*?" She asked, unnerved. Drawn by the shouting, Jade and Ari peeped in, hoping to calm Michelle.

"After you called me I knew something was off. So, I called Jade hoping she could track you down. Then I went to the office," Seina said evenly, in a lulling tone.

"Then I called you," Jade started. "To trace the number, illegally." she added. "You told me you were at Terada Industries and that you would call back. Thirty, forty minutes later Seina and I are looking for you but your phone was turned off. Then some man called with your phone saying he found it in a Family Mart and that you went toward Katamachi and Akebonobashi." Jade leaned on Michelle's dresser, watching for any kind of recollection. There was none. Ari cut her eyes to Seina, the look telling him she was right.

"Why did I say I was at the office?" Michelle asked looking from Jade to Seina and back, before covering her face with her hands.

"Jade corrupted the video before we thought to look." Seina paused. "So, we don't know," he took Michelle in his arms.

"Get off me!" Michelle shouted, forcing Seina to let go.

"Michelle there's nothing to worry about." Ari cut in. "We're all here to help. Once we iron out an alibi, we'll be set. I'm already working on a lawyer. The best in my year, I'm told."

"Help?" Michelle asked giving Ari the one over, "Like you did with Adrien?! And a lawyer?! Why would I need a *lawyer*?!" She looked over the three of them, ready to pounce.

"It's just to be on the safe side. I'm going to keep him on retainer," Seina said. "Aren't you hungry?" he smiled.

Michelle ignored him.

"Here," Ari handed Michelle her phone. A news reel from earlier that morning queued for Michelle to play. The headline: Claudio Terada in Coma, swam across the screen, Ami Suzuki with the story.

"I'm standing outside Dokkyo University Hospital, where Claudio Terada lays comatose after what police have called the drug bust of the year. Last night over two hundred kilos of cocaine were discovered at Terada Industries' offices. Witnesses say, gunshots were fired, resulting in the injury of Mr. Terada and his bodyguard, Ishikawa, Yuzuro. Ishikawa died early this morning due to complications. Terada, is in stable—" The words bled into silence. Michelle turned the video off.

"I don't know what the fuck is going on here but between you two mother fuckers my life has been torn apart." She said pointing to Ari and Seina. "Are you working with them too?" Michelle glared at Jade.

"No," Jade shook her head.

"Really? Cus I had the feeling you two hoes had issues and now you're best friends." Michelle shifted her gaze to Seina, "And why the *hell* would you call her?" Michelle motioned to Jade. "This some *real shady shit*," Michelle eyed all three of them.

"Give us a minute," Seina said to Ari and Jade as a woman with bronzed skin and sand colored hair appeared in the doorway to Michelle's room, pulling Jade and Ari out of the fire. Michelle stopped to take her features in as she nodded.

"I'm Daniele Alves, sorry to meet you under these circumstances." The woman smiled. "If you're hungry there's a bit of porridge," she said in a rushed clipped Portuguese accent, before closing the door, leaving Seina and Michelle in silence.

"Was that your—" Michelle started.

Seina simply nodded.

"Why is she in my apartment?" Michelle stood, clasping her hands as she stared at him.

Seina sighed, then pulled a small jewelry box from his pocket.

"I was going to ask you something last night," he said, deciding not to go on. Michelle just stared at the box in silence.

"You pop into my life and turn it upside down. You *literally* bring press where ever you go, putting me in magazine after magazine. Your weirdo cousin worms her way into my work life, bringing back all kinds of ghosts and bad memories. And don't get me started on your brother! Then I magically got embarrassed for the whole fucking world to see. Then yo damn daddy kidnaps me. And now after all that, you want me to *marry you*?" Michelle froze, staring down at the floor laughing, a hand in her hair. She laughed, hysterically until her face reddened and the tears ran down her cheeks.

"I didn't know about most of that Michelle!" He said much sharper then he meant to.

"Did you know your daddy might kidnap a bitch for trying to date you?" She was irate now, "What the hell is going on Seina?! Why is my life in shambles after I met you, *huh*?"

"I'm sorry Michelle. I don't know why he did that. Nothing like this has ever happened, not even when he paid off my ex. I don't know what to say other than I'm sorry."

"He tried to pay me off, and there was a gun." Michelle teared up, her voice breaking. Seina moved closer to take her in his arms. "Don't touch me!" She pulled away, tensing. "You said you and your father were estranged. You said you had nothing to do with anyone other than your mother, Ari and your sister." Here, the tears were falling with her words, "You said you might not inherit anything. You said you have nothing to do with them."

"I wasn't lying," he stared at her, visibly wounded. "I haven't lied to you since I met you Michelle."

"*That* is a lie. This is too much!" Michelle threw her hands up. "I need you to leave."

"Okay. I'll take a walk," he grabbed his coat.

"Give me your key," Michelle said, wounding him even further. Seina looked at her, and seeing no trace of warmth, he placed the key on the dresser and walked away without a word.

Abnegation
Tokyo, April 17th

Evening arrived with no further news of Claudio's condition. It was then Michelle rose again— after sleeping most of the day. Ari had just sat down for a meal in the living room, and as she picked up her fork. She swung, seeing something appear on the arm of the chair.

"What the— what is wrong with you?!"

"Where's Jade?" Michelle asked unmoved from the sofa.

"She disappeared after you woke up." Ari stared at Michelle, searching for signs of some mental break.

"And Daniele?"

"Teaching Howard Portuguese," Ari eyed her. "—they hit it off when he came by to see you,"

"Hikaru was here?"

"Yeah, he stopped by this afternoon, while you were asleep." Ari paused, trying not to stare. "Are you *really* okay?"

"Why? Don't I look like a killer?" Michelle shot back.

"No, you don't," Ari said flatly.

"Like you really care." Michelle crossed her arms. They sat in silence staring at one another, before Ari spoke.

"I do care about you, now. Now, that I know Seina loves you and that you're not a gold-digging hefa. I'm sorry, I never meant to hurt you." Ari's eyes drifted away from Michelle, "But you should know that my concern comes with all I have at my command. And that I protect the people I care about."

"Words, Naima. Those are all just words," Michelle said coldly.

"Jade left something for you." Ari changed the subject as she reached for the hard drive in her purse. "It turns out you were right about Eva but, you'll want to see this. I have lawyers on standby ready to move forward, if you'd like. For this as well as the other problem. Like I said, he's the best in my year, and here in the city."

Michelle took the hard drive and stared at Ari. Ari handed Michelle her laptop from the coffee table.

"Later we need to prepare our stories separately but with the same base line."

"Okay." Michelle nodded.

In a matter of moments, it became clear to Michelle what Jade discovered and what Ari hinted at— the numbers adding a concreteness to the betrayal. Eva funneled money into several accounts in the Caymans, which were connected to eight companies in South Africa, Nigeria, and India, then three companies in Panama, Spain, and Argentina, and more in this vein of shell companies and trusts, coming to a head at Phoenix corp in Switzerland.

"Ari can you call a car for me?" Michelle called out from her room. "I also need to borrow someone from you."

Some fifty minutes later, in the cool dark night, the light from Eva's office acted as a beacon in the dimmed hallways of the agency, guiding Michelle to her target. It was just after eleven, Eva was alone in her office, this her usual routine since Yu moved out.

"The high and mighty Eva Wong, at work on her throne." Michelle playfully mused. She flung the door to Eva's office wide open, a thick stack of papers in hand. Michelle wore jeans, a white long sleeve shirt and a grey and black North Face jacket, her curls damp with conditioner. "Can I get your autograph?"

"I told you I needed a vacation from you. Clearly you don't speak English either. Shall we try French?" She cut her eyes to Michelle. Then pages flew at Eva's face, connecting. They spilled into her lap, onto the floor and across the desk between them in an instant.

"I own you now," Michelle's mouth folded into a sly smirk. "How does that feel?" Michelle crept closer.

Eva scowled at her, then dabbed at a slight papercut on her nose. "You own me?" Eva repeated with amusement in her tone, earrings bobbing as a grin pulled at her lips. "You don't even own what's between your legs. That belongs to a man. How the—" she stopped as she glanced down at one of the sheets in her lap. Eva's grin crumbled in that moment. Michelle's brows rose and she took a seat.

"That's all of last year's transactions," Michelle crossed her legs.

"Where did you—" Eva started but Michelle cut her off.

"That doesn't matter. But you know what does?" Michelle stared at Eva. "I thought you'd be more fun." Michelle rolled her eyes. "I'll start with my demands." Michelle pulled a sheet of paper from the bottom of the tumbled stack splayed on Eva's desk. Eva froze as she read.

"Jun?" Eva spat. "You think you're going to replace me with my brother?"

"I made a promise to him," Michelle beamed. "So now I'm delivering."

"And Ari as his VP? You're doing all of this for what?" Eva scoffed.

"Consider this your penance to me and my escape from under you. My twenty-seven and a half percent though," Michelle paused to stare boldly into Eva's eyes. "— that was meant to sting."

"I know you didn't obtain any of this legally." Eva's eyes glittered. She threw the paper down on the floor. "So you have no grounds Michelle. You really should do a bit of research before blindly ambushing someone." Eva turned back to her computer—dismissing Michelle.

"Well," Michelle began in a mouse-like voice. "—since Ari joined our team, she's had the press eating out of her hand." Michelle looked down at the floor, hands tucked under her knees. Eva stopped typing. "If I gave her these papers and all the fines you—" Michelle murmured.

Eva leapt to her feet and slammed her fist on the desk. "I will crush you!" She said through clenched teeth.

Michelle grinned, pausing to pick up the sheet of paper on the floor before boldly presenting it to Eva. "Sign it."

"I'll see you in court," Eva retorted.

"Before we go down that route, I thought you might chat with a friend of mine," Michelle turned to the door. "*Friend*, could you help me?" She called.

Out of the dark of the hallway, Darius emerged, slinking into the office and putting on gloves. His caramel eyes were lit with a particular sort of mischief. Eva stiffened. Michelle stood, knocking the office's phone to the floor. Eva dashed for the door.

Darius caught her. "Now—now." He taunted. Eva melted in his arms. "— were just gonna have a chat, that's all." She fought to get loose. He tenderly stroked Eva's hair.

"Just what we talked about, nothing—" Michelle paused. "*Overt.*"

Eva screamed but Darius clapped a gloved hand over her mouth. He tied her hands, then pulled a large colorful silken scarf from his pocket. Michelle moved to the window, closing the blinds when Darius forced the cloth into Eva's mouth, securing it with another of similar hues.

Eva let a muffled scream loose, wriggling to free herself from him as he tied her ankles. Tears ran down her face by the time he pulled a billiard eight ball from his jacket and slipped it into a pair of black socks.

"You will sign it." Michelle glanced over a shoulder at Eva. "And I'll make sure we take long vacations from each other." She said,

then Darius swung.

Here, Again
Tokyo, April 20th

Victoria had known the moment she came. Through the ragged breaths, as she collapsed against Li Jun's body, euphoric, and taking in the scent of skin, hair and sweat— all his. She knew. *She knew.* Li Jun lay with her, giving himself to her so totally, desperately seeking to please her. *What else could have happened?* In the weeks since Li Jun's show, they had returned to all they were, before Michelle— and more. Everything was better, fresh, since that night.

Now, hours after laying together, Victoria slipped from his bed. She quietly went into the bathroom, thinking the dream might finally be ending. She closed the bathroom door behind her, her hair a wild puff of chemically induced waves.

The sun was just coming up, and Victoria knew she had the better part of an hour, *that is unless Li Jun's morning piss comes a bit early. How much did Jun drink last night,* she wondered. She reached into the very back of the cabinet under the sink. Victoria pulled five pregnancy tests from the depths of the cabinet. She placed them on the sink, locked the bathroom door, pulled her hair up into a bun and breathed.

By the time Victoria looked at the last test, it really didn't matter. Her fears were confirmed, though the tests were inconclusive. She knew she was pregnant, again, *at least until I lose this one,* the thought tumbled forth. Victoria sank down onto the edge of the tub, wanting to cry. For the third time in her life, she was pregnant by Wong Li Jun, the unnamed miscarriage in New York, little Hua Lan in Tokyo, and now, this. She wasn't sure how to feel. When she heard Li Jun stir, Victoria threw the tests away, then took out the trash.

She returned to Li Jun's apartment and leaned against the door frame to his bedroom watching him sleep. Everything about him was calling her name in the morning light. She wanted him, Victoria laughed, of course she did, *that's how we got into this mess,* she thought. Though she wanted to tell him, Victoria knew she wouldn't. She pulled back the covers and climbed back into the bed. When she took hold of him, Li Jun opened his eyes.

"You found the ring, didn't you?" He asked half amused.

Victoria froze, staring blankly at him. "What ring?"

16. 'It Girl' Luck

Tokyo, April 23rd-24th

"Hello." Michelle said picking up the phone, setting plates on the coffee table between her and Hikaru.

"Hey," Seina replied, trying to keep the cool tones in his voice. "What are you doing tomorrow night?"

Michelle instantly wished she had screened this call as she glanced to Hikaru on the sofa. Hikaru sat awkwardly pretending to be invisible, or deaf, while trying to eat the Korean fried chicken he bought for them.

"Why do you ask?" She turned away from Hikaru.

"Why don't you want to hear what I have to say?" Seina asked, suddenly. From the tone in his voice, Michelle imagined him looking out the window of his dark office, as light from the city spilled in— lining his profile. "Michelle?" He called, checking that she was still on the line.

"Let's just leave things how they are." She said briskly, then she hung up, recognizing today was the first day she hadn't thought of Seina. Quietly Michelle walked back into the kitchen.

"So it's just me and you?" Hikaru asked pulling her from her thoughts. "What about Jade and slagathor?" He joked. Michelle smirked.

"No clue," she sang out with a shrug, before pulling a bottle of Grey Goose from her freezer. "But Slagi can go straight to hell with her shifty ass cousin-brother."

Hikaru chuckled at that.

"I win-again." Hikaru announced two hours later, with the food finished, and the bottle of vodka nearly empty. He laughed, his competitive streak showing.

"You must be cheating because I kill Uno." Michelle brushed feathered bangs back from her face. She sat on the floor between the sofa and coffee table, while Hikaru remained on the couch. Hikaru wished now that he had done something when Michelle stormed off, back in Barcelona. *Why wasn't it clear I was interested when we met? And why did I let her run off after that amazing kiss in Shinjuku?* he thought, watching her. If he had made a move when they first met, he and Michelle could have spent nearly a year of weekends like this, he thought as she shuffled the uno cards.

"You can't cheat Uno." Hikaru smiled, teeth sparkling and dimples on full display.

"You can cheat *at* almost anything." Michelle raised an eyebrow, emptying her glass. She placed the cards in a pile on the table and picked up Hikaru's cup, not wanting to get up again.

"Cho—" He started, before Michelle jerked the cup away.

She sipped, wincing at the taste. "Did you just splash juice in there?"

He shook his head. "Sake tsuyoi kara." Hikaru took the cup, with a grin.

"No you're just nasty. So, you can hold your liquor? Is that how you say—" She paused, her eyes locked with his, for a moment too long.

Hikaru held Michelle's gaze before he moved in closer, sliding down beside her on the floor. Their lips moved with a slow precision, brought on by the alcohol. Michelle's fingers caressed his jaw cautiously, then his chest, and along his shoulders, then her phone rang, again.

It jerked them away from each other, and the moment they had created. Michelle grabbed the phone, mouth and lips newly reddened. Hikaru closed his eyes, wiping thumb and pointer finger along his lips, *exasperated.*

"Hello." Michelle cleared her throat.

"Michelle!" Ari shouted with music pumping in the background.

"Michelle-we-some-really, really crazy." The sound cut in and out.

"What?" Michelle questioned. "-where are you? You're breaking up."

"I'm-a club." Ari said, the words continuing to fade in and out. "-you dressed-come—"

"What's the name of the club?"

"The name-can't-remember-Roppongi," Ari replied. Michelle moved away from Hikaru, trying to make sense of what she was hearing.

"Roppongi? Ari, where are you right now? Ari, you okay? Hello?"

"Propaganda-the name. Jade's-is taking shots with-Ken-crazy-come." She said with urgency.

"Okay, alright." Michelle stood, leaving Hikaru on the floor. She grabbed her coat from the chair nearest to her room. "Ari I'm coming. I'll be there as soon as I can."

"Wait what is it?" Hikaru stood, stopping her— a hand to her waist.

"Go to a place I can find you." Michelle covered the phone. "You asked about Jade and slagathor, they're at a club in Roppongi-*trashed*."

"What club?" Hikaru came closer. Michelle shrugged. "Ask if she's in Gaspanic or Propaganda or—"

"I'll be-bar-Jade." Ari said.

"Okay. Alright." Michelle nodded, then to Hikaru. "She just said something about Propaganda."

"I know where that is." Hikaru grabbed his jacket from the sofa.

"I'll be there in a minute, stay where you are." Michelle hung up, and Hikaru pulled her back into his arms.

"Hikaru—" Michelle started, then sighed. "This isn't a good idea. Besides, Jade has a thing for you."

"What? You kissed me. I thought you wanted this, or do you just have a thing for Seina and I'm not close enough tonight?" He countered.

Michelle stopped, and slapped him. "If you didn't need liquid courage, I might not even know who Seina Terada is. But Jade is interested in you and so I'm not willing to try this." She said flatly.

"Is that why you kissed me the last time?" Hikaru shook his head smiling. "Your always being nice or flirting, then you kissed me *out of nowhere*, break up with Seina, and invite me over. I guess you just wanted to try me?" He stood up and walked to the front door.

"What?" Michelle leapt to her feet. "What are you talking about?" She called after him. "Hikaru! Answer me! Henji shite!" She grabbed him by the jacket sleeve.

"Wasurete! Come on, we gotta get the drunks." He said, anger evident in his whole demeanor.

"Fucking Ari! Ashewo!" Michelle stomped to the door. "Bitch is lucky I don't want her to get raped," she mumbled, putting on her coat.

When they arrived, as advertised, Jade and Ari were at the bar and maybe a bit trashed, but all was fine. Michelle was less than pleased. It was Jade that waved them over.

"These bitches," Michelle grumbled, their faces all smiles through the thick wave of bodies moving this way and that. *It's a Thursday night, why is this place so packed?* Michelle wondered, walking past Hikaru, who followed, shaking his head and laughing to himself.

"Kenosuke, this is Michelle." Jade smiled to the bartender as they approached. "Michelle, Ken— the owner and one of the best bartenders in Tokyo," Jade beamed.

Ari waved, sipping a vodka cranberry, locked in conversation with a nice-looking guy to her right. Michelle stared, at Jade then Ari disbelief all over her face.

"Wow you're right, she is exactly my type." Ken eyed Michelle. Hikaru stood behind her, surveying the place, his anger becoming more apparent.

"I told you." Jade laughed, the blonde hair a glow.

"Hi, I'm Ken and you are amazing." He smiled extending a hand to Michelle.

"Nice to meet you." Michelle shook his hand, plastering on a fake smile. She couldn't miss the tattoo on his inner wrist: **courage takes strength**, the other tattoos peeking out near the collar of his shirt. Michelle turned to Ari. "You made it sound like you needed me on the phone."

"How?" Ari questioned.

"We some really, really crazy—can't remember—Jade-shots-Ken crazy." Michelle repeated what she could remember of their conversation.

"I'm sorry. I didn't mean to scare you." Ari cut a look to Jade. "Jade's drunk-ass *friend* in that other club sat his drink on my phone and it got wet."

"You didn't hear the worry in my voice?" Michelle retorted.

"I barely heard you." Ari shook her head. "Oh, Michelle this is Danny." She smiled introducing the man to her right.

"Hi." Michelle gave a grim wave.

"He's a halfie too." Ari whispered.

"So, since when are you and Jade best-ies? A month ago, you didn't want to be in the same room."

"We found some common ground." Ari smiled.

"Since you're here, sit down and have a drink." Jade echoed with the same note of cheeriness. Michelle looked at Jade taking in the hair, short skirt, and heels. "I'm sure Ken would *love* to serve you." Jade said, twisting an earring.

"*Unless*, you and Hochimen were *doing something*." Ari sneered, talking to Jade, but staring at Hikaru. "He is such a wet blanket why is he here?" She was a bit too loud, *and oops*, he overheard.

"Hikaru, you up for a drink?" Jade asked.

"Yeah. Yeah, I am." He walked up to the bar, the anger coming to a simmer. "Hey, Ken give me four shots of patron and a salty dog." Hikaru sat down on Jade's right.

"Houston gettin' wild tonight," Ari said to Michelle sarcastically.

"Fine, I'm in." Michelle moved to the other side of Jade, between her an Ari.

"Okay four shots of patron." Ken smiled at Michelle, placing them on the bar. "Your salty dog." He handed Hikaru a brass mug. "And a shot of patron for me."

"Bottoms up," Hikaru held his glass up, then Jade, Ari, Michelle and Ken joined.

"Ken, do you make Long Island's?" Michelle asked, sometime later, brushing hair from her face, still feeling Hikaru's eyes on her.

"Lemonade or Iced Tea?" A twisted sort of smirk over took his face.

"Iced Tea." She reached into her wallet.

"No, Michelle this one is on the house." Hikaru heard him say to her, then Michelle stuffed money into Ken's shirt.

"Right, Ken." Michelle replied, indifferent to Hikaru's stare and Ken's kindness. Jade turned to watch. "On the house," Michelle repeated, her fingers lingering on his chest as she slowly withdrew. Ken leaned forward and she pushed him back, both smiling. "What is going on under that shirt?"

"Come back in the summer on lady's night and you can see for yourself. Or if you want, I can set up a private showing, tonight." He chuckled, then winked pouring Michelle's drink.

Ken gave Michelle the drink, then unbuttoned his shirt to fish out the money, looking at Michelle as he did so. When he walked away, Ken was still smiling with a glance over his shoulder on occasion. Michelle trailed the sway of the long braid down Ken's back, the wheels in her head turning. Hikaru continued to watch the exchange. *An hour ago, we're in her living room making out like teenagers, and now she's eye-fucking Rapunzel*, he shook his head. Hikaru cut his attention from Michelle to Ari, on the dance floor, with the guy she introduced as Danny.

"You jealous?" Jade asked, pulling Hikaru's eyes from the dance floor.

"No." He shook his head.

"You look jealous to me." She turned back to Hikaru. "Look, you like her. It's okay but, you're not the only one. So, make a move or sit back."

"We're friends, but she keeps telling me, to talk to you, you're just not interested," Hikaru smiled, shifting gears. He took a sip of his third salty dog and Jade smiled.

"Ken another vodka tonic." Jade cut her eyes back to Hikaru. "You're nice, too nice. I like you but, just not enough to fuck you." Jade handed Ken the money. "You make a great friend and plus you're clearly into her. So, if Michelle is what you want, go after her."

"Wow, thank you. All I needed was your permission." Hikaru placed a hand to his chest sarcastically. "So you like bad guys."

Jade rolled her eyes, "You're welcome." She sipped her drink. "Hikaru, look at her." She and Hikaru glanced at Michelle, her hair thrown over a shoulder, eyes electrified by the alcohol. "If you get her, you need not be threatened when others are interested. Women like Ari and Michelle have the world at their fingertips, and it costs them something, you just don't know what it is. I never believed that kind of woman existed until I met them. They get what they want out of life, sometimes without trying, but life always takes its pound of flesh. They pay a heavy fine for that 'It-girl luck.'"

"And women like you?" Hikaru questioned.

"We try not to be discovered." Jade beamed. "For fear of being studied and experimented on." She and Hikaru laughed.

"I'm serious."

"So am I." Jade flung her golden bangs aside, her eyes drifting to the dance floor. "Come on." She took Hikaru's hand.

"Whoa, whoa, whoa?" He stopped her.

"Come on," Jade repeated, as the song shifted into Stefflon Don's 'Hurtin' me.'

"I-I don't dance." Hikaru shook his head.

"Hikaru, you're half African you have to have some rhythm, c'mon let's find it," Jade smiled, handing him her drink. "Ken, two shots of your best vodka," Jade let go of Hikaru's hand. "Where are you from again," She asked, taking the shot.

"What are you trying to do?" He asked.

Jade handed him a shot glass. "Relax. I'm trying to loosen you up." She smiled patting his arm. "This brown came from the source. You told us once but I forgot where."

"Angola." He smiled.

"Ahh, that's right. The west coast, the trigger."

"The trigger?" Hikaru questioned.

"If Africa was a gun, your country is the trigger," Jade said, her loaded fingers to his chest. "I sensed something vaguely familiar when we met."

"So, you knew my mom was from Africa before I told you?"

"Something like that." Jade stopped and looked at Ken, "still waiting on my chaser. You know how this goes." She stared at him. Ken poured a glass of orange juice, with a sarcastic smile. Jade handed Hikaru a shot and sipped from hers, then gave it to him.

"You might need it out there." Jade laughed, putting the glass of orange juice down.

"You're right." He took the shot, following with the chaser. "Ikura?" Hikaru asked Ken, wincing from the taste and reaching for his wallet.

"I got it." Jade grabbed his hand again. "Add it to my tab." She said leading Hikaru to the floor. Jade pulled him against her backside, her hips taking control, rotating to the pulse of the music.

"Where's Jade?" Ari exclaimed, sitting down by Michelle.

"There," Michelle pointed with her eyes, "with Hikaru."

"Ohh," Ari lit a cigarette. "I'm glad you made it out, I been trying to get the three of us out for a while." Ari smiled, exhaling smoke. "Ken, another vodka cranberry, and make it strong."

"Coming up," He nodded, "and for you?" He looked at Michelle.

"Are you trying to get me drunk?"

"Absolutely." He grinned.

"*Cute*, then I'll take you oiled down with a vodka cranberry in hand." Michelle handed him the empty glass brushing the hair from her face.

"I can make both of those happen but, it's your choice which one you want," Ken said making Ari's drink.

"I'll just take the drink then." Michelle nodded.

Ken handed Ari her drink. "Come on Michelle!" He said in mock anger.

"Michelle stop flirting and let's dance." Ari took a puff of her cigarette then Ken whipped up Michelle's drink and handed it to her.

"I'd rather not," Michelle said, somewhat pointedly. "I just want to drink and listen to good music right now." Michelle watched Hikaru and Jade, feeling guilt blooming in her chest. She pulled her phone from her pocket, to text Seina.

"It must be the bartender." Ari glanced at Ken as Michelle typed out: **Wednesday @5**, then she hit send.

"Are you drunk?" Ken leaned over the bar. Michelle looked up from the message, his hair smelling lightly of olive oil, the chest piece almost in plain view.

"No, not yet, but your DJ is working on it." She turned to him, fingering the end of his braid. "Has anyone ever told you, you have nice lips." She smiled at him.

"The better to kiss and suck." Seeing her smile, his smile became a grin.

"Kon'ya shinai, ookami-chan." Michelle smiled.

"Ah, she speaks Japanese," Ken beamed. "Soshitara Mattemasu." He said in reply. Ari took that moment to slip back to the music.

The alcohol heightened Hikaru's senses, he and Jade grinding to beat after beat. He lost himself in the rhythm, to Jade, to the vodka, to the scents of pink play, shampoo, and cigarettes flooding his mind. When he found himself again, adrift in Jade's web, he was at her apartment, ears ringing and body tingling. He remembered saying his goodbyes, Ari off with Danny, Michelle off in a taxi, and he walking down the sidewalk, now suddenly with Jade— but no idea of the how or when, only the why.

"You want something to drink?" Jade opened the fridge.

"What do you have?" He closed the front door.

"Water, apple juice, tea—" She opened the freezer. "Oh and vodka and tequila,"

"You're trying to get me plastered." He smiled, walking over to her.

"Why would I do that?"

Hikaru came up from behind, wrapping his arms around her waist. "So you can have your way with me." He whispered, in a tone, with words Jade knew he wouldn't remember. Bodies throbbing, Jade pulled away from him, slowly buffing the advance. Her phone rang, just in time.

"Hello."

"Hey, Jade I just—"

"Hey Michelle," Jade cut Michelle off, looking at Hikaru, who stared at her unfazed.

"I'm just calling to make sure you got home okay," Michelle said as Hikaru left the door to the fridge open— lighting the kitchen.

"Yeah I'm fine, just got here," Jade looked Hikaru over. He mixed a drink. Taking a sip, he came closer and kissed Jade. The taste: vodka and apple juice, sparked a candle wax-melting-sensation on eager lips. Jade held the phone for Hikaru to hear.

"Okay, I'll call Hikaru. Do you know if he got back okay?" Jade pulled away. Hikaru dismissed Michelle on the phone. He removed his shirt and push down her skirt.

"He hopped in a cab and went home." Jade watched him slide out of his clothes, muscles taut. "I got a text a few minutes ago." She said then Hikaru hung up.

"Do I have your attention now?" He whispered.

Manhattan-esque
Tokyo, April 24th

Sunlight slipped through the curtains, glittering on Jade's face. *Too bright*, she thought, waking again, the sun drifted into early evening as she lay in bed. She heard Soo Young trying to quietly slip out, so Jade limped to her bedroom door, moving for the first time since she sent Hikaru packing.

"Soo Young!" Jade paused in the doorway. Soo Young froze, a hand on the door knob. "The rent is due next week and you need to pay me back for last month."

"Oh sorry I had in few day." Soo Young smiled back. "I have

315

problem at soron."

"*Right*. Is that new?" Jade asked, pointing to the burgundy fur vest Soo Young was sporting.

"No." Soo Young mumbled, before running out and down the stairs.

"Soo Young! Bring me my money!" Jade shouted. She hobble-limped to the front door when Yu slipped in. "What the—" Jade started.

"You didn't think I'd find you?" He locked the door behind him. Jade noted the gloved hands.

"So, you came to give me what I asked for?" She grinned backing away from him.

"I came to get what's mine." He inched in closer.

"And what would that be?"

"My wallet!" He retorted.

"I don't have it." Jade said, trying not to laugh.

"So, you think this is amusing?" He grabbed Jade by the throat. "Huh?"

"What kind of amusing?" Jade whispered. Yu tightened his grip.

"You bitch, this is my life!" He yelled, still squeezing. Jade kicked him in the crotch, and he doubled over.

"And here you are trying to end mine." She kicked him in his side, then kicked him again. Jade drew back to kick him once more but Yu grabbed her leg and knocked her to the floor, climbing on top of her.

They slid away each other, out of breath. "Just give me my money and leave me the hell alone."

Jade climbed to her feet and reached into the pocket of a jacket she'd left on the sofa. Yu watched as she pulled out a cigarette and lighter.

Jade blew out smoke, raising an eyebrow at him. "It's unfortunate you wasted time and talent screwing sad, lonely, rich, and old people." Jade took a puff of her cigarette as she circled him.

"I'm tired of playing games with you." He glared at Jade.

"I haven't played with you yet." Jade smiled, standing on the other side of the room, smoking a cigarette and, naked beneath a short black robe. "If you help me, I'll fix everything stopping you from being with Eva."

"How?" Yu asked with a cynical smile, walking over to the sofa between them.

Jade smiled back. "Erasing and rewriting bits of information here and there. It's simple." She walked into her room, grabbing an envelope from her nightstand drawer, then Jade handed it to Yu.

"What's this?"

She sat down putting out her cigarette to save for later. "Credit cards, I.D.s, bank statements." Jade beamed at him. "Obviously fakes, but *imagine* what I could create for you. I can rewrite your history, and then I can deliver Eva, you just have to win her." Jade watched for a long moment.

"How is a fake identity going to do anything for me?"

Jade sighed, "Today's not a bright day I see. Not fake Yu, *new*. I can bring back the money, and you can be the Hiroshi Yu you were meant to be again."

"And what do you need my help with?" He asked with a raised brow.

"Technically you're an engineer. I need those skills."

Yu stared at her in search of signs of weakness, some sort of tell. "Fuck no. That's shady"

"You're so eloquent." Jade scoffed.

"Well not all of us can be well-read Chinese New Yorkers." Yu grinned.

"I'm not—" Jade began.

"I know you're not a *real* New Yorker, but from time to time you stretch your vowels, Brooklyn or Manhattan-esque, and at times you sing them, like when I was choking you. Which, might otherwise be hard for you to do, if your accent wasn't fake. My guess is you're from Singapore or Hong Kong, maybe Malaysia. I can't tell if Mandarin or Cantonese is your first language, *yet*."

"Well done." Jade sat back, dropping her American accent for the Queen's English. "Impressive, and what makes you think I'm well read?"

"All your references, over lunch at the café, Morrison, Tan, Baldwin, Cisneros, Hurston— I'm not just a hooker, you know." Yu was gaining a certain air of confidence again as Jade crossed her legs. "Anatomy, linguistics, body language, finance, syntax, pressure points, marketing, sales, phonetics, literature, nerve endings— that's what I had to study. I've spent three years of my life in books, bars and beds."

"Your B.A. in seduction has paid off in several ways." Jade nodded. "You know how to carry a room, and a good conversation."

"That's the first complement you've actually given me."

"It happens, on occasion." She shrugged.

"So, you speak Cantonese *and* Mandarin. But they weren't you're first languages, were they? What was your first language?" Yu questioned.

"Nihongo." She eyed him.

"No." Yu shook his head, tea-colored eyes lit with intrigue.

"Time is ticking, yes or no?" Jade stared at Yu, feeling more exposed than she ever had.

"I need time."

"That's the one thing you don't have." Jade tucked her hair behind an ear.

"I can't help you if I don't know what's at stake." Yu countered.

"You have information I need and I have something I can give you— it's a simple transaction."

After a long pause, he looked at her. "I'll do it." He said stunned as the words left his mouth.

"Good." Jade walked back into her bedroom. "Come here." She motioned with her head.

After Yu left, Jade walked to a seven eleven for a couple bottles of umeshu. She was hoping to knockout her headache and send her to bed with no problems. The cool night air chilling her fingers while she sorted through next steps, but her phone rang. **Hikaru**, it read. Jade stared at the phone, then turned it over, to stop the ringing. Still she stared at his picture.

The image was a selfie from Hikaru's art show, the three of them, Hikaru sandwiched between her and Michelle. *Michelle was right, the boy was fine,* Jade thought, her baser nature stirring. *If only he had the confidence and charm his brother did, or even Chris.* She allowed her mind to drift, from this to plans for the future, after the dust settled, imagining a life on a beach, with sun, sand and, a man. Some *other* man. *Someone a dark chocolate this time,* she decided.

As Jade left the store and started down the dim narrow side street toward her apartment, her phone rang again. It was Hikaru. She absently looked at the picture, flashes of him coming to mind—his chest, his abs, his face, his— Jade answered, as she neared her block.

"What's up?" Jade asked casually.

"Hi." He said.

"Hello. You called just to say that." The question was erased.

"Yes and no—I have a few bruises I was hoping you could explain to me." Hikaru replied.

Jade laughed turning the corner onto her street, looking down at the asphalt, strolling toward the stairs of her building. "I don't know. You were marked up when I got to you." She lied.

"I want to take you out." He said with sudden bravado.

She heard the echo in the phone and saw an unfamiliar figure coming closer. Jade swung as a reflex, and Hikaru stopped her hand. "That would have been a nice punch," he said before kissing her.

Jade pulled away, slowly, surprised.

"I'm working on a project for a little extra money at the moment, but I turn it in next Friday, we could have dinner Saturday or Sunday." Hikaru sneakily took Jade's hand in his.

Jade scoffed, flinging her blonde hair aside. "Okay." She nodded, though she had no intention of showing.

"Okay." Hikaru nodded back, dimples punctuating his delight, in the dim shadows. "Which one?" He asked.

Jade shrugged.

"Alright Sunday, it is. I'll come here to pick you up." He didn't ask where she'd been. Rather than do that, he looked her over, and kissed her again before releasing her. When Hikaru let her go, Jade watched him walk backward toward Ikebukuro station as she climbed the stairs to her apartment, his gaze never wavering. When she unlocked the door, he waved goodbye and kept walking.

Smitten
Tokyo, April 28th

Rain trickled forth as it often does in Tokyo, windy enough an umbrella becomes useless, yet heavy enough one can never stay dry. *This will never be home, there is no scent to the rain,* Ari thought as she slipped into a quiet tea house in Meguro-Ku, near Jiyugaoka station, the rain's pace gaining speed.

She slid the door closed behind her, then stopped in the entrance hall, to remove her shoes. Sliding her nude Manolo Blahniks off, Ari realized there was something missing. She looked at the large wooden step polished to maple by the shuffle of countless feet. There were no tires slushing, or horns blaring, only the tap of droplets on glass and the gurgle of water somewhere unseen. The tea house was hushed. Ari placed her umbrella in the rack by the door, and then moved past the genkan to the heavy paper sliding doors of the tea house.

"Konichi wa," A waitress greeted Ari as she slid the door open, seated on the other side. In front of Ari was a staircase while to the right and left was a singular hallway. Ari nodded to the young woman in a pale pink kimono and stepped onto the tatami mat, her long golden earrings tinkling. The woman slid the door closed, then stood in one fluid motion. "Kochira e de gozaimasu." She extended an arm while leading Ari down the hallway to the left. As Ari turned, she saw Daniele seated in the tea house's serving room, alone. At the threshold to the room the waitress stopped and bowed slightly and Ari went onward. The door quietly slid closed and Ari smiled at her aunt.

Daniele was bathed in the overcast lighting. The rain knocked incessantly on the wall of glass sliding doors. Her tawny skin glowed from within, and though Ari hated sitting on tatami, for Daniele she would do nearly anything. Daniele watched the rain, her hands folded neatly in her lap and her tea steaming in front of her. Ari moved passed the seven or eight empty tables and sat, greeting Daniele with a hug.

"You haven't been waiting long, have you?" Ari turned to look at the older woman.

"No, not long at all." Daniele's, sandy eyes and sandier hair came alive as she patted Ari's hands. She paused. "Naima why did cut your hair again," Daniele asked again, the frustration heavy in her voice. "And you're too thin, have you lost weight?"

"I don't think so." Ari laughed, relishing in the attention. "This is my look. You don't like my hair?" Ari asked, turning to show off the cut.

"You had such beautiful hair, why do you cut." She sang in a clipped Portuguese accent.

A waiter entered the room making a bee line for the table. "O chumon—" he started.

"Ichigo miruku, onegashimassu." Ari handed him the remaining menu from the table, dismissing him—as politely as she could.

"Hai," he bowed and walked away, then came the sound of the door opening and closing.

"So, you don't like it," Ari turned back to Daniele, asking more as a statement.

"I'm more interest in why, you just move a world away with no word. It wasn't for a man, was it?" The sandy haired woman started off.

"Aunt Dani no. It was for work. I'm the publicist to some very important people."

"People, other than Seina's girlfriend? You leave a whole life to be publis to her? What sense is that?"

"I was unhappy with work anyway. The timing was just right."

"Just your work? Naima I know why you took the job. Seina told me. I know you were looking for your uncle too. Who died recent, I hope you had nothing to do with that. What matters, Naima, is your own happiness. Are you looking after that?"

"I am." Ari nodded, tucking her hair. She glanced down at the table, again becoming a little girl listening to the words of the woman who was like a mother. The sliding door opened and closed again and the waiter silently placed Ari's drink on the table, trying to go unnoticed.

"Happiness is my dream for you, true happiness." Daniele said after hearing the door open and close again.

"I know." Ari nodded, wanting to roll her eyes.

"And, not that all happiness is in a man—but is there no man in your life?" Daniele asked, lifting her teacup to her mouth.

"At the moment, no." Ari smirked.

"Well, that won't last long." Daniele laughed, putting the cup down. "Your mother used to have the boys lined up. And you look so much like her." Daniele paused, running her fingers through Ari's hair.

Ari nodded and took Daniele's hand. "I thought you left for Lisbon, after what happened with Michelle."

"I need to check on you and Seina." Daniele let out a deep sigh. "To see if I need to keep closer eyes on both you."

"I'm fine," Ari laughed. "We're fine. But why are we meeting here and why did you rent out the whole place?"

"Says the sickest patient," Daniele looked Ari over. "I believe Seina is in love." Daniele grinned, "If not, smitten, and these are dangerous times."

"That's true." Ari nodded in agreement.

"Tell me, what is her full name?"

"Michelle Yamato." Ari took a sip of her strawberry milk. "No need for a P.I. I already did the work."

"No middle name?" Daniele probed, trying not to seem too

interested.

"Well legally it's Michelle Sarah Yamato-Jang but—" Ari stopped, seeing a smile come to her Aunt's face.

"You should stop worrying over Seina." Daniele nodded absently.

Ari sat waiting for clarification.

"Many years ago, God told me I would have a daughter who's name would be Sarah. He told me this again just after April was born," Daniele beamed. Then changed the subject. "I had a dream you and Seina had blood on your hands and a man in shadow wiped the blood away, then Seina hide the weapon. You and the man disappeared. Then April shot you, and then Seina."

"What does—" Ari began but couldn't find the words and Daniele changed the topic again without warning.

"Claudio is dying. Everything is shift." She turned back to the window.

"How do you know that?" Ari narrowed her eyes.

"Kohana, I can feel her hand on the media. Since the coma, all has gone silent." Daniele paused. "He is dying and no one knows what's in the will. I'm sure Kohana, Subaru and Tatsuya will fight for everything. With what you have from your parents and the eight million I will leave you, Seina and April each, you will be well. Leave that Terada trust for the lawyers," Daniele shot Ari a look. "When Claudio wanted to take control—"

"Two Teradas died and one went missing." Ari cut in. "You've never explained that."

Daniele turned to Ari, "Claudio's brother killed their father and kidnapped the twins to pressure Claudio into give up his part. When Claudio caught him, he tortured their location out of his own brother and only Kohana was found."

"Seina's uncle killed his own father, then kidnapped Seina's brother and sister? All these years I never knew what that meant," Ari trailed off.

"And Claudio killed him, taking everything." Daniele added. "That blood runs thick Naima, until money is tangled."

"Why did you marry him?" Ari shrank back from Daniele, earrings jingling.

"I only knew this when Kohana's mother told me years after we married." Daniele turned back to the window much calmer now, "Stay out of their way, Naima. April and Seina know this."

"I will Aunt Dani."

"Seina wants, to marry her, I'm sure he will listen. But you and April have always been stubborn. Listen to me, this once." Daniele begged.

"I won't involve myself in a Terada succession war and I will not get tangled up with the trust. I promise." Ari's earrings echoed the sentiment.

"Good," Daniele nodded. "So, tell me, what is Michelle like?" Daniele leaned in closer.

Armored Souls
Kawasaki, Japan, April 29th

Wednesday at five, per Michelle's text, appeared much faster than anticipated. Despite the handsome bartender, with the amazing body, that would have gladly taken her home, and whom Michelle *may* have had some interest in. She texted Seina, unable to simply throw him aside as she planned. Seina responded with an address.

So, not wanting to seem *completely* off balance, Michelle didn't renege on the offer, once she was sober. Instead, she went two hours early to ambush him. For the good of them both, Michelle decided she would hear Seina out, but end the relationship to do some soul searching.

After looking the restaurant up, Michelle found that its best feature was the rooftop patio. That was the place she knew Seina would want to meet. With its view of Tokyo proper to the north, and Yokohama to the south, and the sea lazily stretched in the east, it was grand enough for lovers to begin again, or to simply end.

So, Michelle wore a calf length form fitting black dress with a split down the back. It amplified the movement of waist and hips with a hem that leapt with each step, styled in the vein of Elizabeth Taylor as Cleopatra. She added an oversized black shawl flecked with gold to battle the sea winds, and was more than relieved for the warmth when she cozied up to the rooftop bar.

At the bar, Michelle acknowledged the scenery, looking from city to sea and setting, unimpressed. She noted the cobblestone-like flooring under the glow of string lights, as the sun began its descent. It felt more like a French or Italian restaurant-café, Michelle thought as an aging female Japanese bartender, came toward her.

"Kincho shinai de." Her smile was warm and welcoming. "You look beautiful. What can I get you?"

"Arigato gozaimashita," Michelle blushed, silently questioning what about her looked nervous enough this bartender would comment. "Uokka soda onegaishimasu."

By the time Seina arrived, Michelle was still chatting with Chihiro, the bartender, and on vodka soda number six. When She finally saw him, Seina was being led by the hostess, to a table near the very back of the patio. In the far-right corner, the hostess placed the menus on the table and bowed to Seina before leaving. Between them, stood a sea of tables, and Seina caught sight of Michelle as the live band began 'Whenever Wherever Whatever.'

Seina stood in a flint-colored three-piece suit, tinged with blue, a white shirt and black tie. His hair was parted to the right and slicked down. *He even let the beard and moustache grow out a bit*, Michelle thought. She stared at him, her glass frozen to her lips.

When their eyes met, Seina smiled a nose-widening, eye-narrowing, million-dollar grin. Michelle wanted to cry. This was why she put off seeing him. Why she wanted to pretend he didn't exist. Why she *wanted* to kiss Hikaru. It was the simple fact her mind would be changed, with no warning. That she *knew*, she would forgive him, because of that smile, because of that *joy,* on *his* face, when *he* saw *her*.

How had she been so cruel, to this man that loved her, in this way? Michelle put down the drink, tucking hair behind an ear, and she forgave Seina, for further complicating her illegal stay in this country, and her already tenuous relationship with Eva. She pardoned him for choosing to protect his cousin, while trying *not* to hurt her. She exonerated him for drawing the attention of the world upon her, and by extension her shame, along with the evil intent of his father.

Seina moved toward her, but Michelle held up a halting hand and he stopped, brow wrinkled. She turned to Chihiro saying something before climbing down from her stool. Grabbing her clutch, Michelle moved with cat walk-like strides, bracelets and earrings glittering in the light of a Japanese sunset— the hem, jumping from calf to knee in step after step. In less than twelve paces, Michelle threw her arms around Seina's neck, whispering: *"I'm sorry."* She took in the smell of deep woods and mountain air— the scent of Seina.

Surprised by this, Seina froze. By the time he thought to wrap his arms around her, Michelle had stepped back to appraise him, tears welling, but too unripe.

"Are you drun—" He began, cut off by Michelle's kiss.

"I love you too, and I'm sorry." Michelle repeated as casual observers glanced in their direction.

Seina looked around the room. Then to her. "So, you didn't just ignore me?" He smirked, staring intently at her.

"I did, but I was trying to keep my bladder from emptying at the time." Michelle looked away, not knowing what to do or say next.

She looked to their table, covered by a white table cloth, just in ear range of the band. Here the sea breeze was light but steady, and still carried cool notes on the constant gust. The intoxicating melodies of Maxwell floated to them as the sunset bled-out, taking its final bow. Seina turned her face, quickly kissing her again.

"I'm glad you wanted to see me. I had given up." His smile stiffened. He extended a hand to the table and sat. Michelle's stomach turned, while she debated how this would play out. She sat down, pulling her foreign resident card from her clutch.

A waiter quietly appeared, to light the candle in the center of the table, before covering it with a tall blue glass cylinder. "What would you like?"

"We still need a moment." Michelle said with a glance at Seina.

"Are we celebrating or—?" Seina asked, looking to Michelle, taking in her demeanor.

The waiter readied his pen, and there was a long pause.

"I'll take the Ornellaia Masseto and, your—um charcuterie board, for now," Seina said quickly, with a brief grin to the waiter.

"A bottle, sir?"

"Yes," Seina chuckled. Then it suddenly dawned on Michelle, he was nervous.

"Yes sir, I'll have it right out." The waiter nodded, before walking away.

Heaters sprinkled about the rooftop knocked the chill from the air. The fading sunlight allowing the string lights to mix with the blue from the candles. The waiter returned moments later, the tide of the music shifting to Utada Hikaru's 'Kimini Muchuu.' The waiter presented an Italian inspired charcuterie board and poured the wine, promptly dismissing himself.

"So, you've forgiven me?" Seina broke the silence.

"I need your forgiveness first." Michelle paused to sweep hair from her eye.

"I was hurt, not angry." He clarified, lifting the glass to his lips, drinking deeply. The glass was nearly empty when he returned it to the table.

"That seems to be all I'm capable of," Michelle took in a breath, then placed her ID on the table in front of Seina. "I'm here illegally."

"Wha— Sarah Kim?" Seina picked up the card and stopped, eyes narrowing as he looked it over.

"You asked why I was so hot and cold with you. There's your answer. I have nothing to go back to in California and I only have problems here. Yet here is *all I have*. I like being with you Seina, I do, but—" She started.

"So what's the problem?" He cut her off, handing her the card.

"Everything Seina," she threw the ID into the clutch, "from my work to my family to my status here. My whole family is here illegally except my oldest brother and—" Michelle paused, then sipped from her glass. She let go of a long sigh, fighting to keep her armor at bay. "As much as I want to be with you— you're too famous— too rich— and— this just isn't working."

Seina suddenly became very serious. "Who said it's not working? Neither one if us has been working with all the facts. That's why I wanted to see you. So I could lay it out for you." He sat up, pulling the chair closer. The way he said this made Michelle lookup. "I want to start by explaining why I helped Naima."

"Okay," Michelle nodded.

Seina poured another glass of wine, which made Michelle down hers. She tilted the glass toward him and he poured. After filling the glass Seina sipped from his own.

"Naima's parents were killed in front of her, by her uncle and his friends. They stabbed her dad, burned my mother's sister *alive*, along with the house, then they attacked Ari."

"That's tragic." Michelle paused, clasping the stem of her glass, rummaging for *some suitable* emotion. Anger reached the finish line first. "So, because of that, Ari should just be handed the world to do with as she sees fit?"

"No." He said, the blue light from the candle glowing in his eyes. "That's not what I'm saying. I want you to understand why she's so protective of our family, of me. My mother, sister and I are all she has." Seina paused, searching for a response. There was none, Michelle just sat placidly waiting, the drunken tears still at bay.

"And, a few years ago—" His eyes moved away from Michelle's to the table and the elegant white tablecloth.

"She found you," Michelle blurted out, at the realization. She had seen and felt the slender scar that extended the length of his left arm. Yet it felt wrong in some way to ask, so she waited for the telling. Now that it had finally outed, it seemed callous for her *not to know*. Hardhearted, for her not to have asked— or even been curious.

Seina closed his eyes, licking his lips before covering them with a clasped hand.

"Oh my God, Seina." Michelle closed her eyes.

"She found me." He nodded, licking his lips again, then the back of his teeth. *"—bleeding out."*

"Why did—"

"Hold on," he cut her off, tears welling in his eyes now. "She stopped me, and kept me from doing the other arm." He smiled a sad smile, his brows drawing up. "She was the only person that saw the signs. My dad treated me like shit, then he made my fiancée leave me, I was drinking too much, too often, and—" he paused, his voice a thick whisper with the hurt. "—minutes from death, Ari saved me. Ari made sure I got through it." He stopped to clear his throat.

"I get it." Michelle nodded, sniffing—stunned, and dabbing at her eyes.

"I didn't know she was trying to hurt you, Michelle," he shook his head. "I didn't know she was *hurting you*, until I saw her in Milan and it suddenly made sense. So I wanted to send her away quickly and quietly." Seina continued in an outpour left to marinate for weeks, pleading his case.

Michelle said nothing, allowing his words to mingle with the melody. Silence shrouded the table.

"Why didn't you tell me what she was doing?" Michelle asked, moments later, feeling a familiar pang in her chest, as curiosity and song lyrics finally got the better of her.

"I did, but I wasn't sure so I couldn't stand behind it. Then I thought

329

if I stopped her, and got her out of there, it would be alright."

"Then we end up in the news, I get embarrassed, then kidnapped." Michelle shrugged and a tear fell with little warning. "Now, neither one of you are the bad guy."

"I'm sorry, Michelle" he said, forcefully, as if to wake her from her distress, or her sadness, or her anger.

"Seina I had to give birth." The conversation derailed. "Adrien and Gabriele did that to me. They took me, and drugged me and—" her voice caught. "—your angel, brought *that* back into my life. All the old hurts, just *poof,* and there again."

"Then why have you forgiven her and not me?"

Silence, covered the table, again. Michelle's lips tingled, the rage swelling to eyes, eyelids, and eyelashes, all on fire. Her breastplate surfaced now, from thin air, she with readied bow.

"I forgave both of you the moment I walked away." She stared at him. "But neither of you are trustworthy. Ari is just my publicist, who I'm trying to replace. You, made me think that you might love me—" Michelle started, her words cut off by his.

"I *do* love you!" He insisted, "But you shut me out." The ire accusation in his eyes, held her gaze.

"I never let you in." She countered, that armor-piercing blow.

"You think I don't know, you keep me at arms-length?"

"I never wanted you, in my life, or my bed." She shook her head, the hurt welling in continued tears. "I knew better."

"Then what? I love you Michelle. I've *never* intentionally hurt you." He said, throwing his sword to the wind, *his armor* crashing to the sand. "I'm sorry that I hurt you. How would I have known that you even like me? You've barely shown me. Outside of any bedroom, you don't seem to care about me— and Ari is like my sister, what should I have done?" Seina asked with his hands flung open.

"I don't know, Seina," she wiped her face.

They stared at each other, his welling tears to her slow falling ones anger present in both, and silence encompassed their table again. Ten seconds passed, and then twenty as the song came to its end. Seina sat back in his chair, crossing his arms, his eyes on the sea. Michelle looked to the front of the patio, where a young girl sat alongside a guitarist and the music changed.

The songstress began Emi Hinouchi's 'I love you,' but not like Michelle expected. The sound that poured from her was forceful, overflowing with raw— unfettered emotion.

It seemed strange— *alien really,* Michelle thought. *Such a voice in this, the land of: oppressive obligation, the country of devoted-housewives and mothers, salary man, and OL, of virtuous-hard-working daughters and brilliant-majimei sons, of oiran, maiko, and samurai. This* is out of place, *for not being a role perfected in perpetuation.*

The sound was an archetype of the nail not hammered, of the group ideal not satisfied. *This sound,* this girl, *is an expression* not *of unbridled joy,* or *bottomless sorrow, but* both— *silver lining and sinister underbelly.* This girl, like Michelle, stood apart from every visage and trope this country would craft for itself, in a way so completely her own. *Yet, this singer and her sound belongs,* Michelle thought. The words and melodies floated on the wind as she sang— the voice, filling the patio with beautifully pained note after note.

Years from this moment, be it the birth of a child, weddings or graduations, Michelle will be returned to this point in time, at this table, to this song, and this feeling.

The feeling: that her lungs have collapsed and her heart has simply stopped, and the realization that even in her armor, she is not protected, be it unparalleled contentment or limitless regret. Her bow and arrow fell to the dust, then the armor, in that window of the mind where one views self. Then the words came.

"I still love you," Michelle nodded, turning back to Seina. Seina looked back at Michelle, putting down the wine. "but since I met you, who you are has consumed my life and put me in danger. On top of that I don't trust you, Seina, and you don't trust me." Her eyes darted around the restaurant in an effort to stop more tears from falling.

"Then let's build it." Seina, took her hand. "You hold on to me and I hold on to you." He smiled, leaning forward. "Let's create the trust we need. I even brought some pepto, just in case." Seina pulled chewable tablets from his pocket, with a sad-sad smile.

Oh how Michelle laughed, then cried— creeks turning to rivers.

"Stop it Seina," she pulled her hand away with a sniff, dabbing at her make-up, "You sell a dream, then give me a nightmare."

"I guess that's all I'm good for." Seina wiped a tear from her face, kneeling down at her side he said. "I'm sorry I didn't tell you about my family. If I did, you wouldn't have been abducted. But I promise you, I will never let that happen to you again." Seina took both of her hands and kissed them. "I am the unloved fourth son that no one other than my mother cared about. Being with you I forget all of that. You turn me into just Seina, not Seina Terada, and I want to protect you and everything you've given me. Take another chance with me Michelle. Trust me," he implored in a whisper, looking up into her eyes. "And I'll do the same. Now that I know you, I can't imagine my life without you." Seina felt his heart pool in the cracks of the cobblestone, having told her all that was in it. Expecting another blow from Michelle's sword, he pulled a small square box from his pocket. Then Michelle took his face in her hands and kissed him, her sword and sheath, at last, falling to the sand.

"That's why I'm still here," she whispered, her lips slowly curling into a smirk and her eyes dampening. At this Seina offered up the small jewelry box. Inside was a massive ten karat pink diamond set in gold— the match to the necklace.

"But can you take a chance on me, indefinitely?" He asked clumsily slipping the ring on her finger. They paused staring at each other, Michelle not so much as glancing at the ring.

"Nkem." She whispered. *My own.*

"Huh?" Seina's face went blank.

"Yes." Michelle nodded, pulling Seina into another kiss.

Nkem, Miles' father called her. 'My own' he had dubbed the girl child of his youngest son, whom he bonded with the moment he held her. *Nkem*. Michelle pulled away, smiling. Seina wiped her eyes with both thumbs.

"What is it?" Seina stood, feeling her thoughts drift elsewhere.

"*Fiancé*," she said with a slight laugh. "my brother is getting married next week," Michelle licked her lips, then glanced down at the untouched charcuterie board.

"So I'm your plus one?" He asked, with a raised brow.

"If you still want to be." She swept her hair back from her eye.

"Of course."

"So, her grandparents won't come to Japan. Meaning there are two weddings, one in Osaka and one in Busan." She watched him move back to his seat.

"Then maybe your brother shouldn't be marrying her. He's Japanese, that's not gonna change." Seina shook his head, in a playful response.

"But we're half Japanese and a splash Korean, I'm told. Seina, we're gaijin. You grew up with this Korea-Japan tension. *You're* Japanese."

"I could see that too. But you do know most Japanese people don't just say gaijin, right? It's not an Afro-American saying nigga to another one."

Michelle's mouth fell open. "You are not allowed to say that!" She playfully hit his leg.

"What the life police gonna do? I'm black, from the blackest country in the Americas. You think Italy or Japan made this color?" He held up a hand.

"You're a touch darker than khaki, speak Japanese like a native, with not one black relative to point to." Michelle stared at him.

"Says the tan Japanese girl. Are you sure your dad is black? He might really just be South Asian." He chuckled as the smile melted from her face. "What I'm saying is I was born in Brazil and I grew up in Italy, Portugal, and Japan so if any thing I'm gaijin too. It's not as black and white as you're making it."

"You still grew up with this culture. That's what makes you Japanese." Michelle stared at him, as Seina poured another glass of wine for both of them.

"Michelle you're looking at their situation too one sided." Seina winked.

"Oh, that's all?" Michelle gave a sarcastic smile. "Because white supremacy, and systemic oppression don't have costumes or passports? Those concepts are more internationally known than any song or band. Her family has a right to abstain from Japanese trappings, and it's no problem because my brother is a *Black* Asian American as am I."

"That's not what I'm saying love. We still have to find happiness amongst all of that. What I am saying is that it will start with two weddings, and end with two worlds. But that's for them to sort." Seina changed the subject. "Let's go down to Osaka a few days before the wedding? I would love to take you around."

"I would like that. I've never been," she nodded.

Seina sighed. "But before that," he sobered. "I have to finish telling you about the ugliness with my family."

Cluster
~~Singapore~~ Tokyo, April 20th - 2nd

Though Victoria wanted to get married in her native Singapore, Tokyo was the best option for a quick, quiet, *somewhat* hassle-free wedding. Given their crazy work schedules, paired with Li Jun's unceremonious re-proposal, and what Victoria took to calling *'the little time bomb'*— still unbeknownst to Li Jun. *Now,* seemed like the only possible time. So, Victoria persuaded Li Jun into a spur of the moment wedding, fueled by money and pride.

They agreed on an outdoor ceremony and chose the Chinzanso for its waterfall. They would walk to the Gojo waterfall and exchange vows at sunset, as a symbol to their families that it is truly *never* too late. The family would partake in an elegant banquet at Il Teatro surrounded by close friends, then they would dance and drink into the night with a large reception. Quick, simple, and straight-forward, until they had to pay off a Japanese couple to book the venue for May second. *Bribe to the couple, 1 million yen. Securing the venue 3.2 million. DJ, open bar, 4 bartenders, and catering, 3.5 million yen.*

Li Jun booked hotel rooms at the venue, for their families. Victoria arranged for a florist to deliver lilies, orchids, peonies and lotuses in red, white, and pink, along with any minor décor needed for a *slightly* traditional Chinese wedding. She did most of the planning with help from the hotel and its staff between getting used to her job as Vice President at the agency. *Wedding coordinator, staff, florist, and hotel rooms, 2.1 million yen.*

Victoria and Li Jun planned to fly everyone in with *'last-minute'* tickets, at already high prices. Then, Li Jun really did wait until the last minute to buy plane tickets. There was Victoria's father in Seoul, Hong Kong, or Singapore, Li Jun's two sisters in Australia, the one in Hawaii, the three living in North America, *and even* the pregnant one in Fukuoka— plus their families. Li Jun also told his sisters, *the day of the flight*, the reason he needed them home. This forced each of these traditional Wong women past and present to scour her closet for a lucky red item fit for her brother's wedding. *Last minute airfare, 3.6 million yen.*

When Li Jun called Victoria's father, *three days prior*, and couldn't get in touch, he left a message with Jennifer— the assistant and still hadn't heard back. The dragon and phoenix gown and tux Victoria ordered arrived unfinished and falling apart, though she asked a famous designer and old friend of hers to alter something pre-made. *Wedding garments 130,000 yen. Rushed repairs, 50,000 yen.*

Once everyone had arrived, with no delays— *thank God*, the hotel manager called Li Jun to apologize for the mix up, promising the falls would still be available that day but at an earlier time, while throwing in free services for the wedding party to ease the inconvenience.

"What mix up?" Li Jun asked as he waited at Haneda for the last of his sisters, but more on this in a moment. To add gasoline to the mess, the private rooms of the Il Teatro were booked into early June, and the Wong-Yang party was too large.

Now, here they were, in the calm of Mokushundo's Zanso room overlooking the lush green garden after simply deciding to have a family dinner. Li Jun sat across from Victoria at the head of the table looking incredibly handsome, *screw up though he was. Family dinner at Mokushundo, 230,400 yen*

On Li Jun's right, were his parents, all nine of his sisters along with the five husband-boyfriend-fiancé combos dotting the rest of the table. The five grandchildren were in the nursery as the restaurant had age minimums that both Li Jun and Victoria missed. Twenty-four in all.

Li Jun winked at his wife-to-be and mouthed: *'I love you to the moon,'* under the ocean of Cantonese. They finished the last of the stone grilled feast, while Eva who was sitting on Victoria's left, smiled at her friend.

"Are you nervous?" She asked with a smile.

"Well, there's still another twenty-hours for something to go wrong." Victoria joked, smoothing her long sleek ponytail.

"Don't think like that—" Eva patted Victoria's hand. Though she was listening, Victoria took in the bags under Eva's eyes, concealed by the make-up, and the quiet sadness she carried.

"Eva, what's going on with you?" Victoria whispered.

Eva shook her head. "These next few days are all about you and my little brother, you cougar."

"He's twenty-eight next month," Victoria scoffed, trying not to laugh.

Eva beamed. "I'm very happy for you. *Both of you.*"

"Thank you." Victoria beamed back as the rest of the Wong sisters' squawked around them, discussing one of their latest parenting adventures. *Jesus these women are loud,* Victoria mused, simply trying not to dwell on thoughts of her absent family, or the two empty seats to her right.

For the head count should be twenty-six. Twenty-seven if you asked Jia Lang, Victoria reminded herself, putting down her chopsticks. She carefully wiped her mouth then felt her phone vibrate inside her hand bag. A text from **Ba-ba. Just landed**. It read, sent nearly forty minutes ago.

"Everything Alright?" Li Jun asked standing over Victoria, Eva having freshly joined the Wong sister's conversation. "I hope nothing else went wrong."

"No, Ba-ba landed. He's on the way." Victoria said as a phone lit up on the table, and Victoria saw **Kohana Terada** flash on the screen. Eva quickly picked it up, and excused herself.

"Why is she call—" Victoria tried, but Eva rushed out of the room.

"It's probably work, don't worry." Li Jun shrugged.

"She's been off lately."

"Well, we have a bigger issue." Li Jun said not wanting to go on.

"Bigger issue?" Victoria tensed, with a half-hearted smile.

"Aiyah, Li Jun what is all this?" Mrs. Wong sliced through their conversation and the table fell silent.

"You didn't tell them?" One of the sisters exclaimed. Li Jun ignored this, but Victoria's eyes burned a hole in him with the same inquiry.

"Victoria and I are getting married." He announced.

"When?" Mr. and Mrs. Wong shouted in a panicked unison.

"This time tomorrow." Victoria added.

The husband and wife stared at one another. "Wong Li Jun where are the flowers?!" Mrs. Wong shouted in Cantonese. "Where is double happiness? Where are the lucky fruits?" She was nearly hysterical.

"Where are the phoenix and dragon? And the banquet?" Mr. Wong picked up the thread. "And the tea ceremony, eh!" He rushed over and hit Li Jun across the head. Everyone at the table slowly shrank back from the two of them with lowered eyes.

Outside near the entrance to the restaurant, Eva paced, still on the phone.

"Yes, Ms. Terada, I am well aware of that. I just need—" She said, using Keigo, that formal level of Japanese rarely used outside of business and when deference is commanded.

"Miss. Wong, I don't care what you need. You. Owe. Us. I expect you to do your job—the only one that matters." The phone call ended.

"What do you mean tomorrow morning?!" Victoria's shout rang out of the restaurant.

Eva put down the phone and moved to the front door where she found Victoria's father, removing his shoes to enter the restaurant. He stood in a charcoal grey suit, his silver hair in a crew cut, paired with a black mustache and eyebrows, and complete with a silvering goatee. Next to him stood Jennifer, the beautiful blonde assistant. She wore a green cocktail dress and a coat matching Mr. Yang.

"Miss. Wong," He beamed, looking up at her. "I'm so sorry about the last time we met," he started off, looking abashed. "I thought you were blackmailing me."

"I don't know how that picture got on my computer—it—" Eva started defensively.

Mr. Yang held up a hand. "It doesn't matter. You see, my daughter has been missing for over two years." He looked at the ground, while Jennifer took hold of his hand. Eva's eyes went to their hands.

"It appears Jia Lang died –last—" He broke off, then cleared his throat.

"I'm so sorry, Mr. Yang. Victoria never even mentioned that to me." Eva said taking a step to comfort him.

"Ba-ba?" Victoria questioned, trying to compose herself. "Are you o—" She stopped speaking as her eyes came to rest on Jennifer, with her hand on Liam's back. Victoria was about to walk away but Li Jun stopped in the doorway and bowed to her father.

"Good evening, Mr. Yang. It's good to see you again. I'm so glad you could come on such short notice. We're sorry to rush off but, Victoria and I have some last-minute wedding details to see too."

"Ah, til later then," Mr. Yang nodded to Li Jun, his cool distain only marginally veiled.

Li Jun swept Victoria away into a quiet place in the garden, away from the restaurant and their families. The trees blocked the setting sun, slowly plunging them into shadow. He threw her jacket over her shoulders. At this, Victoria realized he already had his own on. *That was Li Jun, always ready to make an escape.*

"I did everything I could to keep it on your mother's birthday so please don't be too mad. The couple we paid off knew the hotel double booked and just took the money and ran." He changed the subject. "Tori, we did this thing last minute, we're quite lucky you know?"

"I know lah." She pouted; the queen's English dismissed and the tears of frustration falling. "Wah lau eh Why dis happen? Pua chao cheebye!" Victoria shouted. She sniffed, covering her face, the other hand on her hip, the stress of it all finally getting to her. Li Jun had never heard her talk like this, never known her to break character.

"It's alright. This is you and me, and we're getting married tomorrow." He smiled.

She did not. "You're right." Victoria exhaled, the accent firmly in place again. Li Jun grinned harder and stepped closer to her, taking both of her hands.

"I'm going to go upstairs take a hot bath and go to bed." Victoria said matter of fact.

"Okay, I'll walk you up." Li Jun nodded.

"I'm going alone." She kissed him on the cheek, saying 'Good night,' as she strolled back to the hotel.

"Can I join you?" Her father asked, walking with Victoria as she passed the restaurant.

"Ba-ba, thank you for coming. This was thrown together." Victoria tried to smile.

"Read the signs my daughter. This wedding is falling apart because it is not your destiny. Why are you so sure about this man?" Liam clasped his hands behind his back as they strolled.

"Ba-ba we love each other." She crossed her arms and turned to him. The light from the hotel pooled on the ground in front of where they stopped.

"Maybe that is not enough." He said softly.

"If I were Jia Lang, you would be tripping over yourself to help pay for everything." She paused. "Ba-ba, I don't want to do this. Good night." Victoria stormed off toward the hotel.

The next morning, Victoria woke to find she had not rested at all. It was as if the past eleven years of fashion shows and photo shoots had come to collect, with interest. She felt heavy, and tired. She wanted to cry. Victoria sat staring out the half-open curtains at Tokyo coming to life, toothbrush in hand, frozen mid-routine. A soft knock came from the door. She didn't move. After a few moments, Mrs. Wong came in, and froze in the doorway—jasmine tea in hand. She watched the tooth brush fall from Victoria's mouth alongside her silent tears.

"What's wrong?" Mrs. Wong set the tea down and took a place beside Victoria. "I know today will be hard for you. But now that you are to be my daughter-in-law, you will never be alone again." Mrs. Wong said in Mandarin. At this, Victoria crumbled, and more tears slipped from her in continued silence.

Mrs. Wong took Victoria in her arms, while Li Jun's sisters quietly slipped into the room.

"I will never be your mother, and my daughters might never become your sisters, but we will be family." Mrs. Wong cooed as two of the Wong sisters let more sunlight into the room.

Each Wong woman wore a dress or outfit fit to attend a wedding, but with various articles of red. There were red earrings, headbands, hairpins, handbags, shoes, shawls, scarves, bracelets, belts, or blazers, and all the Wong women were watching her. Had Victoria not been trying to land from last night's Ambien induced sleep, she would have found this scene odd, if not cult-like.

Eva was the last to enter the suite, carrying Victoria's wedding dress, the gold glimmering in the morning light. This was a moment Victoria was meant to feel joy, it was the moment she was to be *happy*. She felt nothing. Victoria had forgotten about the photographer she and Li Jun hired, until she saw her, trailing behind Eva, capturing every second.

The other Wong women sat in silence, expecting some reaction from her to the dress, or the lens. This Victoria knew. Yet, all the bride had to offer was her pain, and so it continued to escape, seeping from her being, regardless of all else. Eva laid the garment down.

"She needs a minute." Eva announced to the room, leading Victoria into the bathroom.

By the time the Wong women got Victoria to the Gojo waterfall, her fog was lifting. The sun peaked through dark angry clouds, but as she approached Li Jun, Victoria was regal. Mrs. Wong had arranged Victoria's hair into a chignon, leaving long tresses draping the sides of her face and in front of her ears. The bride wore a red floor-length, long sleeved, off the shoulder gown with a golden phoenix embroidered on the bodice and train, its wings spread, glittering much of the dress.

Li Jun stood on the waterfall's bridge, his hair was pulled into a bun and he wore a red tux with embroidered gold dragons on his shoulders and chest. Behind him the character for double happiness stood on the railing, crafted from lotuses, peonies, lilies and orchids in plumes of pink, red, and white. Following the exchange of vows, Li Jun and Victoria kissed, and the wind picked up. Then the sun vanished behind the clouds, in an instant.

"Aiyah, Li Jun! Smile bigger, big! BIG, *very* big!" Mrs. Wong screeched as the bride and groom posed for picture after picture on the bridge with the wedding party. *Rushed prewedding shoot, 150,000 yen. Prewedding prep photos, ceremony photos, and portraits following the ceremony, 80,000 yen*

Jennifer and Liam looked on in silence. She squeezed Liam's hand as he watched his daughter, a look of sheer sadness washing over him at the sight.

"Liam, this is what she wants. She's a grown woman, but you have to tell her about Jia Lang." Jennifer whispered, with a comforting nod, spotting a thin blonde man in a red fitted cap. He watched the wedding party from the other side of the bridge for a moment then walked away.

Mrs. Wong continued making demands, as gusts of wind rushed by, pulling at curls and skirts alike. By the time Li Jun and Victoria were taking couple photos, the wind had picked-up yet again. This time the gales snapped the fishing line holding the double happiness arch. It toppled over and hit Li Jun. The other half fell into the waters with a splash. Mr. Wong and Yang sprinted to the bridge. The Wong sisters froze then rushed over to help.

In all the commotion, Jennifer spotted the blonde man again on the other side of the bridge, but Mrs. Wong's collapse brushed that thought aside. *Jun and Victoria's wedding, 14,039,400 yen.*

Seeing Mrs. Wong completely overwhelmed, priceless.

欲　望　望　み
17. Yokubo / Nozomi
Tokyo, May 3rd

"Eu quero você." Hikaru practiced, as he walked to Jade's door, heart, hands, and other parts pulsing. He thought to surprise Jade for their date, but Hikaru knew flowers were too cliché. He abandoned that plan all together, opted for Portuguese lessons instead. He planned to seduce Jade properly, this time, over west African food, with the intent to make *her*, his. Or so that was the thought behind asking her out. Hikaru glanced at his watch as he went up the stairs, and knocked on the door.

Soo Young answered. "Karu!" She exclaimed, with a slap on the butt when he passed. He paused, but ignored this. His nerves were getting the better of him, until he made out the word, 'left.'

Soo Young paused in a skimpy yellow romper. "She just left." Hikaru thought he made out through Soo Young's rather strange accent.

"Kanojo doko ni itta." He asked to clarify.

"Shirane." Soo Young shrugged. "tada sarita," she said crossing her arms, with cleavage on display.

Hikaru called Jade, taking a seat on the sofa. No answer. He called again, and again, again three times over.

"Did she say where she was going?" he asked.

Soo Young shook her head.

In a hotel room, in Yokohama, Chris turned on the tv pulling alcohol from the mini bar.

"*Police discovered the body of Air Force Lieutenant Robert Harris today, when local restaurant owners noticed a strange smell coming from—*" the TV went on, but a knock came from the door. Chris moved to the door and opened it. Jade smirked up at him from the other side, then sauntered in. Chris simply closed the door watching her walk over to the bed.

"*Residents of the area claim Harris sold drugs and—*" The reporter chimed. Jade turned the tv off.

"This is the last time." She pulled off her coat throwing it to the floor.

"Where have I heard that?" Chris grinned, taking off his shirt.

"Chris," she paused for their eyes to meet. "I'm leaving Japan." Jade watched him, looking for what, she was unsure.

"We can't stay away from each other for long. You'll come back, or we'll run into each other." He said, watching Jade slip out of her jeans.

Chris' undershirt hit the floor followed by his shorts and Jade's blouse. In the pile of clothes, Jade's phone lit up on silent, the picture of her, Hikaru, and Michelle on the screen.

Fruition
Ashiya Shi, Hyogo, Japan, May 5th – 6th

The taxi driver dropped Seina and Michelle off at the fork of the Oruike Green road, so they could walk to the restaurant, at Seina's request. They strolled down the quiet street, in near darkness, passing a singular house. Hand in hand they moved leisurely, her heels and his dress shoes pitter-patter on the asphalt. Tonight, winter's chill and summer's humidity had come to a truce, becoming the stand-off of late spring in Japan.

They passed a small grove of trees on the right, moving deeper into the quiet. Time seemed to stand still in this little township between Osaka and Kobe but, an owl marked the passing moments, and Seina slowed the pace, as they neared a street light on the left. He wrapped an arm around Michelle's waist then came to a stop in front of the light pole, staring at Michelle.

"Stop it." She beamed, covering his face, to avoid whatever he might be plotting.

"Stop what?" Seina questioned, leaning against the pole with his patented smile. He uncovered his eyes and pulled her into his arms.

"Whatever you're plotting." She re-draped her shawl, laughing non-stop, as they had since arriving in Osaka three days ago.

In the midst of their laughter, Michelle looked longingly into his eyes. He kissed her, the quick peck slowly escalating into a long lingering urge. When Michelle pulled away, he pulled her back, moving to kiss the base of her neck.

Michelle lifted his head. "You've been acting strange. What's going on?" She asked, though she knew. It was the message he read at breakfast, that's where it began. Michelle didn't read it, but saw the effect all over him. He clung to her the entire day— though welcomed, not like him. They shopped and ate wherever they wanted, with no thought of being photographed. Even in New York, they went out cloaked in dark sunglasses. But not here. *Why?*

Seina looked at Michelle and knew there was no way out. "They started the investigation into the shooting this morning." He said, hoping the questions would stop there.

"Oh," Michelle echoed, stepping back to better look at him, to better assess. "Good thing your cousin-sister got a lawyer." She said glibly.

Seina looked at her, haltingly, invoking their yet unvoiced understanding. It was the agreement that began as an awareness of the limits between them and grew into a silent pact. The limits themselves sprang from things like, inquiries neither wished to think about, their unkempt pasts, and their yet untold secrets. Seina's attempted suicide, for instance, or Michelle's affair with Adrien being just the beginning. Instead, they drew comfort in being two magnets drawn together. No story, just action, *this*, simple attraction.

"So, where in the world are you taking me?" Michelle switched topics. She gently pulled Seina away from the light pole. "My feet hurt." She lied, trying to move past the unpleasantness. "And I hate dark wooded areas." Michelle looped her arm in his.

"There's nothing to be afraid of." He looked at her chuckling, as the street zagged to the left.

"Whatever! They don't look for us!" She brushed her hair back from her face, and Seina burst into laughter.

"I'm sorry," he covered his mouth, "That's not funny-it was the way you said it." Seina kept laughing, the faint Florissant light from a row of vending machines playing on his face.

"You're silly," she scoffed.

"You didn't know?" Seina replied, with raised eyebrows.

"Where is this restaurant?" Michelle looked up at the sky.

Seina pointed. They passed the vending machines, and moved toward what looked like an extension of the grove they passed earlier. "I wanted you to try very traditional Japanese food since we're in Japan's kitchen, and because I know you love to eat."

"And you don't?" Michelle retorted, the asphalt suddenly changing to gravel.

"There it is." Seina said, and there, some ten feet ahead stood a grand wooden gate, surrounded by bamboo arching toward its center. There was a sign written in stylistic kanji—that old writing adopted from early Chinese.

"Reiko?" Michelle questioned, reading the sign then thoughts of her grandmother, a woman she only briefly knew, flooded to mind.

"You can read that?" Seina stopped, thinking Michelle completely unlearned in this realm of Japanese culture.

"Yes. I can read it." She elbowed him and they walked toward the gate.

"Even I struggle with Kanji."

"I guess your not as bright as you think." Michelle giggled, patting his cheek, then his buttocks. Seina scoffed and the pair walked into the bamboo forest beyond.

The wood was divided by a narrow sidewalk made wider by a gravel walkway, and lined by lit stone lanterns dotting the path. After a few moments, Michelle stopped when the forest began to thin and they came to a wide foot bridge. Music drifted toward them as they came closer to the restaurant.

It was a Ryoutei, the luxurious type of traditional Japanese restaurant. The restaurant was composed of stone and wood, paper lanterns and doors, and lit on a lake. It was a castle, or so one might think in passing. Even at this distance, Michelle could hear people laughing and chatting on the open-air deck that overlooked the grounds. Seina walked toward the door and slid it open, Michelle's hand in his.

"Irasshimase," A young woman said, dressed in a red Kimono, speaking barely above a whisper from behind the receiving desk. The halls were lined with paper screen doors, and elaborate décor of a world before the war, reminiscent of the time of Edo, Daimyo and Minamoto. The sound of the shamisen poured in from some place unknown. Michelle was enraptured as they slipped out of their shoes.

"We got a VIP table." Seina said to her, moving toward a lantern lit hall.

"I'm not surprised." She shook her head. Attendants appeared from nowhere, opening the door to *their* private dining room.

"Dozou." The hostess extended an arm to the room. Seina walked inside while Michelle took in every sight and sound. The table was sunken into the floor, surrounded by tatami mats. Large bowls of goldfish sat on shelves along the walls of the room. The walls were white and trimmed in gold, and from their table was a view of the inner courtyard. Here, three bridged islands floated in a space that seemed both intimate and expansive, surrounded by the restaurant and the lake, on which the entire dream floated. A large Cherry blossom tree littered the water with its petals. Ponds of colorful koi fish, housed on each isle, glimmered and glowed in the light of lanterns hung from the tree. Seina nodded to the hostess and he sat with Michelle following. The young woman handed out hot towels, poured tea, and discussed the menu, and without Michelle knowing she slipped away saying: "Goyukuri dozou."

"How did you hear about this place?" She asked looking back to the islands.

"It's a hot spot if you're in the area." Seina smiled.

"Sureshimasu," A sweet calming voice said, entering the room. It was the owner, coming to chat with the VIPs. Michelle only caught sight of the black Kimono, fading to red, from the corner of her eye as she listened to the music of the shamisen. Seina froze. *There were two Michelle's.*

Michelle let go of Seina's hand before she had even seen her mother. It was instinctive. The waiters came in next, placing the food on the table. Sashimi, soup, and salad, elaborately arranged in large trays fashioned like boats with several embellishments here and there.

"Good evening Mr. Terada, I was so happy to hear of your coming, although I thought you were your brother." Ms. Yamato said in Japanese, referring to Tatsuya, the right-hand man of the Terada supply chain. Michelle turned at this voice, and felt her heart stop.

Ms. Yamato knelt, her hair elegantly arranged in a traditional fashion. She glanced at Michelle with a warm smile. This was the first time Michelle had ever seen her mother in any color that wasn't white-adjacent. The waiters handed out rice portions, disappearing in an instant, with Michelle staring at her mother still in complete disbelief.

"You said the restaurant was in Osaka," Michelle changed the tide to French.

"If I said 'Ashiya Shi' would you have known where it was? I said *outside* of Osaka." Ms. Yamato responded, not missing a beat, still smiling, placing cuts of sashimi in front of each of them, as the Okami would at such a restaurant, for VIP guests.

Seina looked to Ms. Yamato then to Michelle and back. "You know my brother? Which one?" Seina's eyes met Ms. Yamato, with Michelle trying to keep up with the Japanese.

"Tatsuya." Ms. Yamato smiled, aware of the rivalry between them, long before Michelle, page six, and New York.

"Ah, he does like Osaka a great deal." His eyes drifted from Ms.

Yamato to Michelle again for the nearness of faces, *they could be sisters,* he thought. "I'm sorry about the confusion; I guess that's why we got the private room. I'm Seina Terada." he took this moment to introduce himself, pausing only to fold his legs beneath him and bow before Ms. Yamato.

"Wonderful to meet you Seina, as you may have guessed I'm Michelle's mother, Ayane, or Vivian, if you like."

Ms. Yamato returned the bow, then looked at Seina, and instantly his stats floated to mind: *absent father, three older brothers, soon to be locked in a battle for succession over the ill-gotten Terada fortune. The stakes: the Terada empire, a kingdom unto itself, made up of: private islands and private jets, houses, and land in seven countries, nearly a sovereign nation, ranging from cell phones to media—the tip of the iceberg.*

Terada is gold, but for whom? It is highly unlikely for all four brothers to emerge king of the castle. Two, or three doable but, four— never. And what of the other Terada spawn, the two sisters, April and Ko, Ko— something, she considered. *The stakes are too high, and the odds clearly not in favor of, Seina Terada.*

Seina, the playboy turned corporate, fourth son, from the fourth wife with no proven ability to lead himself, let alone a company, an empire, "or my daughter," she mumbled. "What brings you here?" Ms. Yamato asked slipping into English for Michelle's sake.

"We came for the wedding." Michelle looked to Seina. "Seina was showing me around."

"Wonderful. Your date," Ms. Yamato questioned, motioning to Seina with a slight extension of her hand. She moved like artwork brought to life. A complete change from the woman in court.

"Yes," Michelle nodded.

Ms. Yamato smiled. "I see. Well I'll leave you to your meal. You're a special guest, my only VIP tonight."

"I'm honored," Seina beamed.

"As am I," Ms. Yamato stood. She slipped through the door, closing it behind her.

Seina looked at Michelle, trying to survey the damage. "I swear I didn't know."

"Neither did I." Michelle whispered. "It was going to happen anyway." She grumbled.

"One down," he laughed nervously.

"Only three more," Michelle shook her head and Seina moved to the other side of the table to sit beside her. He pulled her into his arms while Ms. Yamato listened in the hallway, cracking the door to peer in. She watched Seina pick up his chopsticks.

"You know what's strange?" he paused, "It sounds like she knows my brother pretty well."

"That's scary, if you ask me. What does Tatsuya do?" Michelle brushed her hair from her face and over a shoulder.

"He works for my father, on the dirty side of things."

"Ah, right. And how many siblings do you have again?" She asked, avoiding the question of why he might know her mother.

"Naoki, Subaru, Kohana, Tatsuya," Seina counted on his fingers, "Technically four brothers and three sisters counting Ari. But one of my half-brothers died. So, six,"

"And your only whole sibling is April, right?"

"Right. And your brothers are Marcus and Chris."

"Yeah," Michelle nodded "But Marcus' girlfriend, Devina, is my mother's *real* daughter— she loves Devina, and then Chris is marrying Alyson, this beautiful Korean woman."

"Too easy," Seina smiled.

Michelle scoffed. "Because my daddy wasn't Henry the eighth."

"When we get home, I'll draw up a family tree just for you." Seina kissed her before diving into the rice. Ms. Yamato watched as Seina stroked Michelle's back, noting the tenderness.

"So, how did this brother of yours die?" Michelle asked cautiously.

Seina stopped. "My uncle, kidnapped my oldest sister and her twin." Seina paused. "Kohana was found alive but Koji wasn't."

Outside, in the hallway, Ms. Yamato froze, still listening but not wanting to, wanting to walk away, but not able to.

"Yeah, that whole thing was part of how my mother and father met." Ms. Yamato heard Seina say. She looked down the hall, her eyes meeting Chris' eyes, and behind him her eldest, Marcus, fresh from the airport. They both stopped outside the sliding doors. Ms. Yamato held a finger to her lips.

Inside the room, the music from the courtyard changed to a slow, unwinding piece as they ate. Seina continued eating, and Michelle's mind began to drift taking in the beauty of this space. She was ushered into another idea of herself. A self that was aware of this land, its customs and traditions, and its language. A self, equal and opposite to the woman *she is*.

The unwinding notes from the shamisen came to a close, and Michelle's cheeks dampened for the woman she has become. Not soft but, calloused, not sweet but, embittered. She was crying and not realizing, for reasons and feelings she had yet to truly understand. Michelle listened, unknowingly, allowing the crushing reality of her life, and her mistakes, and her complete failures, and this love to wash over her like a monsoon. Seina looked at her and stopped.

"Why are you crying?" He wiped her tears.

"It was a beautiful song." Michelle sniffed, still unable to give her feelings words. In all of this, the door slid open, and Chris spoke.

"It's called Namonaki Oka." He stood in the doorway with Marcus behind him.

Marcus was a tall man, taller than Chris. He was the color of honey and caramel, with a splash of half and half, chiseled features and a dense forest of curly hair that hung to his shoulders. He was familiar to Seina in an instant. The two stepped inside, Ms. Yamato nowhere in sight.

"Congratulations," Michelle beamed as she got up to hug Chris.

"I'm glad you could make it." Chris grinned. "So, what did you get me?"

"You'll see." She said, noting Marcus' defensive demeanor at the first sight of Seina.

"Where's Devina?" Michelle attempted to pull Marcus' attention away from Seina.

"She's visiting family. She flies in tomorrow." Marcus said to Michelle, glancing at her ring before looking passed her, back to Seina.

"So, this is your friend?" Chris pointed with his eyes.

"Chris, Marcus this is Seina. Seina these are my brothers Marcus and Chris." Michelle said, pointing. Seina stood to greet them.

"Nice to meet you, join us, please." Seina extended an arm to the table.

The brothers sat and Michelle quickly excused herself, to touch up her face. This was the first untangling of destinies between houses Terada and Yamato-Jang.

Michelle came back from the bathroom to find Seina pouring sake for Chris, Marcus, and both of her parents. She closed the door behind her, knowing this evening would turn full assault on her love life. All of them had seen the huge diamond ring but, nothing had been said, and yet, the atmosphere was charged.

"Just in time," Chris shouted, seated between Ms. Yamato and Miles, while Marcus sat at the end of the table between Miles and Seina. Chris placed a sake glass in front of Michelle when she sat down on Seina's left. Michelle looked at Seina and then to her father sitting across from him. Miles was the color of cedar wood in this light, and his thick lidded eyes looked tired, but bright as he watched the exchange between Chris and Michelle.

Michelle ignored Chris. "Daddy, when did you get here?"

"Last Tuesday," Miles smiled, bright eyes narrowing. He was greyer then last she saw him, but still so handsome with his slick coils combed back from his face, the gray running rampant in his neatly trimmed beard alongside his full lips the shade of mocha.

"Where are you staying?"

"You know mom lives up the street, right?" Chris cut in, with Seina quietly following the conversation.

"No, I didn't." Michelle stared at Chris.

"Yeah," Chris nodded. "Now take your shot," he pointed. "Me, Marcus and your boyfriend here are four shots in. Mom and Dad got two." He poured another round. Michelle looked at her mother, sitting across from her, tucking her hair with her usual smile of indifference. She had slipped out of the Kimono, and into a simple black Vera Wang.

"This is your brother's doing." Ms. Yamato looked at Chris and Marcus, with a different sort of glance. Chris, Seina, and Marcus took a shot as Ms. Yamato lifted her glass to Michelle.

"You gotta catch up." Chris repeated.

"Hear that sweet pea?" Seina smiled, looking at Michelle.

"I might like you less now." Michelle smiled back.

"Chris slow down." Miles interjected, placing a hand on Chris' forearm. Miles could see a plan taking shape, but he still wanted the Terada boy to live.

"Christopher, this is good nihonsu, not vodka. You're supposed to sip it." Ms. Yamato laughed hitting his shoulder. "You're so much like your father was when we met."

Michelle stared at Seina caught up in all the drinking and family oneness, then picked up her glass. *When did they get like this?* She wondered, eyes and thoughts shifting to Chris and Ms. Yamato. *Viv was always like this with Marcus. But Chris, Chris never made her laugh, at least not when she was willing to admit it. strange,* she thought, *this is wrong in some way.*

"Okay pretty boy, you and my sister are up." Chris smiled pouring them drinks. "Mom you want another?"

"Sure." Ms. Yamato nodded, looking at Seina, his face slightly flushed from the alcohol.

"Dad, Marcus, want one?" Chris asked, turning to each of them.

"Yeah." Marcus agreed, his chest glowing red.

"The food here is delicious Viv." Miles put down his chopsticks, the last of the fresh water eel devoured.

"I'm glad you like it," Ms. Yamato nodded with a smile.

"Drink up." Chris announced, he and Seina rhythmically knocked shots back, while Michelle sipped hers.

"Seina, where is your mother from?" Ms. Yamato toyed with her cup, kicking off her line of questioning.

"Brazil, like my dad. That's where they met." Seina grinned. Michelle sat, eyeing her mother and then Marcus, both listening intently.

"Where does she currently live?" Ms. Yamato's questions continued. Michelle glanced over to Chris, who was also awaiting Seina's answer.

"Lisbon." Seina answered. Chris poured another glass.

"Chris cool it with the shots! I'm not dealing with stumbling idiots tonight." Michelle said, throwing the interview off course.

"Michelle I'm fine." Seina turned to her grinning at the concern. He leaned over to kiss her. So passionate, so intense. So much more than Michelle would like with her family present. Seina pulled away sluggishly, enraptured. Michelle tucked her lips, running fingers through her hair. She tried not to but, couldn't help it. *I won't look,* she thought.

She glanced instead, past Marcus' raised brows, away from her father, unmoved, and skipping over Chris' applause, into her mother's eyes. As if written on a billboard Michelle saw the word, *no*, coldly etched into Ms. Yamato's expressionless face.

"I wasn't talking about you." Michelle looked at Seina.

"Oh. Well, give me my kiss back." He chuckled, inching in for another. Michelle placed a hand on his thigh, stilling him.

How it happened, was like clockwork: first Miles went to help Marcus get settled in, then Chris after he and Seina finished the bottle of top notch Nihonsu. 'Checking on inventory,' was his excuse before leaving. Finally there was Seina's perfectly timed trip to the bathroom. Elegantly planned, fruition. The assault.

Ms. Yamato sipped the last of her sake. "I like him." She nodded, placing the empty glass on the table, then she looked at Michelle, her face and tone saying otherwise.

"What's wrong with him then?" Michelle sighed.

"Michelle, do you know who he is? If you did, you would know, why it won't work." Ms. Yamato fanned herself, the alcohol flush coming over her.

"Why? Because you say it won't?"

"He cares for you but, a good piece is hardly worth your life." Ms. Yamato stated. "I hoped this was mostly rumor but this thing needn't continue. He's a good catch, but his family is the biggest problem."

"This needn't continue? He has nothing to do with the drugs."

Ms. Yamato closed her eyes, taking in another breath. The room spun, but the mission was still clear. "You can't live in his world Michelle."

"You're working with them." Michelle stared at her.

"I'm doing what I was taught to do since I was a girl. You're not equipped to deal with them. You don't even speak Japanese— He seems like a great man but, how can a swan and a dolphin live together?" Ms. Yamato rested her chin on a fist, leaning on the table, recalling similar words from her mother decades earlier. "The surface is where you and he exist, but a hurricane is coming. His father is dying, he has three older brothers and two sisters-and there is no clear indication what will happen when Cláudio Terada is dead. Your life could be at stake. Don't you see the way he looks at you? Claudio hates that boy. How do you think you'll fare?"

"Seina has assured me he has nothing to do with—" Michelle began her counter.

Ms. Yamato stopped her. "It doesn't matter. The Teradas are the suppliers for countless drug cartels in Asia. That's like marrying a prince and expecting to never entertain the press. The legitimate business is just a cleaning machine. Michelle, this might be fun for you, but even the Yakuza is working for them."

"How do you know this?" Michelle glared.

"My friend, Junichiro—" Ms. Yamato started.

"The one they asked you about at the trial." Michelle interjected.

"Yes, he's the head of the Kobe Yaku—" Ms. Yamato began.

"I knew you were lying." Michelle cut her off.

"My point is the Yakuza works with Tatsuya. They arrange a number of their deals in restaurants like these." Ms. Yamato paused, "Seina is very nice, good looking, but there is no future in this."

Had either of them known Seina was just outside the door, the conversation would have long ended,

but Ms. Yamato went on, "We lie, that family kills. Do you know what happen to the last girl he was serious about?"

"His father paid her to disappear," Michelle stared at her mother.

"No, Michelle he did not. Claudio *sold* her into sex work because she was ambitious, like you. A beautiful-young-black girl with her whole life in front of her. She was the kind of woman that *pushed* him to go legitimate without his father's name. Ask Darius next time you see him, because Michelle, like it or not that family is who Seina is." The door opened and Ms. Yamato's eyes met Seina's in a glance. "Am I lying?" Ms. Yamato cut her eyes from him, back to Michelle.

Michelle watched as Seina sat down folding his legs under him, then lower his head to the tatami. "Ms. Jang," he said in Japanese, "I swear to you I have no connection to my family's drug trade. At this point I have cut ties with everyone but my sister, mother and cousin," he kept his head bowed.

"The same cousin who arranged the Depaul fiasco while working for Michelle, so loyal of her." Ms. Yamato said with every ounce of contempt she could muster. "How are you paying for the hotel you're staying in? What about your condo in Tokyo, or that trip the two of you took to New York? Truth be told neither of you know why you have what you have, or how it came to be," she turned to Michelle. "You never cared to know, but I guess that's my fault for not making you care. Michelle, you have always been rebellious, so I won't push you but this will not work. I am just afraid that by the time you realize this it will be too late." Ms. Yamato stood, then looked down at Seina, unmoved from his spot. She looked back to Michelle then walked out, her feet almost silent on the wooden floor of the hallway.

Scotoma
Ashiya, Japan, May 6th

As if by magic, Ms. Yamato found herself in the solitude of the fourth floor, looking out on the lake. "This needn't continue—swans and dolphins," she scoffed, at her mother's words becoming hers. She stood with her bare arms exposed to the elements, and suddenly thought of her mother, Reiko.

Reiko came from Oshima still speaking the island's dialect. She had dreamt of escaping her small life, and left right after high school for Tokyo. She made it as far as Osaka, where her money was stolen. Reiko was hungry and broke, when Yamato Ituski *found her,* trying to salvage food from the trash. He was a bow-legged-man, with cinnamon colored hair. He rescued her, with a job at the family restaurant, then a ring years later.

By the time Ayane, or Vivian, was old enough to work at the restaurant, her mother had given birth to two girls and had six successive miscarriages. Reiko became the Okami, the owner's wife— the hostess, and she performed it well. It was the miscarriages that hardened her. Not the first, for one was nearly expected. Her miscarriages became the first kind of loss she would never give words to. Reiko simply washed the bedding, made an appointment, and went on with her day.

Miles was the first black person Reiko had ever seen up close, in real life. She had smiled, talking with the four Army men, Miles interpreting for all, but she continued to find his skin amazing. Months later, when Reiko saw that mocha skin again, it was wrapped around her daughter. Reiko once said to Vivian in passing, how that moment became her great loss, years later, looking upon her three— nay, two coffee-crème grandchildren. It was the only feeling Reiko had ever opened up about in her last years. The only one she had not taken to the grave. *Regret*, at choosing to let her daughter go with no guidance, no anchor. It was a feeling, Ms. Yamato now understood from both sides. This feeling of danger, with no course of action, and no way to quantify what instinct whispers.

The trees swayed in the wind as the image of lanterns faded one by one in the reflection of her palace on the lake. She stood, a queen in yet another castle. Alone. Ms. Yamato unpinned her hair, hoping to release herself from the headache taking root behind her eyes. She threw the pins to the crème chairs and on the ebony tables, crafted by hand then shipped, all for authenticity. *'An effort to force ancient and modern to exist in harmony, in a space to enjoy the pleasures of life.'* She had boasted to the magazine dubbing this chilled palace 'A glimpse of man and nature on one accord.' The wind blew in through the luxurious open-air deck as Ms. Yamato swirled a glass of red wine—though she shouldn't, per her doctor's orders.

What no one knew, what no one would ever know, is that the tables were designed in Sweden for that true new age 'Asian' affect, fashioned in Washington state by the friend of a friend to give a rooted earthen feel, recreated in mass in China in order to get the job done quickly, then shipped to Osaka, all of which was cheaper than buying or making them in Japan, and like Ayane—Vivian herself, nothing here fit. The land was just woods, when she found it. Everything here was created to affect the eyes, enrapture the mind, all altered for allusion.

Yet every detail from the layout and design that went into every room, to the angle of the trees, and shape of her island garden— it was her will. That iron-will she was always reminded of by her children. If she thought it, she did it and the work just followed, like winter becoming spring becoming summer, just one after the other.

She tired of this, of always moving mountains, of making things happen as if by magic, shifting landscapes, but not people, not relationships, certainly not the heart. Some years ago, Ms. Yamato would have secretly praised the will to imagine this world. It was once a gift, the ability to turn nothing into a vision she birthed. That was before she created and envisioned a thousand-times-over for galas, art shows, and fundraisers, with no real investment in the outcomes. Even now she wonders if all those events, all those things, are the reason her family is so distant.

Ms. Yamato shifted from this thought pushing aside contemplations of illness, moving instead to Michelle. Not of the woman she may have just cut down, but of the girl with pig tails of ringlets that once sprang freely from pony tail holders. The girl she imagined would move mountains in the world of the future, and how it isn't so. Ms. Yamato didn't know when, or how she lost their connection. Only that she and Michelle had become the same as she and her mother, Reiko— distant and walled up. It helped even less that Michelle looked so much like Haruna, Ms. Yamato's older sister, and Sarah, Miles' mother. She took a sip of her wine, empty. Ms. Yamato poured another, tucking hair behind an ear in a tumble of waves.

All have gone: a sister, a father, a mother, a husband, a son, and a daughter— but not Marcus she smiled. He is no more mine than this country. He has Devina— a good match, Chris now has Alyson—a financial match which may lead to love. Let's hope Alyson will be enough. But Michelle and this Terada, for that is all he is— that name, Ms. Yamato shook her head. *And she loves him, though he will fail her. I know, he will. He can only fail her. He's not strong, not like her and yet she doesn't see. She doesn't see him. Then there is the far dirtier business his family deals in.*

"Here you are." Chris threw a coat over Ms. Yamato's shoulders. She stiffened at his touch. "I told—" he stopped, noting something was wrong.

"Thank you." She struggled to hold back tears. "It's beautiful up here, mom." Chris changed the subject. "You really dreamt up an amazing place."

"It is beautiful isn't it? It almost makes all the money worth it. Days

359

like this make me think about the restaurant your grandparents ran, before I met your father."

"Granny ran a restaurant? When?" He jerked his head toward her

"It seems like a dream now." Ms. Yamato's eyes shifted back to the lake.

"Why don't you talk about things like that mom? Where you come from, how you grew up?"

"There are few memories of that life, and even fewer of them are happy ones." She stopped. "I'm proud of you. Alyson is a wonderful girl. Marcus has Devina and now you have Alyson. I don't think I'll worry as much anymore." Ms. Yamato's eyes seemed to sparkle. "Take time to enjoy your married life, okay? Be sure it's the life you want, then have children."

"You're not in a rush to be grandma?" Chris asked, wondering if the sparkle in her eyes were unfallen tears. Ms. Yamato said nothing. Chris continued. "I heard what you said to Michelle."

"Oh? And was I bitching, again?" Ms. Yamato poured another glass.

Chris sighed. "She doesn't hear the point you're making or the reason behind it. She gets what you're saying and how you said it." Chris looked out to the pitch-black water and the moon staining its surface, the restaurant dark, all but where they stood.

Ms. Yamato looked down to the glass in her hand. "Michelle hears what she wants to hear." She tucked her hair behind an ear.

"Okay," he smiled. "Do you remember what you said about the sake?"

"That it's good sake, not vodka?"

"This is good nihonsu, not vodka. You're supposed to sip. So, if you say that to Michelle, she hears you comparing, and takes it as a critique. And the 'you're like your father' part as an insult. But mom, me and Marcus grew up with you, she didn't. And you two just react to what the other says or does."

"Chris," Ms. Yamato began then she put down the wine glass.

"You were different with her, mom. Me and Marcus got ten times what she got: your attention, your time, your affection. To be completely honest, Marcus always got more of you and dad than both of us. You and Michelle are strangers and—" Chris said looking at the floor, he paused, when he saw Miles by the door to the lower level from the corner of his eye. "Never mind, another time." Chris kissed his mother on the cheek. "I'll see you in the morning." He smiled, then nodded to his father. Miles approached his ex-wife as Chris reached the railing.

"Kanojo wo hanashimasu," Chris heard his father say to his mother. "But she's a grown woman Viv," Miles continued as Chris made his way down the stairs and the voices faded.

Echoes of Silence
Osaka, May 6th

Silence. Silence was the soundtrack, from restaurant, to uber and now their hotel room. Seina stood, leaning against the dresser at the foot of the bed.Michelle walked past him, kicking off her shoes, passing him again, suitcase in hand. She threw the suit case to the floor, then sat down on the bed with her back to the front door, In silence.

"Are you angry with me?" Seina looked at the floor, his hands in his pockets.

"No."

"Michelle, talk to me," he paused to look at her.

"Have you heard from your ex since she disappeared?" Michelle looked up from the suit case out the window to the city and the light's below. Seina stared at her profile but said nothing, then slowly shook his head. Michelle opened her mouth to speak. She looked up at the ceiling with a sigh. "So your father, sold her?"

"Michelle—" He started, and moved toward her. She stopped him with a raised palm.

"No," she shook her head, turning to face him. "Full disclosure now. A couple years ago I aborted Adrien's babies. His wife forced my hand but I let it happen. I did it. Drugged or not I didn't fight for them." She sniffed. "That is my big secret. That's my burden to carry. And that's heavy enough, with my family, all the money problems we had, and trying to start over here. Now, my mother and I don't like each other, as you can tell. So, I didn't really expect her to like you." Here the tears sprang up. Michelle looked more pointedly at Seina seeking his eyes, "Given everything with your family it was slim at best. But I love you so here we sit." She stared at him waiting for his response, to determine if she would tell him all of it. *Everything.*

"Babies?" Seina echoed, thinking he misheard.

"There's no record, so no one knows that there was two." Michelle looked away from him to the white pillows at the head of the bed. Seina's jaw went slack and he moved to take Michelle in his arms. She turned and buried her face in his shoulder. "I didn't want you to look at me the way Marcus did went he helped me hide it from our parents." Was the next muffled string that came from her.

"I told you I love you, Michelle. I don't think I can change that at this point, even if I wanted to." Seina pulled away to look at her, her tears staining his dress shirt.

"My father told me she was alive. He even sent a picture once. So, I believed him."

"You didn't ask questions?" Michelle wondered aloud.

"I was a stupid kid," he shook his head. "I just believed what my dad fed me back then, before I really knew him."

"Why does your father hate you?" Michelle brushed her hair back from her face.

Seina shrugged. "Because he doesn't see himself in me." He smiled a sad, sad smile.

"And yet you look so much like him." Michelle ran her fingers through his coiled hair, on this rare occasion with no gel. "What was she like?" Michelle suddenly asked, avoiding his eyes. "Your first fiancée," she shifted to her lap as jealousy pricked her whole body.

"She was as different from you as night and day," Seina placed his thumb to her chin to make Michelle look him in the eyes. "and that was seven years ago; when I thought wallet chains were cool with beanies." Seina paused, licking his lips in the low lighting.

"Seina," Michelle began, slowly sliding back from him. "I can't ha—"

"I love you, that's all that matters," he stroked her face. "I won't let go of this, Michelle. I want nothing more then to be with you."

"I love you too."A different silence ensued now, drawing lovers closer. Seina unbuttoned his shirt and kissed Michelle's forehead, then tenderly her lips, longing to ease her suffering. In a moment, they will make love, possibly for the first time in their lives. For the moment, Michelle brought her hand to his face, her hurts and his insecurities melting away with the feel of his lips on her neck, she slowly undressing him.

Much later, with the dark of 3 a.m. all around, Michelle woke against the weight of Seina's body. She slipped from his grasp, naked, and instantly she felt his absence. She moved to sit on the floor. Quietly, she stared at the hills and valleys of Seina's back, in the barely present light, wishing this moment might go on forever. Then, unthinkingly, she grabbed her phone an snapped a photo. A moment, or maybe an hour later, she climbed back into bed.

"This bed is cold without you," Seina said in a raspy whisper, throwing an arm around her. Michelle kissed him and snuggled in to be his little spoon, in silence.

18. Entangled

Ashiya, Japan, May 8th

For the wedding, Reiko's paper screens on the first floor were painstakingly removed, allowing the central portion of the first floor to function as a pre-ceremony mixer. The sunken tables of each private room allowed Ms. Yamato and Miles to expertly seat and host Chris and Alyson's guest along with their own. The rectangular island courtyard became the centerpiece of the expanse with its stone lanterns, bridged isles, koi fish ponds, and the towering cherry blossom tree. On the islands, a place was made for the bride and groom to exchange vows and share their first dance as man and wife.

The day began with cordial greetings and long unnecessary introductions, for Seina at least. As the boifurendo of the groom's younger sister, whom everyone seemed to forget was not *still* in school, there was little use for Seina— other than arm candy. So, he broke away from Michelle when Ms. Yamato moved from introducing her friends from law school into the ones from high school. Seina made his way to the bar at the back of the restaurant while Michelle remained Ms. Yamato's hostage on the other side of the islands.

"Jin tonikku kudasi," Seina motioned to one of the two bartenders, as Miles came up behind him.

"Ore mo, onegashimasu," Miles added. The barkeeper quickly got to work.

"Mr. Jang, how are you?" Seina's smile slowly turned self-conscious under Miles' long silent gaze.

"I'm well, and you, Mr. Terada?" Miles replied, with a certain level of familiar sarcasm. *Guess that's where Michelle gets it,* Seina thought. The drinks appeared on the bar between them.

"I have no complaints, sir."

"Is that so? Vivian told me you proposed when I asked about the giant rock on Michelle's hand." Miles grabbed his drink, lifted it to his lips and took a sip all while staring at Seina.

"Yes sir, I did." Seina blushed, something Miles would have found endearing or at least cute under different circumstances. Miles ushered Seina away from the bar, through the swirls of conversations in language after language to one of the empty sunken tables in a quiet corner.

"Sit." Miles said, sitting. Seina followed not sure how to show deference to this upper class, third culture black man of a certain age. So, Seina sat, then Miles spoke. "You proposed to my daughter not knowing or even meeting my family. I know Vivian has voiced concerns but, I have my own objections."

"I would expect nothing less, sir." Seina nodded, then sipped his gin and tonic. He paused. "What are they?"

"Ise Wawu," Miles chuckled, "aside from your family being entrenched in the drug and sex trade markets?" He paused for dramatic effect. "You're a trust-fund kid, like my children, but you claim to be independent. You say you have no dealings with your family but you work at your father's company. Look, I can tell you've spent all of what?-twenty-four or five years of your life—"

"Twenty-nine sir," Seina quietly interjected.

Miles paused. "—You've spent your life making people like you. That's a hard habit to break, son, especially when you barely know if your compatible outside the bedroom. The biggest problem is that you know nothing about my family, and I imagine in the three or four months you've known Michelle, there's little you know about her." Miles took a long swig and placed his glass on the table. He peeked past Seina and waves of guest shifting through the restaurant, checking for Michelle. Notes of 'Lake by the Ocean' surfaced from the background.

"Yes sir, I think you're right on a lot of those points. I was hoping to have a long engagement to get to know everyone,"

"Is that so," Miles chuckled. "How long?" He asked amused.

"No more than two years." Seina replied quickly.

Miles shifted in his seat. "That aside I just can't get past how you work for your family's company, yet you claim to have nothing to do with them. Now, if you were to stop working for them could you even support your lifestyle, or my daughter's?"

"Yes sir, I would. Mr. Jang, I've lived on the five hundred thousand yen allowance my family offers, since I was sixteen. That paired with my salary and the access to my family's assets create an image of wealth. I'm not that wealthy. My father is. My family is." Seina said solemnly. Miles nodded, listening to the young man. "One of the stipulations of the Terada trust is that I have to work for at least one of my family's companies for a sum of ten years in order to access my birthright. This year is my last year."

"That means you're even more entangled than we first thought." Miles countered. "Now does that just apply to you and your siblings?"

"No," Seina's eyes shifted to the table. "For now it applies to any of my family's descendants that want the money."

"At least your father wanted to teach you something." Miles sipped his drink.

"That was actually my grandfather's doing." Seina smiled, but it didn't reach his eyes. "Michelle tells me your father ruled a chiefdom before the war."

"You know about the war?" Miles paused.

"Only bits and pieces."

At that, Miles smiled. "My father was a great man," his eyes shifted to Michelle, Ms. Yamato, and the wall of open sliding doors with the lake beyond. "But God has a plan, and if not for Biafra my parents would never have met. So I believe in destiny, not fate. Do you know the difference?" Miles looked at Seina.

"I have an idea but, what is your definition?" Seina asked lifting the drink to his mouth.

"Fate is passive, it's a way to just allow life to happen to you and accepting what comes. Destiny requires action, decisions. It requires that you seek out those things life will offer you." Miles saw Michelle slip away from her mother, zipping in their direction in a blur of red and black designer gown. "Michelle is brilliant, but in growing up too fast and keeping secrets from me and her mother, she hurt herself along the way. So, Mr. Terada I will not fail my daughter again." He shook his head. "If you want a place at my table and in my family, you need to sever ties from yours. I like you, but you're a danger to Michelle." Miles finished his drink and stood as Michelle came to the table.

Michelle looked ravishing in the black and red kimono-styled-dress by Zuhair Murad. Her hair was carefully flat ironed pin straight, deeply parted on the right and tucked behind her ears before ending at her hips in a blunt cut.

"Daddy," She narrowed her eyes at Miles. "What are you two doing, over here, *for so long?*" Her eyes darted from Miles to Seina and back.

"Nothing sweet pea," Miles kissed her on the forehead, "Just seeing how much that ring is worth." He looked at Seina and winked before making his way to the other side of the room and Ms. Yamato. Michelle turned to Seina.

"What did he say to you?"

"He said if I break your heart, he's going to break me." Seina stood smiling smugly. He brought the drink to his mouth. Michelle snatched it, finishing it in four gulps. "You're lucky I love you." He glared at her, still grinning.

"You left me to drown." She was losing her joviality.

"I just wanted a drink and your dad pulled me aside." He paused and looked over at Miles and Ms. Yamato. "You know they're not quite what I pictured when you told me about them."

"You don't know them yet. You see what they allow themselves to be, not who they are."

"Well they look like they're still in love to me." Seina saw Ms. Yamato scrunch her nose and lightheartedly pinch Miles, both laughing like children.

"Shell, have you been avoiding me?" A dark mezzo-soprano emerged from behind.

Michelle scoffed, then chuckled. "Well, Devina, you being my mother's favorite daughter-and-all, I can only try." Michelle turned. "Besides we're sitting together, I can't avoid you."

Seina was confused. Michelle's tone was lighthearted but the smile seemed a tad angry. He looked at this Devina, the woman he was almost certain was the long-time girlfriend of Michelle's oldest brother. Devina looked nothing of the sugar-water sweetness the voice suggested, with its faint notes of both England and India. Her dark sepia skin, long flowing burnt sienna hair and haunting green-blue eyes made Seina stop as Michelle embraced her.

"I'm not the favorite Michelle, I assure you of that." Devina laughed. "I can't believe how many people are here." Seina heard Devina say.

"I know, Miles and Viv are show boating, again." Michelle rolled her eyes, turning and walking back to Seina with Devina on her arm.

"And I love your hair, it's gotten so long." Devina admonished the hip length extensions. Michelle said nothing to this.

"This is Seina," Michelle said. "—my boy—"

"The fiancé," Devina interjected, eyes brightening behind that pencil thin dark eyeliner. "You sir have caused quite a storm."

"It's what I do," Seina laughed and shrugged, with a glance to Michelle. Devina flung her long curls off a bare shoulder and turned to Michelle.

"He's gorgeous Michelle, I approve." Devina said. Seina blushed. "You take care of this girl," Devina pointed at him, her eyes moving to Michelle.

"Shhhh," Marcus is coming," Michelle whispered. Seina wrapped an arm around her waist. Marcus appeared on Devina's right with a glass of white wine and some dark colored concoction in his other hand. His hair was gelled back and his honey caramel-half-and-half complexion was dewy but, the sight of him still disturbed Seina.

"Here you go." Marcus said to Devina, with a slight nod to Seina. When he caught Seina gawking at him, Marcus placed his free hand to the small of Devina's back, feeling more put off by Seina's presence.

"Marcus, I think they make a really cute couple. Don't you?" Devina asked holding her wine glass like a prop. Michelle looked away, aware that Devina was testing the waters, if not Marcus.

Marcus shook his head. "No, I don't," he lifted his drink to his lips. "Not at all." He added after taking a sip. "Are you going to the wedding in Pusan?" He asked Michelle, while trying to avoid direct eye contact with Seina.

Devina and Michelle noted the tension and exchanged glances.

"Yes, but Seina could only make this one." Michelle answered.

"I'm so excited about the next wedding. I haven't been to Korea in years." Devina sipped her wine, trying to keep the conversation going.

"Well why don't we all have dinner once we get back to Tokyo?" Marcus offered, quite insincerely.

"That's a great idea." Michelle agreed, knowing it would never happen. "So, when are you and Devina going to get hitched?" She asked teasingly. Marcus smiled then opened his mouth to speak, when Devina cut in.

"Marcus doesn't want to marry me because my grandfather is avidly against it," she blushed.

"Why?" Seina asked.

"Yeah, Marcus isn't half as bad as Chris, and he's marrying into one of those Chaebol families."

"Because, I'm not Muslim." Marcus interjected.

"And you're not going to convert?" Seina questioned.

"There'd be no point," Devina cut in again. "— and he doesn't want to get married in secret." She playfully rolled her eyes.

"Or out your family for converting." Marcus added, with a smile as he looked down into Devina's eyes.

"So were at a standstill you see." Devina looked to Seina and Michelle laughing, before planting a kiss on Marcus' cheek.

"Aw," Michelle chuckled. "All these years I didn't know that."

"When we go this summer, I'll win him over this year. I feel it." Marcus grinned.

"Get 'em tiger." Devina beamed back. Michelle kissed Seina, who felt a hole bore into his head from Marcus' undisguised glare.

As late afternoon dawned, Reiko's enchantment truly came to life. Having said their vows on the courtyard isles, Chris and Alyson shared their first dance as man and wife, to Vandross' 'Here and Now.' The couple danced, locked in each other's arms, friends and family on looking with smiles and well wishes.

Seina and Michelle sat at their sunken table, watching Chris and Alyson sway under the cherry blossom, thankful for each other. Alyson's creamy beige skin glowed under Reiko's recess lighting. Her hair tinted chocolate and loosely pulled into a bun of curls. Through all of this, her v-neckline wedding dress glittered, highlighting her hour-glass proportions. Chris' beamed as he held her, his squared off features softened by his joy.

Across the table from Michelle and Seina, Marcus sat with an arm draped around Devina, she leaning against his chest. Seina took Michelle's hand interlocking their fingers, before he kissed the back of her hand. Michelle watched Chris and felt his happiness, Seina saw a joy come to her face that she tried to wipe from her eyes, unable to extinguish the warm smile on her lips.

"I wish I knew you were such a softy when we first met." Seina chuckled. Michelle looked at him, still smiling, then clicked her tongue. When the song changed to 'Fortunate,' Seina stood and asked Michelle to dance. They danced, to Tess Anne Chin's 'Hideaway', through Alaine's 'Love U Loud & Clear', until three songs later to the very end of Utada Hikaru's 'Addicted to You'. By the time 'Square Biz' came on, Ms. Yamato had pulled Miles up from their table to dance along with Marcus and

Devina. Michelle pinned up her hair and took off to join them, as Seina lost the blazer and tie then went after her.

In the uber en route to the hotel, Michelle watched Osaka go by in a blur as she had with countless other cities. It was then Seina turned to her.

"Michelle I don't get it."

"Get what?" She turned expecting some joke.

"Your family, they seem to really like each other. Why don't they come together often? I mean both your brothers live in Tokyo but you don't see them."

"Ahh, that," he saw her smile fade in the near dark of the car.

"I'm sorry my family won't be as," Seina trailed off, looking for the word. "I'm sorry my family isn't like yours. But you'll meet them at some point." Seina said seeming to collapse in on himself. Michelle reached over and placed her hand on his and slowly Seina gripped it, in silence.

Wanting & Having
Kyoto and Tokyo, May 16th -17th

It was 2 a.m., Darius picked up his phone to find a missed call from Ari. He called back hoping she would answer.

"Come here," she whispered, ending the call.

And come he did. At one fifty-three the phone rang amidst a drug deal in Kyoto's Gion district. When it happened, Darius was wrapping up, finalizing the details of a shipment meant for Thailand. So, he ignored the call without as much as glancing at the name.

But Darius made his way to her door, after calling in a favor with a friend to get one of the unmarked Terada helicopters. A mere 2 hours later, Darius and Ari lay on the floor in her living room, hearts, thoughts, and breaths moving too fast—both spent but wanting more.

Later in the morning, while sunrise played out on the patio Ari lit a cigarette. She was seated on the white sectional-like patio-set. Darius was stretched out beside her along the length of the chair, asleep. A blanket haphazardly covered his naked body, this imagery, a sight she was already well acquainted with by now. Ari looked at him, bare arms exposed to grey dawn and, like Ari knew she would, she thought of Jade, then Victoria, not seeing either in him. Not only was his chocolate caramel skin *worlds away from that pasty Vickie*, Ari remarked to herself, *but there are no common features between the three of them.*

He was the centerfold to the sibling trio, she now knew, or rather pieced together in London. He had said 'I'm protecting family'. Yet the words gave way to a double meaning that forked again once more. *For what did he mean by 'protecting,'* and given the new creeping tattoo she spotted, *what kind of 'family' was he referring to.* This Ari clearly remembered thinking, not wanting to confirm her suspicions. She expelled the smoke from her lungs, put the cigarette in the ash tray and looked to one of his biceps. Ari licked her thumb before rubbing it over what looked like a bruise. The make-up came away with little effort to reveal a tattoo. She pulled the blanket down and moved to his ribs, then his thigh.

Ari closed her eyes, feeling deflated. She sat back on the patio sofa, soundlessly. Though she couldn't make out what it was, she knew what it meant. What he was. Though she had planned it all, from the late-night phone call, to the alcohol and the baby oil she lathered on each time he wanted her, she wasn't prepared to be right.

Ari had hoped it was her hyper active imagination, that this time her sixth and seventh senses for this sort of thing were completely off. She prayed her skills had been dulled, by jealousy, or insecurity, or one of those other bottom-feeding emotions. But she was right, again. Then suddenly her thoughts circled back to him, to them: on the floor, in the kitchen, in her bed—on her patio. Ari exhaled and crushed the cigarette in its ashtray, snuffing out the urge to be with him again just as quickly as it came into being.

"I need you gone in fifteen minutes." She said waking him.

"Why?" He asked, thinking she might be role playing.

"I can't do this anymore," then, "This is our forever goodbye." Ari threw on an oversized t-shirt lying on the ground and walked inside without another word.

On the other side of the city, later that evening, Seina sat on the floor of Michelle's bedroom in his boxers, combing through the books tucked under her bed. The shower came to a stop as he sifted through the pages on the other side of the bed. Seina's eyes widened as he read a few pages of White Fragility, and he quietly nodded as he thumbed through Playing in the Dark. A few moments later, Seina felt the heat from the bathroom on his neck as he read. Michelle stretched across the bed peeking over his shoulder.

"What are you doing?" She asked, the cloud of limp curls dripping water.

"This is some heavy reading, young lady." Seina turned the page. Water dripped from her hair to the book.

"I read fiction too," Michelle took the book from him and sat up on the bed. Seina turned toward the bed to look at her.

"Okay. Favorite book— go."

"No." She shook her head laughing at him. "Give me a theme or genre or something."

"Fantasy."

Michelle scoffed and rolled her eyes. "I don't read fantasy. Try again."

"Great books about hope and destiny." Seina came to his feet, leaned in, and kissed her. Michelle smiled a sly grin as he moved back, mere inches from her face.

"Ghana Must Go," Seina kissed her. The Tea Girl of Hummingbird Lane," he kissed her again. "Purple Hibiscus," he kissed her a third time. "The Kitchen God's Wife," another kiss, Michelle smiled again. "The Joy Luck Club, and let's not forget The Bluest—"

"Okay." Seina cut her off. He sat across from her on the bed, touching her hair.

"Jade insisted I read Amy Tan and Lisa See." Michelle paused. Seina's hand sank into her hair through the drying curls. "What are you doing?" She stared at him, her hand on his forearm.

"Seeing you." He chuckled. He touched the flat wavy and loosely curled sections altered by the constant heat. Michelle clicked her tongue at him and pulled away. "I always wondered what you looked like in your natural state."

"As opposed to my unnatural one?" She smirked, and then kissed his nose before standing.

"Where are you going?" Seina asked as Michelle walked into the bathroom and picked up a bottle of a Keratin treatment. "Oh my God Michelle." He fell back on the bed. "You got any of those books here?"

"Yeah. Look for Purple Hibiscus," Michelle said before closing the door and shifting to the task of doing her hair.

In the nearly two and a half hours it took Michelle to straighten her hair, it was only as she ran the flat-iron through the last portion, that she noticed the hush of the apartment.

"Seina," Michelle called, unplugging the flat-iron. She opened the bathroom door. Seina was seated on the bed still reading. He looked up at his fiancée, the dense fog of limp curls replaced by that famous black waterfall. Michelle stared at Seina noting that something was bothering him.

"Are you okay?" She asked.

"I thought you said this was about hope and destiny. She met the priest and her life is still trash."

"Seina," Michelle sat on the edge of the bed. "By Kambili meeting father Amadi does that not inspire hope for her and the reader, and is it not her destiny to find happiness in the face of so much unhappiness?" She moved across from him, seeing his frustration with the story. "I recommended this book because I thought there were a lot of parallels between you and Jaja, maybe even Kambili." Seina nodded, and his eyes locked with Michelle's. She crossed her legs, brushing bangs from her face.

He scoffed. "There are, some." Seina nodded. "Your father was right." He took the hair tie from her wrist and dropped it in the book, before closing it. "You're brilliant and you just might be right about this book." He said, restoring the stare.

"You needed another man to tell you that?" Michelle rolled her eyes. She moved to her side of the bed as Seina watched her.

"Not another man, *the* man." Seina moved to the head of the bed, elbowing Michelle. "You're dad's pretty cool." He said in a serious note now.

Michelle picked up another pony tail holder from the nightstand on her right. She pulled her hair into a bun at the top of her head, snickering. "Don't tell me you have another crush." Michelle stopped, closing her eyes and biting her lip.

"Another?" Seina echoed, "And who might the other-others be?" He asked playfully, but Michelle turned to lay on her side and saw the wrinkled brow.

She smiled. "Marcus asked me if you were gay or something. He thought I was paying you to help me piss off our parents." Michelle said hesitantly, pushing the comforter back.

"What?" Seina's face went blank, his shoulders limp.

"He told me you were staring at him," Michelle tucked the stray hairs back from her face through her laughter. "He asked me not to say anything." She tucked her lips.

Seina's stare was cold. "And what did you say?" He countered, stretching out beside her, getting under the cover. He turned to lay on his side, facing Michelle with a hand to his temple, placing the other hand on her hip, where it stayed. "Did you dime me out for being a hoe-bag?" He asked with a chuckle.

"I did," Michelle nodded, trying not to smile. Seina jerked back with his smile crumbling. "I told Marcus you could do any and everything you put your mind to," she added. Seina's head crashed on the pillow. "I'm sure he knows I was joking, maybe."

Seina sat up. "Only you could deal a complement to hurt like that. Now every time I see him he's going to think I'm making googly-eyes and he's probably going to tell Chris, or your dad." Seina covered his face, still smiling but embarrassed.

"So why were you making googly-eyes at my brother?" Michelle asked gleefully, but there was something in her voice that let him know she wasn't joking.

"Is Marcus adopted?" Seina redirected the conversation.

"No." Michelle paused. "He looks just like my father."

Seina shook his head.

"Why do you ask?" Michelle tilted her head waiting for his answer.

"He looks a lot like someone I used to know." Seina said vaguely

"Oh, was he, just a friend?" Michelle teased.

"She might be, *sometimes*." Seina kissed Michelle, pulling her closer. "In fact, friend might be a stretch." He said, wrapping an arm around her, then he slid a hand into her shorts. By the time he was kissing her neck, Michelle said his name in a note too serious for sex. He pulled away to look at her. "What's wrong?"

"When this investigation is over," she paused, her eyes darted across his face to take in all his features. "I want to marry you."

A smile swept across Seina's face-uncontrolled. "We will. But let's not rush it." He said to her in a hushed tone.

Michelle looked at him, with a sad sort of smile. "I just keep thinking what if he wakes up. Seina, I still can't remember anything."

"Shhhh," He cradled her in his arms. "I'm here for you no matter what." Seina looked directly into her eyes. "You will not go away for this." He said this with such conviction, that to this day it gives her chills to think about it, though, she only *almost* believed him then.

誰 に も 言わない
Darenimo Iwanai
Tokyo, May 18th

Seina woke to the smokey jazz notes of a saxophone, alone in Michelle's bed, her vanilla scent wafting through the fog of music. He sat up, recognizing the song and tracing the light source to Michelle.

She was standing by the window peering out to the street. Michelle had a coffee mug in hand, huge rollers in her hair, and Utada's 'I won't tell anyone' on her lips. He watched her for a long moment listening to the song as the sax came back with its sultry smokey solo. Seina stood up and walked over to the vanity table where Michelle's phone sat playing the music. He turned it off.

"You were just talking about getting married. You think this a hit it and quit it situation? I care what happens to you," He said gruffly. "Do you even know what she's talking about?" Seina asked, walking over to Michelle still by the window. He slowly wrapped his arms around her.

"The rollers are hot," she said in a whisper. "I know what she's saying— I just love that saxophone." She spoke absently, her eyes out the window as she leaned against him.

Seina smirked. "Man is ensnared by the words of his lips." He said before letting go of her. Seina kissed her on the lips, then walked to the bathroom.

Michelle turned to face him, but the bathroom door was already closed, then one of the heated rollers fell to the floor with a clang, her hair unfurling like a black ribbon. Her eyes darted to the roller as it stopped mere inches from the bed. Michelle pulled her hand from the curtain plunging the room into nude-colored shadows. She heard the sounds of urine hitting water, then the toilet flush. Seina stepped out, turning off the light then climbed back into bed.

Michelle picked up the roller and opened the curtain rather than turn on the light, then she leaned over the vanity to take the rollers down. Only now did Seina see that she was wearing a blue silk robe over the white tank top, the shorts from last night replaced by his much baggier sweatpants. He smiled at this wanting to sleep, yet he laid there watching her in silence—the saxophone's notes still swirling in his head.

"Where'd that come from?" Michelle asked, brushing her hair from her face with a hand.

"What?" He asked, puzzled by the question. He closed his eyes.

"Man is ensnared by the words of his lips." She repeated turning to face him, looking at his skin in the morning light.

"Oh," Seina scratched his head. "—the bible, I think—my mother used to say it all the time." He was suddenly gripped by the smell of vanilla and lavender, then there was the caress of her hair on his chest. He opened his eyes to Michelle, and she kissed him, slowly climbing into his lap. This would be the first time he saw the Vivian-Yamato-spark in the woman he loved, but somehow, he knew this was only the surface. When Seina woke again it was to voices in the living room. There was a woman that spoke in a hesitant but steady stream of English who asked:

"What time did you call Terada Seina san?"

"It was around eight thirty. I think." Michelle offered.

"What did you talk about?" The woman asked. Seina began the search for his underwear.

"I told Seina I was running late and that I would be there as soon as I could. Then he told me it was fine and that his mother was excited to meet me. I didn't know his mother was there, and I told him I wasn't ready for that and that turned into an argument and I hung up." Michelle said as if going through a shopping list— almost bored. Seina pulled the comforter from the bed to search for his clothing. His underwear, sweatpants, shorts— something. And where was his bag.

"What happened after you end the call?" The woman Seina knew had to be a detective asked.

"I told the driver to stop the car and I got out." Michelle said. Seina searched the room frantically. It was then he realized his overnight bag wasn't in the bedroom or the bathroom. *She moved it.* He sat back on the bed shaking his head with a sigh.

"Yes, I was with Hiroshi Hikaru," Michelle said. Seina stopped, realizing he missed something the detective had asked. "My friend Jade took her time meeting me at the bar so I called him to drink with me."

"What bar did you go to?" the Female detective asked, Seina turned to the door left ajar as if he could see Michelle.

"That is where things get fuzzy. I know we went to a few. Umm, Box bar, Indulge, Olive-something I that's all I remember but we went to a lot.

"How did the night end?"

"I lost my phone and I'm pretty sure Hikaru and I got into an argument and then Seina came and picked me up."

"What time did you and Hiroshi san go apart?"

"I don't know."

"Do you know what time Tarada san came to get you?"

"No." Seina head Michelle say. He slumped down on the bed feeling useless.

"Thank you, Miss. Yamato san." The detective broke off and Seina heard the rustle of socks on the floor. "We will call if we have more questions." The detective added. There was another pause then Seina heard the door lock. He waited until he saw Michelle in the doorway before he spoke.

"Are you crazy?" His voice leveled with anger. He sat on the corner of the bed wrapped in Michelle's comforter tracing up to her face.

"No." She spoke with her eyes first on the floor, then locked on him. "We— I needed to look as innocent as possible."

"You think I don't know that Michelle? What if they misunderstood you? What if—" Michelle cut Seina off.

"I was advised by the lawyer you told me to trust, to leave you out of any initial interviews." Michelle came into the room then, and stood inches from him. Seina looked up at her not wanting to admit she was right. "I had to answer their questions and I had to do it alone so it wouldn't look suspicious. And I'm sorry about Hikaru. Evan dug up the facts and we put together a story, whether its truth or not I can't tell you." She whispered. Seina grabbed Michelle's hand and she continued. "There's footage and witnesses confirming Hikaru and I out and about all over Shinjuku. So, I told them a story." Michelle looked away, breaking the stare. "I also didn't want you in there because I was hoping I would remember and would be able to tell you the truth."

"Fine. I got the why, I understood what you were doing when I realized my bag was gone." Seina pulled his eyes from Michelle to the window. "Did he attack you?" He narrowed his eyes waiting for her answer. "Your dress was ripped."

"No. I think I may have hurt him," Michelle sat down on the bed beside him, placing a hand on his bare thigh. "You'll be really late today if you don't get going."

"Doesn't matter, I'm already pretty late. You turned off my alarm." Seina kissed her on the cheek and got up; dropping the comforter to the floor then he walked to the bathroom and turned on the shower.

19. Absence
Tokyo, Japan, May 19th - 22nd

"This is our forever goodbye." Ari had said that to Darius two days ago now, and never looked back— or so she claimed. With Jade's reappearance and their "rekindled friendship," Ari thought it necessary to cut carnal ties with the girl's older brother. Despite that fact, thoughts of him lingered at the edge of Ari's imagination.

Ari started the day with a call to Michelle, stating she was taking the week, and would work remotely if needed. She watched standup comedy and didn't laugh. She turned on the heat and still felt cold, and though Naima 'Ari' Arion Louien knew the source of this disconnect, she didn't know what to do. Ari had never dealt with this kind of living loss, or the continued missing someone that came with breaking up. It was like the death of her parents, yet on a much smaller scale— more like an aching mosquito bite than anything.

"My God, all those poor saps I dumped." Ari gasped, clutching her chest as she sat watching tv with the heat on high. "Those sad poor men." This, her version of empathy.

She took a "nap" and woke up the next afternoon on her sofa, heat and tv still blaring and a tray of Indian food on the coffee table. Now that the source of her sequestration had been identified, and the problem *thoroughly* examined, Ari headed to Omotesando to shop herself better. She searched the high-end stores but, didn't even bother to go in, nothing enticed her.

"I don't know Shahir." She said chatting on her phone. Ari strolled down the sidewalks dressed to the nines in a white pants suit. "I need a project, something big. You sure there are no open cases?" She stopped at a Turkish food cart. While a text came in from Michelle, asking Ari to come over to her apartment. "Shahir I call back." Ari hung up to call Michelle but got no answer.

Ari called Michelle a few more times, inching near Shibuya and the crossing, phone in one hand, warm shawarma in the other. Eating merrily all the while, it was then she saw it: Claudio Terada wakes from coma… The scrolled bar of the One-o-nine building swam away and was gone before she could make out the rest. But by then, her mouth was open and red shawarma sauce was dripping onto her white leather Christian Louboutin's. She screamed. Then felt the sauce on her foot. She screamed again before dropping her food. Ari open the uber app, but stopped when she saw the sign for Shibuya station.

"Shit! It's a emergency bitch!" She shrieked, twitching and jerking in an effort to convince herself to go.

90 minutes later, Ari sat in the arm chair by the door in Michelle's living room. The stain on her shoe had faded but was clearly present, her clothes were slightly disheveled, and dingy. Michelle and Seina sat across the coffee table shocked by Ari's state. Michelle sat in a chair that matched Ari's with Seina seated on the arm, in a tan three-piece suit, both of them staring at Ari.

"Did you hear us?" Seina looked from her to Michelle. Ari's face was blank. "Ari? Ari."

"We broke her. I finally did it." Michelle mused. "I broke the unbreakable." She laughed, brushing her hair away with a hand. Seina cut a look at her then stood. "I'm sorry it was coming her way." Michelle shrugged.

Ari jerked, coming back from the trauma of the subway ride. "You knew and you want me to do what?!" Ari shouted. "How does that make any sense? And why didn't you call me before the news broke?!" Ari held up a hand. "I took the subway and got seven kinds of lost in this birds'-nest-of-a-city and you two knew?!"

"No, we didn't know." Seina said, his hands in his pockets. "Mom warned me that it might be coming."

"So now you two wanna get married? I'm just not following." Ari stared at Michelle and Seina aghast.

"Ari, they plan to disappear." Jade sighed, slamming the door and kicking off her sneakers. She plopped down on the sofa, in tight skinny jeans, a white graphic tee and a fitted cap. *She look like a man*, Ari thought ogling Jade realizing Michelle and Seina were doing the same thing. *So it isn't just me, this hefa was being weird.*

"Why are you—" Ari started.

Jade rolled her eyes. "Next question," She looked to Michelle. "So you want us in the wedding?"

"Yes," Seina nodded.

"But we want Ari to plan it." Michelle added.

"Why would I do that?" Ari smiled. "I am not some lowly wedding planner. Running a company, that would be more me." Ari grinned.

"It would be an apology and a wedding gift to us." Seina smiled, as he walked back toward Michelle. "I told you, you don't get to walk away from this, didn't I?" Seina's grin turned sly.

Ari scoffed. "Fine. When? Where? What decor? What's the budget?" She rolled her eyes. "This still makes no sense."

"Cape Town or Morocco, or Seychelles." Michelle smiled and Jade tensed. "I was thinking blue and white or gold, with a water-fire theme." Michelle looked to Seina. Ari nodded.

"Let's just keep it under 20 million." Seina chimed in as Jade forced herself to relax again.

"That all sounds good. I can work with it." Ari looked to the ceiling flinging her bangs aside. "So were thinking September? October?"

Michelle beamed, "June 20th."

Ari stopped, to glare at Michelle.

"I just got you a new job, once we get married you can start moving the pieces as you like." Michelle leaned in closer. "I'll stay out of your way too."

"Actually," Seina cut in. "We can't do Cape Town," he scratched at his temple, looking at the floor. "I can't go there at the moment. Wild-party-punched-the-mayor of Cape-Town-long story."

"That's what you're marrying," Jade snorted. "And there's red tide in Seychelles right now." She lied.

"Morocco it is then." Michelle shrugged. "Somewhere by the water."

"A wedding like that is impossible, even for me," Ari cleared her throat, cutting her eyes from Michelle to Seina.

"Well it's a good thing the wedding is invitation only." Seina smiled. "Love you sis."

Commodity
Tokyo, May 29th - June 1st

"Why did you call me here," Yu stared at Seina. The red and blue string lights overhead cast a purple hue over Seina's face. He didn't hear Yu; instead, he sipped his drink— a world away. He was thinking of his father, and how feeble he looked this morning, in that bed, barely breathing, surrounded by his *other* sons, when Yu hit him across the arm with the back of his hand.

"Hey."

"Hey stranger." Seina smiled. "Good seeing you. Have a seat." He stood to hug Yu, who glared at him and took a half step back.

"What do you want?" Yu asked.

Seina sat. "I needed to talk to my best friend. The last time we were here our friendship ended. I thought this would be the best place to start again." He smiled. "Have a drink."

"I have nothing to say to you."

"Ogane-san," Seina called, holding up his drink. "Mo hitostu onegai, toriaizu." The old woman nodded in silence.

"You're fucking drunk." Yu scoffed, still standing.

"So, are you up for it? I haven't met anybody who can drink like we could." Seina pulled out a stool.

"I hate you." Yu stared at Seina. The bartender put a drink in front of him.

"I know you do." Seina slid the drink closer. Yu looked at the drink and sat. He took a sip and stopped; brow wrinkled. Seina laughed. "You remember?"

"Kuru kuru pa." Yu nodded. "That shit is nasty. How are you sipping on it?"

Seina shrugged, putting the glass on the bar. "It's not too bad, after three of 'em," he beamed. Yu looked at Ogane-san and she shrugged.

"What's goin on?" Yu asked suddenly. A couple walked up to pay their tab. Ken the 390's 'Winter Song' the only sound for a few long moments.

"Will you be my best man?" Seina grinned while the front door slammed.

"What? No." Yu lifted the glass to his mouth. "God! How did we drink this?!"

"We were young-er and stupid." Seina chuckled. "And brave." His smile faded, along with the brightness in his eyes. "You know Eva's still hot. You should do something before she marries the wrong guy."

"We were engaged." Yu mumbled.

"What?!" Seina jerked his head toward Yu. "What happened?"

"Her parents hate me. Plus, work is always first."

"Just work through it." Seina turned to the bartender. "Mo hitotsu." He asked and the woman nodded.

Yu scoffed again.

"I know you and Eva work," Seina said. "Make it happen."

"How long have you been drinking?" Yu asked, trying to mask the growing concern. Seina smiled when Ogane-san placed another glass in front of him. He lifted the drink to his lips and paused.

"Really need a best man." Seina took a gulp. He cleared his throat. "If you say no, I'll have no one but Naima."

"No one likes you?" Yu questioned.

"Looks that way. What have you been up to?"

"Just working. You know traveling here and there." Yu finished the drink, still wincing at the taste. Seina heard about a job with National Geographic, from Eva. He even went as far as trying to reach out, wishing to congratulate his old friend. That was a dead end. No one knew who Yu Hiroshi was, and Seina said nothing, not then— not now.

A lie from Yu Hiroshi is simply mountain made mole hill, rarely the reverse, but two? Seina mused. *It was never what Yu said, but the way he said it, the delivery, too fast, too slow, too nonchalant, or lacking confidence. Yu Hiroshi never lacked confidence, until it came to a lie. Even with, no money, no food, and holes in his clothes and shoes, Yu Hiroshi could own the room. He always could.* Seina thought watching him.

"Getting Eva back is your mission, right?" Seina leaned back in the chair.

"No, we're over this time."

Seina stopped. "It can't be that bad."

"It is." Yu grumbled, looking at the floor. *She hates that I worked as an escort.* Yu thought, *she hates that I screwed other people, while we were engaged— for work, that I lied to her bold face, paper thin and she trusted me. She hates me for making our life a lie. She hates me,* Yu thought wishing he could tell this man he once called friend.

Instead, there is this hate caged and stoked by Yu's abject poverty. If Yu hadn't told Seina about the Hiroshi's plan to break into real estate to recover their dwindling wealth, Yu and Seina might still be friends. In those days the name Hiroshi Isao still meant something, even in Tokyo, but not as much as Claudio Terada.

Alas, Yu told his best friend, and with no malicious intent— while trying to make conversation with his father, Seina mentioned buying Shinjuku Park Tower. The very building Yu said his father was scraping to buy, the property that would become Terada Fifteen-o-Seven and indirectly seal the Hiroshi's decline. Claudio had seen the genius in this move, recalling that Seina had, at the time, started dating a Georgetown International Business major. Claudio planned to make one or two of his oldest sons his successors, and so kept an eye on that girl.

Yu ordered a Tequila sunrise. "So, you're getting married?" He questioned. Ms. Ogane, the bartender, peeped at him as she poured the drink.

"Yeah." Seina nodded.

"To what?" Yu laughed as the woman placed a drink down in front of him. "What was crazy enough to fall for you?" He asked looking Seina over.

Seina let out a sigh. "Michelle Yamato." Yu heard the name and there was the face. Sneering at him from the restaurant, arms folded, eyebrow raised. Then her blatant disdain at the Wong's, she flinging hair aside. '*They can keep their bull and his shit. I don't woo.*' She had said. Yu remembered the icy way she looked at him— *no past him. Colder than ice*, he thought with something like rage rumbling in his chest.

"You really wanna marry *her*? Does this have something to do with your dad almost dying?"

"No." Seina shook his head. "I love her." He laughed. "Like you love Eva. So, will you be my best man?"

"No." Yu shook his head. The bartender stopped. Seina paused also, drink half way to his mouth. "I hate you and your family, for destroying my life."

"Yu, I didn't do that—that—" Seina started.

"Your father right? You didn't mean to tell him?" Yu questioned. "You're still living off my father's plan, Seina. While he doesn't even remember me or how clever he was. So, yeah, fuck you and I still hate you." Yu motioned to stand.

Seina put his hand on Yu's shoulder. "Yu, you're the only real friend I have and I want our friendship back. I have to make this right."

"Make our friendship right?" Yu repeated.

"Yes." Seina nodded.

"300 million."

"What?"

"300 million yen." Yu repeated, his eyes cold, expressionless – almost lifeless.

Seina stopped. "Okay." He said after only a moment.

He wanted to hurt Seina, Yu remembered, thinking back to this moment. He wanted Seina to hurt, in the way *he* was hurt, the way Yu *still hurts*. He had given up a dream that still lived, crippled in the shadows of loss, and disappointment, and desperation. Yu turned their friendship into numbers, into something to be traded back and forth— something he became. Yu now knew, that Seina agreed, with no hesitation because he missed his friend. Yu's hurt was only worsened, of course, when the money arrived in his account three days later.

But after two years being a host, and three as an escort, how else would he see himself, but numbers, trailed by zeros? His net worth— the value of his soul, a mere 300 million yen. A commodity rented, traded, and turned in, a movie, a costume, a hooker.

Reprise
Somewhere on the Coast, Morocco, June 9th

Ari stared at the giant tent positioned on the beach and leading into the shallows. The construction crew broke for lunch having firmly established the tent's skeleton. For everything to be on schedule Ari needed the shell on, and the floor installed along with the lights and HVAC unit by Friday. Next Thursday and Friday, the decorators and florists would tap in, but Ari didn't care. It would get done.

She strolled to the water's edge, the wind in her hair, bare feet in the sand, and somehow, Darius loitered from sunrise to sunrise, masking a more sinister thought. He was in the notes of joy Daniele poured out over the phone when Ari found the time to call, for instance. He was in the fabrics Ari, Michelle, and the wedding planner sorted through over skype and messenger yesterday. Darius was in the posts erected where the ceremony will take place, on this beach in Morocco, in the sand itself. It seemed—he was here, nearly flesh and bone and Ari wished him gone. *I hate this*, she thought, thinking she had gotten over him.

Still in all this, Ari can't shake the thought. Though it hides shyly among the images of Darius. She felt the shift when she read the scroll bar in Shibuya— a yet unseen storm building on the horizon. Only now did Ari realize what that storm had been, what it truly meant, as she once sat on her patio in Algeciras, before she even went to Japan.

Claudio is awake now. Claudio is the thread all their destinies are linked to. Whether alive, dead, or somewhere not either, their lives will be severely altered. And Terada anger ripples. Does he remember that night? Is he a vegetable? Who is managing the companies? And who the drugs? How then, can these two plan to marry and just disappear? It makes no sense. How then can any of us hope to move forward, and thinking this, she felt her lungs collapse.

"I should have never sent Kohana that package." Ari mumbled. *I should have never called her in Paris,* she thought. "My God, how can I fix this?" She said, feeling the murder of Samir encircling her, as only destiny and misfortune can, in those moments, when they return wanting their encore.

Enemy of thy Enemy
Tokyo, June 11th

Li Jun sat in the bathtub of his apartment with the weight of silence ringing in his ears. The front door opened and closed, followed by the sound of heels and grocery bags.

"Jun." Victoria called. *How long was I gone,* she wondered unpacking the groceries. Li Jun remained unmoved. In his lap, lay a sonogram, beside it an invitation, white and light blue with gold lettering.

It was hand delivered— with a warning shot, fired from Michelle's camp. '*Keep your tired ass out of her life.*' The words and eyes cutting past insult to existence. He didn't know who she was until she left. Darkened eyes, wing tipped in blue-black eyeliner, blonde hair. She smiled and sneered through the blonde bangs, then disappeared.

Li Jun flushed the toilet and washed his hands, running water over his face. He opened the door to Victoria humming – 'Rolling in the Deep,' he noted. The scent of her food filled the apartment as she turned to him.

"Jun are you okay?" Victoria tucked her hair behind an ear.

"Yeah. When did you get back?" He said trying not to meet her eyes.

"About fifteen minutes ago. I'm worried about you." She stroked his chin, the wedding band shining.

"Don't worry, I'll be around for *our baby*." He grinned.

Victoria froze. "How—" She paused again.

"I found it this morning," he said, holding the sonogram. "Jade dropped off her wedding gift." He pointed to the coffee table, with his chin, where a small box that suggested jewelry sat.

"I wanted to tell you later in the pregnancy, in case—" She trailed off.

"There's nothing to worry about." He stared into her eyes. "It'll be fine. We'll be fine." Li Jun took Victoria in his arms. "I love you." He said hugging her, and Victoria closed her eyes in relief.

"I love you too, Jun. I just want this to work." She gripped him tightly then kissed him on the cheek.

"I'm still sick Tori."

She smiled with tears brimming, then Victoria stopped again. "Why was she here?"

"Like I said, she came and dropped off her gift." Li Jun replied almost laughing at her. "I was waiting on you to open it."

"What else did she do?"

"She used the bathroom, Tori." Li Jun blinked staring at her.

"Okay," Victoria sighed. "Are you going to be okay with me hanging out with Eva tonight?"

"I'll be fine." He laughed. "Are you gonna open Jade's gift?"

"No. Later." Victoria shook her head. "Take care. Dinner's almost done. Let it sit for—" She began.

"I got it. Have fun." Li Jun nodded to her. "I promise I'll still be in one piece when you come back."

"Okay." Victoria smiled. She walked toward the door, looking back at this dream accomplished. "Bye, I love you." She said walking out.

"I love you too!" Li Jun called after her.

Eva, by stark contrast, sat on the counter of her kitchen. Her gaze was on her cell phone, in the living room, but shifted to the last of a bottle of red wine. *I don't drink,* she thought, senses dulling. *At least not like this.* She scoffed pushing the glass aside to pick up the bottle, drinking it down with ease. She walked into the living room and grabbed her cell phone to call Yu. He didn't answer. His voicemail chimed.

"Why couldn't you be a man and tell me you're a whore, huh? I hate you, Yu Hiroshi." Eva paused. "I still wish you were here," she wiped her eyes and mouth with the backs of her hands. "right now I could use a hug." Her voice cracked. "They took my company from me. You flaky whore!" The voicemail recording, ended.

After the third such call, Eva threw the phone to the floor and the doorbell rang.

"Did you bring what I asked?" Eva questioned, before wiping her mouth with her palm.

"Yeah. Are you okay? I heard you down the hall." Victoria said, looking Eva over. She stepped inside, and saw the apartment was dark with blankets and pillows on the floor and sofas.

"I'm fine." Eva said flatly, slamming the door.

"How much have you had to drink? You clearly started without me and it's not even eight o'clock." Victoria laughed with the feeling something was again very off with her friend.

"Tori sit."

"Okay. What about the wine?" Victoria asked, taking a seat at the kitchen table. Eva grabbed a cork screw.

"Do you want a glass? I'm drinking it from the bottle." Eva looked up, taking the wine.

"Wow that's out of the ordinary. Are we celebrating?"

"No. You want a glass?" Eva croaked.

"No." Victoria said. "I can't." She smiled. Eva missed her cue, popping the cork instead. "Did you hear me? Eva you're going to be an aunt, again."

"They took the agency."

"What?"

"Those fucking bitches, took my company from me." Eva repeated, this time with venom as she glared at Victoria.

"Who?"

"Michelle and the other one, that sand bitch, Ari." Eva snapped.

"So you called Kohana Terada?" Victoria leaned in closer to Eva, hands clasped together.

"Yes! For help Victoria." Eva retorted, exasperated.

"I didn't know you were close with her. Or any of the Teradas for that matter."

"Look Detective Himekawa, that doesn't matter and she wouldn't help me anyway."

"Okay." Victoria nodded. "So now we fight for it." She took Eva's hand. "Pushing them out will be easy."

"What do you think I've been doing the last month and a half?!" Eva covered her face and stopped. "I can't let Jun screw up all my hard work?" She moaned.

"What are you talking about?" Victoria sat back in her chair. "I thought you said Michelle took the agency." She stood up and poured a glass of water for Eva, knowing her friend needed to sober up.

"She did and Jun helped her." Eva glowered. "I work too hard making this thing legit."

"No, Jun would never do that." Victoria handed Eva the water. "Eva what are you talking about?"

Eva huffed. "How do I know you didn't help them? For Jun's sake." Eva spat. "Jun controls everything now! And I have to announce his promotion by the end of the month. In with Jun in June!" Eva started to cry now.

Victoria took Eva in her arms. "It's going to be okay. We will get it back,"

"We can't just get it back you loon!" Eva broke free of the hug. "Make Jun decline it."

Victoria realized Eva was losing it now.

"I helped you get that ring on your finger, you wouldn't have Jun if it wasn't for me. The least you could do is come through for me!"

"You're way off base, Eva. Stop it before you—" Victoria was cut off.

"Before what!" Eva spat. "Before you spawn some needy brat my brother doesn't want? I did everything for you! I kept you relevant when the calls stopped coming!"

"You selfish bitch," Victoria paused. "You kept me relevant? Then you clearly have less power than you think! And Everything I did to be with Jun got me here because I did it, and our first child did it. You've never liked sharing the spotlight, but that's why Yu disappeared, right? Well now it's your turn to play second chair. *Enjoy it.*" Victoria stood and grabbed her purse then slammed the door behind her.

20. Gaslighting

There stood a large white tent, lined in gold with light blue accents, on an undisclosed beach in Morocco. The grand oddity rose from the landscape, spilling from the beach and into the sea. As the dry Moroccan heat gave way to cool and evening, Hikaru slipped out of the groom's suite, and into the hallway with his thoughts locked in on Jade.

The hallway was in the shape of a cross with Hikaru on the left arm. As he searched for Jade, he contemplated where to look first. Not only had Jade stood him up and disappeared, she simply ignored him, at the rehearsal dinner and all the other rushed wedding festivities. Jade had been unresponsive to him, and she remained that way since that night at her apartment. Hikaru thought perhaps she was playing it cool, but this was ice. He couldn't forget how Jade glared at him, as he attempted to make conversation this morning leaving the hotel.

Hikaru walked toward the sitting room, at the base of the cross, just past the entrance to the tent, and there she was. He motioned to enter but stopped when he saw Ari.

"There's no time for this Lia," Ari protested as Jade sat her down.

"There's something you need to look into."

"Lia this can wait."

"No, it can't." Jade shook her head. "the agency—" Jade started then stopped. When Hikaru looked at what caught her off guard, Darius was standing on the threshold to the sitting room. Darius was here. Here, in Morocco—

Ari paused as she caught sight of him and crossed her arms.

"What are you doing here?" Jade asked.

Darius looked at Ari in silence. Her hair was curled, and adorned with a blue tipped white lily. She was stunning in the floor-length backless light-blue gown, even through her evident exhaustion.

"Naima." He said sweetly, a smile curling his lips.

"Now is not the time." Ari stared at him. "There are too many things that need to be in place. So, I really can't do this right now." She looked at him, drained of all emotion, from the last three weeks of planning and bribing to make this wedding happen.

"Will you give us a moment?" Darius said to Jade now, ignoring Ari's protest.

Jade handed Ari another flash drive and walked away without a word, still debating whether or not to drop the whole thing and go on with her plans.

"I don't want to lose you." Darius pulled Ari closer, as Jade ran into Hikaru at the entrance to the hallway.

"Hey." Hikaru stopped her. From moved in the opposite direction.

"You finally caught me." Jade turned to face Hikaru.

"Okay," he said, looking confused. "I don't know what I did to make you so angry but I thought we had something."

"Yes, we did, Hikaru we did. But you're still pining over Michelle."

"That's not true." He shook his head, moving closer to her.

"It is." Jade stared at him.

"I can't stop thinking about you." He grinned.

"Then why did you call out *her* name?" Jade said in a horse whisper.

Nina, the wedding planner, with her blonde Anna Wintour bob, popped her head out of the bridal suite. "Sorry to interrupt, the guest are ten minutes away. Where in the world is Ms. Louien?"

"It's fine, Nina. We're done." Jade said flatly, turning away from Hikaru. "Ari's in the sitting room." Jade pointed, before marching down the hall toward the bridal suite. Hikaru jumped in front of Jade while Nina went into the sitting room.

"What are you talking about?" He asked, genuinely confused.

"You called out Michelle's name in your sleep— after fucking me." Jade stared at him, her face twisted in disgust, blonde bangs draping her eyes and adding to the visage. She turned away and walked down the hall to the bridal suite leaving Hikaru in shock.

"What?" He questioned, confused. "Wait." He said as Jade disappeared.

"Will you give us a moment?" Darius said to Jade. Jade handed Ari another flash drive and walked away in silence.

"I don't want to lose you." Darius pulled Ari closer.

"What does that mean?" Ari paused to look at him, hoping he would say the right thing.

"We love each other. We can be happy together." He took her hand.

"No." Ari shook her head. The soft blue around her eyes growing cold, the wing-tipped eyeliner cutting— she suddenly cottoning-on to his logic. "No, no we can't." She said. "I like you Darius-Cole, whoever you are." Ari kissed him on the cheek. "but I love me."

"Why are you doing this?" Darius narrowed his eyes in disbelief. "Naima don't do this." He said in Arabic, as she slipped from his grasp.

"I don't want to be a gangster's wife, or this variation of a Japanese-jet-setting trap-queen your trying to sell. So, Cole you have to choose." Ari took a step back from him, feeling the drain of this second break-up. It was then Nina came in asking something. Ari responded not hearing the words. Nina set her sights on Darius then Ari went off in search of a red bull, *and maybe some Vodka,* she thought.

"Sir, I'm going to have to ask you to leave." Ari heard Nina say as she left the sitting room.

One by One

Outside Asilah, Morocco, June 20th

In the bridal suite, Jade walked past Michelle seated in front of a vanity mirror. Her hair was pulled up on the sides then forward in three large twists that draped her left eyebrow before being pinned to their source. She was curling long extensions that swept the floor then placing them in rollers.

Jade sat down on the white chase lounge of the sectional, directly across from Michelle's dress as it lay in the garment bag displaying splashes of gold and blue against the long white sofa.

"You look amazing." Jade heard Ari say to Michelle. Ari strolled into the suite with a red bull in hand, adding it to her vodka on ice.

"Thanks, for all of this Ari." Michelle smiled, the golden eye shadow and flaming red lipstick taking away from her fear.

"Like you said, I owe you one. Besides you're my sister now," Ari took hold of Michelle's hand to stop her from fidgeting with the hem of her silk robe.

"Sorry." Michelle beamed, then inhaled. "I'm a little nervous."

"Don't be," Ari smirked warmly, still holding Michelle's hand. "You got this girl." She said in a whisper.

Swallowing her tears, Jade turned to Michelle. "Be afraid, of not showing your love, of taking him for granted. Fear not making each other happy. Love Seina with hope and passion and heat, love him with kindness and respect, with no regrets." Jade looked at Michelle not wanting to think about her eminent departure or the next phase in her plan, yet the tears welled in her eyes, again— this time for a different reason.

Michelle was taken aback and let go of Ari's hand. *Where had that come from*, she wondered with tears of her own, too unripe to fall. Both she and Jade teetered on an edge with emotions born out of fear, uncertainty, peril, and abandonment as Ari stood frozen, wine glass and slushy vodka red bull in hand.

No one will know what would have happened, had this moment been left to play out. Perhaps, a flicker of honesty could have been sparked, freeing each of these women from the years of their lying facades. Perhaps, there would have been a way for each to warn the others of the deathtraps up ahead. Confession *is* good for the soul, but instead, Ms. Yamato entered, and the sparked embers were cast to the sea.

Thirty-six hours before Michelle and Seina's wedding, Ari lured the Yamato-Jang's to Morocco under the guise of Michelle being injured in a boating accident. Ari called Miles and Vivian telling them that Michelle asked for her family before the doctors sedated her.

"We can't airlift her until her condition is stable." Ari lied, knowing Ms. Yamato would pry, so she had Hikaru on standby to interject something about the doctors needing Ari to sign release forms.

After she got off the phone with Ms. Yamato, Ari got away from further questioning by sending her two plane tickets alongside a picture of the driver that would be waiting for them at the airport. She repeated this for all three couples then sent texts and emails explaining that the driver would bring them to the hospital where Ari would be waiting with Michelle. Ari's next move was to avoid the successive calls from both Ms. Yamato and Marcus while sending the five Yamato-Jangs plus Devina to the hotel in Asilah.

For Seina's mother and sister, it was a bit easier, with both of them living in Europe. Ari used the same story but with Seina as the lead, telling them early the morning of, and to come right away. So, needless to say, both sides were stressed and confused after landing in Casablanca and being whisked over two and a half hours one way to an undisclosed hotel with a driver who was as clueless on the matter as they were.

One by one and couple by couple they arrived at the airport, then the hotel where they all waited. Each couple dialed Ari repeatedly but there was no answer. Once all eight guests had arrived, Nina made her appearance at the hotel wheeling a luggage rack full of garment bags and hotel keys ready to explain the situation.

"Well said. That's a good bit of advice." Ms. Yamato said presently, stepping into the suite, smiling her signature icy smile. She stopped by the vanity table, pulling Michelle's robe closed before she went on. "Though, I worry if this union is worthy of such dedication." She looked from Michelle to Ari then Jade, each feeling as if the air were sucked from her lungs.

"It is." Daniele chided, appearing as Ari would at this juncture from another entrance at the back of the room. "Hello, Daniele Alves, mother of the groom." She introduced herself coming closer to the group.

"Vivian Yamato." Ms. Yamato extended a hand, and they shook. To Jade, Ms. Yamato was nothing like what Michelle described. *Elegant and beautiful with a certain air of intrigue,* Jade thought, watching her. Ms. Yamato's attention shifted to the dress, on the sofa across the room. The fashionista winning out against the mother— for the moment. "Exquisite." She said, inching toward the gown seeing only the bits of gold and blue. "Who is the designer?" She unzipped the garment bag for a better look.

"Zuhair Murad." Michelle answered, turning to face the room. "Ari asked him to design it as a personal favor." She said, glancing in Ari's direction while touching one of the rollers near the nape of her neck. By then Daniele was eyeing the dress and smiling.

"I'll check in on the groom." Ari interjected, suddenly feeling able to move.

Daniele nodded her approval, and sat down beside Jade.

"A moment," Ms. Yamato turned to Ari. "You're the one that outright lied to me on the phone." She cut her eyes into Ari's soul. Ari lowered her head, then her drink and stood saying nothing to this.

"I asked her to do that." Michelle intervened. "I didn't think any of you would come if I told you Seina and I are getting married, in Morocco, in secret."

"That speaks to how foolish of an idea you knew it was." Ms. Yamato said, the ice in her words beginning to melt, then to Ari. "You're that same Ari that brought that Depaul creature back into the picture, no? Seina's cousin?"

Ari nodded and Ms. Yamato huffed, a smirk appearing on her lips.

"Careful Naima." Ms. Yamato smiled, the older woman's gaze was soft and yet so intense. "Lie to me again," she said letting the threat remain veiled. "Well here we are, lie or no lie." She said to Michelle sighing. Ms. Yamato smiled at Daniele and left the dress to rest on the chair before turning back to Ari. "You may go." She said dismissing her—like a servant. Ari silently scurried down the hall.

Still enthralled by Michelle's mother, Jade was unable to break away. Not only for how she commanded the room, but no one talked to Ari that way for as long as Jade had known her. But clearer still, Jade was caught in the push-pull of wanting to give privacy and a taste for this moment between mother and daughter.

Daniele sat back in her seat, looking at Jade. "I'm sorry, you look familiar. We met in Japan but," she trailed off.

Jade who had been trying not to make eye contact with Seina's mother, glanced at Daniele and smiled.

"Lia!" Daniele hugged her. "Lia darling, how are you? You grow up so beautiful. Oh Lia, Naima was heartbroke when you left TASIS. I'm so glad you reconnect." Daniele gushed. Jade simply smiled.

Michelle's brow rose at this. *Lia? So, they did know each other before I introduced them,* she thought.

Jade opened her mouth to correct Daniele. "Ms. Alves, there's been a mis—" Jade began hesitantly, when Ms. Yamato cut-in talking to Michelle.

"Are you aware your future father-in-law is dead?" Ms. Yamato asked watching her daughter. Like an owl, Michelle turned to her mother, in utter disbelief.

"Yes," Daniele and Ms. Yamato nodded. "It happened early this morning, respiratory failure. The news should have broken by now."

"That's part of why we rushed here with so few questions." Ms. Yamato added.

It was Daniele's turn to speak now. "Vivian, I'm sorry they lied to all us, but I'm not sorry to be here. Seina loves Michelle, I only wish the timing were better. Love will wait for its match." She said looking at Michelle.

"Only the timing?" Ms. Yamato echoed as a cool stab, holding her clutch under an arm. "Daniele what do you think will happen to this marriage with Seina's father dead and no successor? How will your son at the very least protect her from your family?" Ms. Yamato smoothed flyaways on the side of Michelle's head. Michelle closed her eyes, bringing a hand to her forehead, exasperated with her mother. Jade ate up every minute of it, her concern for Hikaru's hurt feelings completely evaporated.

"Seina has clearly expressed, even in writing that he will not have hand in Terada Industries. Michelle's life is in no danger from successor fall out." Daniele admonished, in her clipped Portuguese tones.

"Knock, knock," Miles called from the hallway.

"Come in Daddy." Michelle looked up, hoping he might stop Ms. Yamato's tirade.

"Are you alright?" Miles said to someone in the hall. "Come in and sit." He commanded, not waiting for a reply. Miles came into the bridal suite with Ari leaning on him, she holding her head. Ms. Yamato's eyes went stone cold as she watched them cross the room. Miles walked Ari over to the sofa with the dress, and Ari plopped down. He ignored the cold war standoff between his ex-wife and the bronzed-skin, sandy-haired woman, and walked over to Michelle. "What were you thinking lying to us like that?!" Miles said, showing a rare flash of anger, brow raised and notes sounding mildly equatorial.

"Would you have come if I said I was getting married?" She asked, child-like. She stood still looking up at her father.

"After a very long lecture, yes." he kissed Michelle on the cheek. "I'm wholeheartedly against this but I love you, Sweet Pea. And you are an adult. I would stop this if I could, but I can't." Miles said to her staring long and deep into her eyes. He sighed and let go of Michelle, wanting to say more but deciding to wait.

Michelle sat down again and Miles shifted to Daniele.

"Miles Jang." He moved toward her, offering a hand.

Daniele shook it "I'm glad to meet you, I am Seina's mother, Daniele

Alves." She beamed.

"Is Uncle Claudio really dead?" Ari interrupted near tears.

"Yes," Daniele said softly.

"Oh no," Ari covered her face.

"Naima, he isn't worth your tears," Daniele cooed. "We can only pray that he went to God seeking forgiveness."

"To do o inferno está prestes a ser desencadeado," Ari tried and, Daniele shot her a look.

"You see," Ms. Yamato chimed in, turning to Michelle, then she shot a look at Miles, who didn't follow the Portuguese.

"Daniele we are completely opposed to this wedding, not because of Seina but because of your ex-husband and his *other* children." Miles stood leaning against the sofa near Michelle's dress.

"I stand in agree with you. My daughter April is in the other room convincing Seina." Daniele pointed.

"Wedding or not murder is in his blood." Ms. Yamato said crossed her arms and Daniele sighed, trying not to be rude. Ms. Yamato shifted to Michelle. "This is all rather rushed Michelle. And given this Claudio thing, we should just repurpose all this as an extravagant engagement party."

"Mother that makes no since." Michelle shook her head.

"No, it makes too much sense. Michelle when you rush you don't think." Ms. Yamato sighed. *All valid points*, Jade noted—silently. "Hurry is the enemy here. Don't rush this, Michelle," Ms. Yamato pleaded.

"Your mother is right. There is no rush." Daniele smiled. She turned her attention, to Ari then Jade, "Come. Ari, Lia." Daniele said, attempting to give Michelle and her parent's privacy.

"Why are you so opposed to holding off on this wedding?" Miles suddenly asked as Ari, Jade and Daniele left the room.

"Seina and I wanted all of you to have unforgettable memories before we vanished for a while." Michelle quietly said.

Ms. Yamato scoffed. "I should have known. Well, that is that." She said sarcastically followed by a sigh. "Run off, with another man. Your destiny is not tied solely to a man, Michelle. I thought you might know that by now. This," she gestured to the tent, "all of this is a mistake that you may not ever recover from. And yet you run faster into the lion's den. For what?! That boy will be there for you in a year or so after the waves settle if you're meant to be. But you want to play house. Well, your father and I will still be here when Seina fails you and all of this falls apart." Ms. Yamato said before exiting the room.

Miles exhaled and closed his eyes. When he opened them, he cleared his throat trying to keep his voice level. "What do you mean vanish?" He asked.

Michelle stared at her father. "Abba, sekulu ani."

Miles cautiously watched his daughter as he took a seat.

"I mean we're going to go on a honeymoon and we will disappear until it's safe. Ke ife ilo?" Michelle took his hand, and he pulled away.

"Ina apu ala? Michelle this is childish. Why do you think we'd be okay with this?! Marry him after all the trouble fades. Do you already have the license?"

"Yes," she nodded.

"You're not on the family registry, are you?" Miles stood up again and Michelle shook her head. "Then let us do what yo motha suggested, um? Then we—"

"Daddy I'm getting married today." Michelle said.

"My only doughta, gettin married in secret, and disappearing like a tief in the night, eh! Tufiakwa!" He shouted. "He is not worf your life, he is barely worf you. Ahh, doughta, I beg, it is too soon for all of this." Miles petitioned, his home dialect getting away from him. Michelle looked at her father, her gentle amber eyes welling with tears.

"Daddy, I don't think Seina and I will get another chance." She stifled a sob. "Will you still give me away?"

Miles released a long sigh, realizing once again that Vivian was right. Michelle's mind was set, and this was the road they would now travel. Houses Terada and Yamato-Jang would be united, for better or worse.

Light Blue
Sunset, A Beach Outside Asilah, Morocco, June 20th

Light blue strips of fabric in nearly every imaginable shade, draped the wedding hall from the height of the tent, down along the walls where it came to rest at the edges of the room. Here, the strips of material met the lagoon-like moat that encapsulated the enchanted world Ari work so hard to create. A candle-lit bridge arched over the largest expanse of the lagoon, leading past the two guest tables to the alter. Each candle along the way was surrounded by a light blue cylinder that glowed brilliantly. Seina stood at the end of the aisle, in his tuxedo, atop a short staircase. Just beyond him and the minister, on the right, was a table for the wedding party, and an orchestra on the far left.

Seina glanced to Ms. Yamato, his mother and sister at a table to his left, and only now did he notice how much more beautiful his sister April had become.

April had the long slender nose of the Alves, the piercing and sometimes chilling eyes of the Terada's, straight hair, with brown skin too dark to just be white, and a dash of Asian for good measure. It was the look their father praised, the look Seina longed for when they were children. When Seina finally showed Michelle a picture of his 'amazing little sister' she said the girl had 'dead eyes' and looked hungry, but that she and Seina had the same lips.

April crossed her legs. She surveyed the sanctuary, bored. She looked across the aisle, to check out the in-laws, once again. There were the newlyweds, Chris and Alyson who sat blissfully together. Alyson's hair pulled back and thrown over a shoulder, her arm on the back of Chris' chair. Chris kissed her hand as he stared into Alyson's eyes, raised his brows then smiled. April rolled her eyes. Then there was Devina, who she had met at the hotel. She was sitting with— April stopped. *Is that the other brother? Marcus?* She turned to Daniele hitting her leg.

"Ma-ma," April whispered. "Who is that?" She pointed with her eyes.

"Don't." Daniele said without looking in Marcus' direction.

April stared at Devina poking the cheek of a man that look less than pleased to be here. When the man turned to face her, Devina kissed him. *He must be Marcus,* April thought staring long and hard at him in disbelief.

Sea shells and sand lay scattered around the sanctuary. At the center of the tables, stood a six-inch tall cyclical vase where lit tea candles floated encircling an arrangement of long-stemmed white jasmine and Casablanca lilies tipped in light blue.

Housed in the vase were brightly colored blue beta fish. At the center of the arrangement, surrounded by the lilies and jasmine was a larger lit candle. The scent of the flowers permeated the air while the light of the candles littered about the room grew stronger with the darkening sky. There was electricity in the air, with only the sounds of conversation, soft music from the orchestra, and the shhh of sea to quell the feeling— but to no avail.

An unseen piano came to life in a crescendo, then the electricity surged. It was in this moment, that blue cylinders overhead covered the candles strewn about, on the tables, and across the room, changing the atmosphere to light blue.

Tea candles were released on the water of the lagoon, and beneath the raised translucent floor where Seina stood. The music slowly built in its complexity, then to the far left of the alter, just past the orchestra, a singer came to stand behind a sheer curtain. Ari and Hikaru stepped forward at the end of the aisle. The vocalist began 'Finally Found,' releasing a sound that pierced the soul, from the very first note. Jade walked in with Yu alongside her. Her eyes instantly met Chris'. Alyson held Chris' hand absently, his hunger re-emerging to Jade's cold forward drawn gaze.

"What's that about," Yu asked, noting the look.

"Shut up."

"Complicated, aren't we?" He laughed as the weight of the

atmosphere wrapped itself around him.

Though she tried to fight it, Jade too felt the magnitude of being here. There was the testimony of this voice, her anger, and her fears, and the growing desire to remain Jade Wang, all tangling and vying for her attention. Yu glanced at her as they crossed the bridge, but took pause seeing her glassy eyes. After a few long painful moments, Jade quickly let go of Yu, taking her place beside Ari.

Jade was breathless, as the tears came to rest like dewdrops along her eyelids. Not an emptying out, the tide washing in and returning to sea, but emptiness, an echo— a thing taking shape in, and from absence. She pushed the tears aside as the grip on her lungs tightened, the cold numbness becoming a sharp biting ache. Ari took her hand in silence. Yu watched, Jade's eyes drift to Chris, and his kiss on Alyson's cheek, her hand on his back. Then they stood awaiting Michelle, the singer taking a dramatic pause.

Ms. Yamato placed her champagne on the table, taking in a breath. She saw a smile come to Daniele's face and knew her daughter was breathtaking. Jade along with Ms. Yamato felt the world closing in, a weight building in the lungs, and the urge to fight— to maintain composure. Miles beamed with a warm sort of sadness, as he walked his daughter down the aisle.

Michelle appeared in an ocean of white, accented by blue and gold. The embroidery of waves flowing along the waist and out to the train, following some six feet behind. The dress draped at the hips, the fabric folded, pressed and creased like the waves in an ocean, fading from white with a golden tint, into a light blue at it's edges. Interwoven curls swept back from her face, down her back, and to her thighs. She was a vision in all this uncertainty, complete with red lips and golden smoky eye shadow.

Captivated by this sight and the moment, Yu's thoughts drifted to Eva, and the messages she left, and how she would look on the day they might be man and wife— if they were still together. Though he swore he wouldn't listen to the messages, and he swore he would not think of her on this day.

Hikaru saw the tears come to Michelle's eyes, as the lyrics rang to the bone. Yet his thoughts remained with Jade, wiping her eyes. Hikaru watched Ari wipe Jade's face, in an effort to keep the face in one piece.

The song quieted, then slowed, along with Michelle's pace. Miles froze and looked at her. No one will know what it was in this moment, that caused Michelle to stop short of the alter— not even Michelle herself. Perhaps, it was wedding jitters turned full terror. Or Maybe the thoughts of 'future' and the ramifications of 'I do'.

Whatever the case, with the ball in his court, Seina took the four short steps between them and took her hand. She kissed him, long and deep. Seina pulled away from her, laughing. He nodded to Miles then looked back at Michelle.

"Way to scare me there." He whispered, still smiling.

Michelle laughed. "You're so handsome I blanked." She whispered back, as they ascended the stairs to the altar.

愛 だ け が
Ai Dake ga
Plage Sidi Mghait, Morocco, June 20th

As it goes with champagne events, glass one took the edge off, easing the threat of impending tension, but paired with Travis Greene's 'Finally Found', it sombered the beach, the atmosphere, and the ceremony. Glass two, lifted the spirits and swept away the tears unbeknownst to the viewer. Man and wife sat smiling and laughing under the sound of live music at their table at the front of the room.

For their first dance, the tiny Asian girl from the restaurant made an appearance, singing Emi Hinouchi's 'I Love you' just as before.

"Beautiful," Daniele smiled.

"What?" Ms. Yamato leaned over while Miles stood chatting with April about who knows what. *The man could charm and angry rattlesnake*, Ms.

Yamato thought cutting her eyes in their direction.

"They are absolutely beautiful." Daniele repeated looking from bridesmaids and groomsmen at their table in the front of the room to Seina and Michelle on the dance floor.

"They are," Ms. Yamato agreed. "I still worry." She said under her breath.

"I would worry if you were not concerned." Daniele paused. "We can only pray and have faith that God will not allow them to ruin their lives or each other."

"And what god might we be discussing?" Ms. Yamato raised a brow, with a smirk on her lips.

"The God of Abraham, Isaac and Israel." Daniele replied, then paused. Her eyes locked with Ms. Yamato. "Do you pray for your children?" Daniele asked hesitantly.

"I'm not—" Ms. Yamato began.

"For as many as are led by the spirit of God, they are the sons of God." Daniele said with her eyes trained on Seina and Michelle she continued. "If you are willing to have real relationship, He will use you." Daniele went on with Ms. Yamato half listening.

Ms. Yamato felt she was the only one who seemed implicitly aware of this union's impending and disastrous end. So aware, and yet it was her only daughter's wedding. And yet, she didn't and couldn't feel joy. She could not find the delight in her daughter finding a man to love and be loved by. *He cannot match her strength*, she thought. Nor could she find the pleasure in her daughter's happiness— *fleeting as it is*.

"Vivian, you have been the best mother you know to be. Just like your mother. Your example was not who you become. Don't worry. God will have the final say. Pray for them, forgive yourself, and give yourself to Him, then He will heal you of this sickness." Daniele shifted to look at Ms. Yamato squarely.

It may have been the music, or perhaps the three and a half glasses of champagne—which she shouldn't have had, per her doctor's orders. It was certainly Daniele's eyes, incisive, almost all-knowing eyes. Daniele held Ms. Yamato's gaze, unable to dismiss her— or what was said. The words rang absolute, down to the very heart of the matter, bringing Vivian Yamato-Jang's standing tears to the point of overflow.

"Miles doesn't even—" Ms. Yamato started.

Daniele produced a napkin, wiping the shallow tears before Ms. Yamato knew they were there. "God knows of all things in all places, Ayane. And he wants you to know you have done all you can do and raised you children well. And that he loves you so much. You have done your best. Now let go and let God move in their lives. Your gift of foresight is no accident." Daniele tended to Ms. Yamato's tears punctuating the exchange with an embrace. Not absolution— a forgiveness born out of both effort and failure, but understanding. *This was a path Daniele too had walked,* a voice told her.

"Mom?" Michelle interrupted, concern on her face with Seina at her side.

"I'm Fine." Ms. Yamato answered briskly, taking Michelle's hand in her own.

Miles pulled April, Daniele and Seina to pose for an impromptu photo. The entire exchange of these two women was somehow missed by him, but not unseen. For later, when Ms. Yamato shifted to glass four, Miles brought her attention to the ceremony's photos in print. Ms. Yamato's lips parted, and the tears returned, this time from a different source, and neither of them were alarmed by her elation amidst the sadness.

By the collective third glass of champagne, the eating gave way to a dessert of crème brulee and wedding cake. Ari smiled from the wedding party's table, watching the newlyweds pose while cutting the cake. Ari was proud in this moment; of so much she could not give words. Jade, on the other hand, looked bored— Hikaru noted. Not yawning falling asleep bored, no. It was a viewing, but from some great distance. She was on glass six or seven, when Hikaru caught her eye for the first time since before the ceremony, then she rolled her eyes to break the stare.

"You've been rejected." Yu leaned in on Hikaru's right, with Jade on the opposite end of the table from them, he had seen the entire exchange. "Whatever you're selling she doesn't want it."

"Is that what Eva told you?" Hikaru stared at his brother hoping to make the wound sting.

"No." Yu said matter of fact. "Because unlike your cock sucking-punk-ass, I know when to walk away and when to fight." Those words seared Hikaru's heart, dredging up memories he long ago cut away from his existence.

Yu's cold tea-colored eyes cut away from his brother to Ari chatting with the wedding planner, before coming to rest on Michelle dancing with her father.

In the light of half-burned tea candles floating around the arrangement at their table, Chris sat in silence as Alyson stroked his hair, her ring lit even in the flickering candlelight. Chris yawned then turned to her, kissing an eyelid.

"We can tell my parents on the way home." Chris said placing a hand on Alyson stomach.

"You'd better hope my mother doesn't get to them first." Alyson is smirked.

Chris beamed, then chuckled, "We'll just have to dodge some calls for a bit." They burst into laughter. Meanwhile Marcus and Devina slow danced to 'Heaven Sent' alongside Michelle and Seina.

"Tell me about it," Devina prompted, her head on Marcus' chest.

"I don't know what there is to tell Devina," Marcus sighed. "My baby sister is throwing her life away and I'm supposed to be happy about it?"

"She's not throwing her life away." Devina said sweetly and Marcus sighed. "Well you're going to be an uncle. That's something." Devina lifted her head to look at him.

"Yeah, that's exciting," he smiled.

"There's the man I love. Marcus you've been so sulky lately, I'm worried."

"There's been a lot of bad news lately Dee," he sniffed.

"Like what?" Devina's green eyes zeroed in on him.

"My mom is sick." He said simply.

"What does she have?" Devina leaned back, halting the dance.

"I haven't confronted her yet."

"How long have you known?" Devina glanced at Ms. Yamato taking in the sight of her children.

"I found out right before Chris' wedding. She's keeping it a secret so it must be bad." He said, and Devina pulled him closer. "I'm sorry, I'm so sorry Marcus." She wiped his tears and kissed his cheek.

21. Kagami
鏡

Plage Sidi Mghait, Morocco, June 20th

Jade slipped from the sanctuary, the champagne heavily poured, the toasts said and done, her tear ducts feeling empty, and the tears finally evaporated. Hikaru noticed the exit and decided to follow.

At the front of the sanctuary, Seina and Michelle sat down again at their table looking out on their family and friends. When there was a lull between songs Michelle heard a slight hum, but Seina turned to her champagne in hand.

"Wife." He smiled, handing her a glass.

"Did you hear that?" She asked throwing heavy curls off her shoulder.

"Hear what?" He questioned, leaning into a kiss. He lifted his glass to hers. "To us. Mr. and Mrs. Terada."

Absently, Michelle toasted with her husband. She wanted to correct him, that her name would be double hyphenated but, her thoughts lingered on that unaccounted-for hum.

"To us." Michelle kissed Seina, then she turned to Ari in a whisper.

"I'll have Nina get security to do a sweep." Ari nodded, getting up from the table.

"Something wrong?" Seina prompted. Ari casually left the sanctuary.

"No. I just asked Ari to get security to check on things." She leaned on Seina's shoulder. "Shouldn't we say a few words in memory of your father?" Michelle asked placing a hand on Seina's thigh. "I know you weren't close but he's your father and its okay to grieve." Michelle's brows rose.

Seina beamed. "There's no need to." He kissed her. When they pulled apart, Ari was rushing back over the bridge, at odds with Sade's 'Lover's Rock' and the whole atmosphere. She moved over to the wedding party's table, and within seconds Ari squatted down between Michelle and Seina.

"Nina just told me the security team saw a Terada helicopter land. I told them to—" Ari's eyes went wide. "Kohana is here." She said in a voice too small even for a whisper. Something about how Ari said that name echoed of reverence. It was the way Michelle's grandfather spoke of God and his father's conversion to the Christian faith— the west African variant, after being the voice of Chi-naeke.

"I don't know how she found us." Ari muttered to no one in particular. Her eyes locked on an approaching figure.

Michelle broke free from the conversation and was immediately drawn to the tall woman that floated down the aisle with two bodyguards in tow. She had to have been six feet at least, skin the color of honey and caramel, mixing a bit of half and half. Powerful legs in a purple floor length dress with a split in the middle, silver high heels and shapely bear arms. April and Daniele simply paused, while Ms. Yamato and Miles sat stunned with their eyes glued to this woman. Across the aisle, Chris was visibly disturbed and sat wide eyed staring at her. Devina's smile faded and she stopped talking, her face completely soured.

Alyson looked up from her phone. "I can't find it. The service here—" she tucked her hair, following Devina's gaze as Kohana and her men passed their table. "Omo-omo!" Alyson clapped a hand over her mouth, then eyeballed Marcus. Marcus stood up, with Devina watching him and slowly he moved toward Kohana and her guards.

At their table, Seina stood as Kohana came better into view. "I'll explain." He said to Michelle, leaving the table.

Kohana's hair was braided into a crown, golden highlights on display with long strings of curled hair dangling freely. That was when Michelle saw the face— her brother Marcus' face. There were the identical almond eyes lined in black eyeliner, Marcus' long chiseled nose covered in bronzer, the similar thick eyebrows but arched. Kohana had Marcus' lips only cloaked in purple lipstick, the matching jaw line yet softened.

Suddenly it dawned on Michelle why Seina gawked at Marcus every time he was nearby, along with the comment about him being adopted and not looking like their father. '*He looks like someone I used to know.*' Seina had said and Michelle turned it into a joke. Had Seina still been sitting next to her, she would have hit him, but by then he was moving to meet this Kohana as she made her way to the cake table directly across from her. Michelle stood up, and followed her husband, but Ari grabbed her wrist.

"She's dangerous," Ari said, hesitantly letting go of Michelle's arm. Yu saw the determination on Michelle's face, so he sat back at their table waiting for the sparks to fly. Kohana's bodyguards were posted a mere three feet behind her. She grabbed one of the stylish golden forks and a white plate flecked in gold and light blue. Marcus was inching closer, and the bodyguards slowed his approach.

"Sir, step back." The bald guard on the left said, a hand on Marcus' chest.

"Let him through," Kohana replied without looking up.

The greasy haired body guard on the right patted Marcus down then let him through. Kohana picked up the cake knife to cut one of the remaining pieces. Marcus laid a hand on hers and the two guards pulled out their guns. There where gasps around the room and Alyson fainted.

"Alyson, Alyson!" Chris shouted as he caught her.

Marcus didn't notice, he didn't even look back. "I'm going to have to ask you to leave." Marcus said, taking the knife. Kohana smirked, switching the plate and fork to her other hand.

"Kohana Terada, sister of the—" she jumped, dropping the plate and fork, suddenly feeling all eyes on them— but now knowing the why of it. Kohana was stunned by Marcus' honey-caramel complexion; by the same chiseled features, the same dense forest of curly hair.

"Ko-ji?" Kohana whispered.

"Marcus Jang. This is a private event. I need you to leave." He examined her face, staring hard at her features— his features made womanly.

"Lower your weapons." Kohana, said slowly gaining her composure, and the two men did as they were told.

"I see you two have met." Seina smiled, glancing up at the two mirrors. Michelle strolled over to Seina's side staring at Kohana, arms crossed.

"You must be Michelle." Kohana smiled. "Between you, Seina, and this whirlwind romance our issues featuring you two can't stay on the shelf. Magazine sales alone could have paid for this little party you threw together." She turned and ran her finger along the edge of the half-eaten cake, pausing to taste the frosting. "Our father died today Seina." Kohana leaned against the table, crossing her ankles and leaning back on her palms.

"I realize that, but as you can see, I was a little busy." He motioned to Michelle with his head.

"I see, e com a cadela that killed him. I know you erased the evidence but, there's always more. I know you were there Michelle. I sent the car to get you myself. Once I find the evidence you will pay—then I'll hand you over to the police." She looked at Michelle and though they were the warm eyes of her oldest brother, Michelle could only see the cold reptilian eyes of Claudio and April— Terada eyes.

Kohana stood up and smiled. "Baby brother," she said looking pleased, something between a smile and a sneer, "I apologize for what my men did to your guards, if only I'd had an invitation. Good night." Kohana turned, grabbing a handful of cake. She stared at Marcus, then took a step closer to him. "I'll see you again, Marcus Jang." Kohana kissed him on the cheek, leaving a deep purple stain that looked like a bruise. She started eating the cake in her hand then walked toward the sanctuary's bridge. She gave a halfhearted wave to Daniele and April. "Nice finally meeting you Michelle!" Kohana called from the bridge before throwing the cake in hand into the lagoon with a splash. One of the bodyguards pulled a hand towel from his blazer and handed it to Kohana as they walked out of the sanctuary.

Dragon Lady
Plage Sidi Mghait, Morocco, June 20th

Jade slipped from the sanctuary, the toasts said and done, and the tears finally evaporated. Hikaru noticed the exit and decided to follow. Down the hallway and through the sitting room, he trailed her at some distance. When he saw her slip through the foyer and out of the tent, Hikaru knew Jade was plotting something, so closed the gap.

He watched Jade creep down along the north side of the tent and over to a wooden crate. From the shadows, she grabbed a bag partially hidden in the sand. After changing her shoes, Jade sat on the crate to light a cigarette looking at the waves. Hikaru appeared on her right like a shadow himself, arms crossed with a smile— dimples visible even in the moonlight. *God he's sexy*, but Jade looked away.

"Your feet hurting that much?" He came closer.

"No." She glanced over at him, trying not to look at his face.

"Then what are you doing?" He sat down beside her, skin tingling on contact through their clothes.

"I needed a moment."

"You've been avoiding me." Hikaru looked at her with soft loving eyes.

"I haven't." Jade shook her head. Hikaru cleared the blonde hair from her eyes.

"You've been dismissive."

"Yes. Maybe." She pulled a laugh to her face, and the cigarette from her lips.

"What's going on then?"

She paused to consider what words to form, stringing the most hurtful with no will to harm, and with little effort they poured free from her lips. "It's clear to me now that you just used me to get off." The blonde hair draped Jade's face in the breeze as the moonlight turned it silver. "You like Michelle." False tears trickled from her eyes. "She told me you were her alibi," Jade lied. "—and that you two were drinking together before you came to the club." She turned to look him in the eyes, finding the stone-heart and iron-will to move forward with her plan. "Then you called out her name after you had sex with me."

"Jade that's not possible you're all I think about." Hikaru said without flinching, without missing a beat.

"After you were rejected." She stood up to stop the tingling where their bodies were in contact. "I don't want to be your runner-up."

"Michelle kissed me when she used me as her alibi. Yeah, I kissed her that night when we were drinking, because she was sending signals. But you came on to me and I liked it. So I want to keep seeing you. I know you're doing some crazy illegal stuff but—" he paused to stare at her as Jade looked down at him in the moonlight. "I want to be with you Jade." Hikaru leapt up and kissed her, with the same passion Jade had sparked that night in Roppongi. He cupped her face in his hands and Jade pulled away, placing her hands on his neck. "What are you doing?" Hikaru croaked in a whisper.

"Close your eyes. Don't fight." Jade heard voices. Hikaru started hyper ventilating, remembering a similar moment of trauma in his childhood. His mind went blank. Jade's face morphed into that of a young man, piercing icy blue eyes and dark brown hair.

"Call Naoki as soon as we get in the air." A female voice said moving away from the beach. Hikaru's breaths became shallow and quick and his eyes glistened with wetness.

"Yes, Ms. Tarada," said a male voice in response.

"As soon as we land in Tangier, I need the jet ready to go back to Tokyo." Kohana said, their sounds became more distant.

"Stop. please." Hikaru croaked again, with tears in his eyes, spilling down along his cheek and onto Jade's hands.

"Go to sleep." She said before Hikaru went limp. Jade let his body gently fall to the ground, she wiped her eyes trying to trace the voices. She rushed to the entrance to the tent and saw Kohana and her two guards climbing the path uphill to leave the beach. "Damn dragon lady." She sighed, torn. Should she make her escape or— Jade looked back at Hikaru then stopped.

She moved over to the crate at his feet and opened it. Then she smiled. Jade took off after Kohana, taking as many fireworks as she could and making sure to grab the launcher. She ran across the beach dropping one or two here and there but couldn't slow down. Jade climbed up the path leading away from the beach with damp sand lining her sandals and dress.

When she reached the field at the top of the hill, Jade saw the helicopter doors closing. The helicopter was about forty feet away, and in the white, red, and grey of Terada Media Holdings it was an easy enough target. Yet, Jade knew she would only have a matter of moments. She dropped the fireworks on the ground, and between the light of her phone and the moon she lit three of the bigger bulbs and dropped them in the launcher.

Jade pointed the launcher at the blades, the wind from the helicopter blowing her hair and dress in every direction. The chopper lifted, with its blades sounding like gun shots. The first firework shot out and Jade lost sight of it. Some eighty feet in the air, the firework exploded near the tail blades. It became a huge glittering sky bound flame that surrounded but missed the vehicle, the golden flakes, hitting the ground.

Jade aimed the launcher at the overhead blades and the second firework disappeared into the jet-black sky with a pop and a hiss. The chopper swiveled and swerved away as a flash of gold bloomed above blades.

"Damn you Dragon Lady!" Jade exclaimed as the second and third wave of flashes bombarded the body of the aircraft. The helicopter was moving north toward Tangier and the strait of Gibraltar when the third firework exploded out of the launcher with a resounding boom, followed by the screams of the firework itself. Jade saw a small fire on the helicopter's tail. When the final golden bomb swallowed up the tail, its fire, and the helicopter, a splitting headache came with the sight, one that was somehow linked to the knots in Jade's stomach. The helicopter caught fire, and spun out near the water. Jade felt numb, except the stomach-linked headache. The gold glitter turned red flash then went dark as it crashed on the hillside north of the tent.

By the time the helicopter fell from the sky, still on fire, Jade and her bag where gone. But not before she sent a text to Ari.

Nina and Ari ventured out of the tent with five of the remaining security guards to see why the fireworks were going off earlier than scheduled. As they search the beach, Ari's saw a message on her phone. She unlocked it to find Jade's text. **ALL ROADS LEAD TO TERADA! Ps. find Hikaru**

Nothing more.

"Ms. Louien!" Nina called running toward her. "There's a fire." Nina stopped. Ari slumped to the sand.

"Ma'am we found Hikaru Hiroshi, but no sign of Jade Wang." The security team leader said to Ari.

Yet Ari knew Jade was gone. As soon as Nina said fire, she understood what must have happened. Claudio was dead. Kohana was likely dead. Jade absconded. Seina and Michelle married. While she was in the middle of an impending war.

Omission
Seoul, South Korea, June 23rd

In Seoul, it was ten thirty-nine a.m. Soo Young tip-toe-hobbled into the lobby of Yang Wei Plastics in silver heeled stilettos far too high for daylight, or office work. She walked up to the reception desk, sporting a tight black and white pants-suit, a set of silver earrings, and a matching necklace. The clank of Soo Young's heels on the marble floors, echoed throughout the lobby, her purse swinging heavy as she came to the desk.

"Hwajangsil eodiyeyo?" Soo Young asked in nearly accent-less Gyeonggi dialect. The receptionist, an uninterested pixie-haired-thirty-something, pointed without even looking up from her computer. Soo Young sighed, flipped her hair and glanced at her watch before heading in the direction the woman pointed.

Once in the bathroom, Soo Young rushed into the stall nearest the AC vent, trying not to be seen. She closed then locked the stall door and pushed her purse behind the toilet.

"It's in position." She spoke into the mic wired under her clothing.

"*Good,*" Jade answered through Soo Young's earpiece. "*Remember, as soon as you can, I need you to get out of there. Stall for a bit, lay the terms, get out of there.*" Jade reiterated in Korean.

"Ya, geojeong haji mala." Soo Young chuckled. She walked out of the stall and found a man peeing in the urinal across from her. The man stopped mid-stream when he saw the feminine figure, long orange hair like flames down her back, and the semi-autonomous butt cheeks in the tight pants suit.

Soo Young slipped into the lobby and back to the reception desk, acrylic nails poised on the receptionist's screen.

"I have an eleven o'clock with Liam Yang." She said as if picking up where she left off. "Jia Lang Yang." The instant that name rolled off her tongue the receptionist's whole body tensed. Soo Young felt everything around her change. Before she knew it, four men in black suits appeared from nowhere, escorting Soo Young to an elevator.

"*Soo Young, what's happening—are you okay? Soo Young!*" Jade shouted, hearing the commotion. Meanwhile in the bathroom of the lobby, hundreds of black and blue marble-like spheres quietly spilled forth from Soo Young's purse, directing themselves up the wall and into the HVAC system.

When the elevator chimed their arrival, two of the guards stepped out and the fat stubby one on her left held the door, in case Soo Young might try something. Soo Young met his eyes, blew a kiss and floated out of the elevator amongst the quiet hum of meetings and phone calls. Soo Young passed a row of eerily quiet offices, two guards in front and two behind.

Each office was awash in mostly white, with glass for walls and doors. The whole floor had a deathly silent atmosphere. The sight of these typical findings gave away no sign that Yang Wei could be under siege. Even Soo Young was unaware of this. And no one could have imagined how this day would end, two down, and three billion in damages, the final amount still being tallied.

Jade painted this scam to Soo Young as a way to steal money from the already rich man who killed Jade's mother. There was mention of a way to steal more money after the initial robbery. But with Soo Young's money pit of a salon and increasing rent rates in the greater Tokyo area, more money was all Soo Young could hear. Soo Young had no way of knowing what would really happen.

The men led her to a conference room, the wall shared with the hallway was made of glass, while a wall of windows on the opposite side faced the Han. The fat stubby guard took Soo Young by the elbow and forced her into a chair at the conference table.

"Yeogi anj-a!" Stubby grunted in a heavy Chinese accent, and Soo Young crossed her legs. Stubby took a small remote from the doorframe and pressed a button, making the conference room look empty from the hallway. He barked and order and the other three: skinny, muscles and broke nose posted along the wall with the hallway.

"*Soo Young let me know if you're okay. What's going on?*" Jade chimed.

Soo Young turned to look at each of them uncrossing then re-crossing her legs. "Why I'm I locked in this conference room with the four of you?" She asked looking at stubby, who was clearly the leader.

"You're playing with a very dangerous man," stubby replied as he came to sit on the table. The door opened and then skinny, muscles and broke nose snapped to attention.

"Is there a reason you're posing as my daughter." Mr. Yang asked, standing in the doorway.

Soo Young glanced at her watch and looked at Liam Yang with a smile. "To met you." She grinned slyly switching to English. Mr. Yang slowly walked around the table. He barked an order in Mandarin to stubby, whose name was Zhang Yong, Soo Young had gathered. Zhang and his men left, leaving Soo Young to the infamous Liam Yang.

Seated on the bed of her hotel room at the Seoul Times Square Marriott. Jade put on a white shirt and a pair of blue jeans, trying to imagine her father's expression as he and Soo Young sat in silence. Just blocks away from Yang Wei, this was the closest Jade had been to her father in three years— barring Victoria's wedding.

"*Met?*" Jade heard her father's deep rumble of a laugh.

"*We make deal.*" Soo Young stated.

"*You want to make a deal?*" Mr. Yang questioned, almost scoffing at Soo Young.

"*Yees.*" Jade heard Soo Young say. "*Good deal. We have the Jia Lang, you can buy.*"

"*Why do you have my daughter?*"

Soo Young sighed then switched to Korean again, "*I'm sorry to tell you this but she's a junkie and she owes us quite a bit of money. I was sent to broker a deal.*"

Jade heard her father scoff at that and could almost picture his sneer. "*Jia Lang is an addict? I find that hard to believe.*"

"*Mr. Yang that's your problem.*" Soo Young said quickly, almost sharp. Jade was impressed.

Back in the conference room, Soo Young tossed her hair off her shoulder and smiled.

"And do you have proof of any of this?" Liam Yang interlocked his fingers on the table.

Soo Young paused and held up a finger, her eyes drifting up to the ceiling, blue contacts catching the light. The sound of footsteps came down the hallway, and Zhang rushed in again, with Soo Young's empty purse. Zhang threw the purse on the table, holding up a silvery blue camera, conferring with his boss in Mandarin. Zhang placed the camera in front of Mr. Yang.

"You can go." Liam Yang said to him. Zhang bowed then left the room. "You left your purse in the men's room. I take it this is your proof? Why would you only come with a camera?" Liam Yang turned to Soo Young, his eyes narrowed in confusion at her. "What else was in the bag?"

"Yeongsang bwajuseyo." Soo Young urged him, saying nothing else but crossing her arms.

Yang promptly picked up the camera and turned it on. He came across a video—the only item for viewing. He saw Jade gagged in a dark room with today's newspapers from Singapore, Tokyo, Seoul, and Hong Kong thrown on the floor at her feet— seven seconds, no more.

His brows rose, then fell. Mr. Yang stared at Soo Young, nostrils flaring. "Fine. You have my attention." He put the camera on the table, the blue of his Italian bespoke suit glistening in the light of the conference room. "The last time Jia Lang came up, the woman claimed not to know anything about her." Liam Yang sneered. "She even passed a lie detector. Now you come in pretending to be her. So, Let's hear your deal." He crossed his arms, sitting back in his chair.

"Two mirron." Soo Young said with long legs crossed and French manicure on display.

At this juncture Jade accessed the central computer for the building's security system, slowly disabling all sensors for everyone but her.

"What?" Liam scowled.

"That's plice for her. I think it pair." Soo Young stared at him blankly.

"*Get out of there.*" Jade said through the earpiece. "*The fire starts in twenty minutes.*" She lied.

"Two mirron, U.S. and two mirron when get she." Soo Young asked, no inflection, pulling a card from her bra.

"Four million dollars?" Mr. Yang asked.

Soo Young nodded— after she and Jade agreed on two million.

"Half now, and half when I get my daughter?"

"Of course," Soo Young placed the card on the desk and winked, shifting back to English. "We talk later. If I not meet boss, she dispear. Account on za back." Soo Young slid her chair back.

"No," Mr. Yang smiled. "Call your boss. Here." He pulled the phone from his pocket and handed it to her. Soo Young's face went blank as she took the phone, hands trembling.

"Soo Young you have to get out of there! I think he knows something's up." Jade shouted.

Soo Young knew what she had to do.

She went to google and typed in "김밥" then dialed the first number that popped up. Putting the phone to her ear, Soo Young plastered a smile on her face, "Ye, annyeonghaseyo." She looked at Mr. Yang. "Oh, you can keep talking since you want to waste time," she retorted in Korean, then to the phone. "Ah ye joesonghandego, chijeu gimbab se gae wa sogogi du—"

Liam Yang reached over the table and knocked the phone from her hand. "You think you can play with me?! Where is my daughter!"

"I'm. Not. Leave. She. Not. Safe." Soo Young's brows rose. "You waste time, I eat." she shrugged.

"Go. Call your boss." Liam Yang dismissed her. Soo Young stood and he watched her go, committing the face to memory.

"I'll call you when I hear something." Soo Young said switching to Korean again. "If you love your daughter, pay." She said from the doorway, her hand on the doorframe. "She might be missing a finger or a hand or worse if you don't." With that Soo Young left.

Liam Yang scoffed, then picked up his phone and called Jennifer. "Jennifer, have *Miss. Yang* tailed and get someone from accounts up here."

Soo Young walked into an elevator, feeling danger enveloping her surroundings and the quiet melt away.

"Get on the subway, go to Seoul Yuk," Jade's said cutting through Soo Young's thoughts on the earpiece, guiding with urgency as the elevator doors opened on the ground floor. *"—take the ktx to Pusan, then, in Pusan take the ferry to Fukuoka, the ticket will be waiting under Yukina Tanaka. I'll meet you at Hakata Eki, in front of the bakery."* She lied. *"Do you understand?"*

"Yes." Soo Young whispered.

"Good. Go. Do exactly what I said." Jade pulled the earpiece from her ear, then she cut the mic.

Though Michelle cared for her, Jade realized in New York, Michelle would have asked too many questions—poked too many holes for this to take place. This Jade thought, knowing that Soo Young would pull her father's suspicions away from the building as the temperature began to climb and the H.E.X.D.—the High Energy X Devices moved into position.

After getting the initial access code from Robert, in death, Jade and Ah Fan realized the devices were limited to its test mode functions. The initial access code brought the H.E.X.D. online but only with limited capabilities. That was why Jade had to risk overnighting to each of the respective offices.

No matter, Ah Fan and his team started tinkering with them as soon as Robert gave up the codes. Jade only needed the H.E.X.D. to travel a short distance before carrying out their final commands. Ah Fan told her that extreme heat or cold would also trigger them whether activated or not. How he knew that, she would never know. But Jade realized, this was why the H.E.X.D. were still more concept than tool. How could one's secret weapon be effective if it overreacted because of the temperature?

Hence the reason Robert fought not to give her any information as he lay caked in his own blood on the floor of that storage room, begging that monster— begging *her* to stop. That's why she had to torture him. To get what she needed, she thought, deciding to order room service.

Burn the Dreams
Seoul, June 23rd, 2:45 p.m

Jade decided to do away with the gradual increase she used while Soo Young was still in play, and raised all three building's internal temperature from 29 degrees Celsius to 35 on her laptop. She forced down a late lunch of seafood cream pasta and salad, keeping an eye on the three locations.

"The red H.E.X.D. will blow out at 35 degrees Celsius while the black and sometimes the blue H.E.X.D. hold out til 49 degrees." Ah Fan had told Jade on her way to the airport, after leaving Hikaru to the sand and Kohana in the flames.

From the mint green arm chair of her hotel room, Jade used the blue H.E.X.D. as the eyes of her operation. She came to the end of her lunch and cut the water supply to each of the sprinkler systems, then her phone lit up again with another call from Soo Young. Jade let the phone ring, then let it go to voicemail. *The money will hit her account by Wednesday and Soo Young should find the foreign resident card once she gets back to Tokyo*, she thought, shifting back to her computer screen.

Inside the buildings, Yang Wei employees, took off blazers, loosened ties, rolled sleeves, unbuttoned blouses and broke out fans. In Hong Kong and Singapore, 'HVAC system under repair, work from home until further notice,' was the email Jade sent to all the tenant companies that shared the building. The notice and unbearable rising temperatures paired with the unseasonably warm weather caused the work day to be cut short.

'Wah lau, why so hot today?' was the resounding cry heard over and over as wave after wave of workers braved the hot monsoon rains for home. But in Seoul they stuck it out, despite the email. The clack of keys quieted, while the constant ringing of phones annoyed everyone within ear range.

Even always peppy Jennifer Martin was over it. "Yang Wei Rubber and Plastics," she said sluggishly in Korean, wiping sweat from her temples. "Liam Yang's Office. What? Fire?!"

When Jade switched tabs to check the progress, the fire had already broken out. Alerted by smoke billowing into the hallways from the mailroom, all Yang Wei employees were forced to evacuate. A group of young men tried to extinguish the fire, they empowered it instead.

The fire department was called and Jade watched the firemen leaping into action, storming the building— fighting the flames but to no avail. The smoke from Yang Wei quickly billowed skyward from Yeouido to Gangnam in thick unyielding plumes, in protest of the heavy June rainfall. It was later reported in both Hong Kong and Singapore that the fire leapt from floor to floor, and the flames gleefully devoured every drop of the monsoon rains.

Jade could even see the smoke here, from her window, as sirens echoed from what seemed like a far-off place. Fire hoses began their assault on the growing blaze from the building's exterior, but still floor after floor lit up with the red-orange bloom of flames, and just as with Michelle and Seina's wedding, Jade watched absently— as if it were a movie.

With the black H.E.X.D. placed at all the critical points Yu had identified months earlier, the blue H.E.X.D. surveyed the crowds pooling across the street, while the firemen valiantly worked to clear the building. Had it not been for Jade's blackmail of Yu, she would have blindly placed the black H.E.X.D. and simply let it go. She wouldn't have known a way to save as many lives as she did, and perhaps would have cost these cities billions more in damages.

Still her anger was palpable. Anger at the lives she couldn't save—that her father wouldn't save because it cost too much, because it took away from the bottom line. *Two million each year: Malaysia, Indonesia, Thailand, Cambodia, and others. No one batted an eye because Liam Yang paid them not to. They would say nothing because their pockets were lined. With three new plastics factories opening in Nigeria next year there was no end in sight. This rogue privilege had to be stopped*, Jade thought, as she had a thousand times over. Yet she was a blossoming beauty even in this shade of rage, skin glowing.

The rage up-ticked, as the blue H.E.X.D. panned over to her father.

He stood out somehow, pacing in his rain-soaked vibrant blue suit, searching for something. *Probably that blonde secretary he's screwing,* Jade thought, watching him place a hand to his hip, the other on his head. She wanted to hurt him, to make him feel her pain, her rage, her loss— though she would never admit it. *Will he?* She wondered. Though she thought she wouldn't.

Hours, the fireman bravely tussled with the hoses to combat the blaze, but to no end. The rain came more steadily as it does on days when time stops, and the shape of one's grief has yet to reveal itself—while calling all feelings into question. Jade sat quietly on the subway, under a cap pulled low as she thought of all it took to do this. She thought of Robert, bloodied and on the floor in the storage room of that Chinese restaurant. She remembered the feel of the pliers in her hand as she pulled each tooth from his mouth. Then she thought of Kohana, that last fireworks, and how she only wanted to buy Michelle more time. Jade adjusted the surgical mask over her face, feeling her stomach turn. She grabbed her duffle bag from the floor and threw it over her shoulder.

"Incheon International Airport." The intercom chimed. Jade stood with her duffle on her shoulder and her laptop under an arm. Once she made it through security, she found an empty gate and returned to the camera feed, a morbid curiosity getting the best of her. She watched the camera in Hong Kong as they tried to contain the fire.

"I guess suppressing it seemed out of the question," Jade murmured. By then the blaze consumed at least ten floors above the old Yang Wei office.

In Singapore, Jade saw four helicopters dump water onto the building as seven or eight hoses hammered the flames. She felt a pang of guilt and nostalgia for her home but she could do nothing now. Three years and at least four million American dollars stolen and invested in this, she would see it through, no matter how much it hurt.

Jade turned her attention back to the cameras in Seoul. The firemen valiantly scoured the building, assuring its emptiness where they could. She saw her father on his phone, pacing, and running his fingers through his wet hair. A pilot and two female flight attendants walked past Jade and she flinched, almost closing the laptop entirely.

When her heart rate slowed again, Jade opened the laptop and saw the last two fireman surface from Yang Wei's front door. Jade checked the buildings again. All three were clear. The fires raged on. She locked the buildings down— leaving the fire to take care of the rest. Jade brought the blue H.E.X.D. out of survey mode switching over to broadcast with a 30-minute delay on the playback. Then Jade opened a movie file on her laptop and pressed play.

Three years ago, the last time Jade saw her father, she helped Ah Fan map the network layout of all three Yang Wai offices through a printer in Hong Kong. With Ah Fan's help in coding and hacking she was able to disappear, to become Lia, dropping the Yang, before becoming Jade Wang. By stripping away many of the costly protective measures in its manufacturing process, Yang Wei Rubber and Plastics, became a very lucrative company under Jade's father. These cuts paired with growing profits, allowed the company to open offices in Seoul, and Singapore while exposing many of its workers to a number of chemical agents, unknowingly—or so was the claim.

If Jade's mother had been healthy enough to lead the company, Yang Wei would have never become the monstrosity it is today. Alas, Mia Yang, Jade's mother spent years of working in the plant, learning the business, and this resulted in lymphoma. Though no one said it, they all knew where it came from. It was the independent studies, years later, that confirmed the truth of the matter. Yet those too were swept under the rug by her father, allowing Yang Wei to become a cancer in its own right.

Jade wiped her eyes, and licked her lips moving her mind back into the present as her flight called for boarding. Jade looked at the three buildings rapidly burning to hollowed frames, then she closed the laptop. She stood, dropping both laptop and phone into the trash and walking toward the gate. *I needed those codes*, she thought, tears coming to her eyes.

"You've run out of nails. I'll have to pull teeth now. Just give me what I want Robert." The words played from memory, reminding Jade how she dumped the body in that alley after she shot him up with whatever she could find.

A flight attendant scanned Jade's passport and ticket. "Have a nice flight Ms. Fang," The man said before handing Jade her British passport back.

Jade heard the hiss of fire crackers, then was left to relived the moment the flames consumed the Terada helicopter. But as she sat down and buckled her seatbelt, Hikaru's face floated to mind, again, wet with his tears in the moonlight along with his plea for her to stop. There were countless other things that plagued her, but these were the moments Jade knew would live on, the ones she would have to live with, just below the surface of whomever she would become next.

When the plane took off, the tears came. Jade closed her eyes and simply allowed them, she had avenged her mother, grandfather, and all of Yang Wei's victims, but at what cost. Robert had called her a monster, now she truly felt it. Seeking some comfort, she unzipped her bag searching for the small container of keepsakes from the last year.

It wasn't there. It wasn't in the bag. Panic and terror spread, blooming from Jade's neck, stomach and knees like branches and leaves. *Okay, okay calm down, calm down,* she thought.

It's at the hotel, a voice said to her.

NO! No! No! This, was Jade's seventh grave mistake, *the one that kept on giving.*

Simultaneously, electronic devices around the financial districts in Seoul, Hong Kong, and Singapore cut out and restarted. As they rebooted a video played, broadcasted from blue H.E.X.D.'s stationed near the site of the fires.

The first image was of a baby holding dad's finger in some tropical place. Mom waves from behind the camera, as baby tries to take her first step. The dad lets go and baby remains standing, then she takes a step. Dad beams with pride pointing to the camera. The infant coughs taking another, then a third step, before vomiting up blood. The baby collapses. Blood and vomit pooling. The body stiffens. Mom drops the camera screaming, then a glimpse. She neither dashes nor runs but scoots with all her might, dragging shriveled legs behind her, to her child. The clip freezes, and words appear first in Korean, then Chinese, and finally English:

The parents featured here, worked in one of the over 1,800 factories owned by Yang Wei Plastics. Direct exposure to the chemicals Yang Wei uses in its rubber plants cost the mother the ability to walk, then her job after which she discovered she was pregnant.

The infant was given less than a year to live. Due to a weakened heart and other complications from lymphoma, minutes after this video the infant died. Three months later the mother followed.

The father was diagnosed with stage three cancer from working at one of Yang Wei's plants, he committed suicide one week after his wife. They are three of the estimated two million lives Yang Wei Plastics has destroyed each year since Liam Yang has owned the company.

An image appeared of the mother and father, young, healthy—vibrant, prior to Yang Wei. More pictures appeared one after the other of the nameless deceased, by the thousands as more words appeared.

We are **L**iberty **i**n **A**sia, **i**n **A**frica, **i**n **A**merica,
in **a** world with no humanity
in **a** world, where life is given no value.

Like the nameless left to die around the world, Yang Wei will take no more steps.

The words faded. Three, five, ten explosions went off one after the other, giving way to countless detonations. People on the streets ran for cover. The roar of the blasts rumbled through the air as a deep sinister growl echoed forth from the bowels of each building in time. Metal, steel and concrete whined and groaned in thunderous claps as Yang Wei, Seoul,

Hong Kong and Singapore crumbled in on themselves. Plumes of dust surged like tidal waves, dimming the lights of each of these dazzling cities and shaking their very foundations.

Dampened by the rains, the ash clouds roamed about each of the three cities. The video of baby played on repeat, in the deafening silence. This time there was the added message from LIA:

Burn the hopes, burn the dreams, watch the cinders fly,
What good are they if they light the way, to hopelessness and emptiness?
They are but endless ambition lit by desire.

The hands of destiny have tied mine as I watch this world crumble only to be rebuilt, better, I hope.

– signed,
New Beginnings

Coming Soon

If you enjoyed Fragments Shattered and Shattering, keep an eye out for

Fragments II
Lies and Liars

Fragments III
That Which was Broken

And

Kingdom Veiled

About The Author

Author Gary Battle Originally from Goldsboro, North Carolina Gary now lives in San Antonio, Texas where he currently works for the United States Air Force as a Cyber Analyst.

A graduate of the Global Studies Program at Appalachian State University and the Organizational Development and Leadership Program at the University of the Incarnate Word. He served six years in the Air Force following three years of teach in Japan, South Korea, and his hometown. He is current working on the second book in the Fragments series. His writings can also be found on amazon and the link below in addition to countless query letter emails linked to the phases, "I'm sorry" and or "going to pass" up and down the US eastern seaboard.

https://www.fruition-literaryagency-shop.store/

Instagram: speaking.of.mr.batalhar

Made in United States
North Haven, CT
09 May 2023

36409915R00243